PROLOGUE

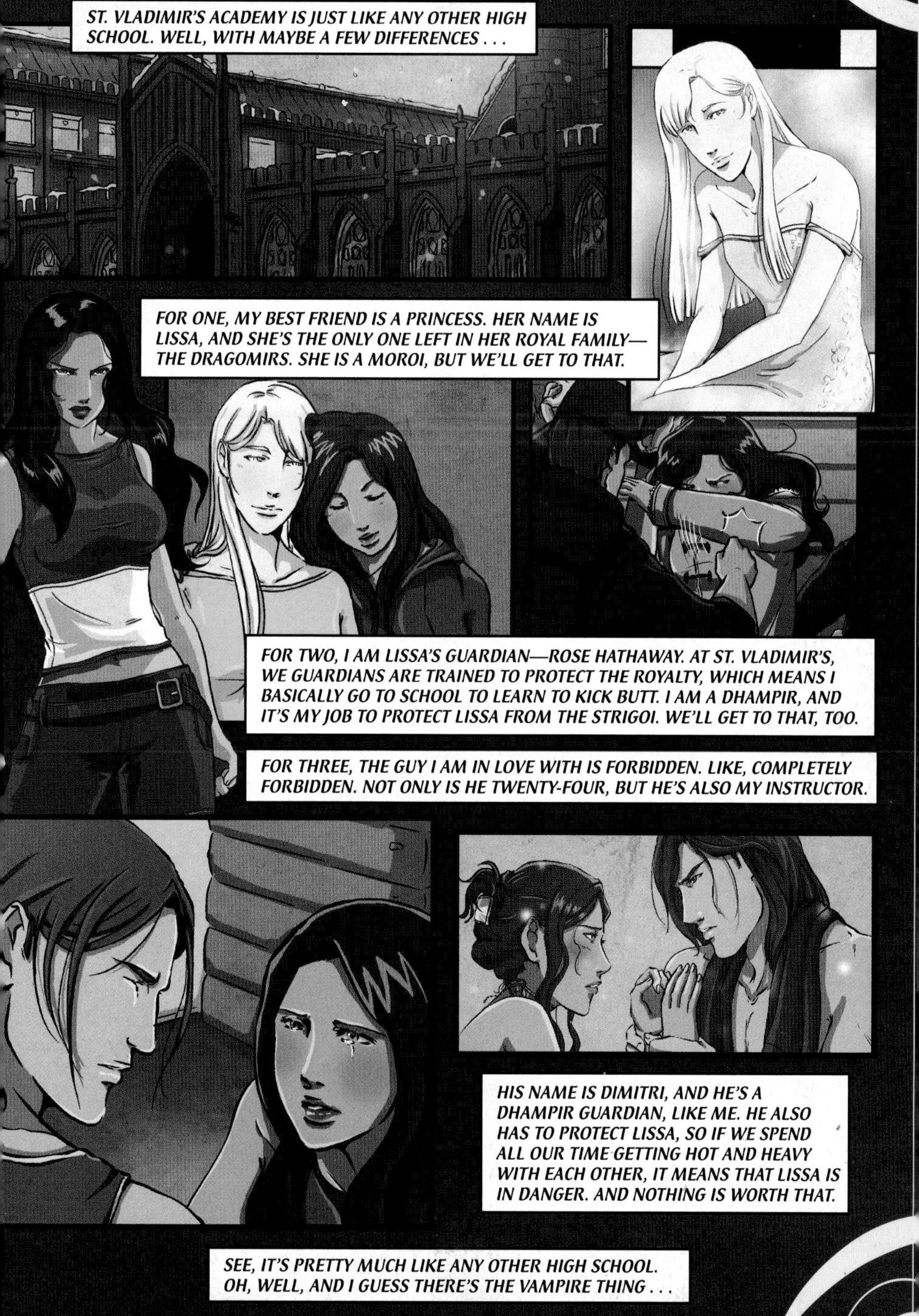
ST. VLADIMIR'S ACADEMY IS JUST LIKE ANY OTHER HIGH SCHOOL. WELL, WITH MAYBE A FEW DIFFERENCES . . .
FOR ONE, MY BEST FRIEND IS A PRINCESS. HER NAME IS LISSA, AND SHE'S THE ONLY ONE LEFT IN HER ROYAL FAMILY—THE DRAGOMIRS. SHE IS A MOROI, BUT WE'LL GET TO THAT.
FOR TWO, I AM LISSA'S GUARDIAN—ROSE HATHAWAY. AT ST. VLADIMIR'S, WE GUARDIANS ARE TRAINED TO PROTECT THE ROYALTY, WHICH MEANS I BASICALLY GO TO SCHOOL TO LEARN TO KICK BUTT. I AM A DHAMPIR, AND IT'S MY JOB TO PROTECT LISSA FROM THE STRIGOI. WE'LL GET TO THAT, TOO.
FOR THREE, THE GUY I AM IN LOVE WITH IS FORBIDDEN. LIKE, COMPLETELY FORBIDDEN. NOT ONLY IS HE TWENTY-FOUR, BUT HE'S ALSO MY INSTRUCTOR.
HIS NAME IS DIMITRI, AND HE'S A DHAMPIR GUARDIAN, LIKE ME. HE ALSO HAS TO PROTECT LISSA, SO IF WE SPEND ALL OUR TIME GETTING HOT AND HEAVY WITH EACH OTHER, IT MEANS THAT LISSA IS IN DANGER. AND NOTHING IS WORTH THAT.
SEE, IT'S PRETTY MUCH LIKE ANY OTHER HIGH SCHOOL. OH, WELL, AND I GUESS THERE'S THE VAMPIRE THING . . .

LISSA HAS POWER OVER SPIRIT, WHICH SHE CAN USE TO CONTROL PEOPLE. SHE ALSO KIND OF BROUGHT ME BACK TO LIFE ONCE. WE NOW HAVE A BOND BETWEEN US, SO I CAN FEEL WHAT SHE FEELS, AND I KNOW WHEN SHE IS IN DANGER.

I FEEL HOW MUCH SHE CARES FOR HIM.

LISS, DRINK.

BLISS SETTLES OVER ME.

JOYFUL.

LIKE BEING IN A DREAM.

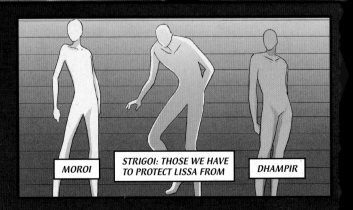

MOROI

STRIGOI: THOSE WE HAVE TO PROTECT LISSA FROM

DHAMPIR

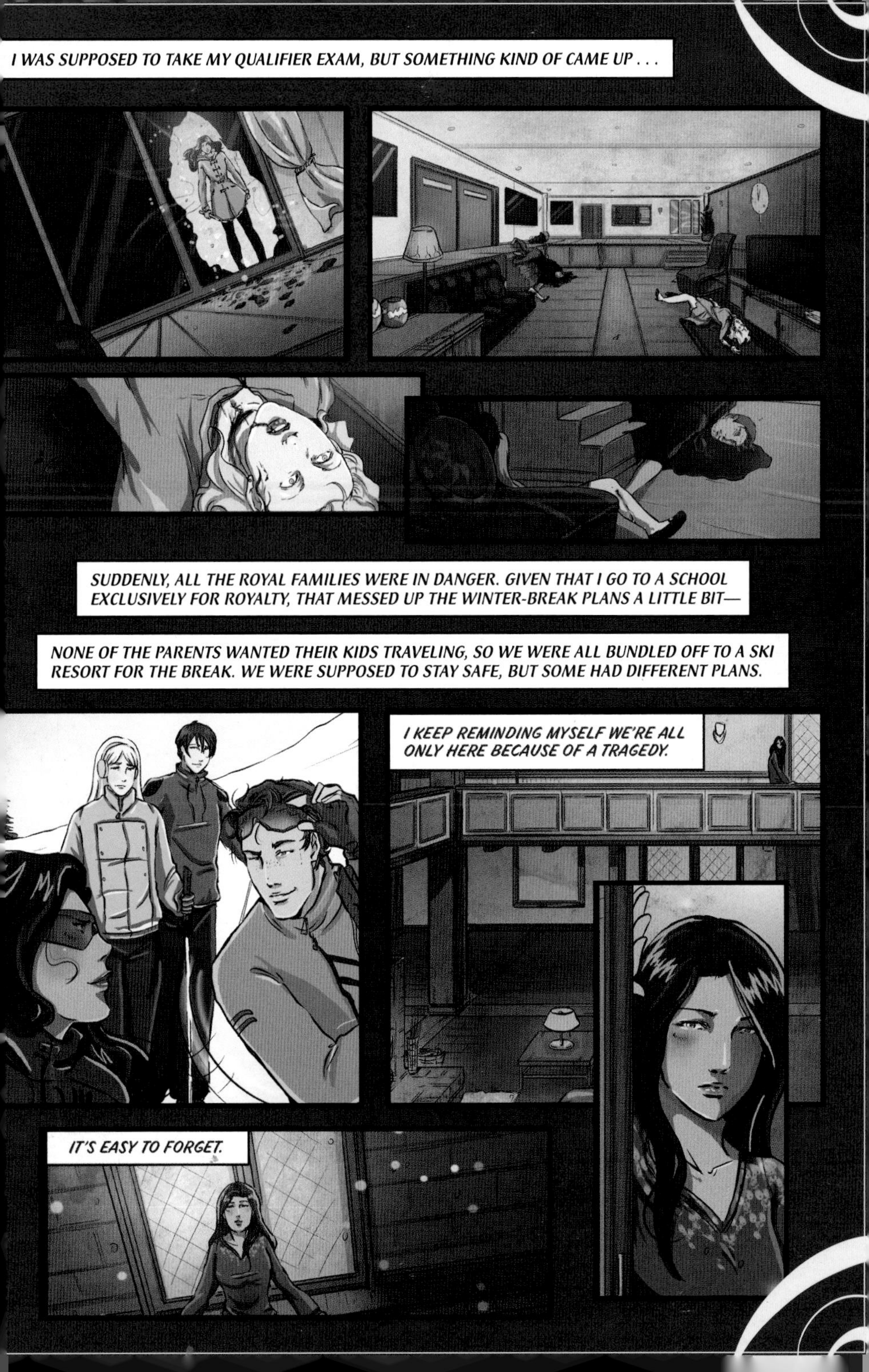
I WAS SUPPOSED TO TAKE MY QUALIFIER EXAM, BUT SOMETHING KIND OF CAME UP . . .
SUDDENLY, ALL THE ROYAL FAMILIES WERE IN DANGER. GIVEN THAT I GO TO A SCHOOL EXCLUSIVELY FOR ROYALTY, THAT MESSED UP THE WINTER-BREAK PLANS A LITTLE BIT—
NONE OF THE PARENTS WANTED THEIR KIDS TRAVELING, SO WE WERE ALL BUNDLED OFF TO A SKI RESORT FOR THE BREAK. WE WERE SUPPOSED TO STAY SAFE, BUT SOME HAD DIFFERENT PLANS.
I KEEP REMINDING MYSELF WE'RE ALL ONLY HERE BECAUSE OF A TRAGEDY.
IT'S EASY TO FORGET.

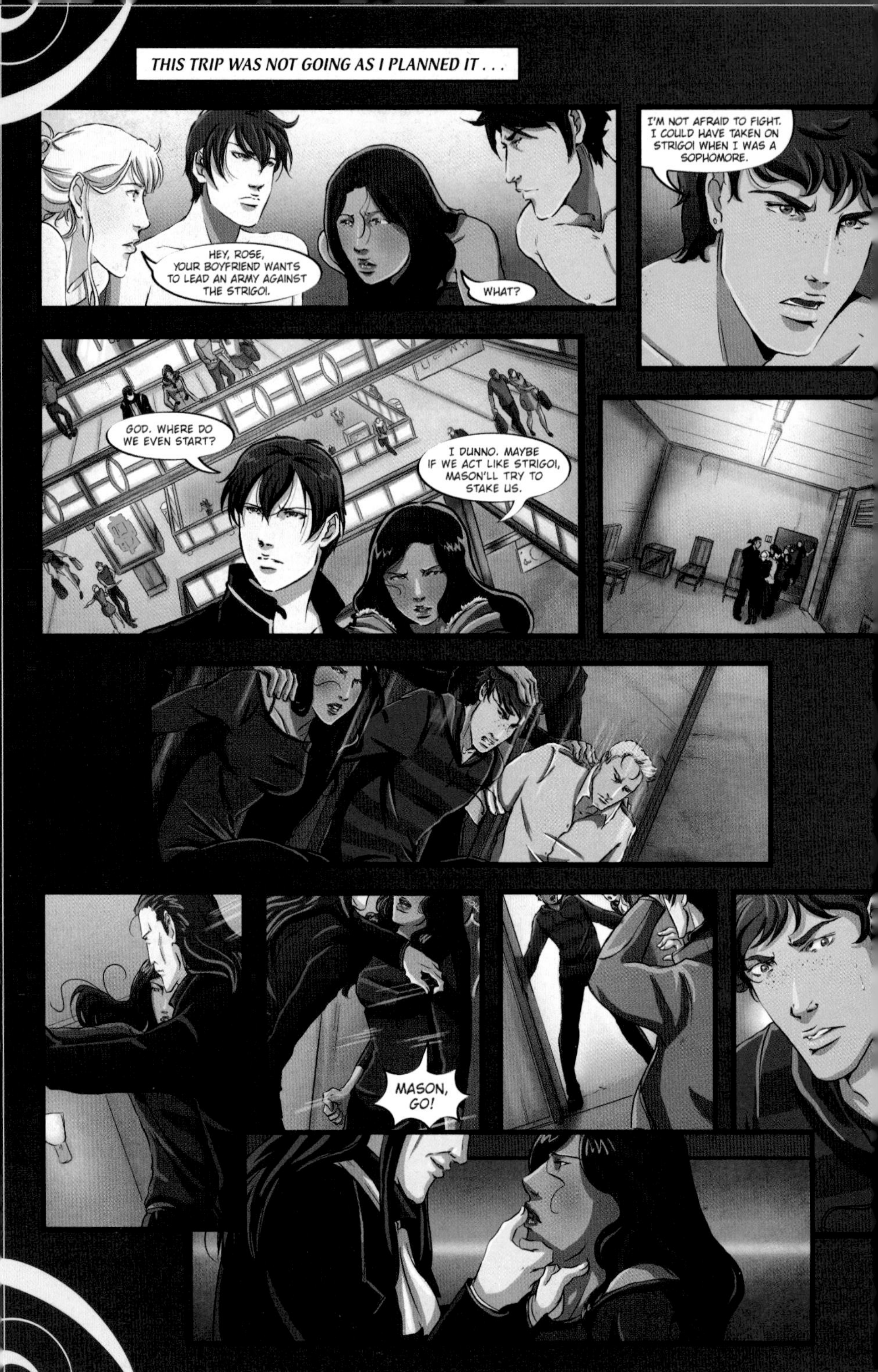
THIS TRIP WAS NOT GOING AS I PLANNED IT . . .
HEY, ROSE, YOUR BOYFRIEND WANTS TO LEAD AN ARMY AGAINST THE STRIGOI.
WHAT?
I'M NOT AFRAID TO FIGHT. I COULD HAVE TAKEN ON STRIGOI WHEN I WAS A SOPHOMORE.
GOD. WHERE DO WE EVEN START?
I DUNNO. MAYBE IF WE ACT LIKE STRIGOI, MASON'LL TRY TO STAKE US.
MASON, GO!

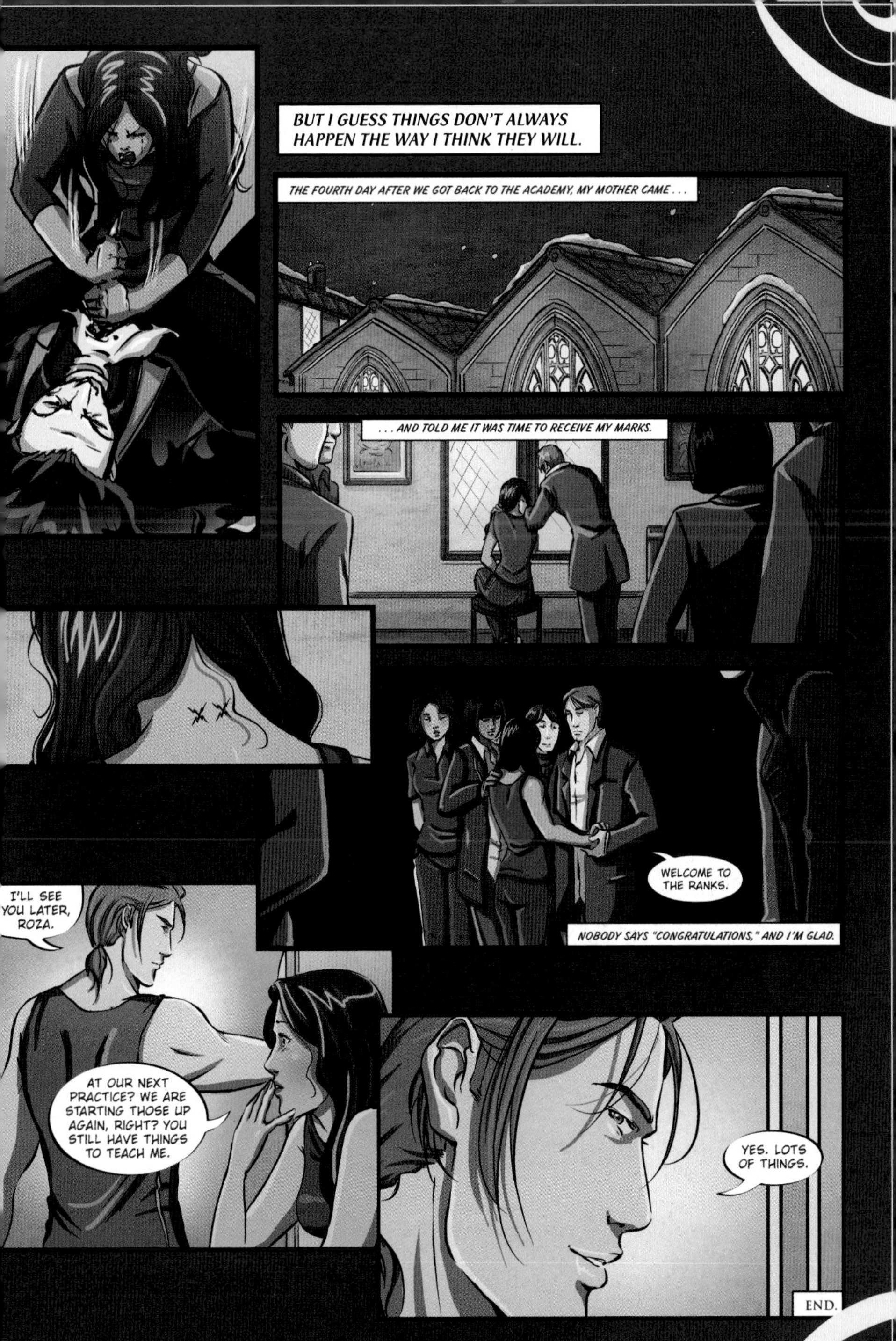
BUT I GUESS THINGS DON'T ALWAYS HAPPEN THE WAY I THINK THEY WILL.
THE FOURTH DAY AFTER WE GOT BACK TO THE ACADEMY, MY MOTHER CAME . . .
. . . AND TOLD ME IT WAS TIME TO RECEIVE MY MARKS.
WELCOME TO THE RANKS.
NOBODY SAYS "CONGRATULATIONS," AND I'M GLAD.
I'LL SEE YOU LATER, ROZA.
AT OUR NEXT PRACTICE? WE ARE STARTING THOSE UP AGAIN, RIGHT? YOU STILL HAVE THINGS TO TEACH ME.
YES. LOTS OF THINGS.
END.

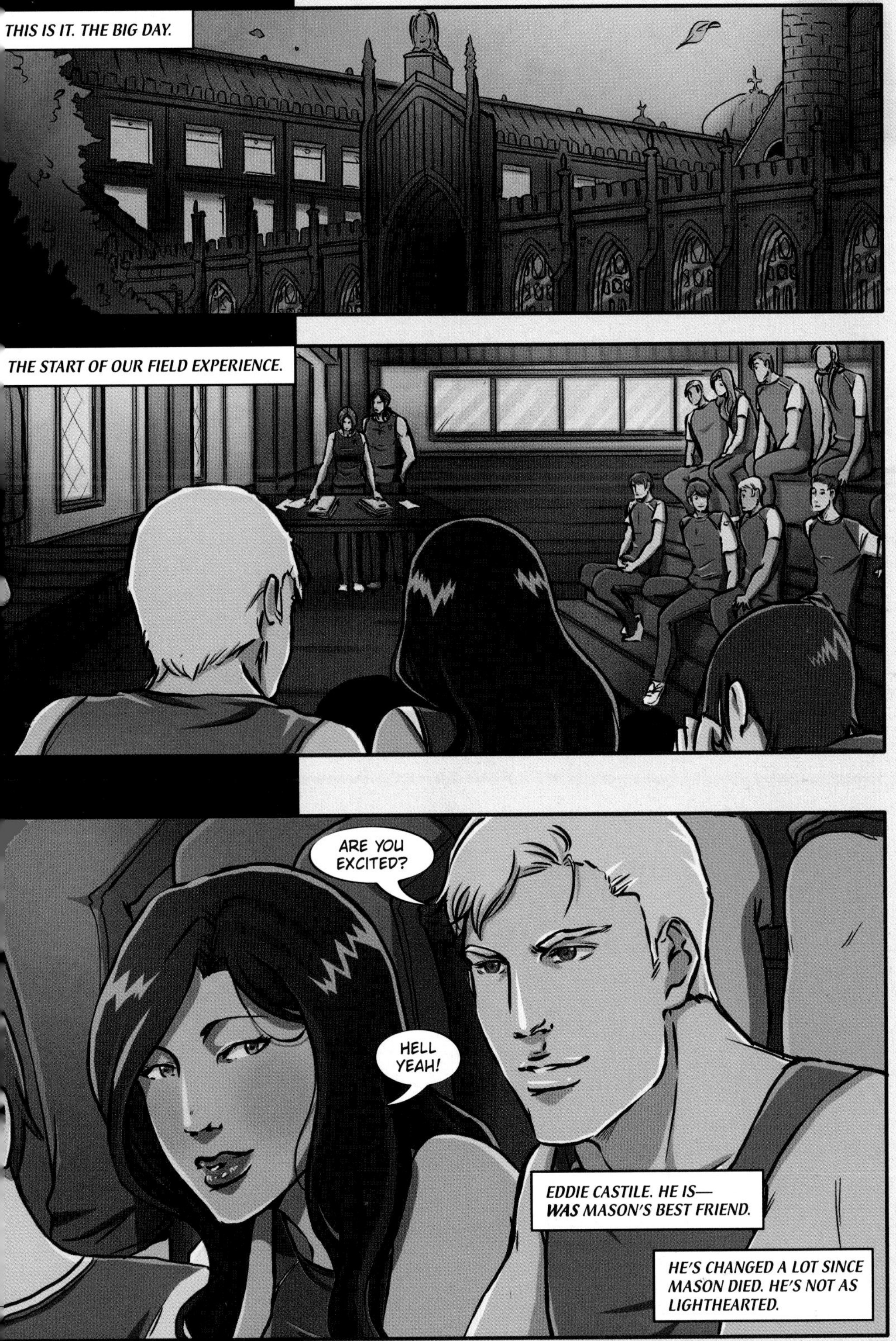
THIS IS IT. THE BIG DAY.
THE START OF OUR FIELD EXPERIENCE.
ARE YOU EXCITED?
HELL YEAH!
EDDIE CASTILE. HE IS— **WAS** MASON'S BEST FRIEND.
HE'S CHANGED A LOT SINCE MASON DIED. HE'S NOT AS LIGHTHEARTED.

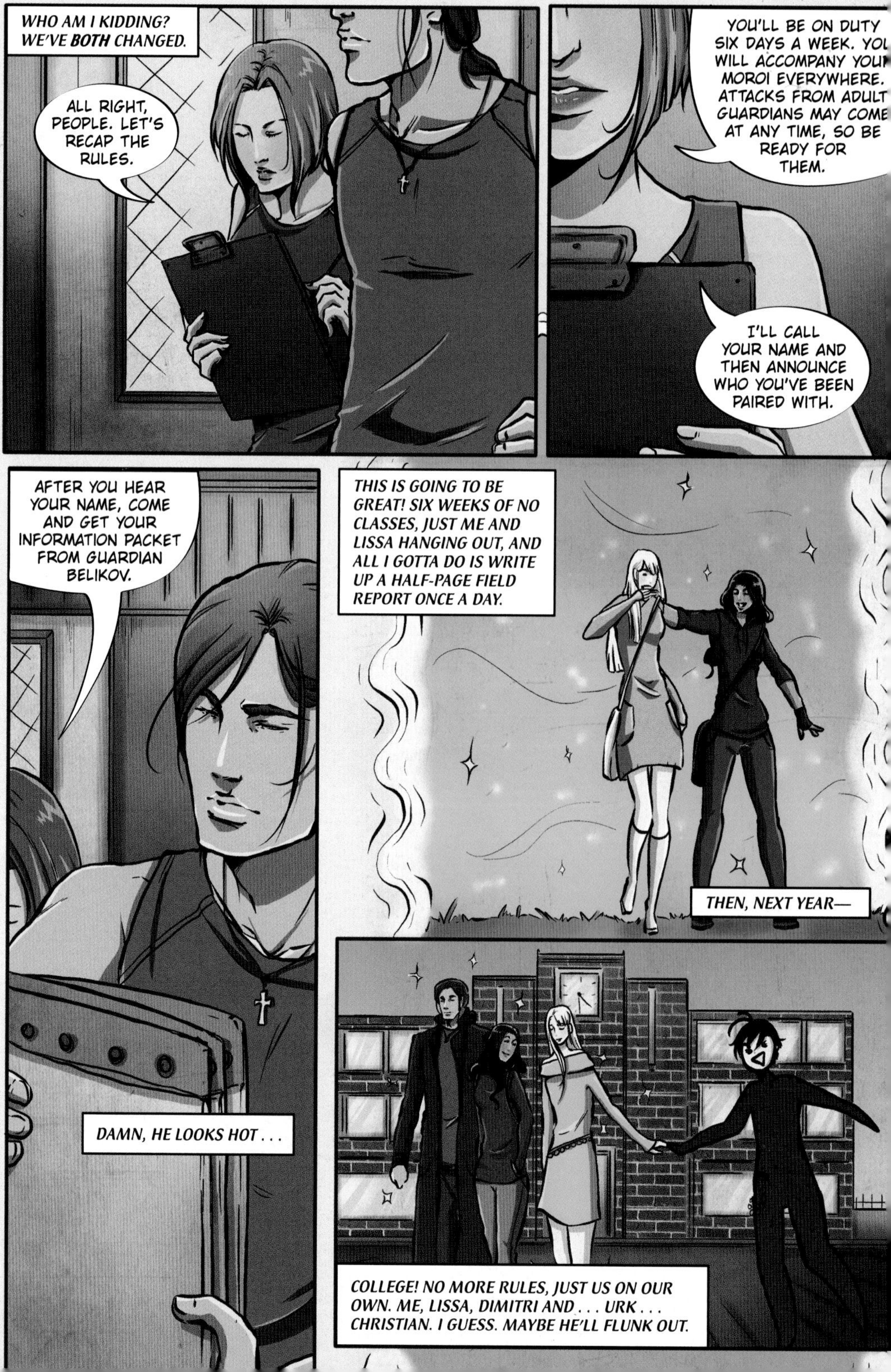
WHO AM I KIDDING? WE'VE BOTH CHANGED.
ALL RIGHT, PEOPLE. LET'S RECAP THE RULES.
YOU'LL BE ON DUTY SIX DAYS A WEEK. YOU WILL ACCOMPANY YOUR MOROI EVERYWHERE. ATTACKS FROM ADULT GUARDIANS MAY COME AT ANY TIME, SO BE READY FOR THEM.
I'LL CALL YOUR NAME AND THEN ANNOUNCE WHO YOU'VE BEEN PAIRED WITH.
AFTER YOU HEAR YOUR NAME, COME AND GET YOUR INFORMATION PACKET FROM GUARDIAN BELIKOV.
DAMN, HE LOOKS HOT . . .
THIS IS GOING TO BE GREAT! SIX WEEKS OF NO CLASSES, JUST ME AND LISSA HANGING OUT, AND ALL I GOTTA DO IS WRITE UP A HALF-PAGE FIELD REPORT ONCE A DAY.
THEN, NEXT YEAR—
COLLEGE! NO MORE RULES, JUST US ON OUR OWN. ME, LISSA, DIMITRI AND . . . URK . . . CHRISTIAN. I GUESS. MAYBE HE'LL FLUNK OUT.

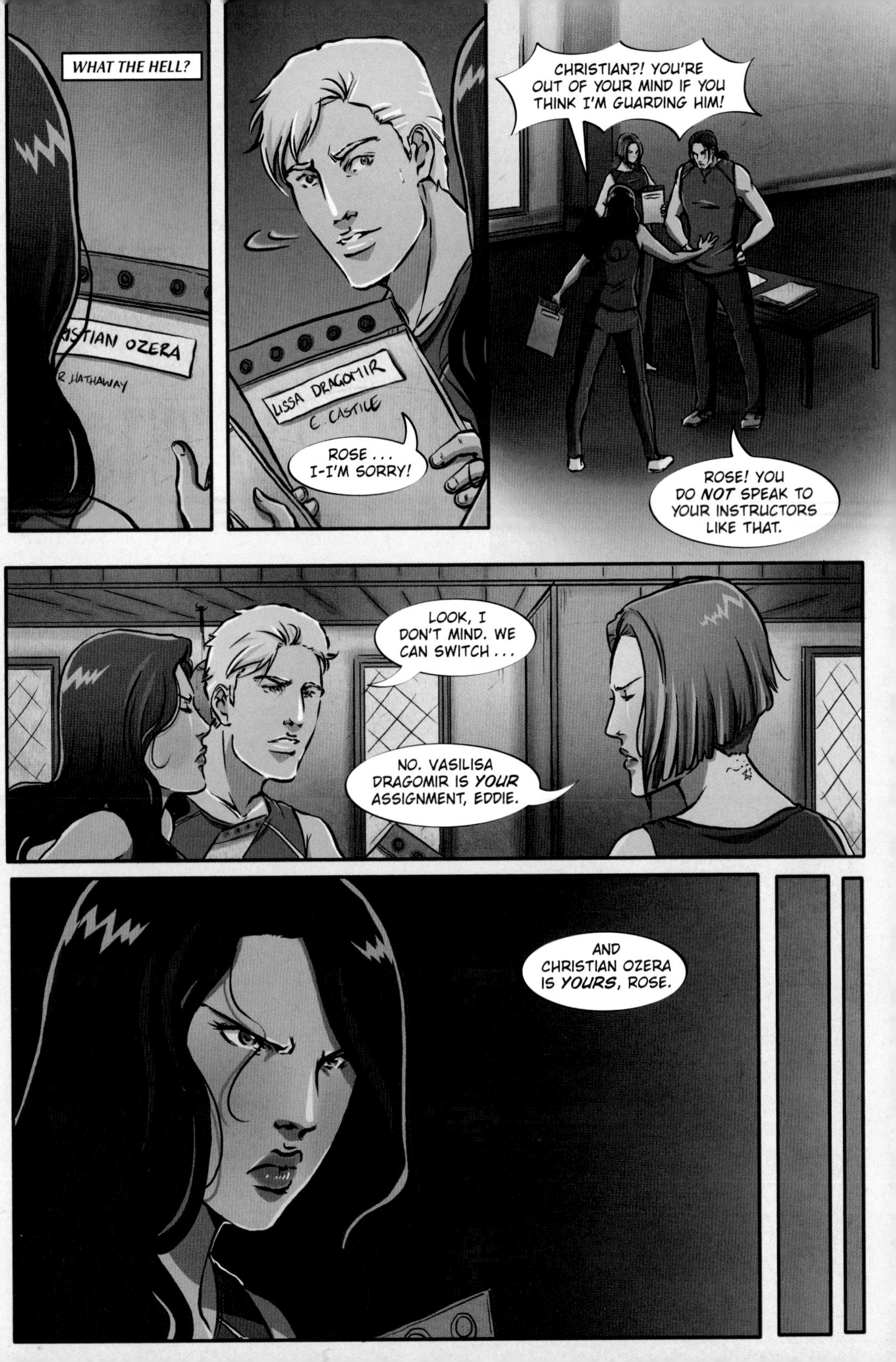
WHAT THE HELL?
ISTIAN OZERA
R. HATHAWAY
LISSA DRAGOMIR
E. CASTILE
ROSE . . . I-I'M SORRY!
CHRISTIAN?! YOU'RE OUT OF YOUR MIND IF YOU THINK I'M GUARDING HIM!
ROSE! YOU DO NOT SPEAK TO YOUR INSTRUCTORS LIKE THAT.
LOOK, I DON'T MIND. WE CAN SWITCH . . .
NO. VASILISA DRAGOMIR IS YOUR ASSIGNMENT, EDDIE.
AND CHRISTIAN OZERA IS YOURS, ROSE.

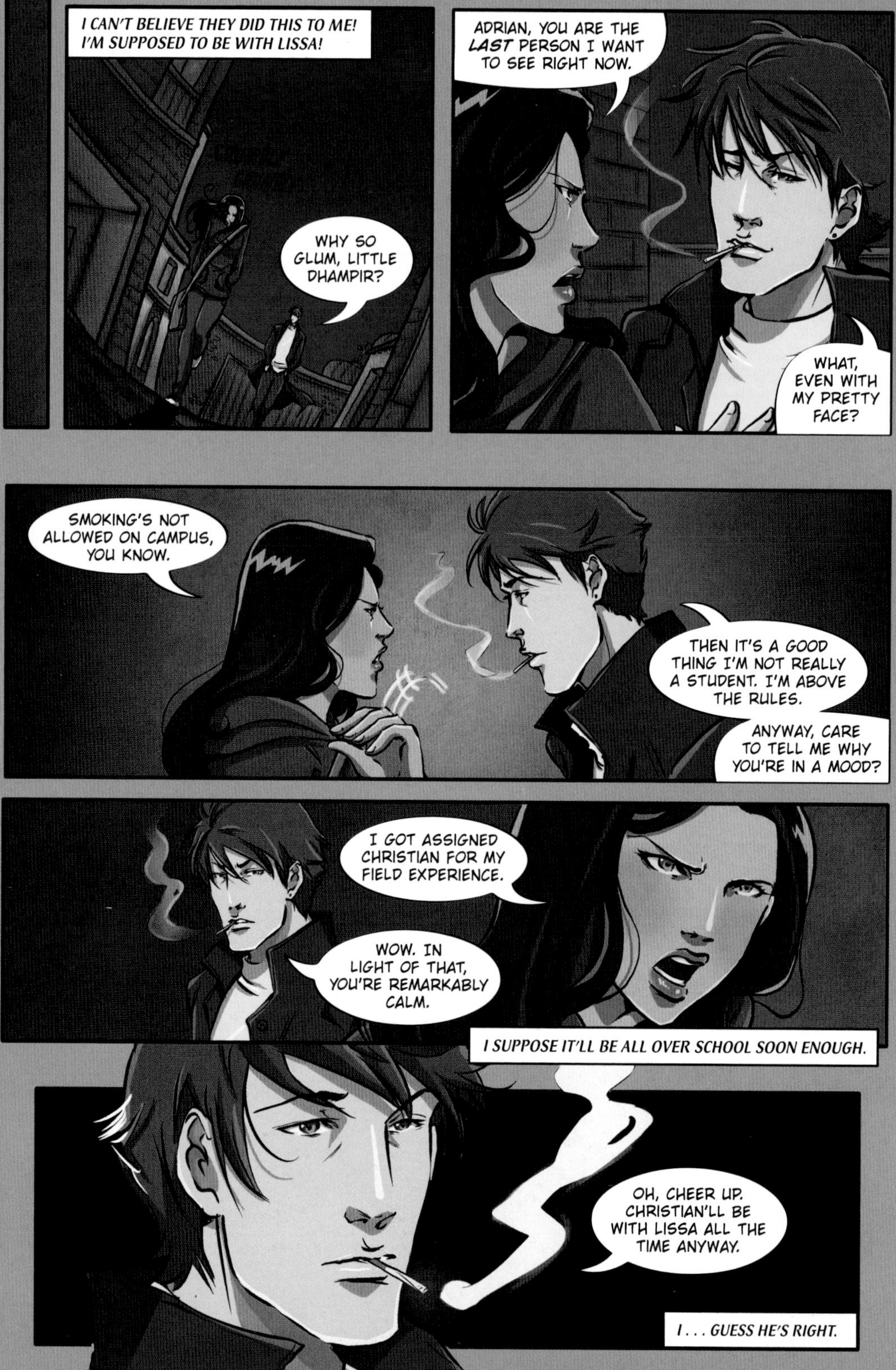
I CAN'T BELIEVE THEY DID THIS TO ME! I'M SUPPOSED TO BE WITH LISSA!
WHY SO GLUM, LITTLE DHAMPIR?
ADRIAN, YOU ARE THE LAST PERSON I WANT TO SEE RIGHT NOW.
WHAT, EVEN WITH MY PRETTY FACE?
SMOKING'S NOT ALLOWED ON CAMPUS, YOU KNOW.
THEN IT'S A GOOD THING I'M NOT REALLY A STUDENT. I'M ABOVE THE RULES.
ANYWAY, CARE TO TELL ME WHY YOU'RE IN A MOOD?
I GOT ASSIGNED CHRISTIAN FOR MY FIELD EXPERIENCE.
WOW. IN LIGHT OF THAT, YOU'RE REMARKABLY CALM.
I SUPPOSE IT'LL BE ALL OVER SCHOOL SOON ENOUGH.
OH, CHEER UP. CHRISTIAN'LL BE WITH LISSA ALL THE TIME ANYWAY.
I . . . GUESS HE'S RIGHT.

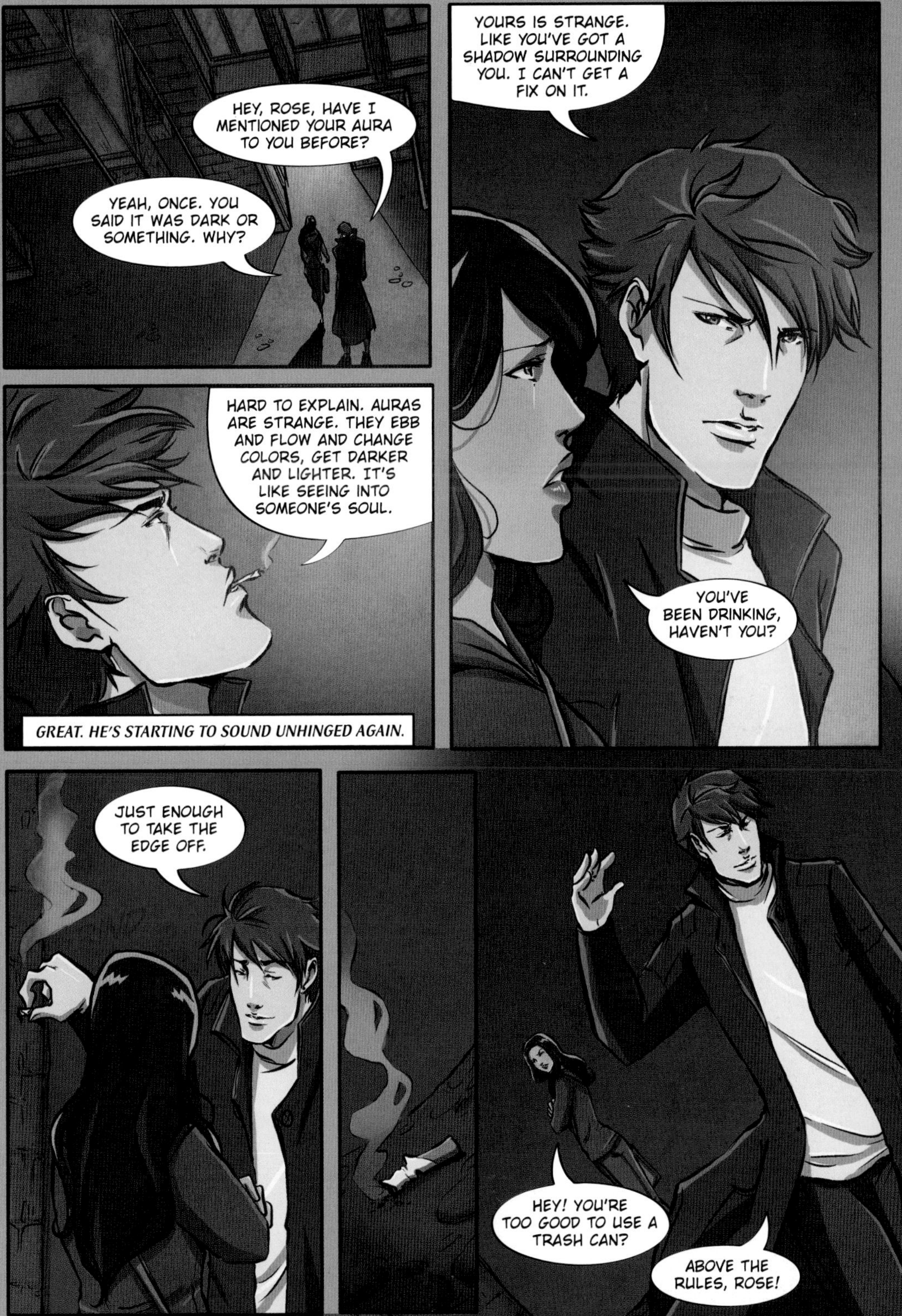
HEY, ROSE, HAVE I MENTIONED YOUR AURA TO YOU BEFORE?
YEAH, ONCE. YOU SAID IT WAS DARK OR SOMETHING. WHY?
HARD TO EXPLAIN. AURAS ARE STRANGE. THEY EBB AND FLOW AND CHANGE COLORS, GET DARKER AND LIGHTER. IT'S LIKE SEEING INTO SOMEONE'S SOUL.
GREAT. HE'S STARTING TO SOUND UNHINGED AGAIN.
YOURS IS STRANGE. LIKE YOU'VE GOT A SHADOW SURROUNDING YOU. I CAN'T GET A FIX ON IT.
YOU'VE BEEN DRINKING, HAVEN'T YOU?
JUST ENOUGH TO TAKE THE EDGE OFF.
HEY! YOU'RE TOO GOOD TO USE A TRASH CAN?
ABOVE THE RULES, ROSE!

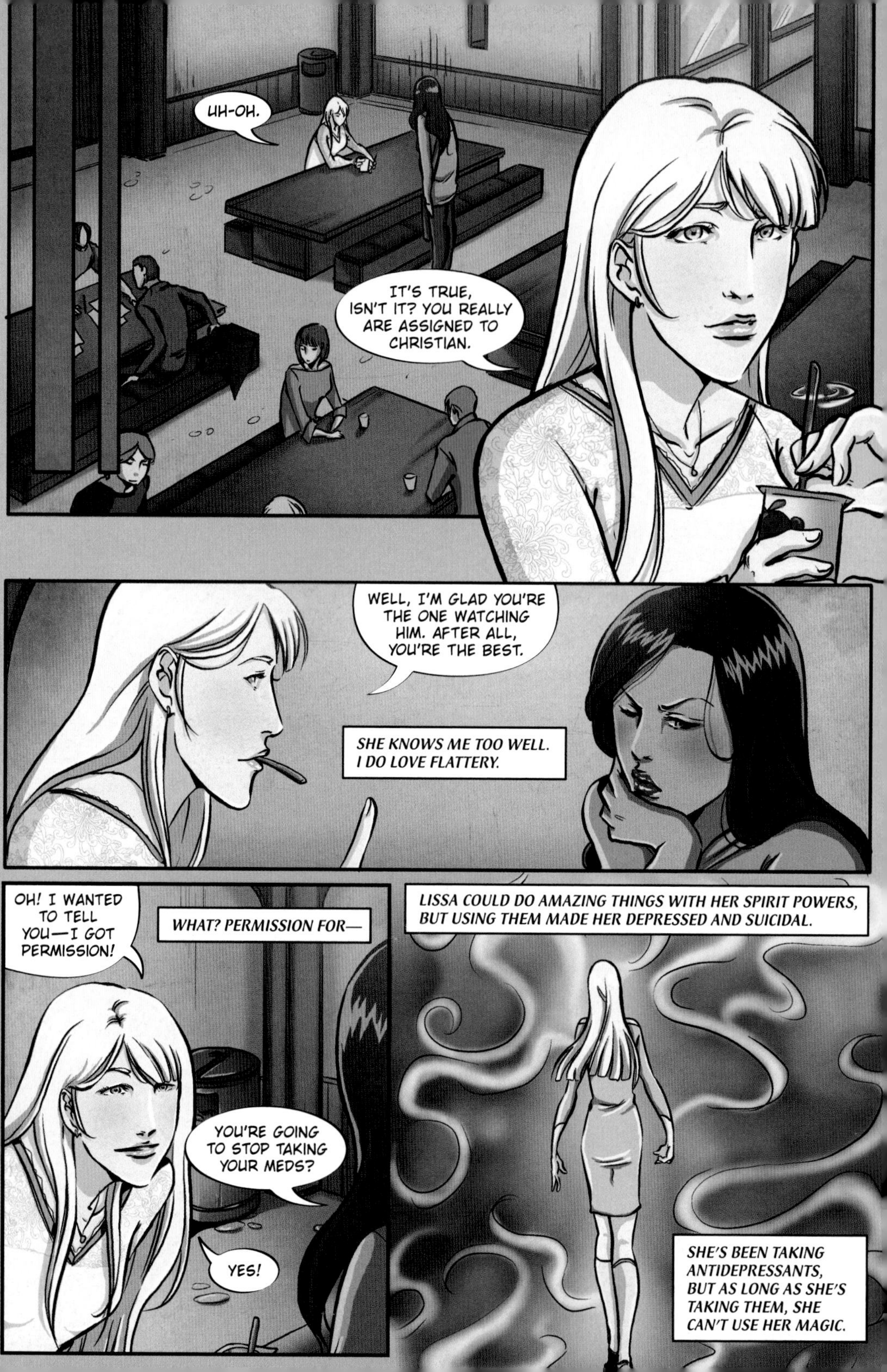
UH-OH.
IT'S TRUE, ISN'T IT? YOU REALLY ARE ASSIGNED TO CHRISTIAN.
WELL, I'M GLAD YOU'RE THE ONE WATCHING HIM. AFTER ALL, YOU'RE THE BEST.
SHE KNOWS ME TOO WELL. I DO LOVE FLATTERY.
OH! I WANTED TO TELL YOU—I GOT PERMISSION!
WHAT? PERMISSION FOR—
YOU'RE GOING TO STOP TAKING YOUR MEDS?
YES!
LISSA COULD DO AMAZING THINGS WITH HER SPIRIT POWERS, BUT USING THEM MADE HER DEPRESSED AND SUICIDAL.
SHE'S BEEN TAKING ANTIDEPRESSANTS, BUT AS LONG AS SHE'S TAKING THEM, SHE CAN'T USE HER MAGIC.

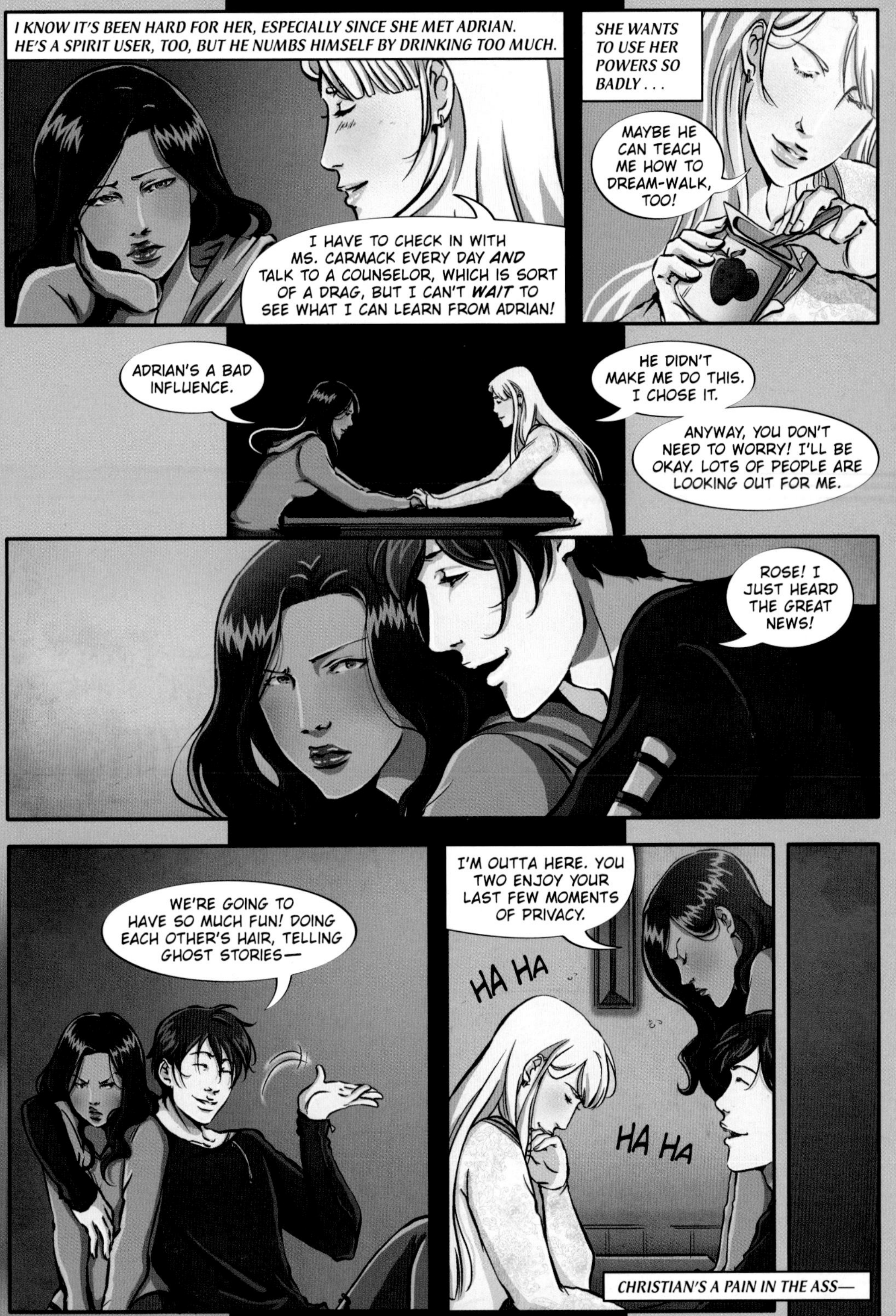
I KNOW IT'S BEEN HARD FOR HER, ESPECIALLY SINCE SHE MET ADRIAN. HE'S A SPIRIT USER, TOO, BUT HE NUMBS HIMSELF BY DRINKING TOO MUCH.
I HAVE TO CHECK IN WITH MS. CARMACK EVERY DAY AND TALK TO A COUNSELOR, WHICH IS SORT OF A DRAG, BUT I CAN'T WAIT TO SEE WHAT I CAN LEARN FROM ADRIAN!
SHE WANTS TO USE HER POWERS SO BADLY . . .
MAYBE HE CAN TEACH ME HOW TO DREAM-WALK, TOO!
ADRIAN'S A BAD INFLUENCE.
HE DIDN'T MAKE ME DO THIS. I CHOSE IT.
ANYWAY, YOU DON'T NEED TO WORRY! I'LL BE OKAY. LOTS OF PEOPLE ARE LOOKING OUT FOR ME.
ROSE! I JUST HEARD THE GREAT NEWS!
WE'RE GOING TO HAVE SO MUCH FUN! DOING EACH OTHER'S HAIR, TELLING GHOST STORIES—
I'M OUTTA HERE. YOU TWO ENJOY YOUR LAST FEW MOMENTS OF PRIVACY.
HA HA
HA HA
CHRISTIAN'S A PAIN IN THE ASS—

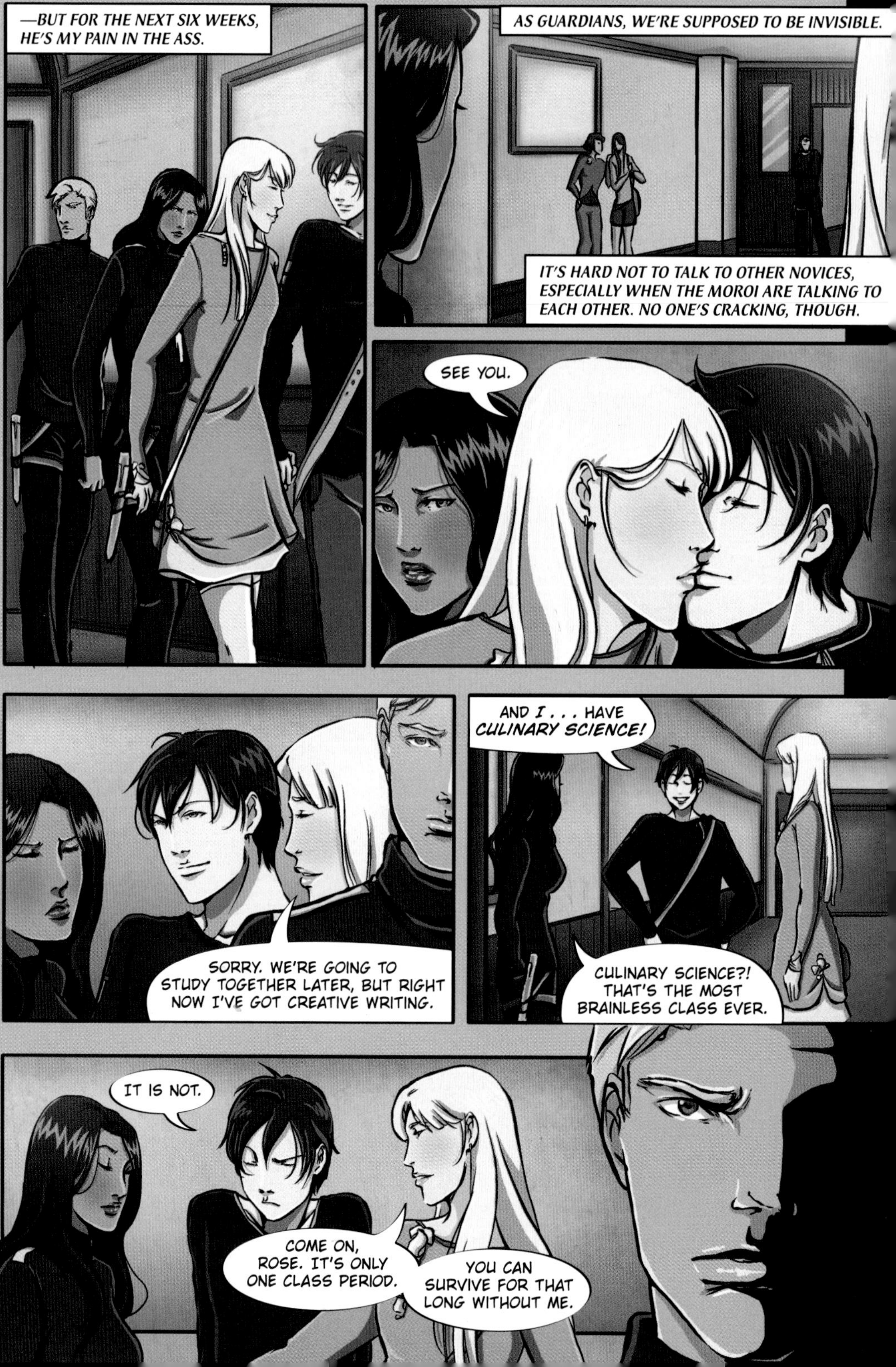
—BUT FOR THE NEXT SIX WEEKS, HE'S MY PAIN IN THE ASS.
AS GUARDIANS, WE'RE SUPPOSED TO BE INVISIBLE.
IT'S HARD NOT TO TALK TO OTHER NOVICES, ESPECIALLY WHEN THE MOROI ARE TALKING TO EACH OTHER. NO ONE'S CRACKING, THOUGH.
SEE YOU.
SORRY. WE'RE GOING TO STUDY TOGETHER LATER, BUT RIGHT NOW I'VE GOT CREATIVE WRITING.
AND I . . . HAVE CULINARY SCIENCE!
CULINARY SCIENCE?! THAT'S THE MOST BRAINLESS CLASS EVER.
IT IS NOT.
COME ON, ROSE. IT'S ONLY ONE CLASS PERIOD.
YOU CAN SURVIVE FOR THAT LONG WITHOUT ME.

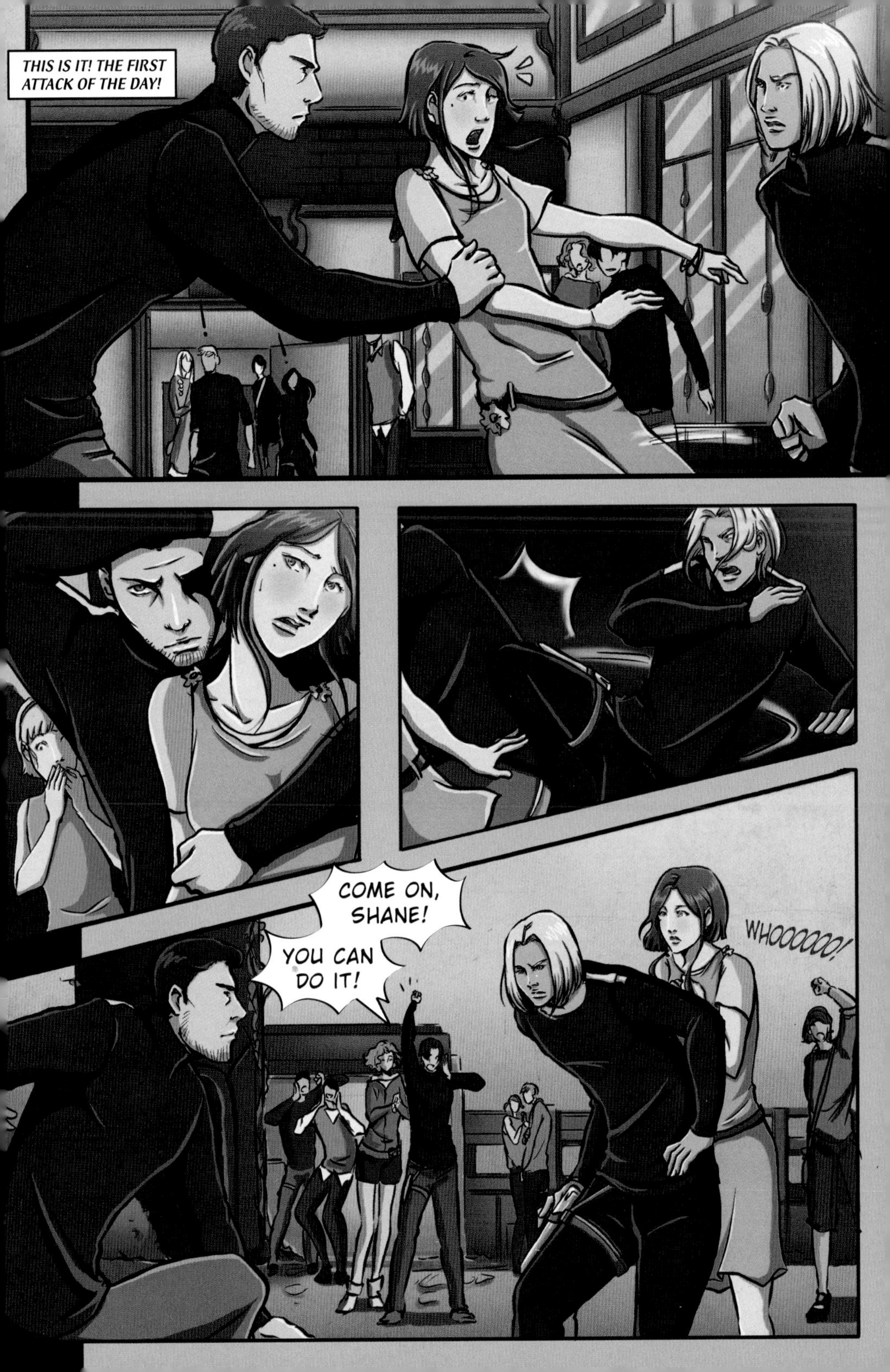
THIS IS IT! THE FIRST ATTACK OF THE DAY!
COME ON, SHANE!
YOU CAN DO IT!
WHOOOOOO!

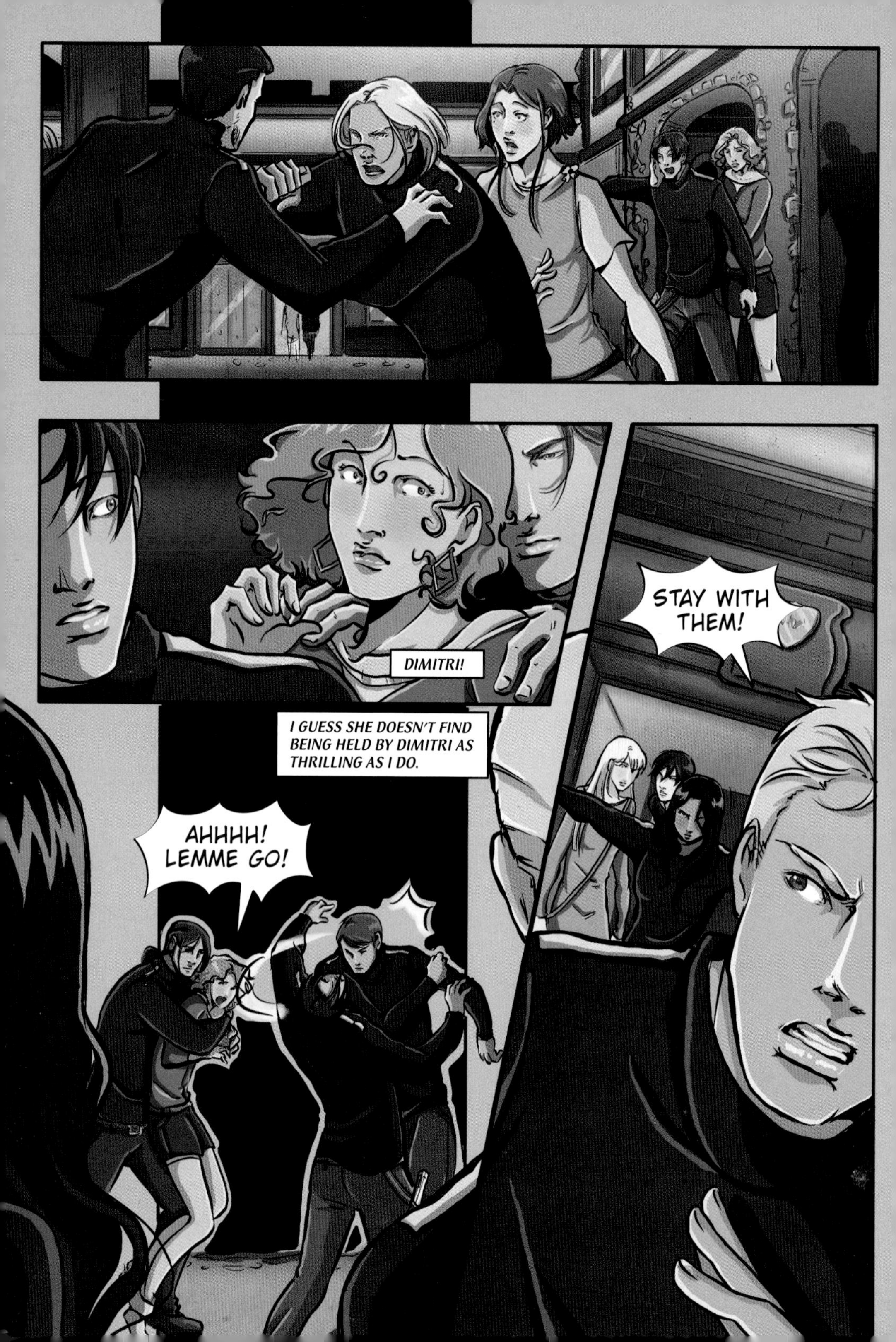
DIMITRI!
STAY WITH THEM!
I GUESS SHE DOESN'T FIND BEING HELD BY DIMITRI AS THRILLING AS I DO.
AHHHH! LEMME GO!

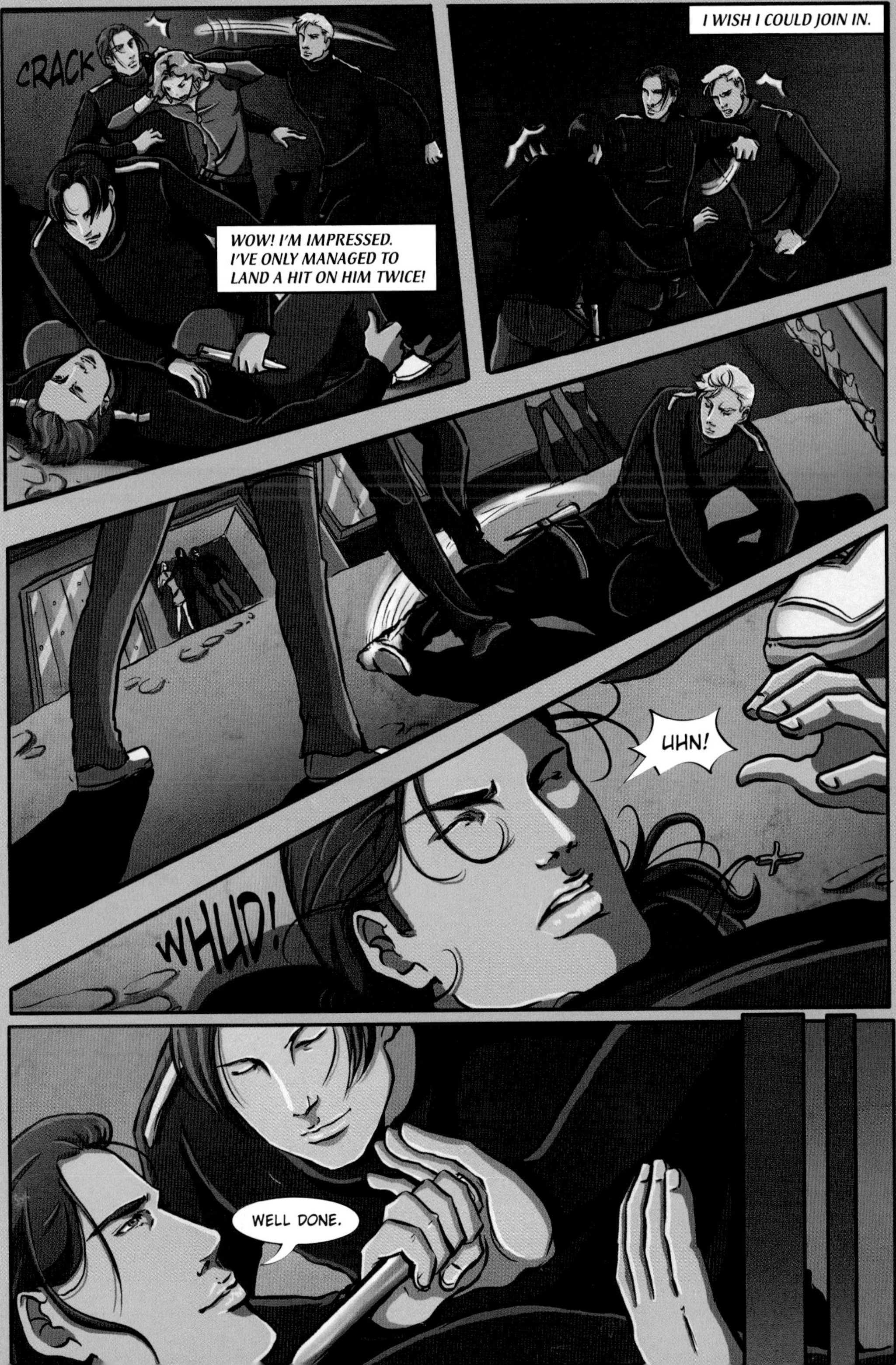
CRACK
WOW! I'M IMPRESSED. I'VE ONLY MANAGED TO LAND A HIT ON HIM TWICE!
I WISH I COULD JOIN IN.
UHN!
WHUD!
WELL DONE.

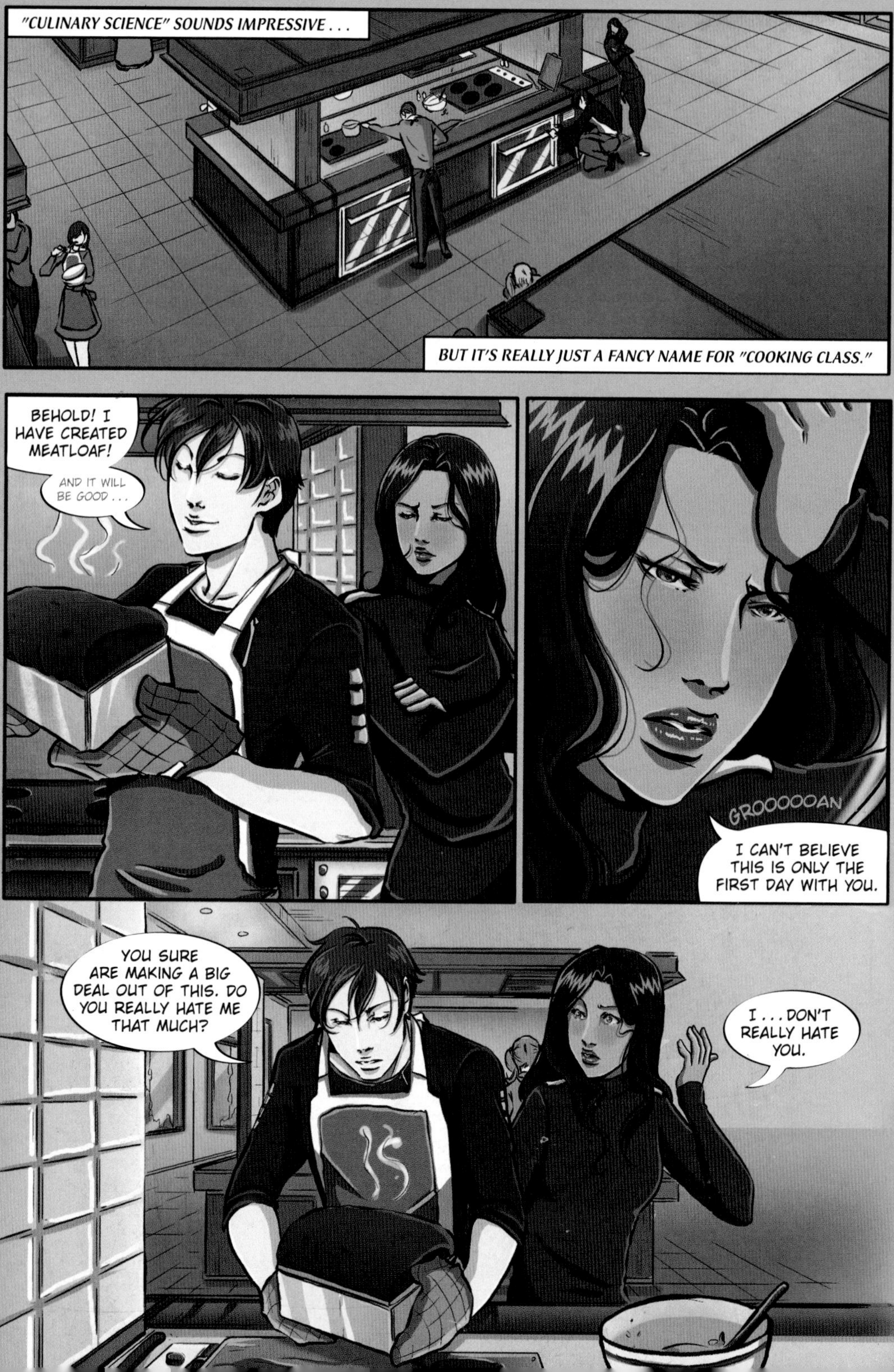
"CULINARY SCIENCE" SOUNDS IMPRESSIVE . . .
BUT IT'S REALLY JUST A FANCY NAME FOR "COOKING CLASS."
BEHOLD! I HAVE CREATED MEATLOAF!
AND IT WILL BE GOOD . . .
GROOOOOAN
I CAN'T BELIEVE THIS IS ONLY THE FIRST DAY WITH YOU.
YOU SURE ARE MAKING A BIG DEAL OUT OF THIS. DO YOU REALLY HATE ME THAT MUCH?
I . . . DON'T REALLY HATE YOU.

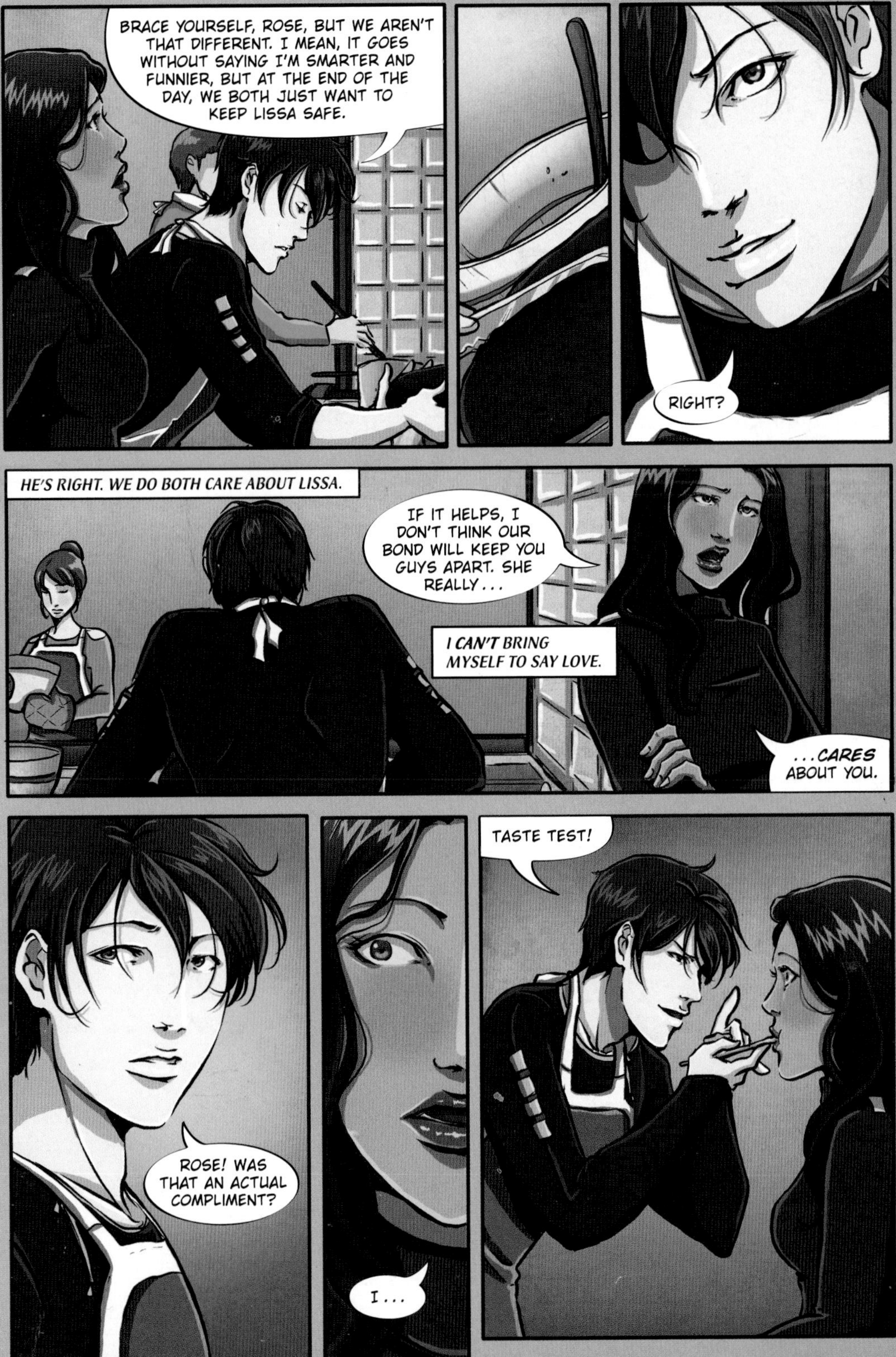
BRACE YOURSELF, ROSE, BUT WE AREN'T THAT DIFFERENT. I MEAN, IT GOES WITHOUT SAYING I'M SMARTER AND FUNNIER, BUT AT THE END OF THE DAY, WE BOTH JUST WANT TO KEEP LISSA SAFE.
RIGHT?
HE'S RIGHT. WE DO BOTH CARE ABOUT LISSA.
IF IT HELPS, I DON'T THINK OUR BOND WILL KEEP YOU GUYS APART. SHE REALLY . . .
I CAN'T BRING MYSELF TO SAY LOVE.
. . . CARES ABOUT YOU.
ROSE! WAS THAT AN ACTUAL COMPLIMENT?
I . . .
TASTE TEST!

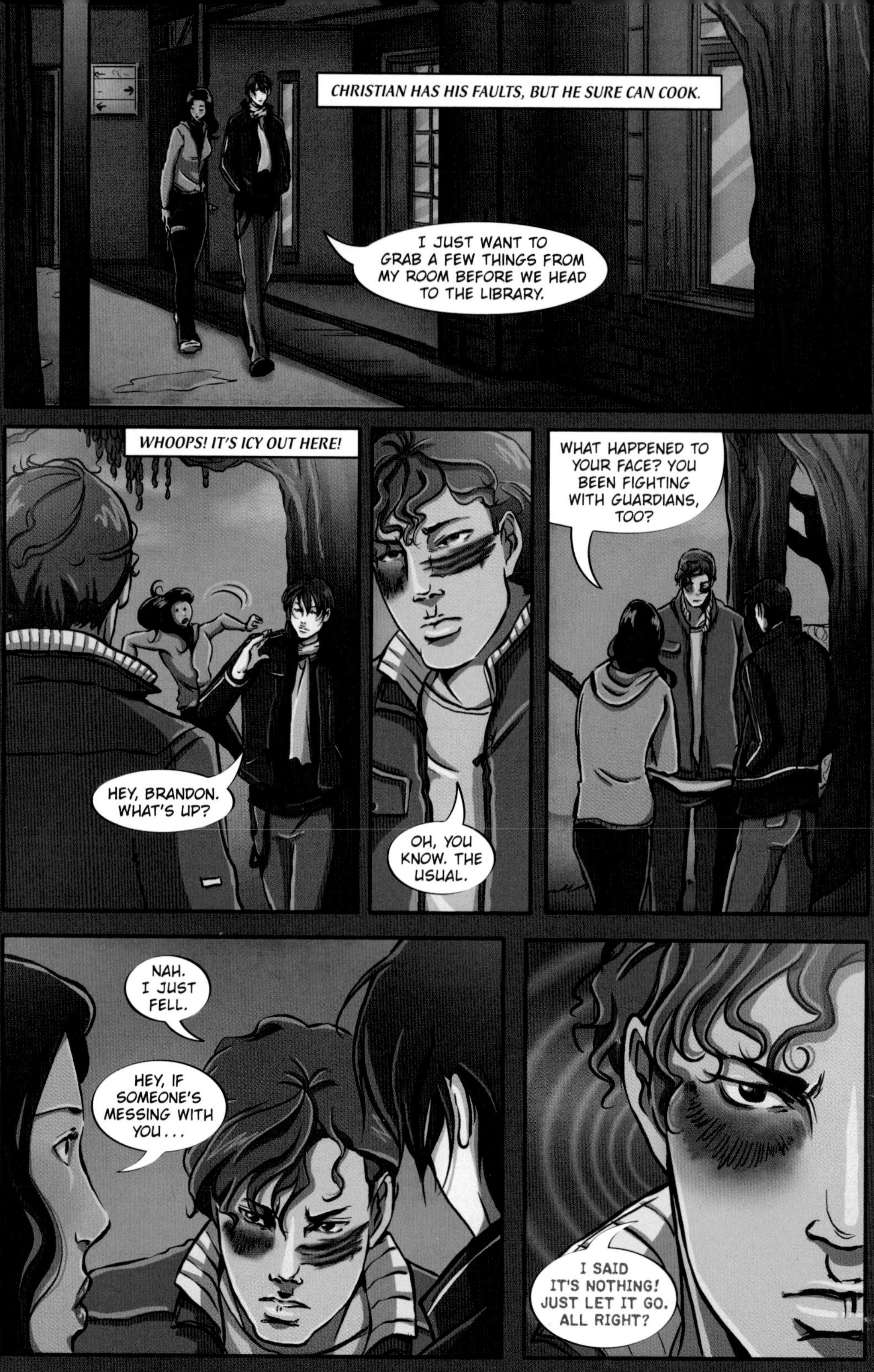
CHRISTIAN HAS HIS FAULTS, BUT HE SURE CAN COOK.
I JUST WANT TO GRAB A FEW THINGS FROM MY ROOM BEFORE WE HEAD TO THE LIBRARY.
WHOOPS! IT'S ICY OUT HERE!
HEY, BRANDON. WHAT'S UP?
OH, YOU KNOW. THE USUAL.
WHAT HAPPENED TO YOUR FACE? YOU BEEN FIGHTING WITH GUARDIANS, TOO?
NAH. I JUST FELL.
HEY, IF SOMEONE'S MESSING WITH YOU . . .
I SAID IT'S NOTHING! JUST LET IT GO. ALL RIGHT?

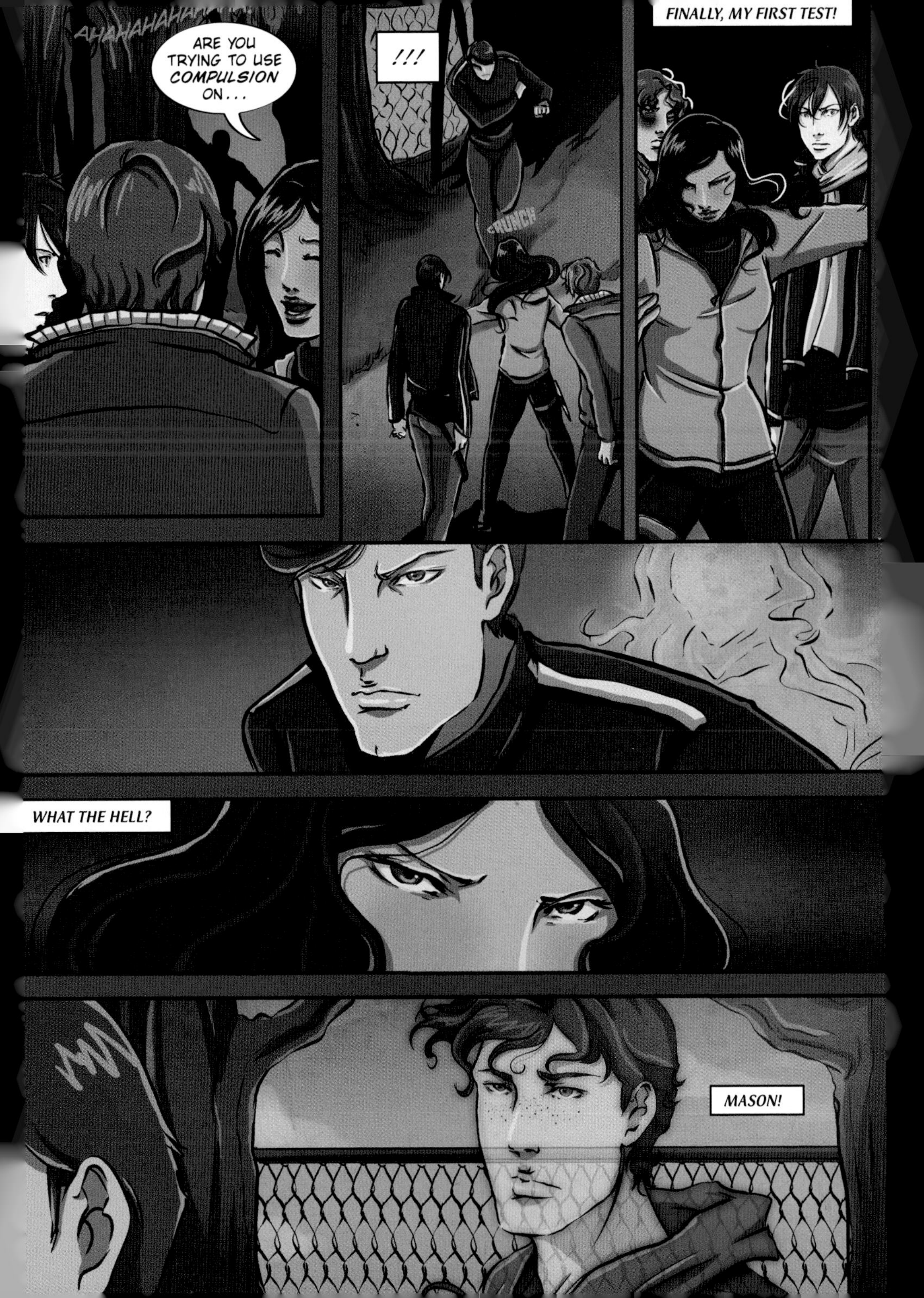
AHAHAHAHAH
ARE YOU TRYING TO USE COMPULSION ON...
!!!
CRUNCH
FINALLY, MY FIRST TEST!
WHAT THE HELL?
MASON!

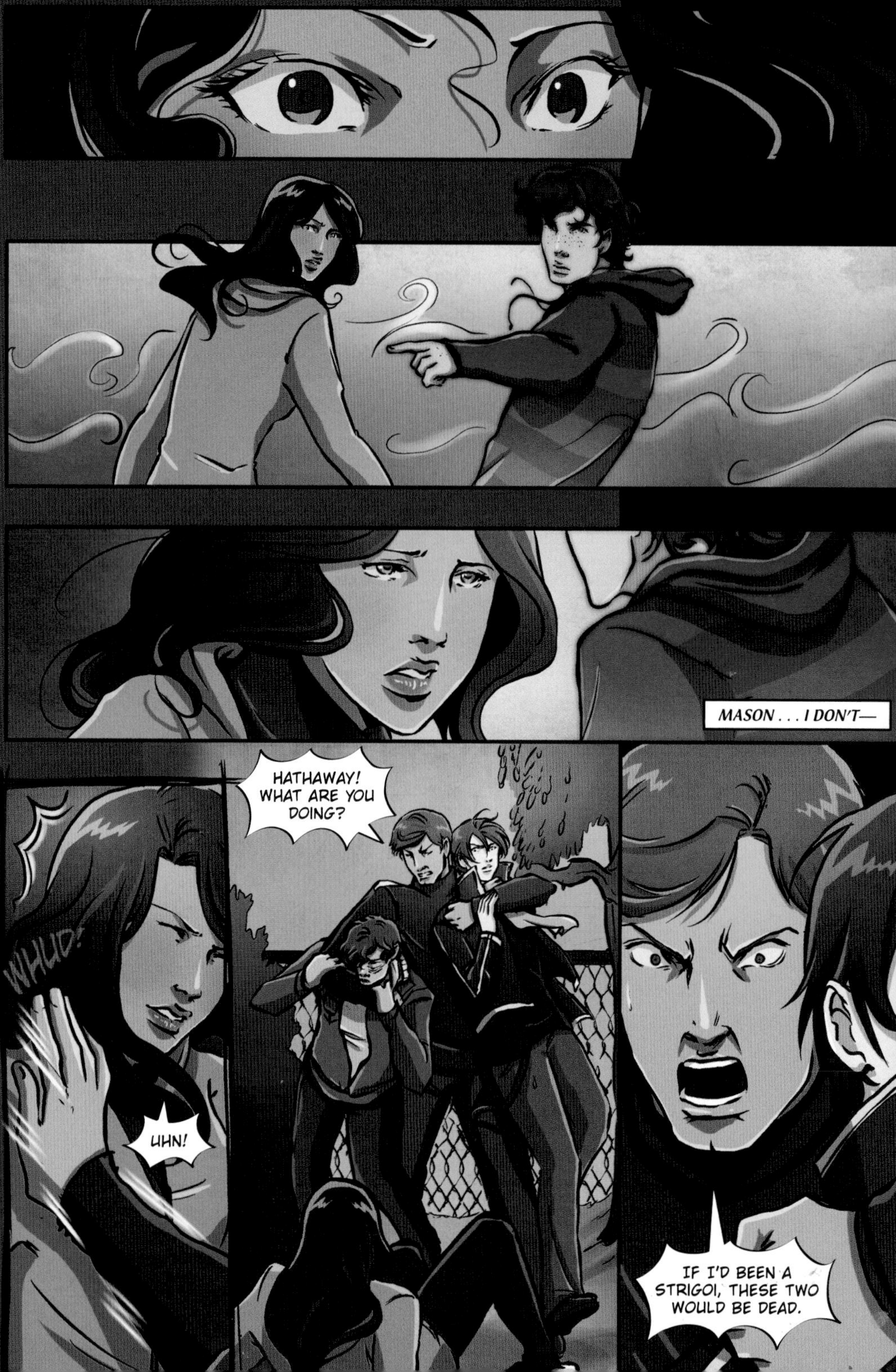
MASON . . . I DON'T—
HATHAWAY! WHAT ARE YOU DOING?
WHUD!
UHN!
IF I'D BEEN A STRIGOI, THESE TWO WOULD BE DEAD.

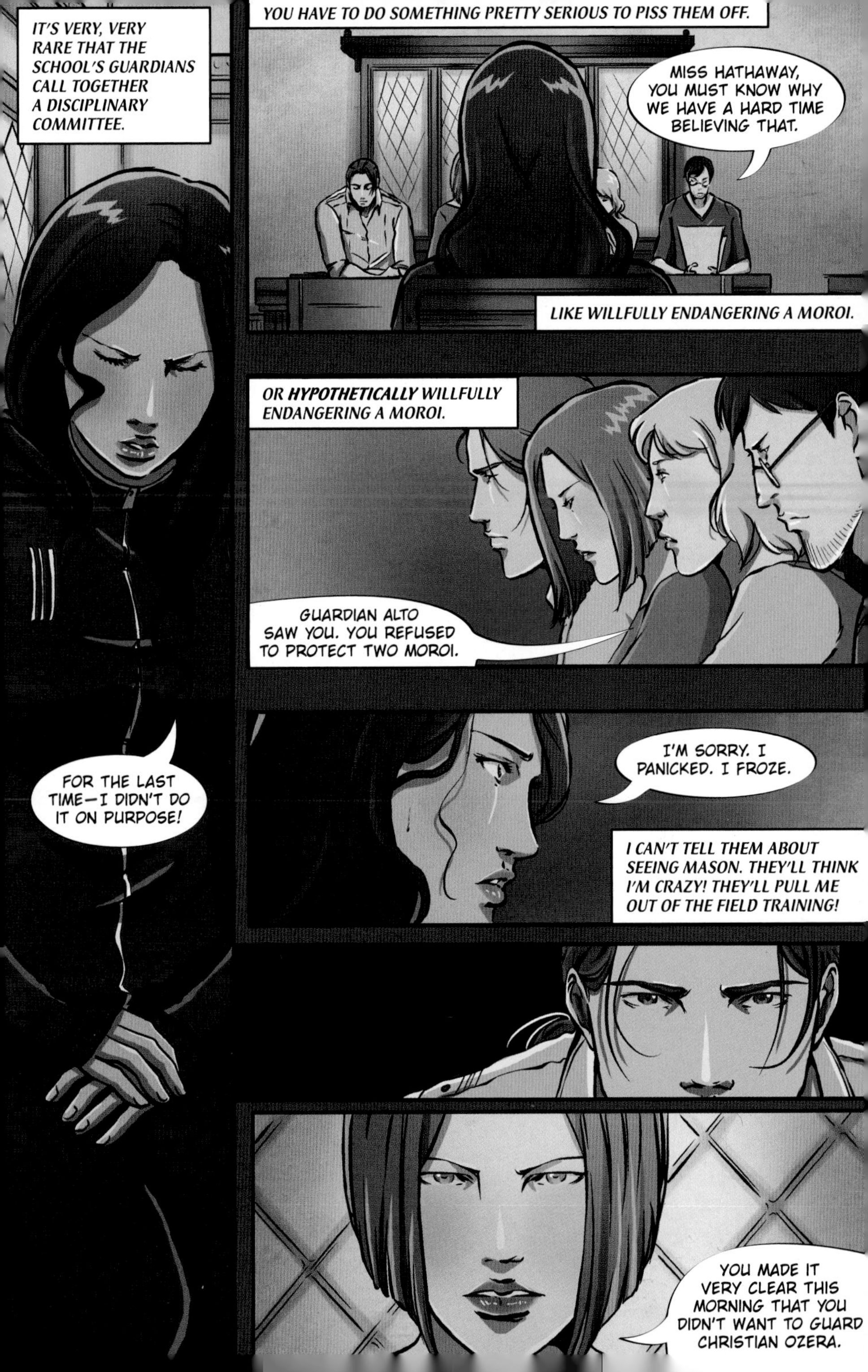
IT'S VERY, VERY RARE THAT THE SCHOOL'S GUARDIANS CALL TOGETHER A DISCIPLINARY COMMITTEE.
YOU HAVE TO DO SOMETHING PRETTY SERIOUS TO PISS THEM OFF.
MISS HATHAWAY, YOU MUST KNOW WHY WE HAVE A HARD TIME BELIEVING THAT.
LIKE WILLFULLY ENDANGERING A MOROI.
OR HYPOTHETICALLY WILLFULLY ENDANGERING A MOROI.
GUARDIAN ALTO SAW YOU. YOU REFUSED TO PROTECT TWO MOROI.
FOR THE LAST TIME—I DIDN'T DO IT ON PURPOSE!
I'M SORRY. I PANICKED. I FROZE.
I CAN'T TELL THEM ABOUT SEEING MASON. THEY'LL THINK I'M CRAZY! THEY'LL PULL ME OUT OF THE FIELD TRAINING!
YOU MADE IT VERY CLEAR THIS MORNING THAT YOU DIDN'T WANT TO GUARD CHRISTIAN OZERA.

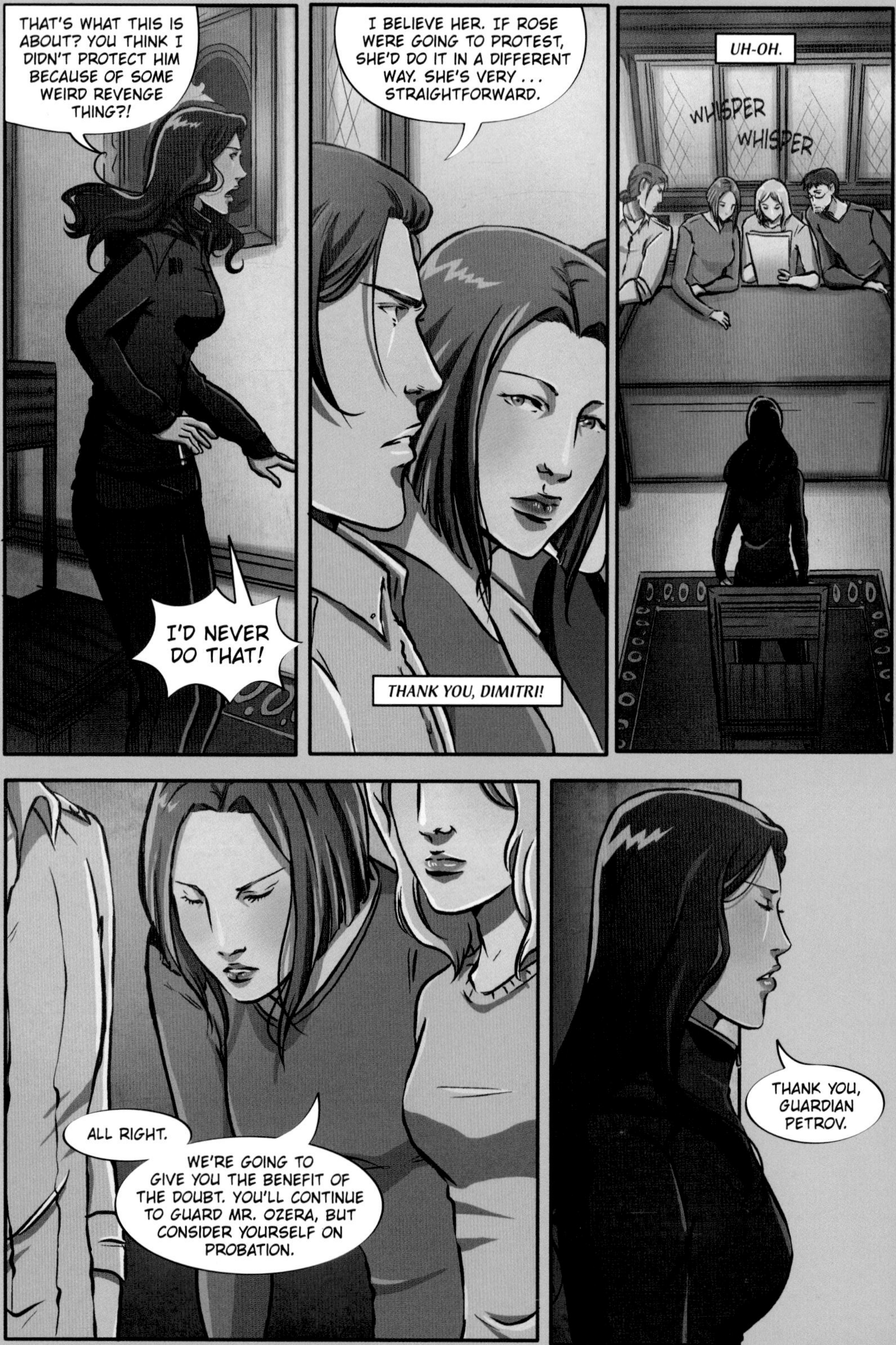
THAT'S WHAT THIS IS ABOUT? YOU THINK I DIDN'T PROTECT HIM BECAUSE OF SOME WEIRD REVENGE THING?!
I'D NEVER DO THAT!
I BELIEVE HER. IF ROSE WERE GOING TO PROTEST, SHE'D DO IT IN A DIFFERENT WAY. SHE'S VERY . . . STRAIGHTFORWARD.
THANK YOU, DIMITRI!
UH-OH.
WHISPER
WHISPER
ALL RIGHT.
WE'RE GOING TO GIVE YOU THE BENEFIT OF THE DOUBT. YOU'LL CONTINUE TO GUARD MR. OZERA, BUT CONSIDER YOURSELF ON PROBATION.
THANK YOU, GUARDIAN PETROV.

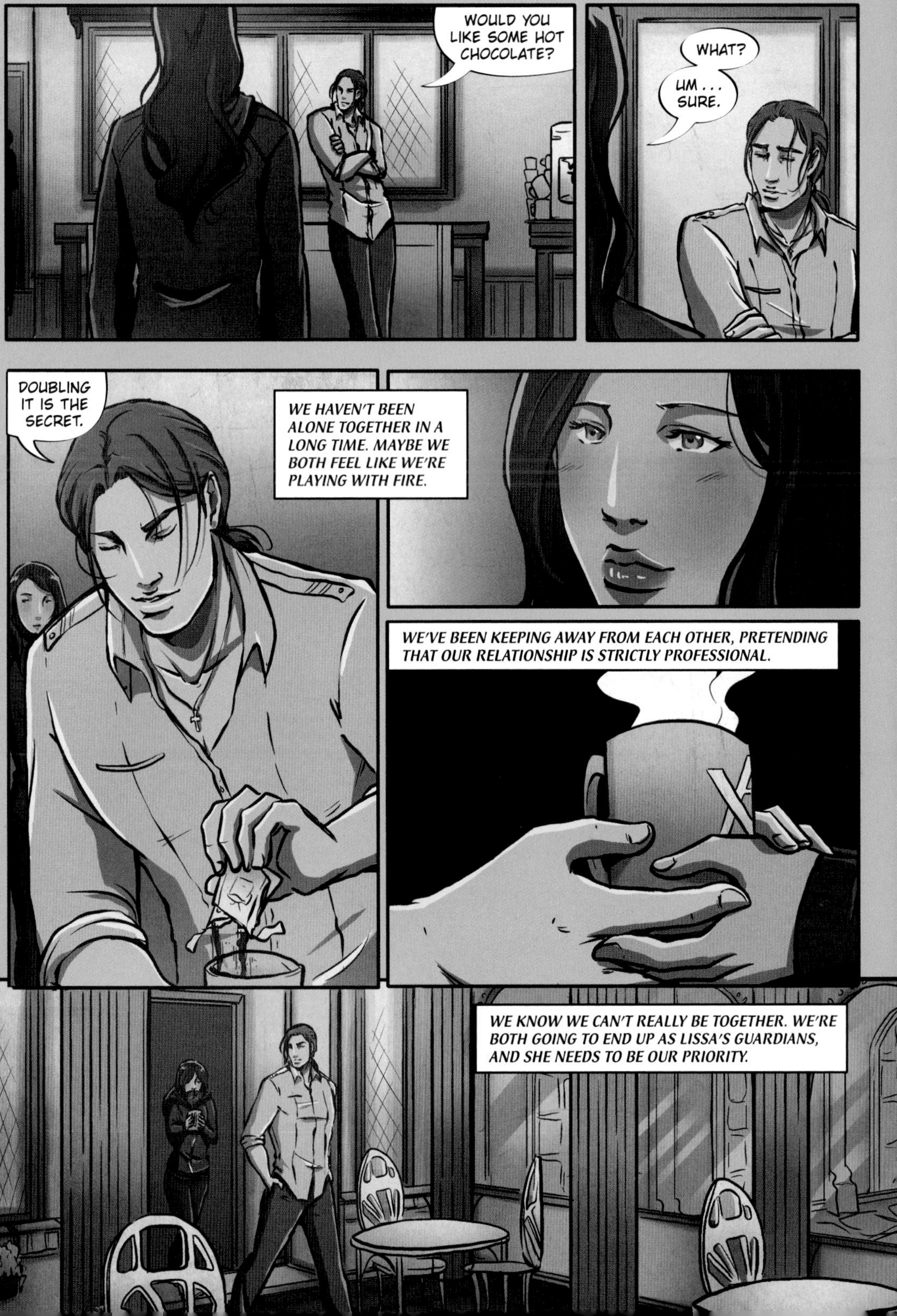
WOULD YOU LIKE SOME HOT CHOCOLATE?
WHAT?
UM . . . SURE.
DOUBLING IT IS THE SECRET.
WE HAVEN'T BEEN ALONE TOGETHER IN A LONG TIME. MAYBE WE BOTH FEEL LIKE WE'RE PLAYING WITH FIRE.
WE'VE BEEN KEEPING AWAY FROM EACH OTHER, PRETENDING THAT OUR RELATIONSHIP IS STRICTLY PROFESSIONAL.
WE KNOW WE CAN'T REALLY BE TOGETHER. WE'RE BOTH GOING TO END UP AS LISSA'S GUARDIANS, AND SHE NEEDS TO BE OUR PRIORITY.

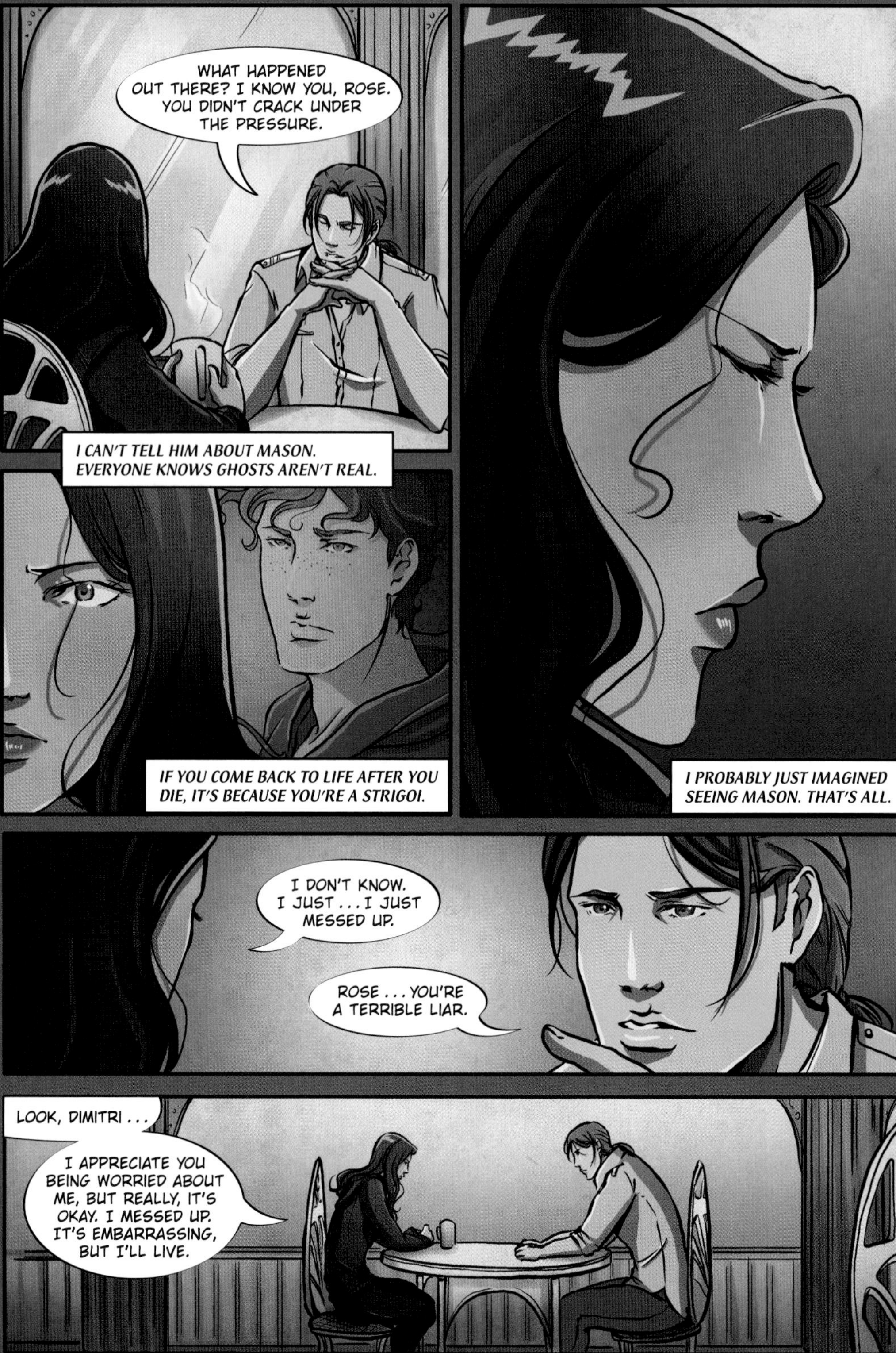
WHAT HAPPENED OUT THERE? I KNOW YOU, ROSE. YOU DIDN'T CRACK UNDER THE PRESSURE.
I CAN'T TELL HIM ABOUT MASON. EVERYONE KNOWS GHOSTS AREN'T REAL.
IF YOU COME BACK TO LIFE AFTER YOU DIE, IT'S BECAUSE YOU'RE A STRIGOI.
I PROBABLY JUST IMAGINED SEEING MASON. THAT'S ALL.
I DON'T KNOW. I JUST . . . I JUST MESSED UP.
ROSE . . . YOU'RE A TERRIBLE LIAR.
LOOK, DIMITRI . . .
I APPRECIATE YOU BEING WORRIED ABOUT ME, BUT REALLY, IT'S OKAY. I MESSED UP. IT'S EMBARRASSING, BUT I'LL LIVE.

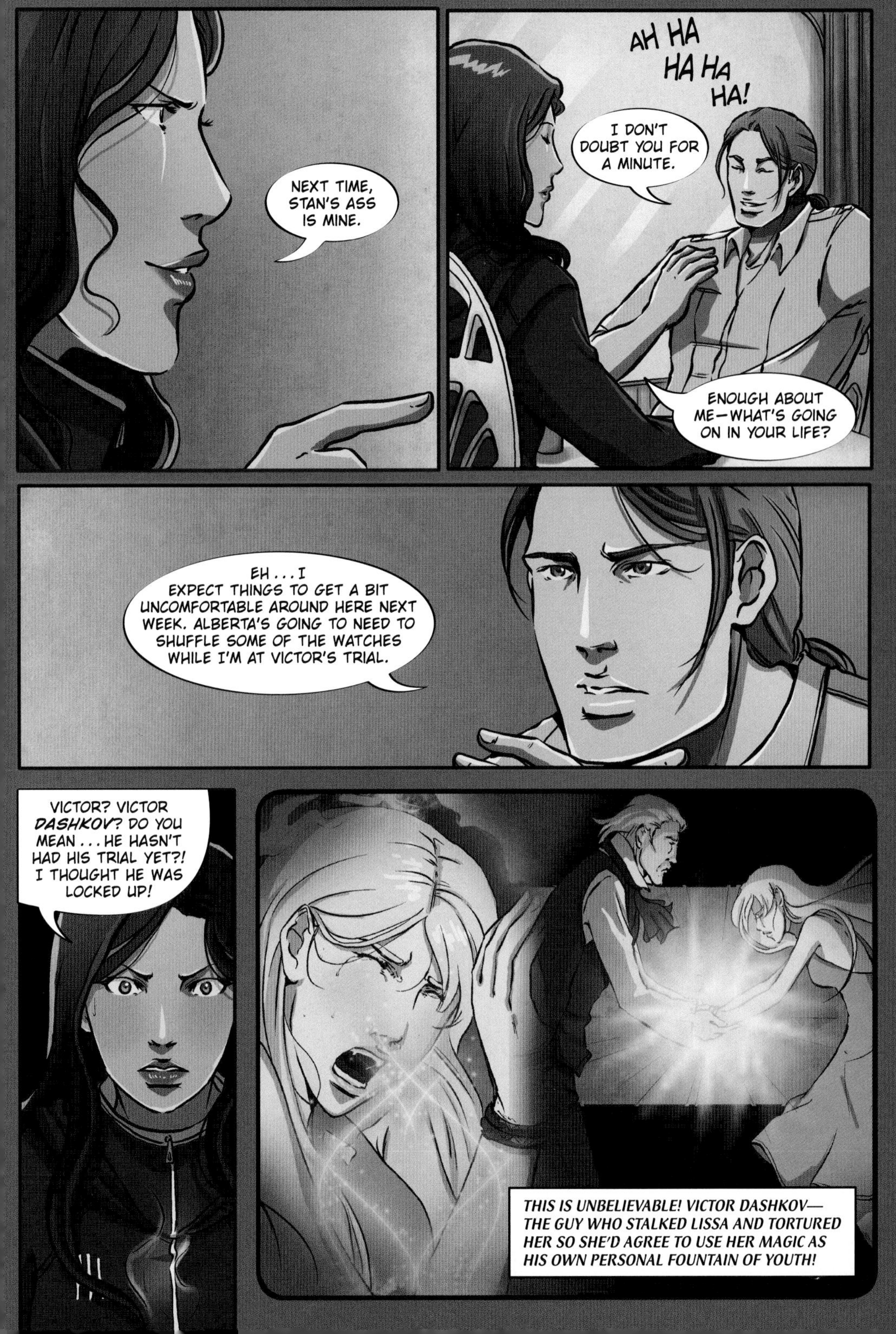
NEXT TIME, STAN'S ASS IS MINE.
AH HA HA HA HA!
I DON'T DOUBT YOU FOR A MINUTE.
ENOUGH ABOUT ME—WHAT'S GOING ON IN YOUR LIFE?
EH . . . I EXPECT THINGS TO GET A BIT UNCOMFORTABLE AROUND HERE NEXT WEEK. ALBERTA'S GOING TO NEED TO SHUFFLE SOME OF THE WATCHES WHILE I'M AT VICTOR'S TRIAL.
VICTOR? VICTOR *DASHKOV*? DO YOU MEAN . . . HE HASN'T HAD HIS TRIAL YET?! I THOUGHT HE WAS LOCKED UP!
THIS IS UNBELIEVABLE! VICTOR DASHKOV—THE GUY WHO STALKED LISSA AND TORTURED HER SO SHE'D AGREE TO USE HER MAGIC AS HIS OWN PERSONAL FOUNTAIN OF YOUTH!

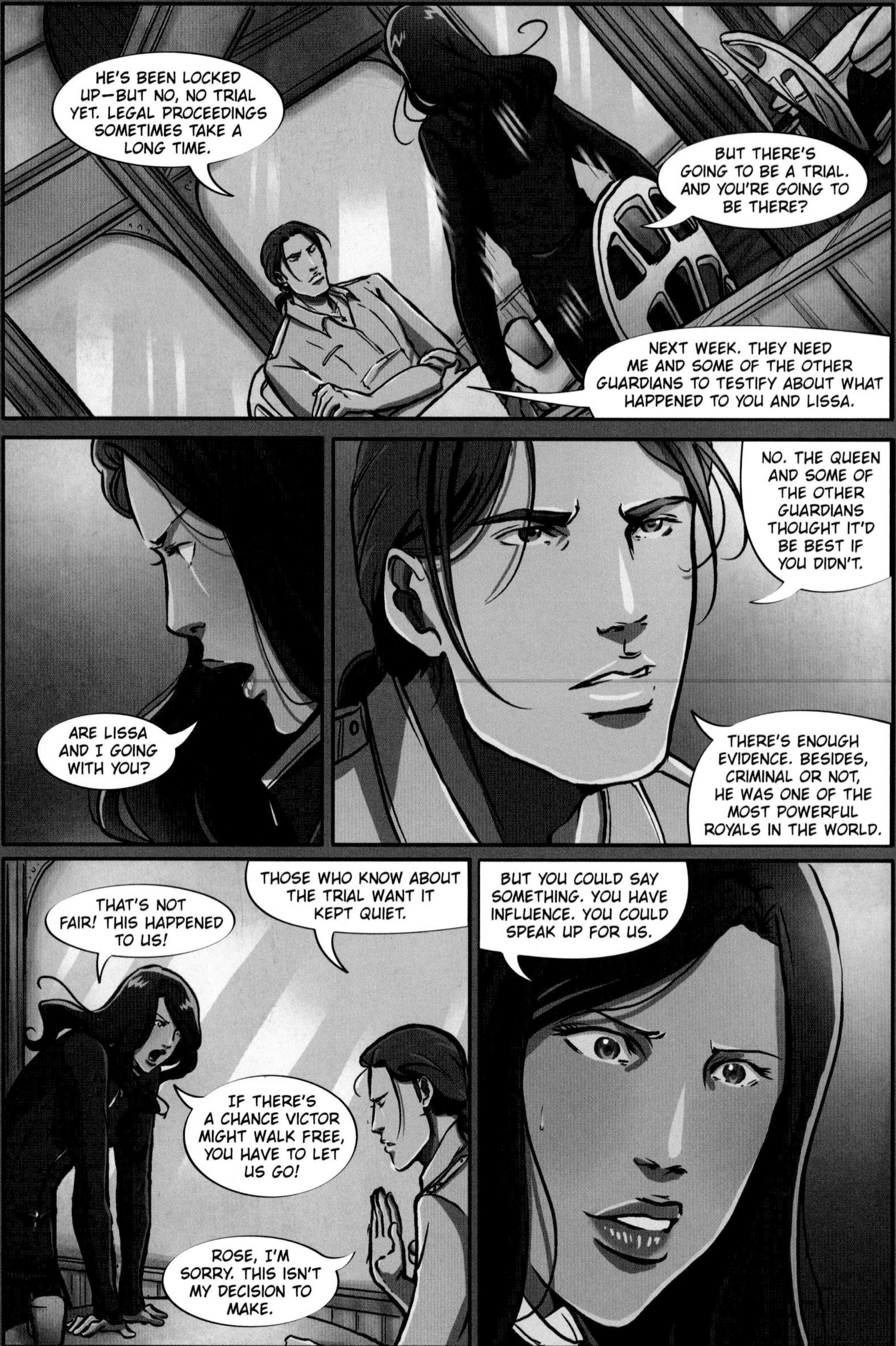
HE'S BEEN LOCKED UP—BUT NO, NO TRIAL YET. LEGAL PROCEEDINGS SOMETIMES TAKE A LONG TIME.
BUT THERE'S GOING TO BE A TRIAL. AND YOU'RE GOING TO BE THERE?
NEXT WEEK. THEY NEED ME AND SOME OF THE OTHER GUARDIANS TO TESTIFY ABOUT WHAT HAPPENED TO YOU AND LISSA.
ARE LISSA AND I GOING WITH YOU?
NO. THE QUEEN AND SOME OF THE OTHER GUARDIANS THOUGHT IT'D BE BEST IF YOU DIDN'T.
THERE'S ENOUGH EVIDENCE. BESIDES, CRIMINAL OR NOT, HE WAS ONE OF THE MOST POWERFUL ROYALS IN THE WORLD.
THAT'S NOT FAIR! THIS HAPPENED TO US!
THOSE WHO KNOW ABOUT THE TRIAL WANT IT KEPT QUIET.
IF THERE'S A CHANCE VICTOR MIGHT WALK FREE, YOU HAVE TO LET US GO!
ROSE, I'M SORRY. THIS ISN'T MY DECISION TO MAKE.
BUT YOU COULD SAY SOMETHING. YOU HAVE INFLUENCE. YOU COULD SPEAK UP FOR US.

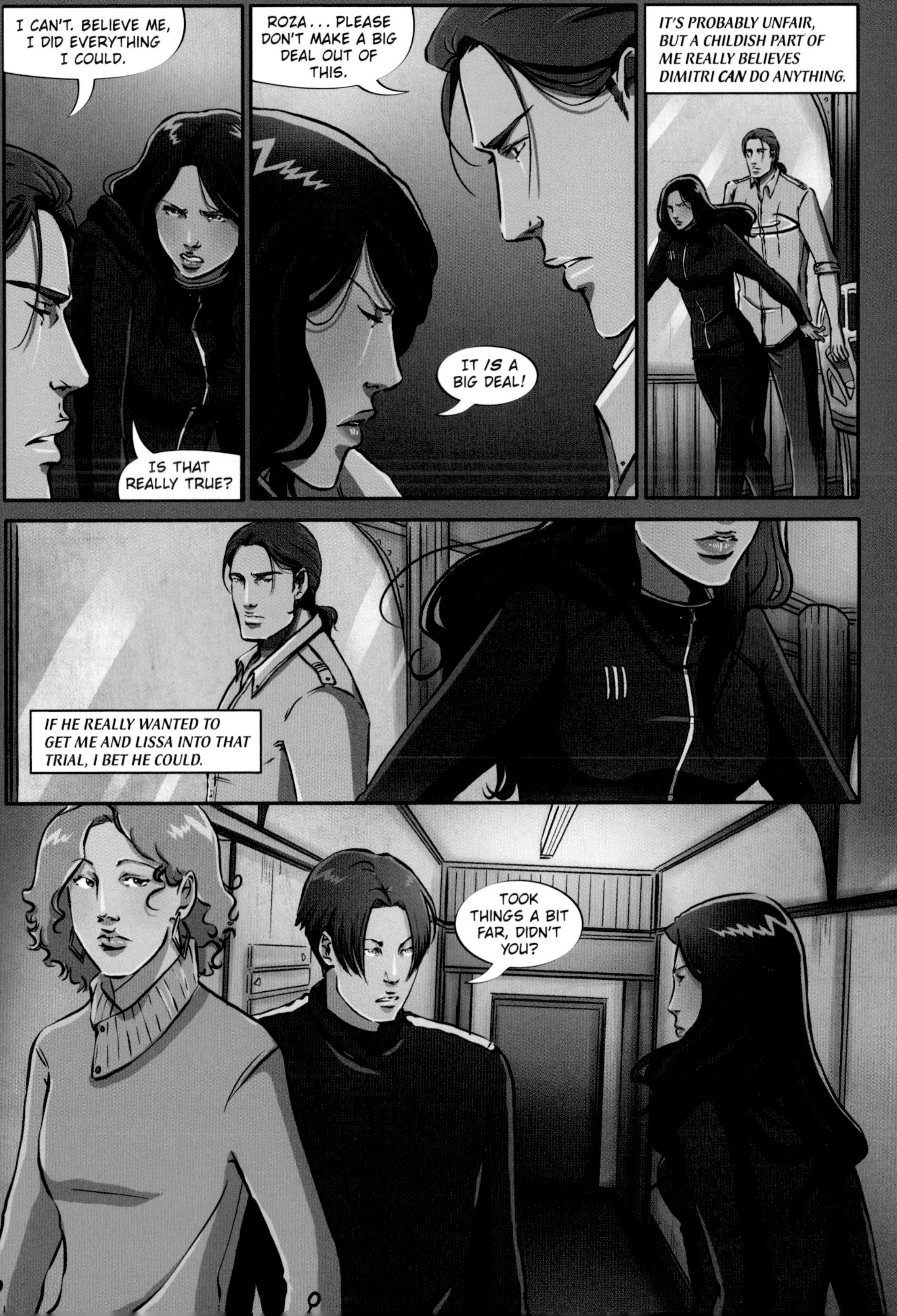
I CAN'T. BELIEVE ME, I DID EVERYTHING I COULD.
IS THAT REALLY TRUE?
ROZA . . . PLEASE DON'T MAKE A BIG DEAL OUT OF THIS.
IT *IS* A BIG DEAL!
*IT'S PROBABLY UNFAIR, BUT A CHILDISH PART OF ME REALLY BELIEVES DIMITRI **CAN** DO ANYTHING.*
IF HE REALLY WANTED TO GET ME AND LISSA INTO THAT TRIAL, I BET HE COULD.
TOOK THINGS A BIT FAR, DIDN'T YOU?

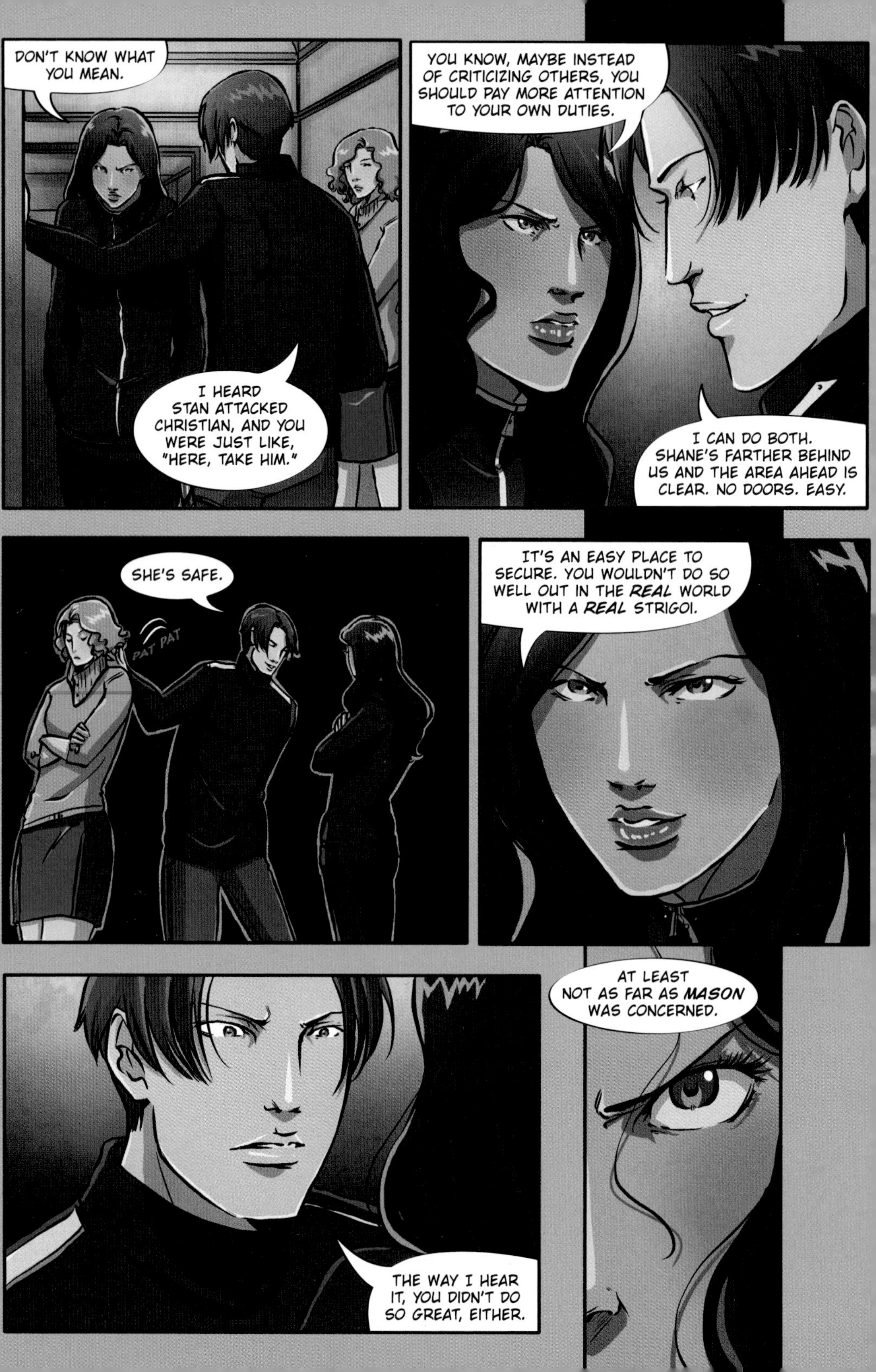
DON'T KNOW WHAT YOU MEAN.
I HEARD STAN ATTACKED CHRISTIAN, AND YOU WERE JUST LIKE, "HERE, TAKE HIM."
YOU KNOW, MAYBE INSTEAD OF CRITICIZING OTHERS, YOU SHOULD PAY MORE ATTENTION TO YOUR OWN DUTIES.
I CAN DO BOTH. SHANE'S FARTHER BEHIND US AND THE AREA AHEAD IS CLEAR. NO DOORS. EASY.
SHE'S SAFE.
PAT PAT
IT'S AN EASY PLACE TO SECURE. YOU WOULDN'T DO SO WELL OUT IN THE *REAL* WORLD WITH A *REAL* STRIGOI.
THE WAY I HEAR IT, YOU DIDN'T DO SO GREAT, EITHER.
AT LEAST NOT AS FAR AS *MASON* WAS CONCERNED.

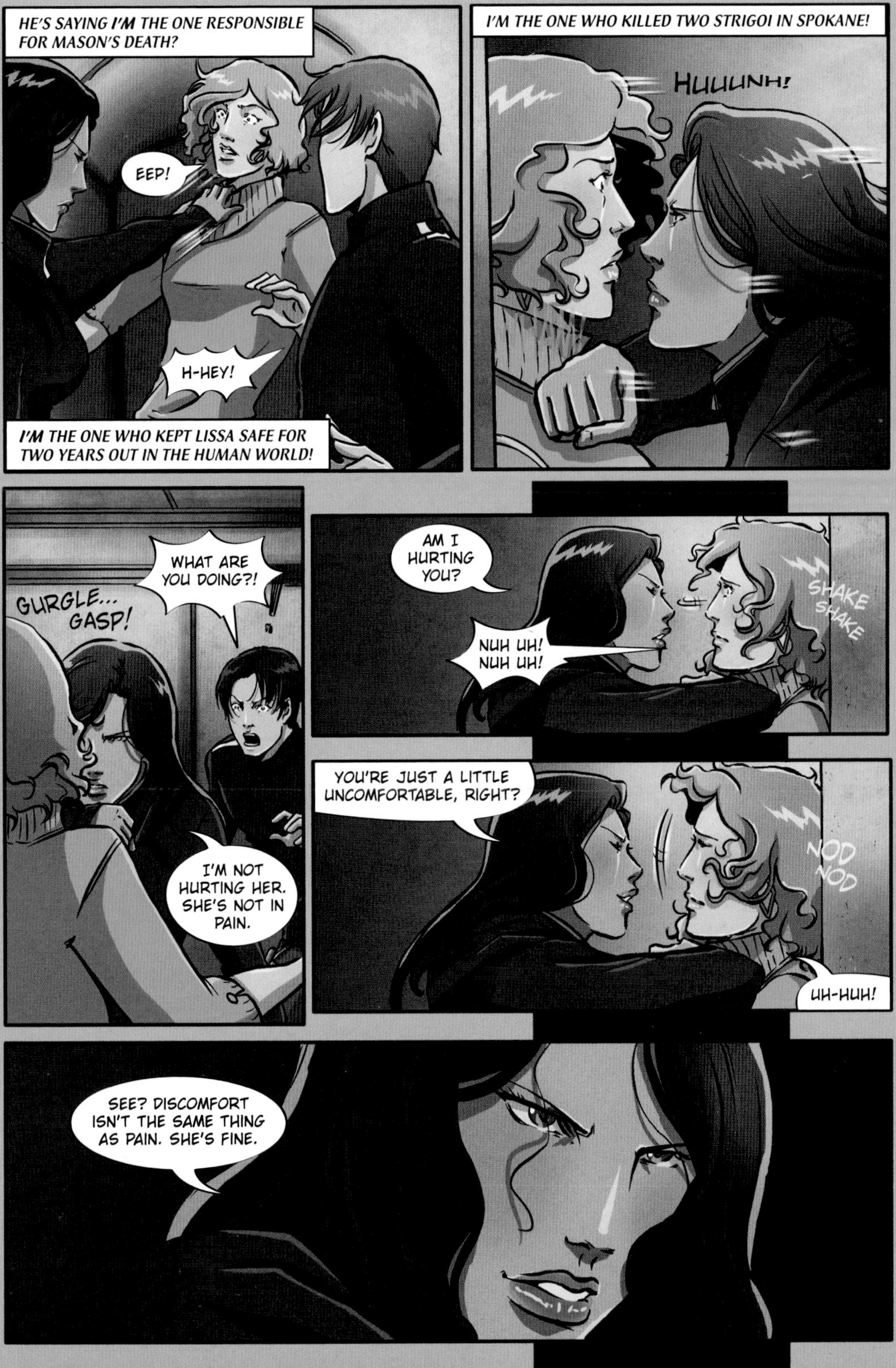
HE'S SAYING *I'M* THE ONE RESPONSIBLE FOR MASON'S DEATH?
EEP!
H-HEY!
I'M THE ONE WHO KEPT LISSA SAFE FOR TWO YEARS OUT IN THE HUMAN WORLD!
I'M THE ONE WHO KILLED TWO STRIGOI IN SPOKANE!
HUUUNH!
GURGLE... GASP!
WHAT ARE YOU DOING?!
I'M NOT HURTING HER. SHE'S NOT IN PAIN.
AM I HURTING YOU?
NUH UH! NUH UH!
SHAKE SHAKE
YOU'RE JUST A LITTLE UNCOMFORTABLE, RIGHT?
NOD NOD
UH-HUH!
SEE? DISCOMFORT ISN'T THE SAME THING AS PAIN. SHE'S FINE.

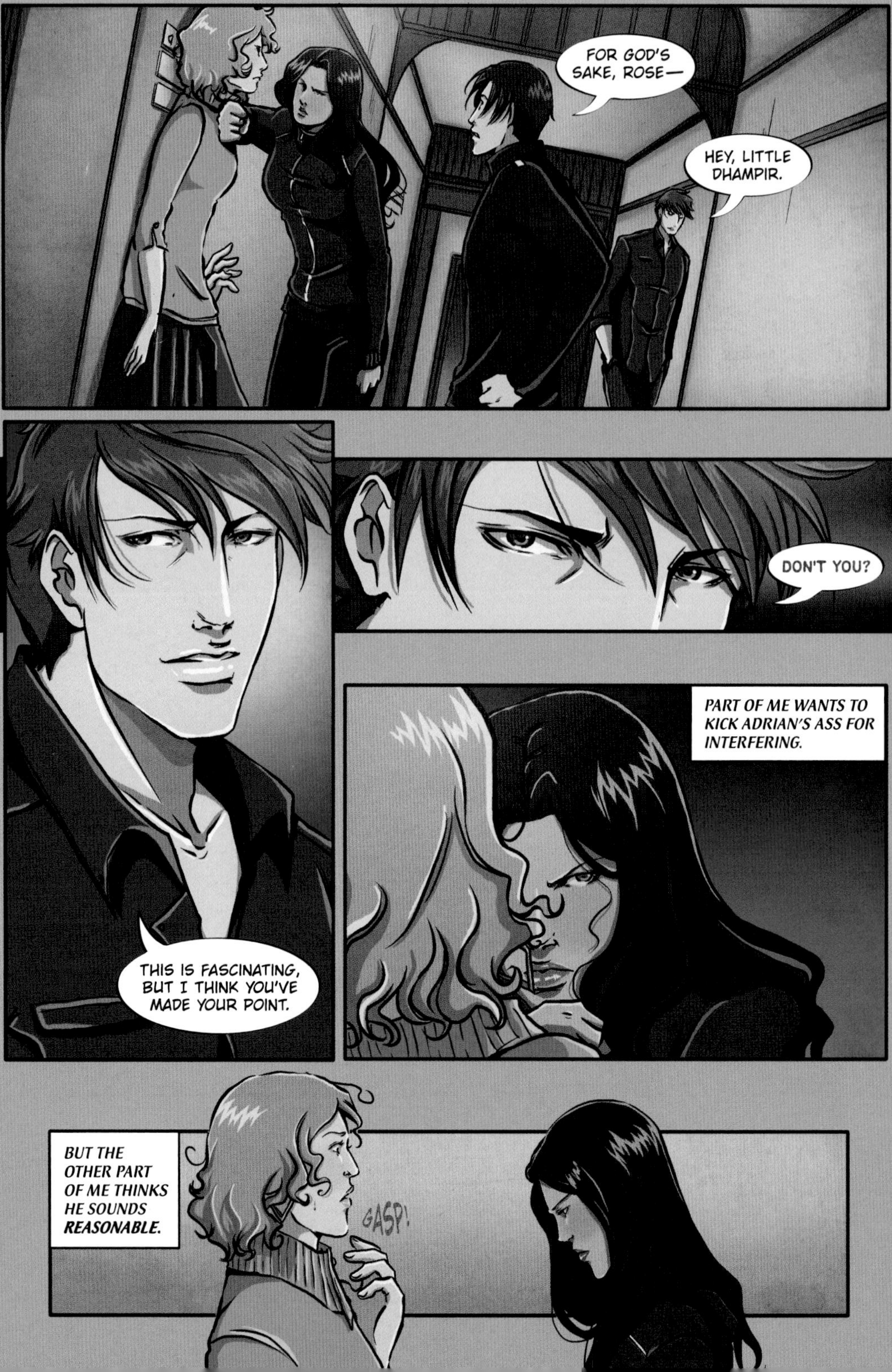
FOR GOD'S SAKE, ROSE—
HEY, LITTLE DHAMPIR.
DON'T YOU?
THIS IS FASCINATING, BUT I THINK YOU'VE MADE YOUR POINT.
PART OF ME WANTS TO KICK ADRIAN'S ASS FOR INTERFERING.
BUT THE OTHER PART OF ME THINKS HE SOUNDS **REASONABLE**.
GASP!

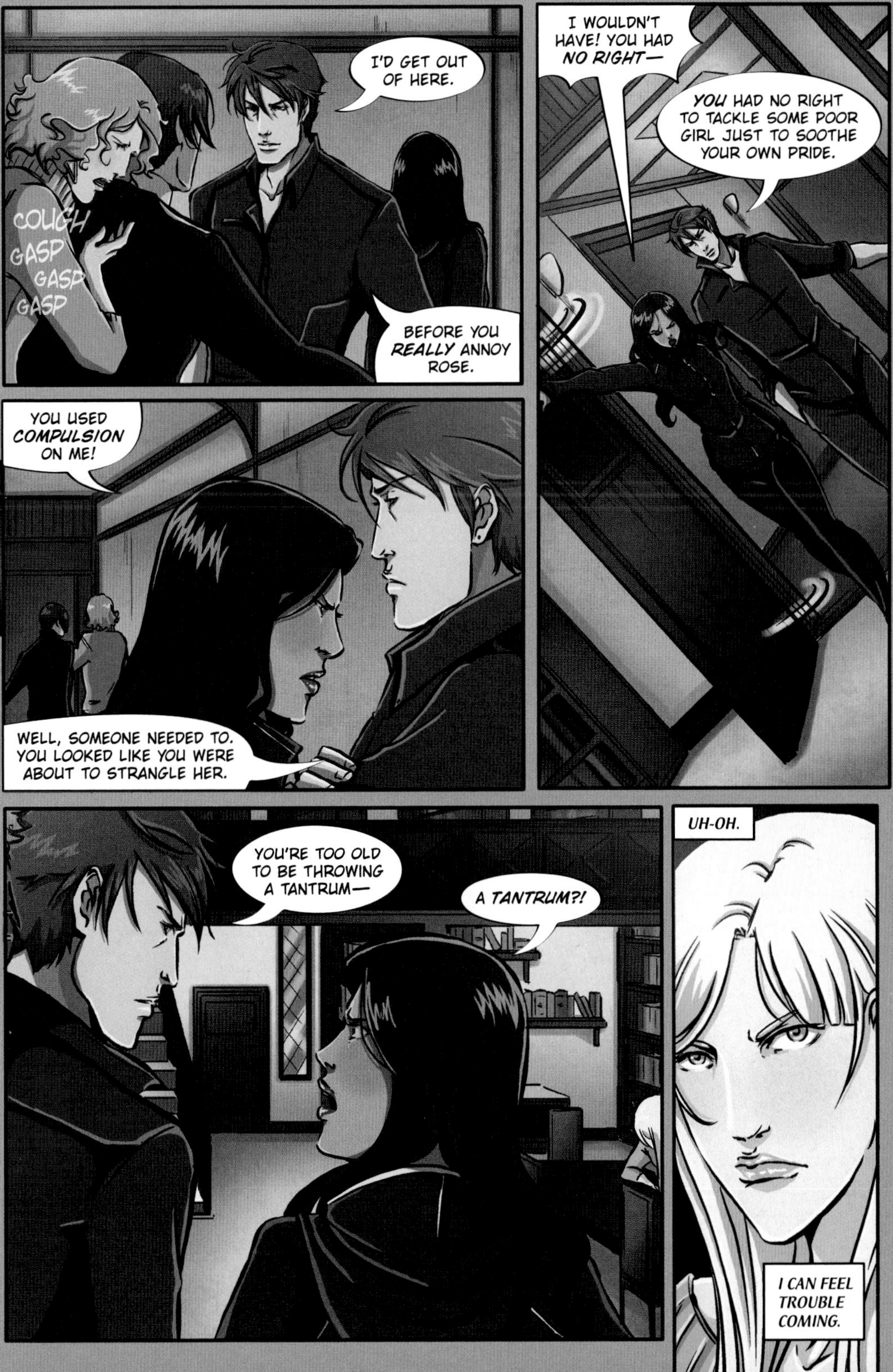
I'D GET OUT OF HERE.
COUGH
GASP
GASP
GASP
BEFORE YOU *REALLY* ANNOY ROSE.
I WOULDN'T HAVE! YOU HAD *NO RIGHT*—
YOU HAD NO RIGHT TO TACKLE SOME POOR GIRL JUST TO SOOTHE YOUR OWN PRIDE.
YOU USED *COMPULSION* ON ME!
WELL, SOMEONE NEEDED TO. YOU LOOKED LIKE YOU WERE ABOUT TO STRANGLE HER.
YOU'RE TOO OLD TO BE THROWING A TANTRUM—
A *TANTRUM?!*
UH-OH.
I CAN FEEL TROUBLE COMING.

UH . . . HEY.

I WAS WONDERING WHEN YOU'D SHOW UP.

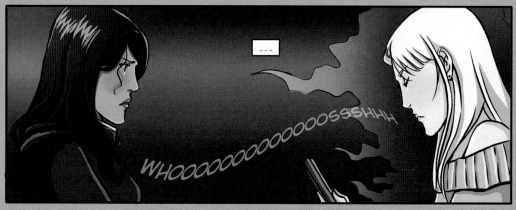

. . .

WHOOOOOOOOOOOOOOSSSHHH

SIIIGH

SLAM

OKAY, TALK TO ME, LISS. I KNOW YOU'RE MAD.

I HEARD ABOUT YOU AND CHRISTIAN. I CAN'T BELIEVE YOU'D DO SOMETHING SO CHILDISH!

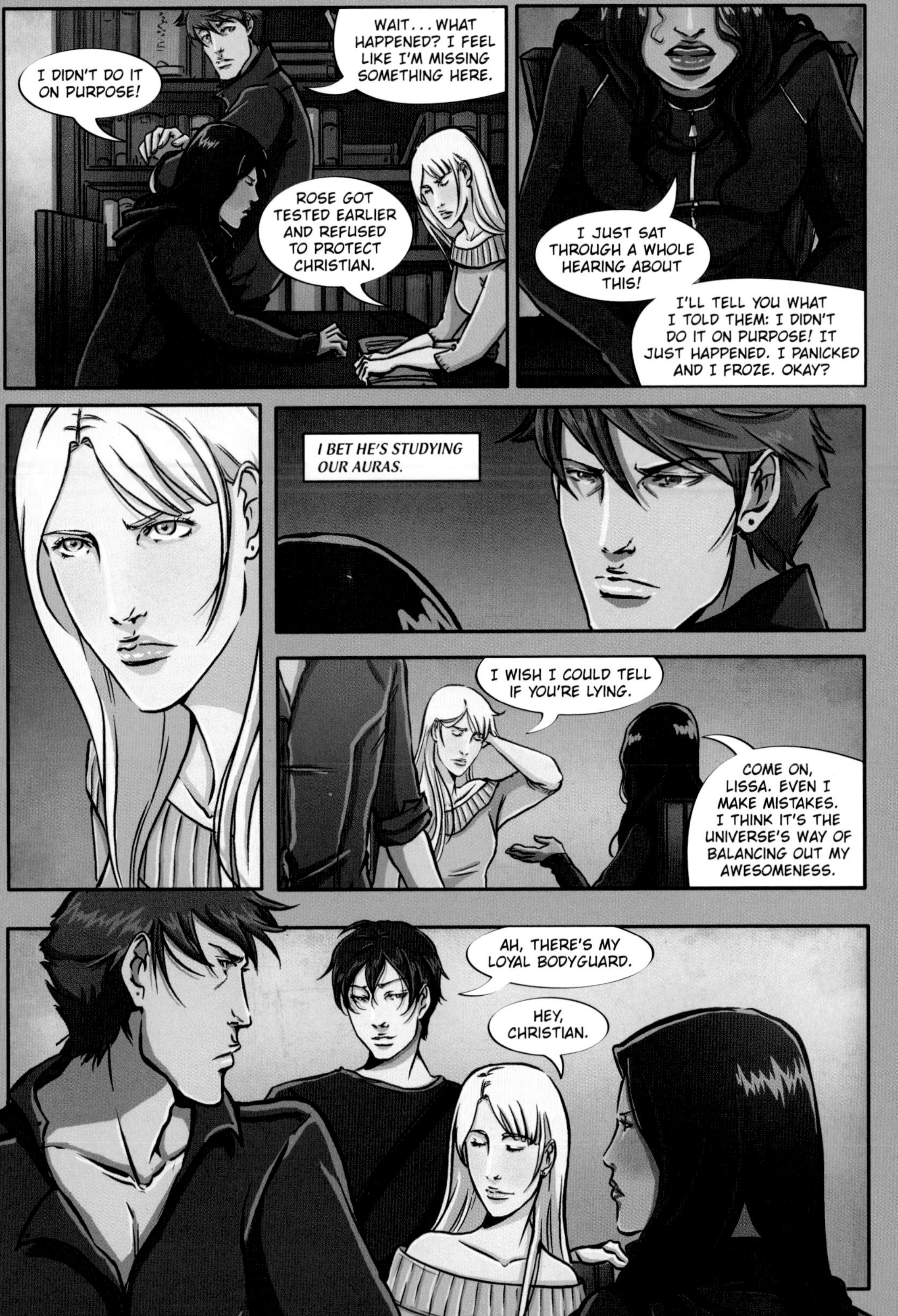
I DIDN'T DO IT ON PURPOSE!
WAIT... WHAT HAPPENED? I FEEL LIKE I'M MISSING SOMETHING HERE.
ROSE GOT TESTED EARLIER AND REFUSED TO PROTECT CHRISTIAN.
I JUST SAT THROUGH A WHOLE HEARING ABOUT THIS!
I'LL TELL YOU WHAT I TOLD THEM: I DIDN'T DO IT ON PURPOSE! IT JUST HAPPENED. I PANICKED AND I FROZE. OKAY?
I BET HE'S STUDYING OUR AURAS.
I WISH I COULD TELL IF YOU'RE LYING.
COME ON, LISSA. EVEN I MAKE MISTAKES. I THINK IT'S THE UNIVERSE'S WAY OF BALANCING OUT MY AWESOMENESS.
AH, THERE'S MY LOYAL BODYGUARD.
HEY, CHRISTIAN.

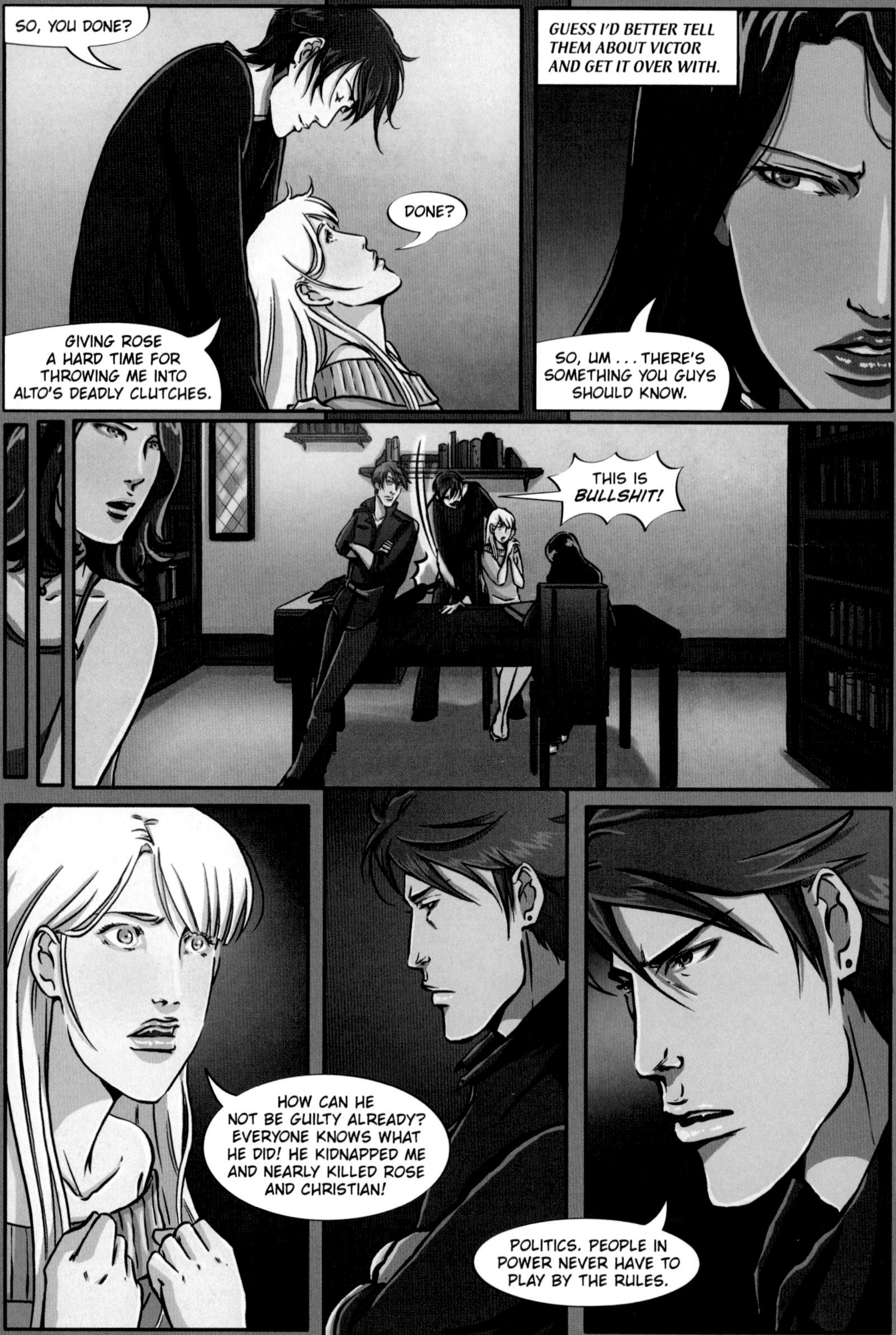
SO, YOU DONE?
DONE?
GIVING ROSE A HARD TIME FOR THROWING ME INTO ALTO'S DEADLY CLUTCHES.
GUESS I'D BETTER TELL THEM ABOUT VICTOR AND GET IT OVER WITH.
SO, UM . . . THERE'S SOMETHING YOU GUYS SHOULD KNOW.
THIS IS BULLSHIT!
HOW CAN HE NOT BE GUILTY ALREADY? EVERYONE KNOWS WHAT HE DID! HE KIDNAPPED ME AND NEARLY KILLED ROSE AND CHRISTIAN!
POLITICS. PEOPLE IN POWER NEVER HAVE TO PLAY BY THE RULES.

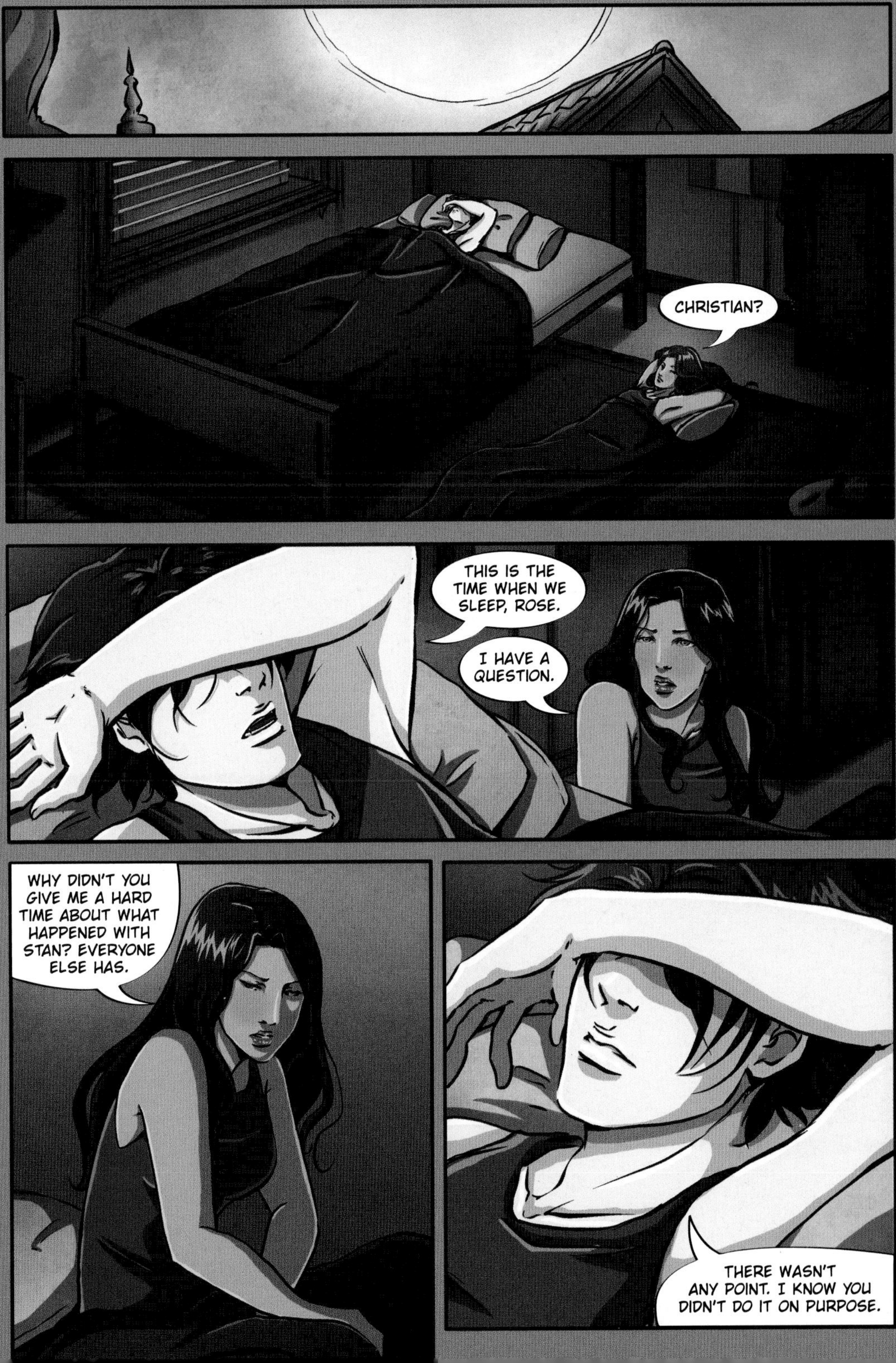
CHRISTIAN?
THIS IS THE TIME WHEN WE SLEEP, ROSE.
I HAVE A QUESTION.
WHY DIDN'T YOU GIVE ME A HARD TIME ABOUT WHAT HAPPENED WITH STAN? EVERYONE ELSE HAS.
THERE WASN'T ANY POINT. I KNOW YOU DIDN'T DO IT ON PURPOSE.

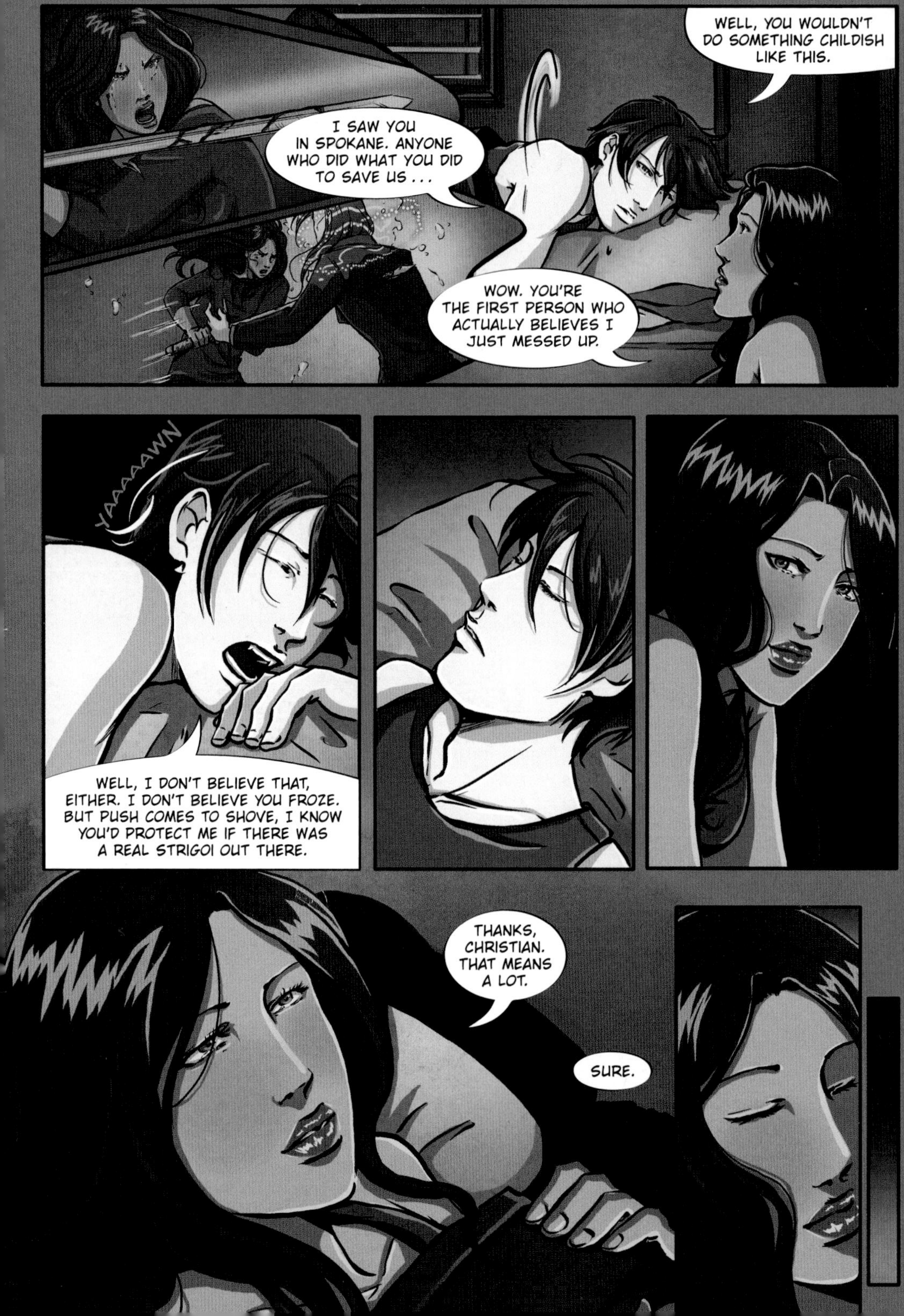
WELL, YOU WOULDN'T DO SOMETHING CHILDISH LIKE THIS.
I SAW YOU IN SPOKANE. ANYONE WHO DID WHAT YOU DID TO SAVE US . . .
WOW. YOU'RE THE FIRST PERSON WHO ACTUALLY BELIEVES I JUST MESSED UP.
YAAAAAAWN
WELL, I DON'T BELIEVE THAT, EITHER. I DON'T BELIEVE YOU FROZE. BUT PUSH COMES TO SHOVE, I KNOW YOU'D PROTECT ME IF THERE WAS A REAL STRIGOI OUT THERE.
THANKS, CHRISTIAN. THAT MEANS A LOT.
SURE.

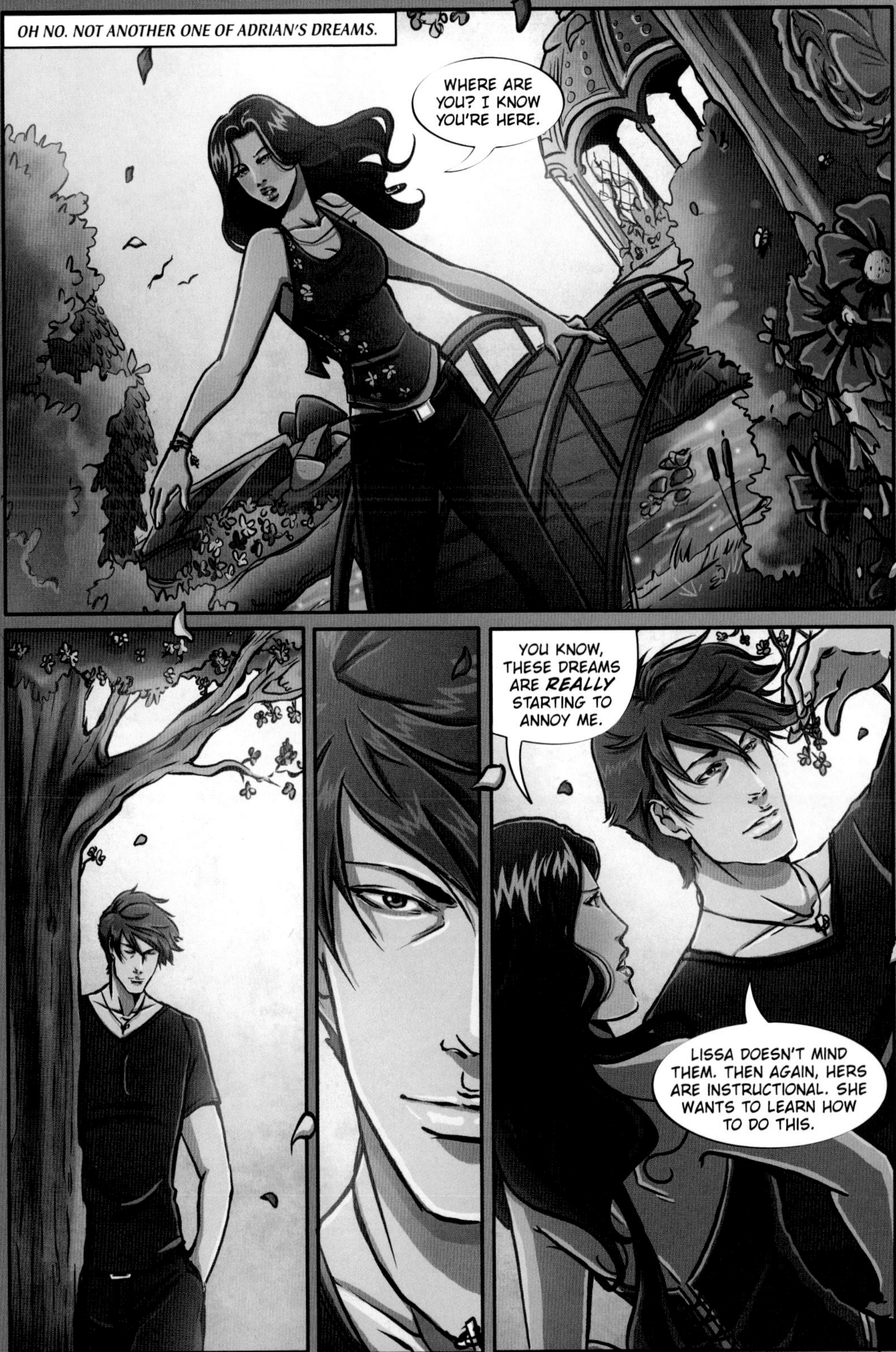
OH NO. NOT ANOTHER ONE OF ADRIAN'S DREAMS.
WHERE ARE YOU? I KNOW YOU'RE HERE.
YOU KNOW, THESE DREAMS ARE *REALLY* STARTING TO ANNOY ME.
LISSA DOESN'T MIND THEM. THEN AGAIN, HERS ARE INSTRUCTIONAL. SHE WANTS TO LEARN HOW TO DO THIS.

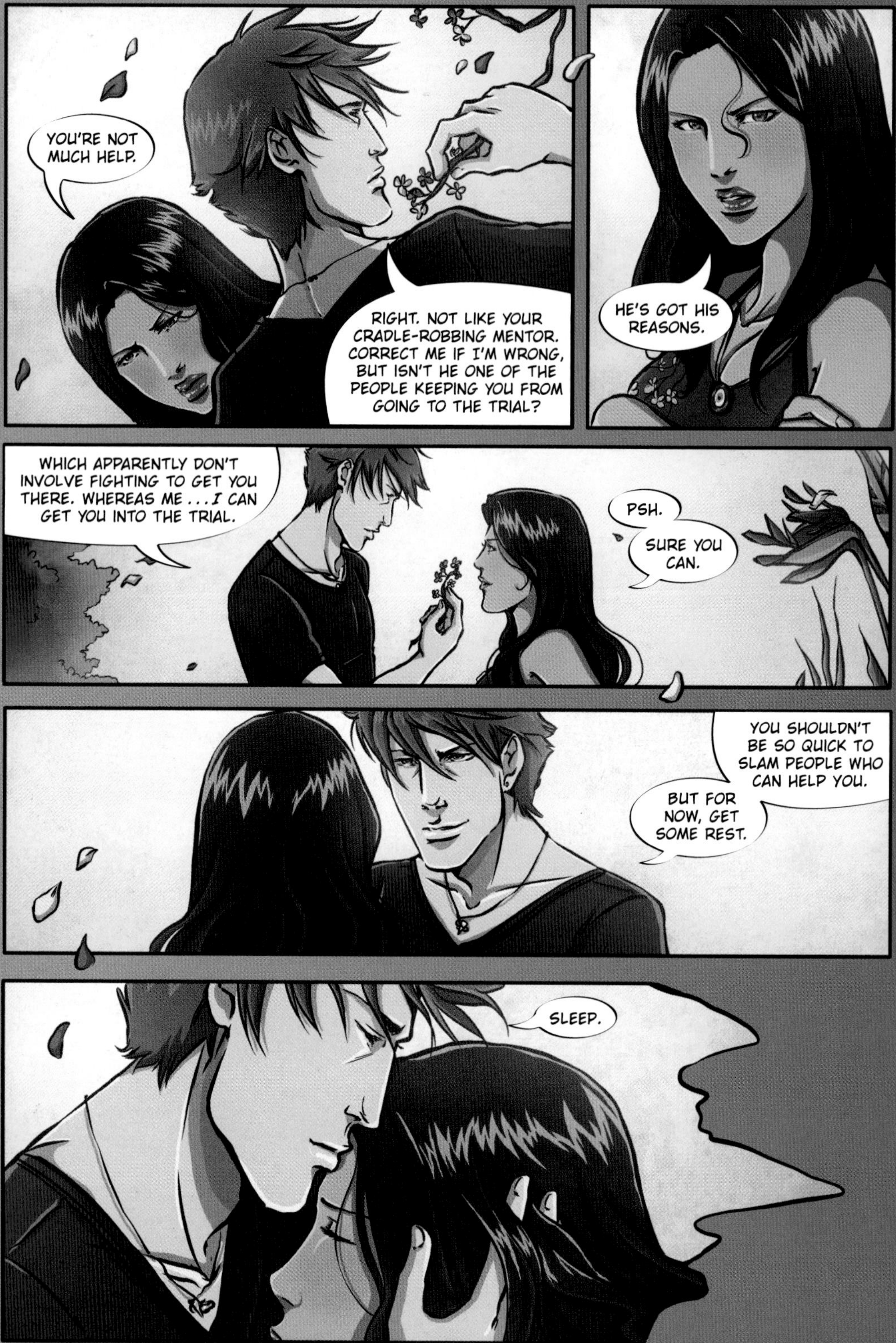

YOU'RE NOT MUCH HELP.
RIGHT. NOT LIKE YOUR CRADLE-ROBBING MENTOR. CORRECT ME IF I'M WRONG, BUT ISN'T HE ONE OF THE PEOPLE KEEPING YOU FROM GOING TO THE TRIAL?
HE'S GOT HIS REASONS.
WHICH APPARENTLY DON'T INVOLVE FIGHTING TO GET YOU THERE. WHEREAS ME . . . I CAN GET YOU INTO THE TRIAL.
PSH.
SURE YOU CAN.
YOU SHOULDN'T BE SO QUICK TO SLAM PEOPLE WHO CAN HELP YOU.
BUT FOR NOW, GET SOME REST.
SLEEP.

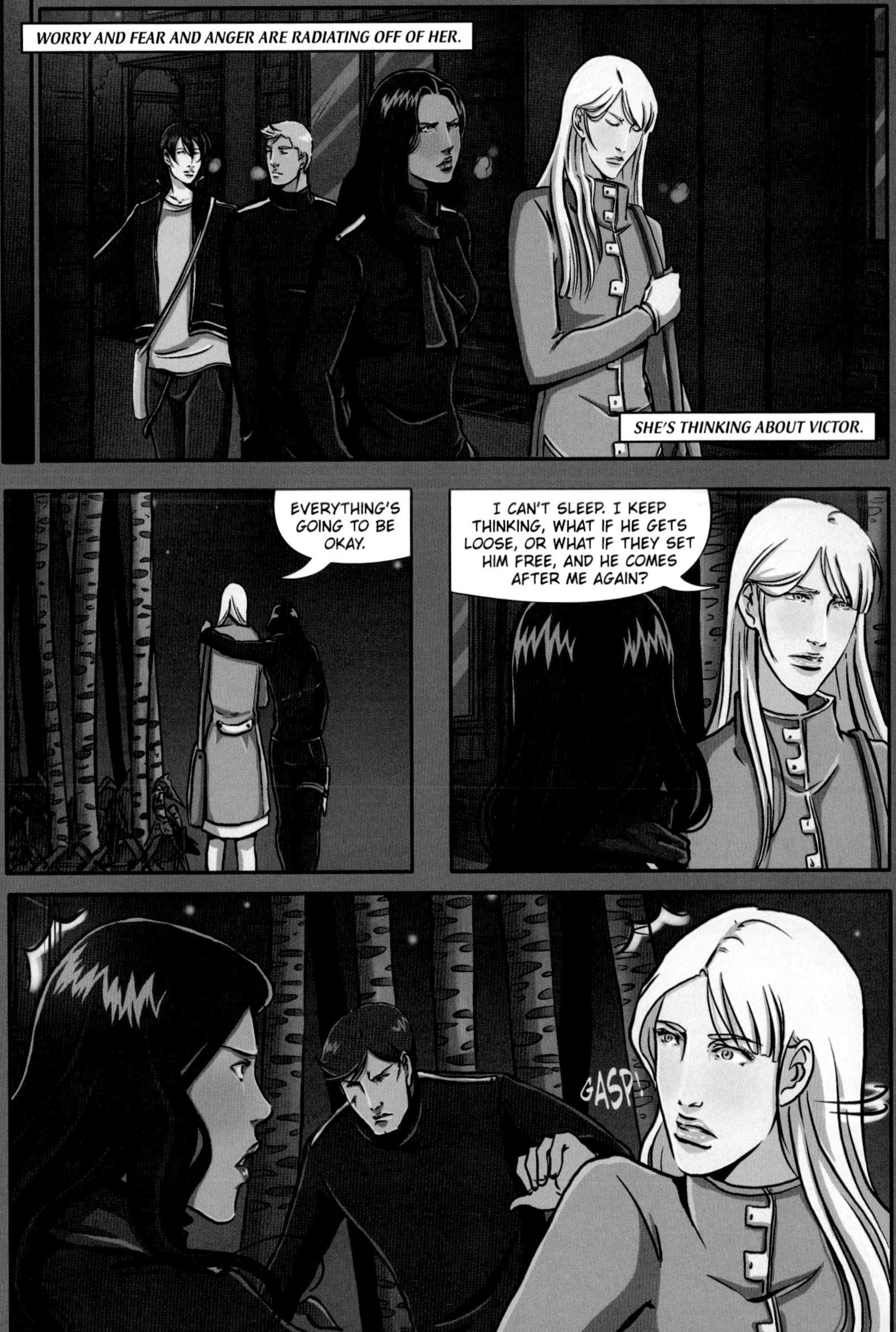
WORRY AND FEAR AND ANGER ARE RADIATING OFF OF HER.
SHE'S THINKING ABOUT VICTOR.
EVERYTHING'S GOING TO BE OKAY.
I CAN'T SLEEP. I KEEP THINKING, WHAT IF HE GETS LOOSE, OR WHAT IF THEY SET HIM FREE, AND HE COMES AFTER ME AGAIN?
GASP!

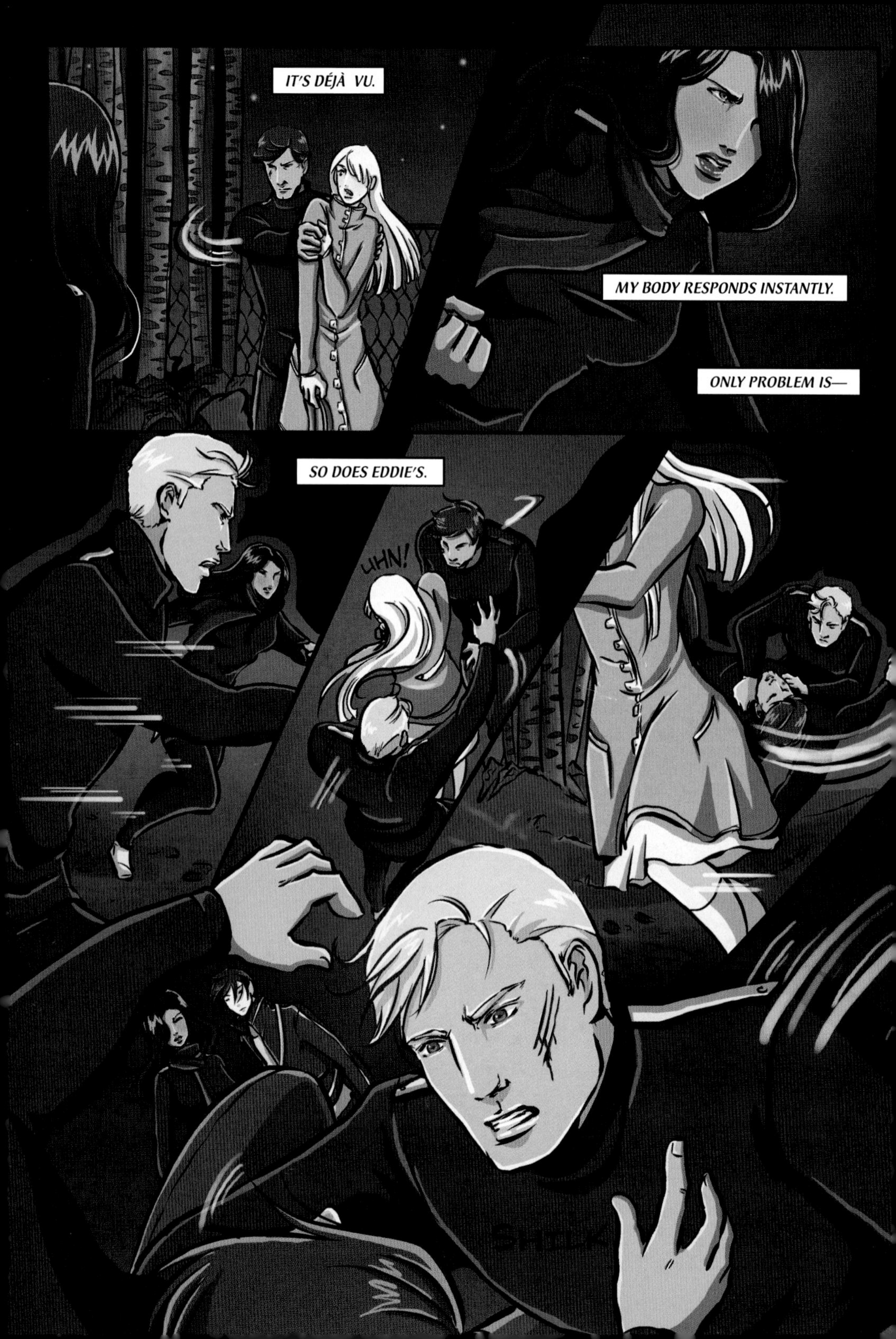
IT'S DÉJÀ VU.
MY BODY RESPONDS INSTANTLY.
ONLY PROBLEM IS—
SO DOES EDDIE'S.
UHN!

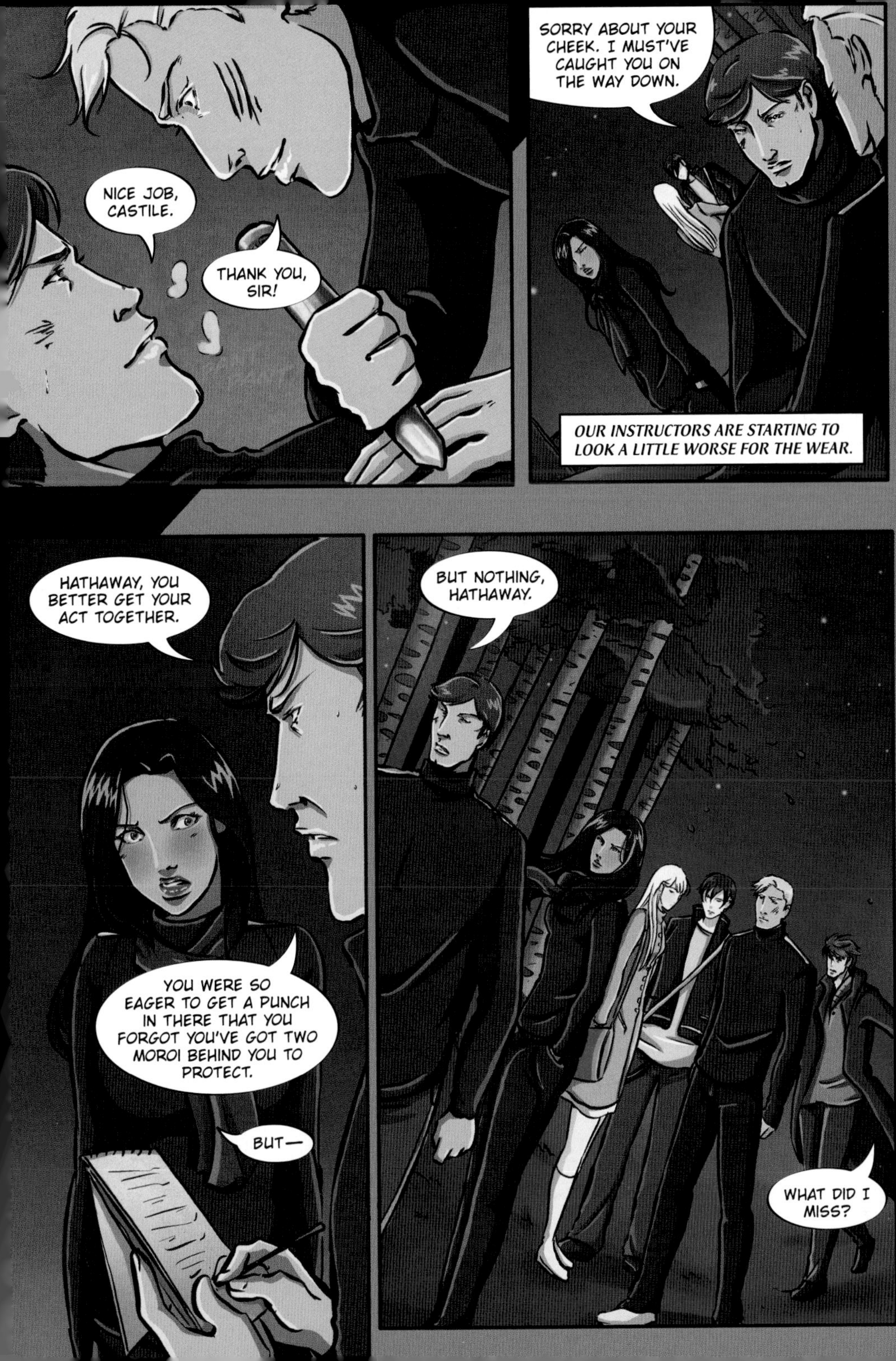
NICE JOB, CASTILE.
THANK YOU, SIR!
SORRY ABOUT YOUR CHEEK. I MUST'VE CAUGHT YOU ON THE WAY DOWN.
OUR INSTRUCTORS ARE STARTING TO LOOK A LITTLE WORSE FOR THE WEAR.
HATHAWAY, YOU BETTER GET YOUR ACT TOGETHER.
YOU WERE SO EAGER TO GET A PUNCH IN THERE THAT YOU FORGOT YOU'VE GOT TWO MOROI BEHIND YOU TO PROTECT.
BUT—
BUT NOTHING, HATHAWAY.
WHAT DID I MISS?

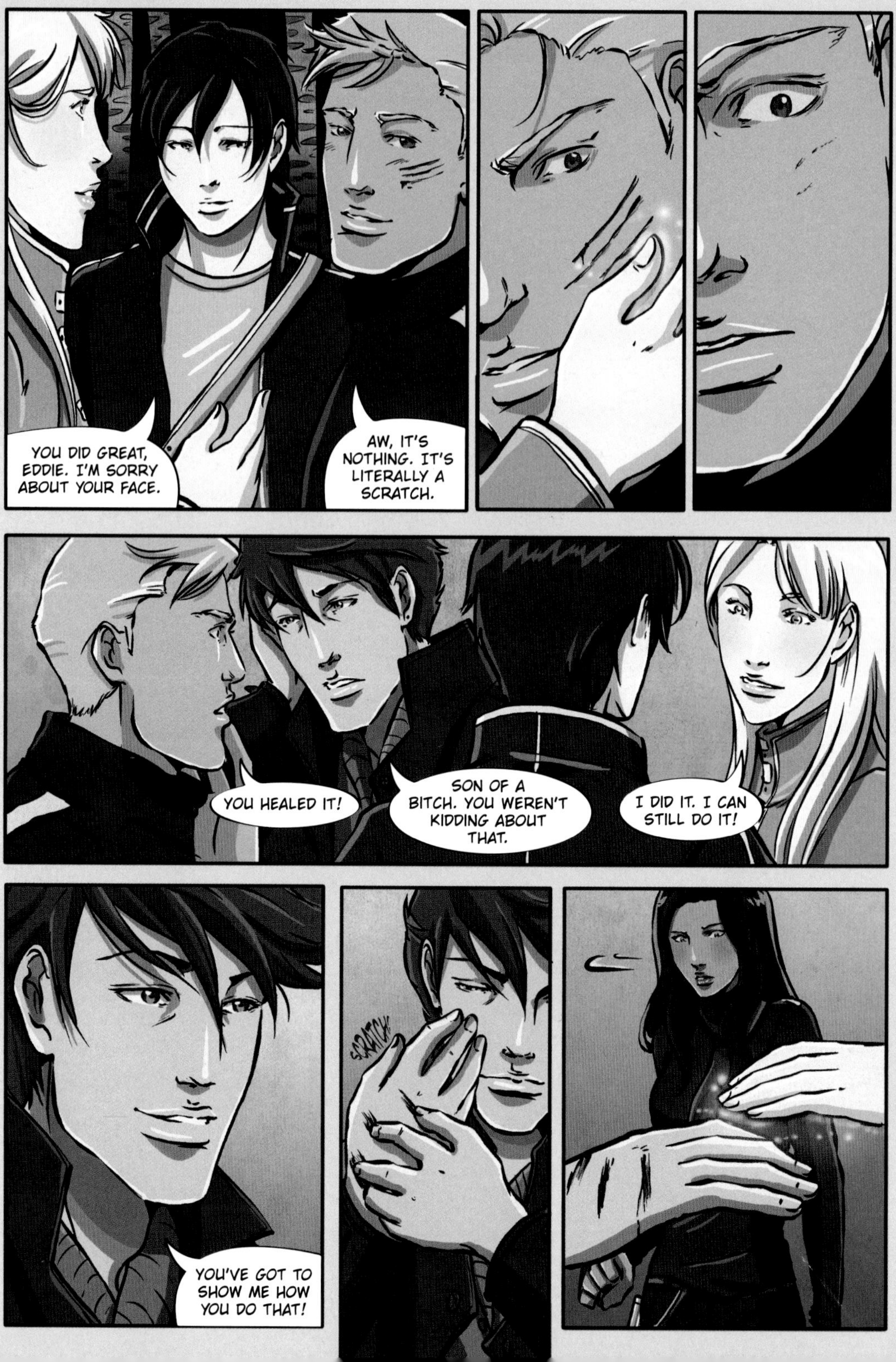
YOU DID GREAT, EDDIE. I'M SORRY ABOUT YOUR FACE.
AW, IT'S NOTHING. IT'S LITERALLY A SCRATCH.
YOU HEALED IT!
SON OF A BITCH. YOU WEREN'T KIDDING ABOUT THAT.
I DID IT. I CAN STILL DO IT!
YOU'VE GOT TO SHOW ME HOW YOU DO THAT!
SCRATCH!

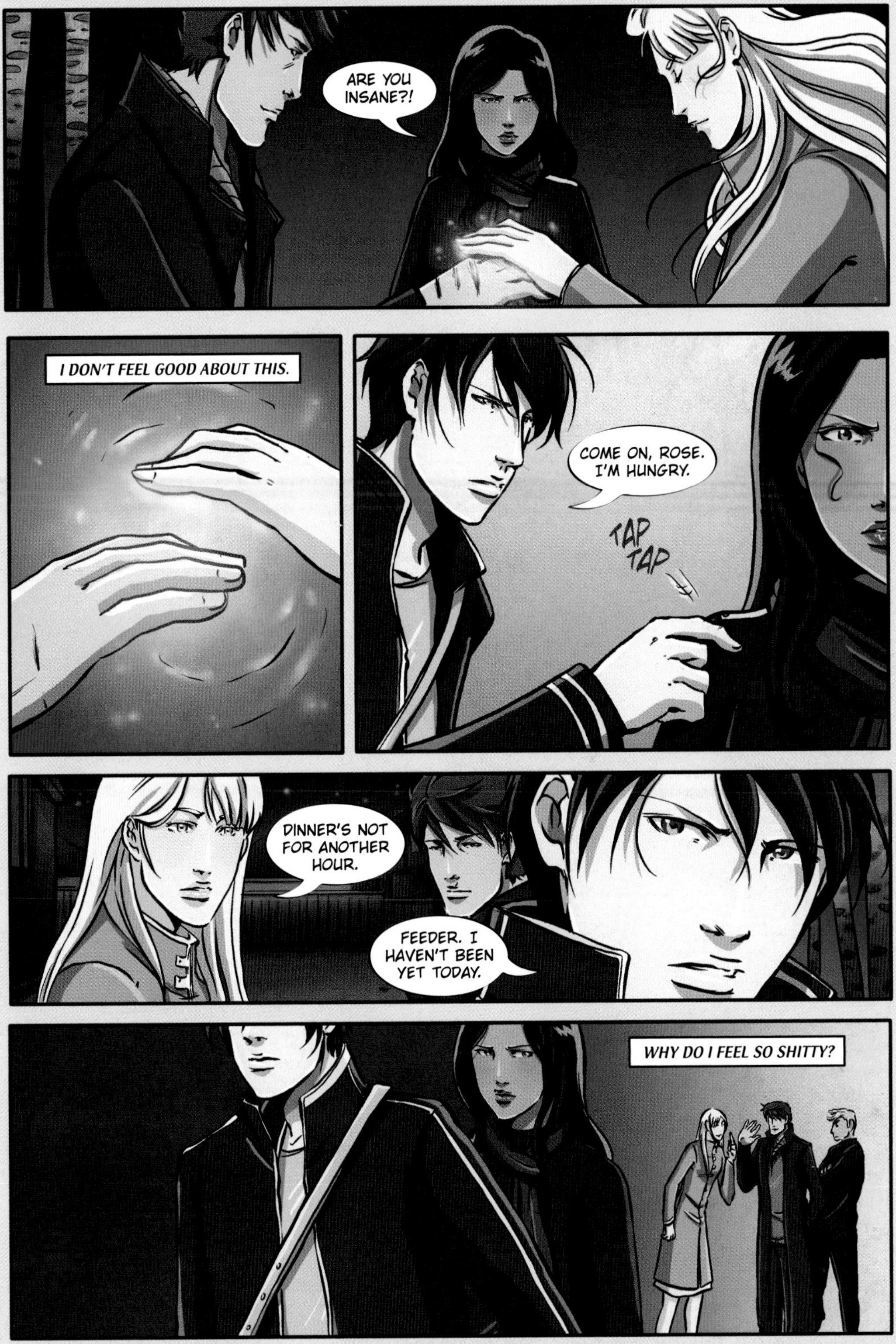
ARE YOU INSANE?!
I DON'T FEEL GOOD ABOUT THIS.
COME ON, ROSE. I'M HUNGRY.
TAP TAP
DINNER'S NOT FOR ANOTHER HOUR.
FEEDER. I HAVEN'T BEEN YET TODAY.
WHY DO I FEEL SO SHITTY?

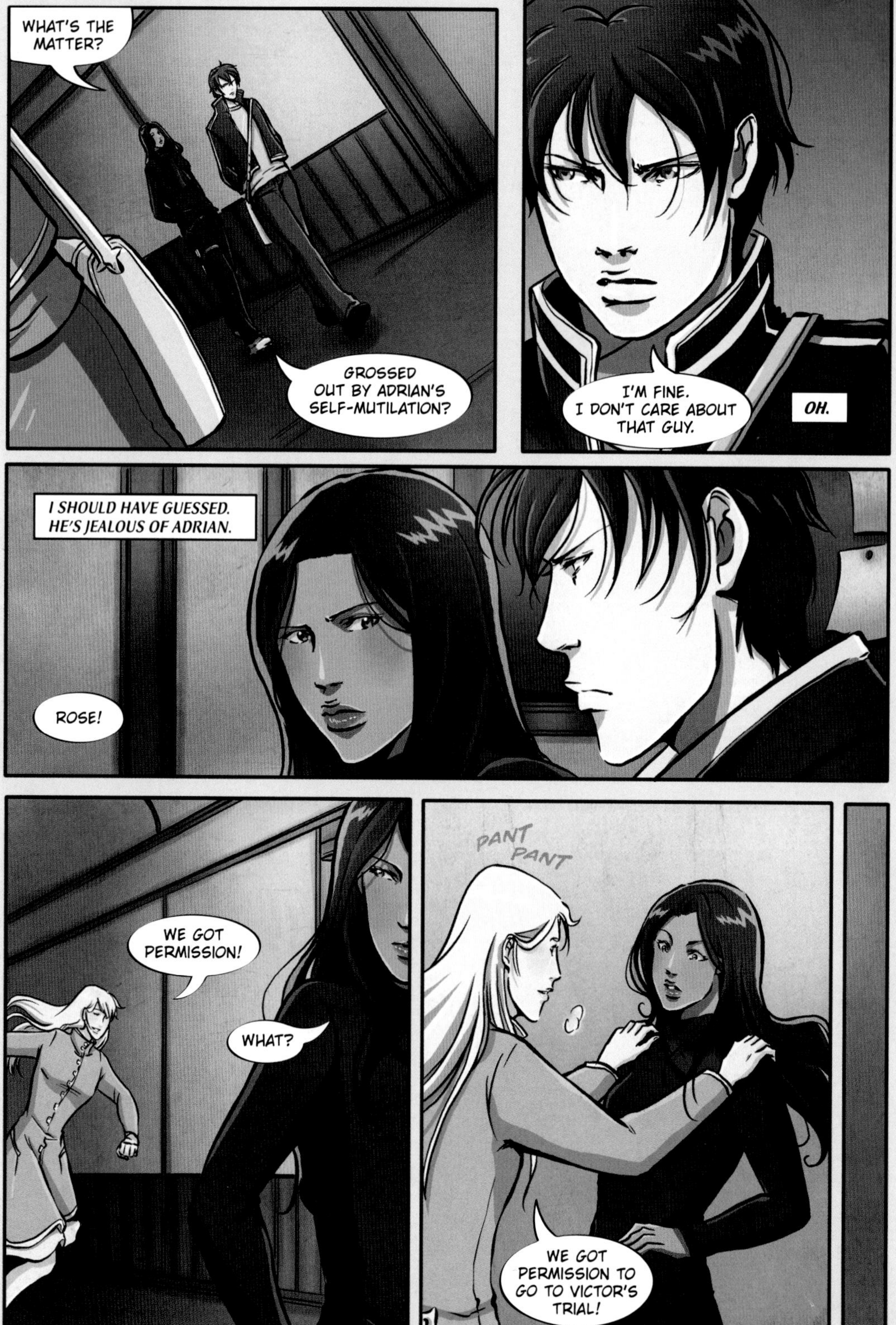
WHAT'S THE MATTER?
GROSSED OUT BY ADRIAN'S SELF-MUTILATION?
I'M FINE. I DON'T CARE ABOUT THAT GUY.
OH.
I SHOULD HAVE GUESSED. HE'S JEALOUS OF ADRIAN.
ROSE!
WE GOT PERMISSION!
WHAT?
PANT PANT
WE GOT PERMISSION TO GO TO VICTOR'S TRIAL!

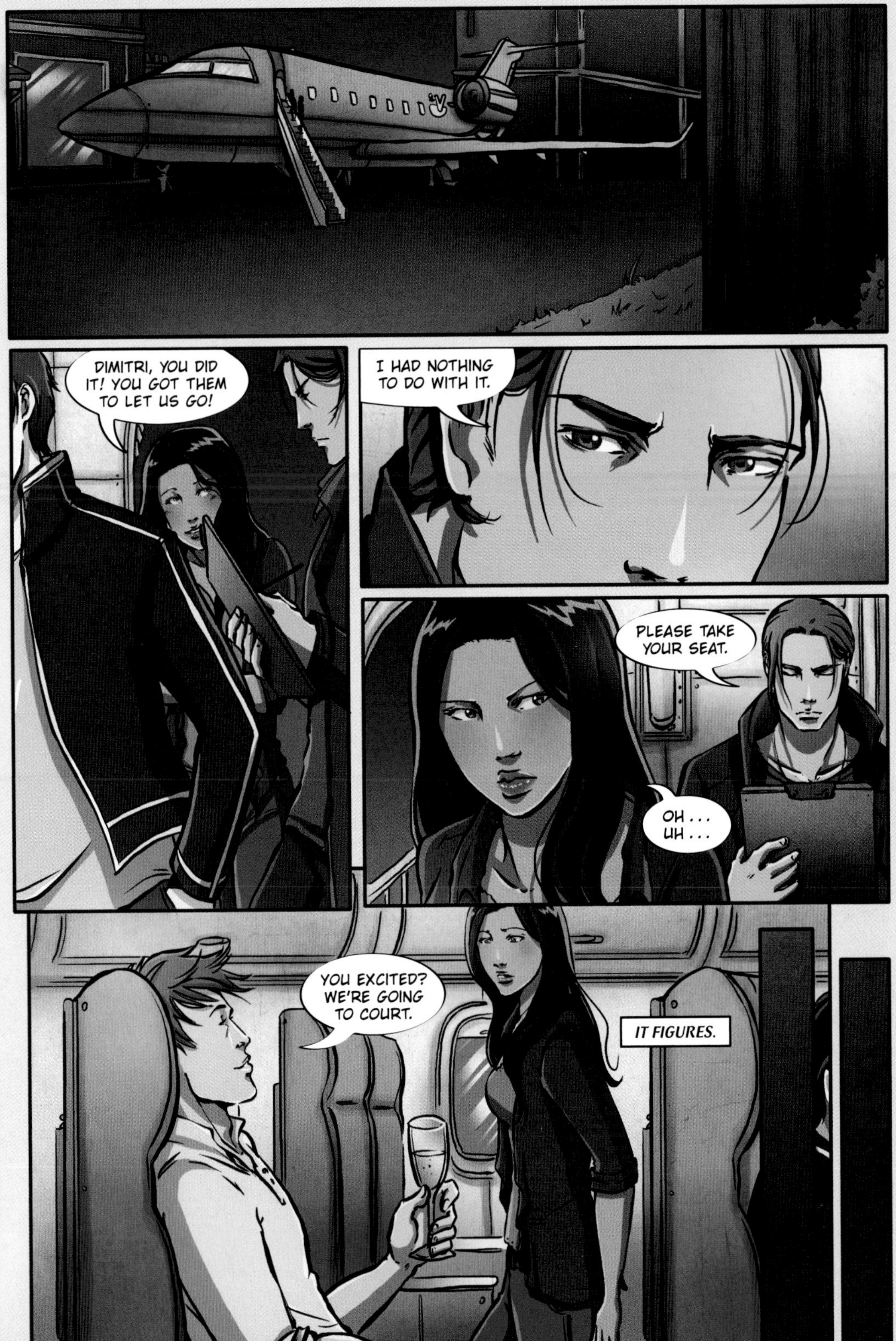
DIMITRI, YOU DID IT! YOU GOT THEM TO LET US GO!
I HAD NOTHING TO DO WITH IT.
PLEASE TAKE YOUR SEAT.
OH . . . UH . . .
YOU EXCITED? WE'RE GOING TO COURT.
IT FIGURES.

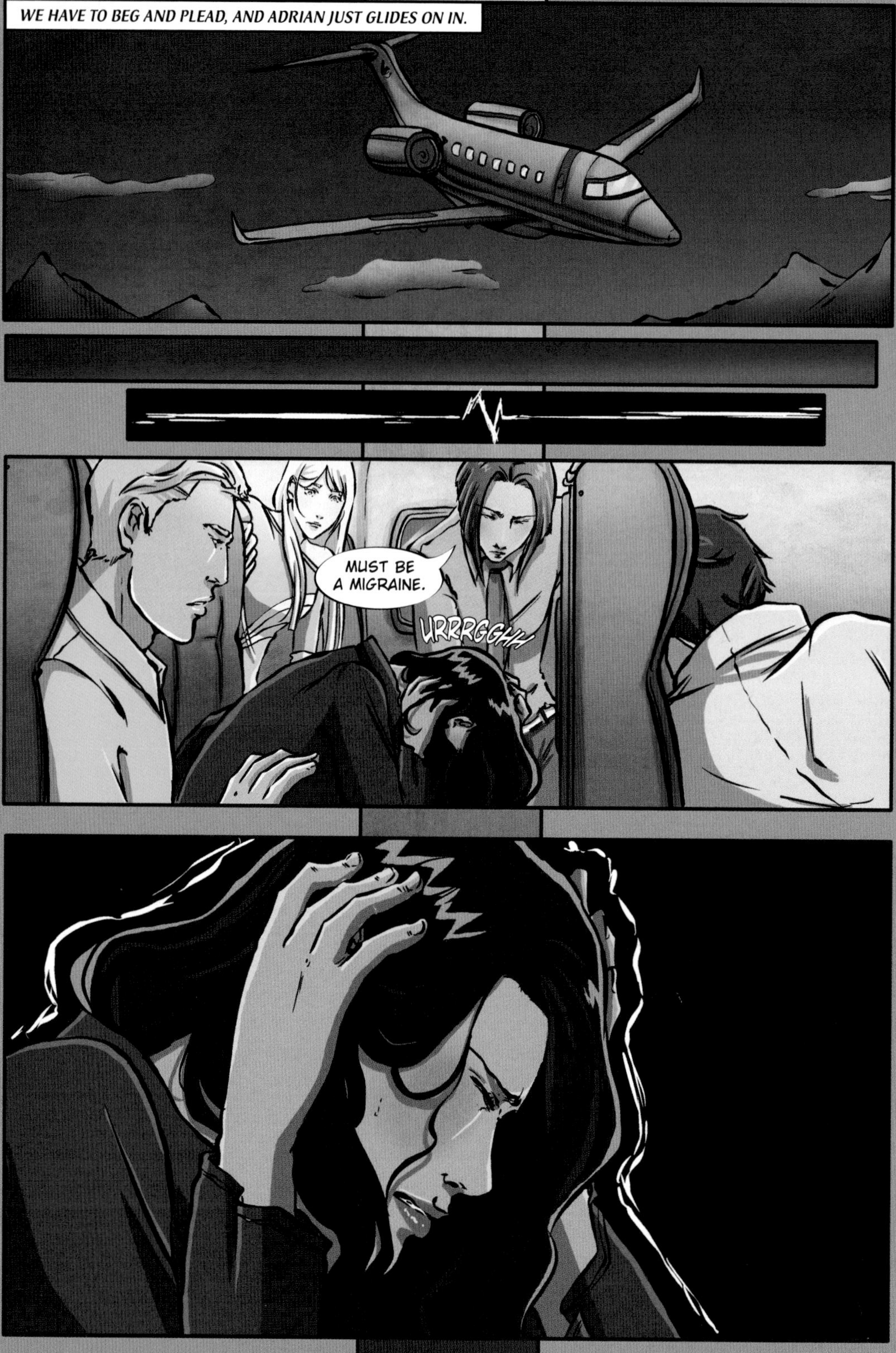
WE HAVE TO BEG AND PLEAD, AND ADRIAN JUST GLIDES ON IN.
MUST BE A MIGRAINE.
URRRGGHH

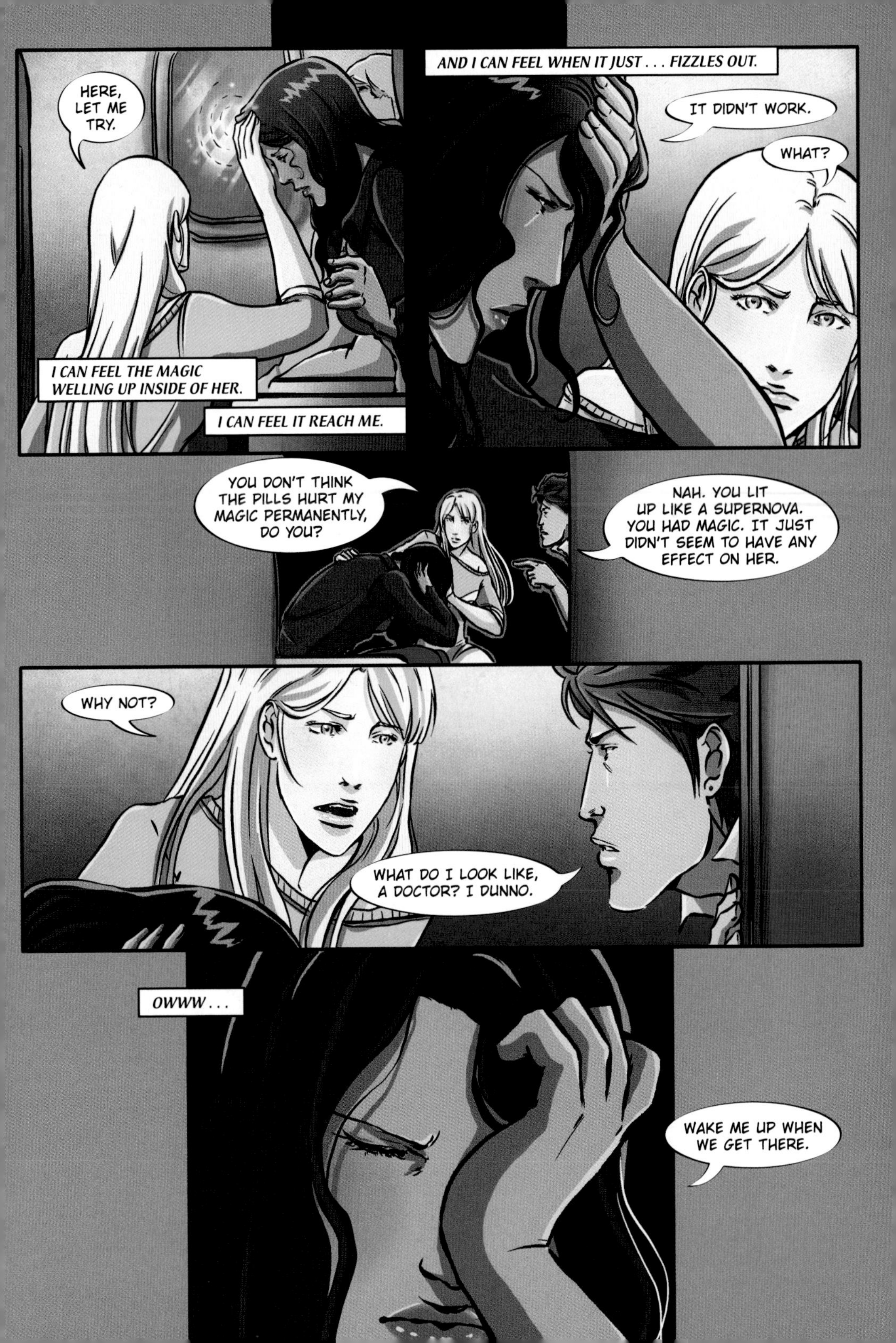
HERE, LET ME TRY.
I CAN FEEL THE MAGIC WELLING UP INSIDE OF HER.
I CAN FEEL IT REACH ME.
AND I CAN FEEL WHEN IT JUST . . . FIZZLES OUT.
IT DIDN'T WORK.
WHAT?
YOU DON'T THINK THE PILLS HURT MY MAGIC PERMANENTLY, DO YOU?
NAH. YOU LIT UP LIKE A SUPERNOVA. YOU HAD MAGIC. IT JUST DIDN'T SEEM TO HAVE ANY EFFECT ON HER.
WHY NOT?
WHAT DO I LOOK LIKE, A DOCTOR? I DUNNO.
OWWW . . .
WAKE ME UP WHEN WE GET THERE.

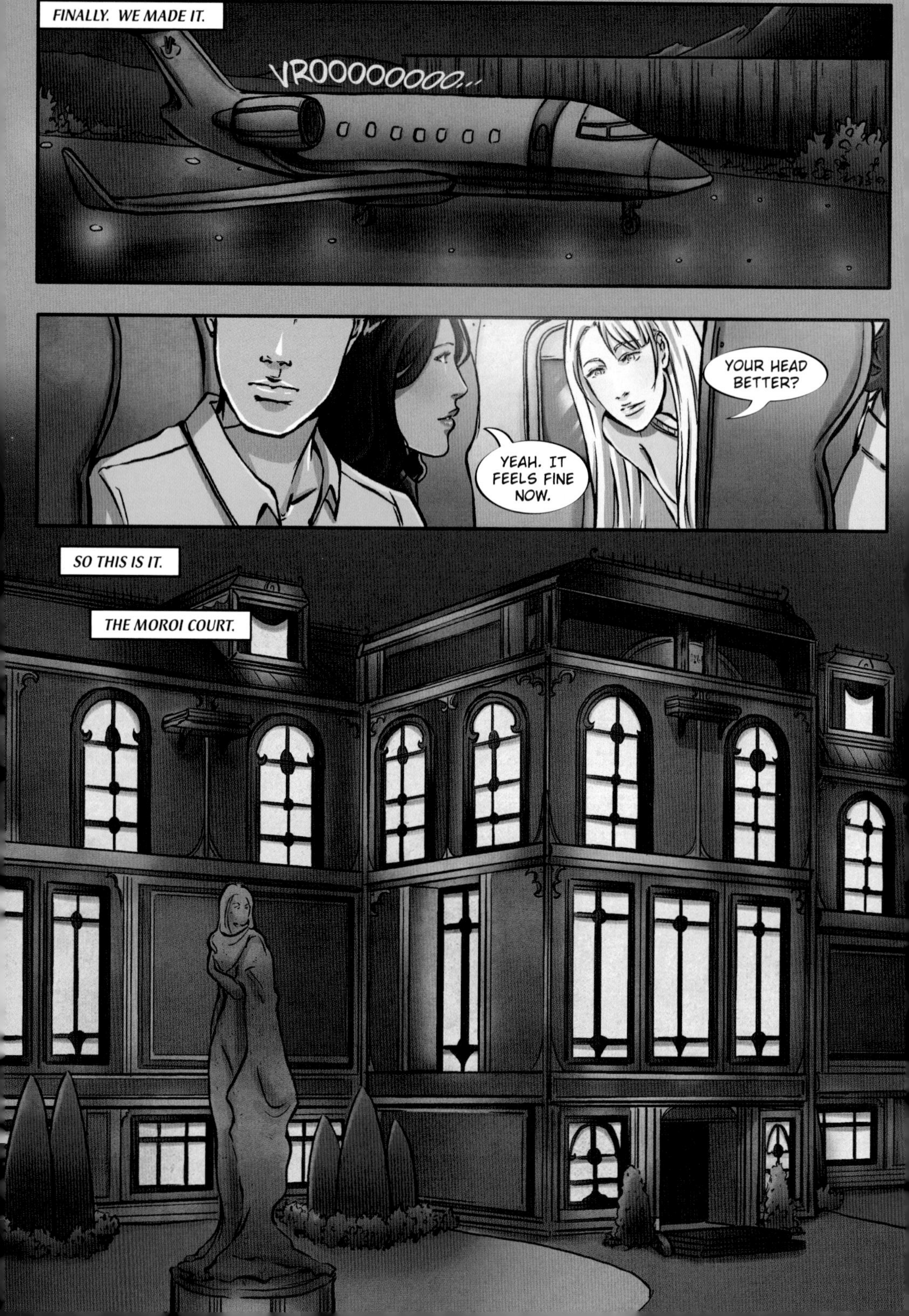
FINALLY. WE MADE IT.
VROOOOOOOO...
YOUR HEAD BETTER?
YEAH. IT FEELS FINE NOW.
SO THIS IS IT.
THE MOROI COURT.

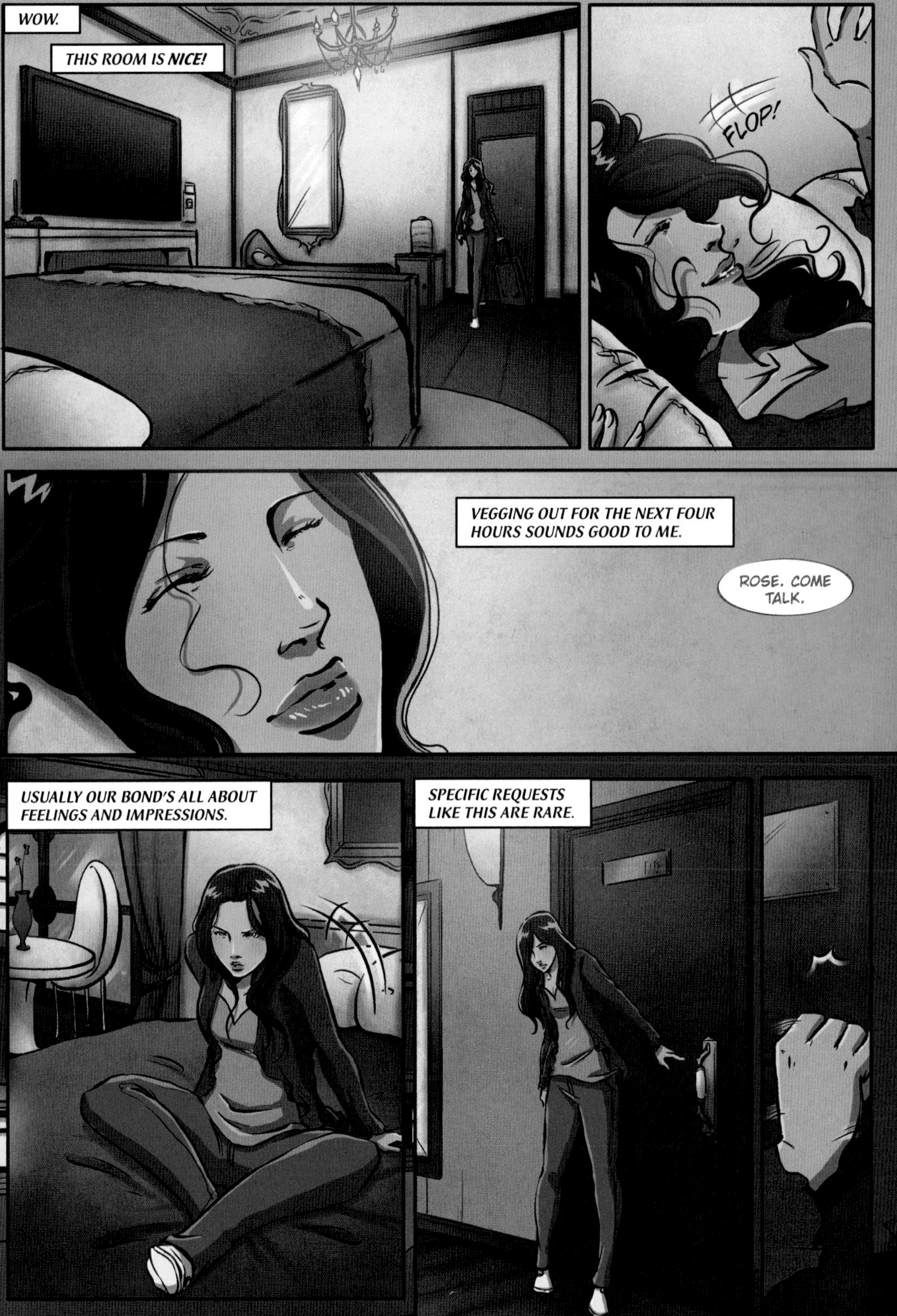
WOW.
THIS ROOM IS NICE!
FLOP!
VEGGING OUT FOR THE NEXT FOUR HOURS SOUNDS GOOD TO ME.
ROSE. COME TALK.
USUALLY OUR BOND'S ALL ABOUT FEELINGS AND IMPRESSIONS.
SPECIFIC REQUESTS LIKE THIS ARE RARE.

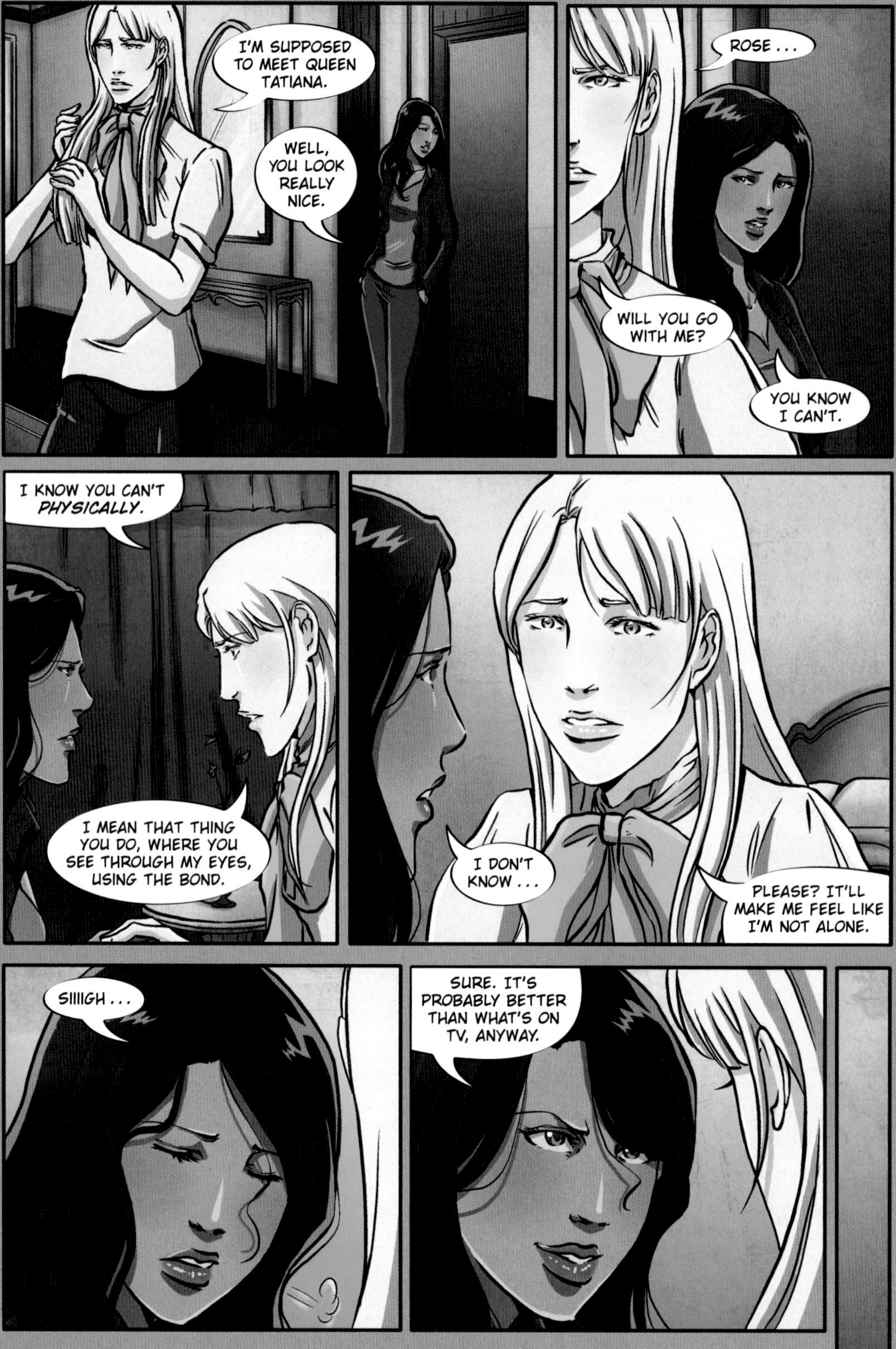
I'M SUPPOSED TO MEET QUEEN TATIANA.
WELL, YOU LOOK REALLY NICE.
ROSE . . .
WILL YOU GO WITH ME?
YOU KNOW I CAN'T.
I KNOW YOU CAN'T *PHYSICALLY*.
I MEAN THAT THING YOU DO, WHERE YOU SEE THROUGH MY EYES, USING THE BOND.
I DON'T KNOW . . .
PLEASE? IT'LL MAKE ME FEEL LIKE I'M NOT ALONE.
SIIIGH . . .
SURE. IT'S PROBABLY BETTER THAN WHAT'S ON TV, ANYWAY.

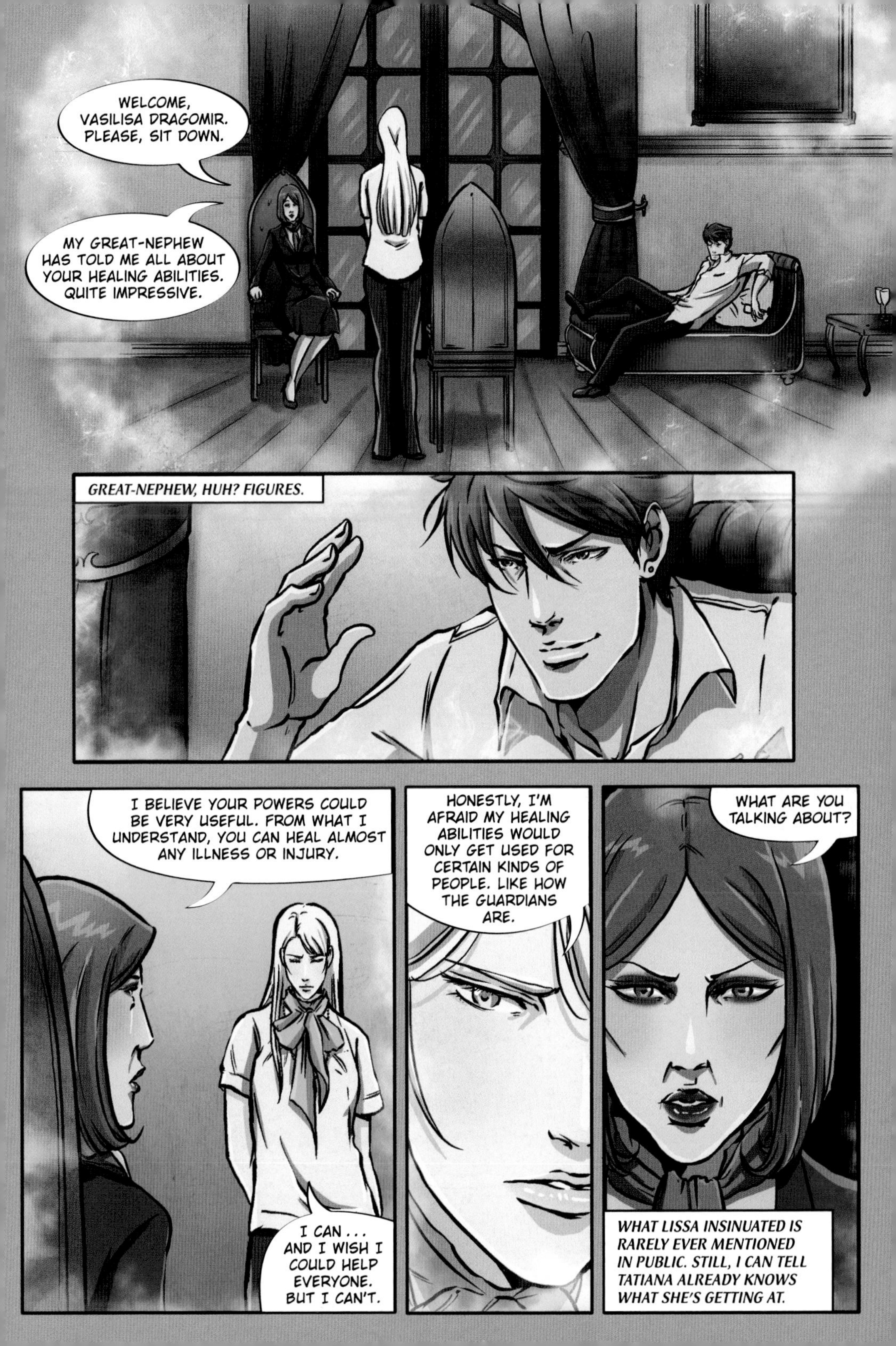
WELCOME, VASILISA DRAGOMIR. PLEASE, SIT DOWN.
MY GREAT-NEPHEW HAS TOLD ME ALL ABOUT YOUR HEALING ABILITIES. QUITE IMPRESSIVE.
GREAT-NEPHEW, HUH? FIGURES.
I BELIEVE YOUR POWERS COULD BE VERY USEFUL. FROM WHAT I UNDERSTAND, YOU CAN HEAL ALMOST ANY ILLNESS OR INJURY.
I CAN . . . AND I WISH I COULD HELP EVERYONE. BUT I CAN'T.
HONESTLY, I'M AFRAID MY HEALING ABILITIES WOULD ONLY GET USED FOR CERTAIN KINDS OF PEOPLE. LIKE HOW THE GUARDIANS ARE.
WHAT ARE YOU TALKING ABOUT?
WHAT LISSA INSINUATED IS RARELY EVER MENTIONED IN PUBLIC. STILL, I CAN TELL TATIANA ALREADY KNOWS WHAT SHE'S GETTING AT.

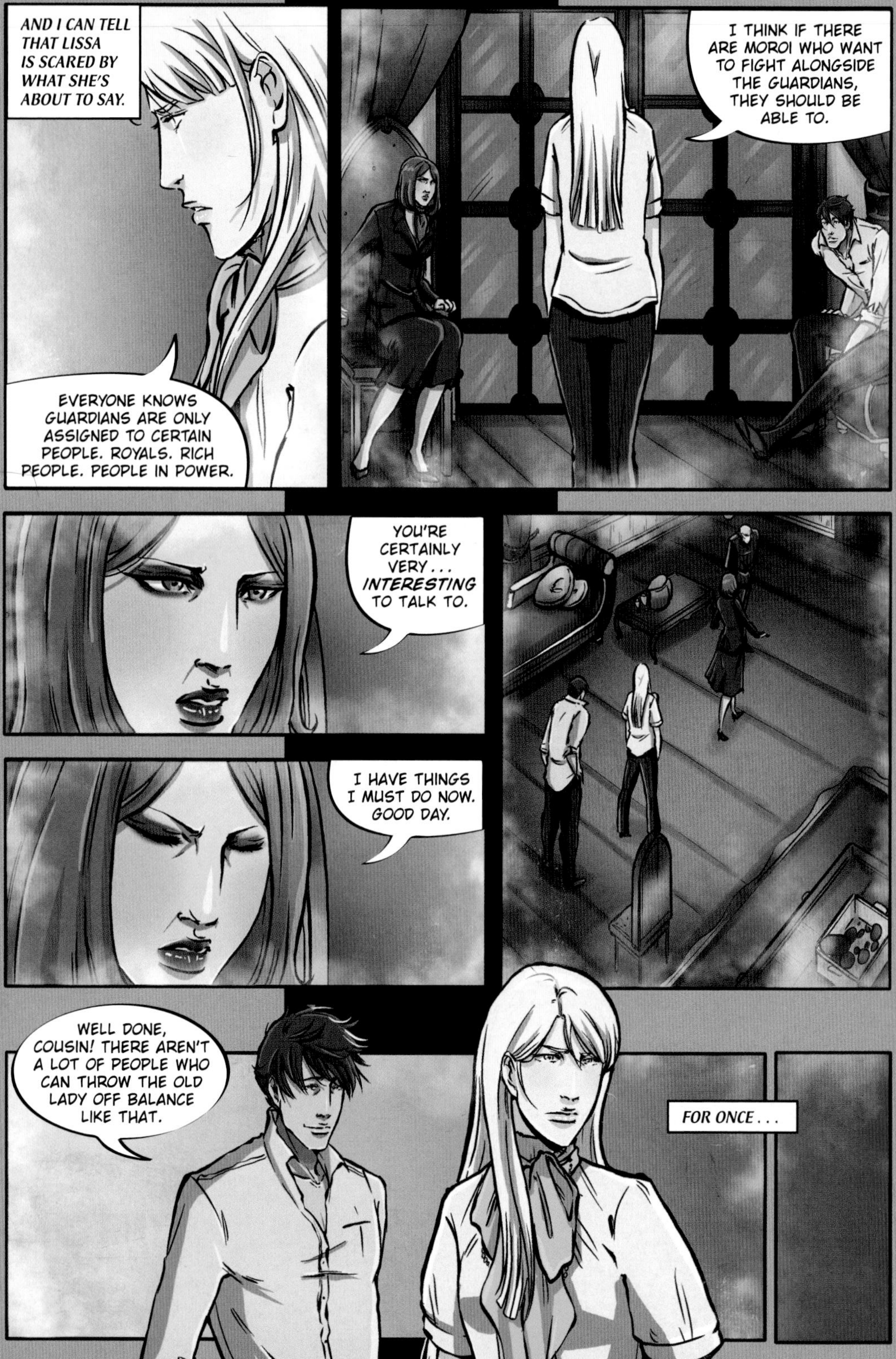
AND I CAN TELL THAT LISSA IS SCARED BY WHAT SHE'S ABOUT TO SAY.
EVERYONE KNOWS GUARDIANS ARE ONLY ASSIGNED TO CERTAIN PEOPLE. ROYALS. RICH PEOPLE. PEOPLE IN POWER.
I THINK IF THERE ARE MOROI WHO WANT TO FIGHT ALONGSIDE THE GUARDIANS, THEY SHOULD BE ABLE TO.
YOU'RE CERTAINLY VERY . . . *INTERESTING* TO TALK TO.
I HAVE THINGS I MUST DO NOW. GOOD DAY.
WELL DONE, COUSIN! THERE AREN'T A LOT OF PEOPLE WHO CAN THROW THE OLD LADY OFF BALANCE LIKE THAT.
FOR ONCE . . .

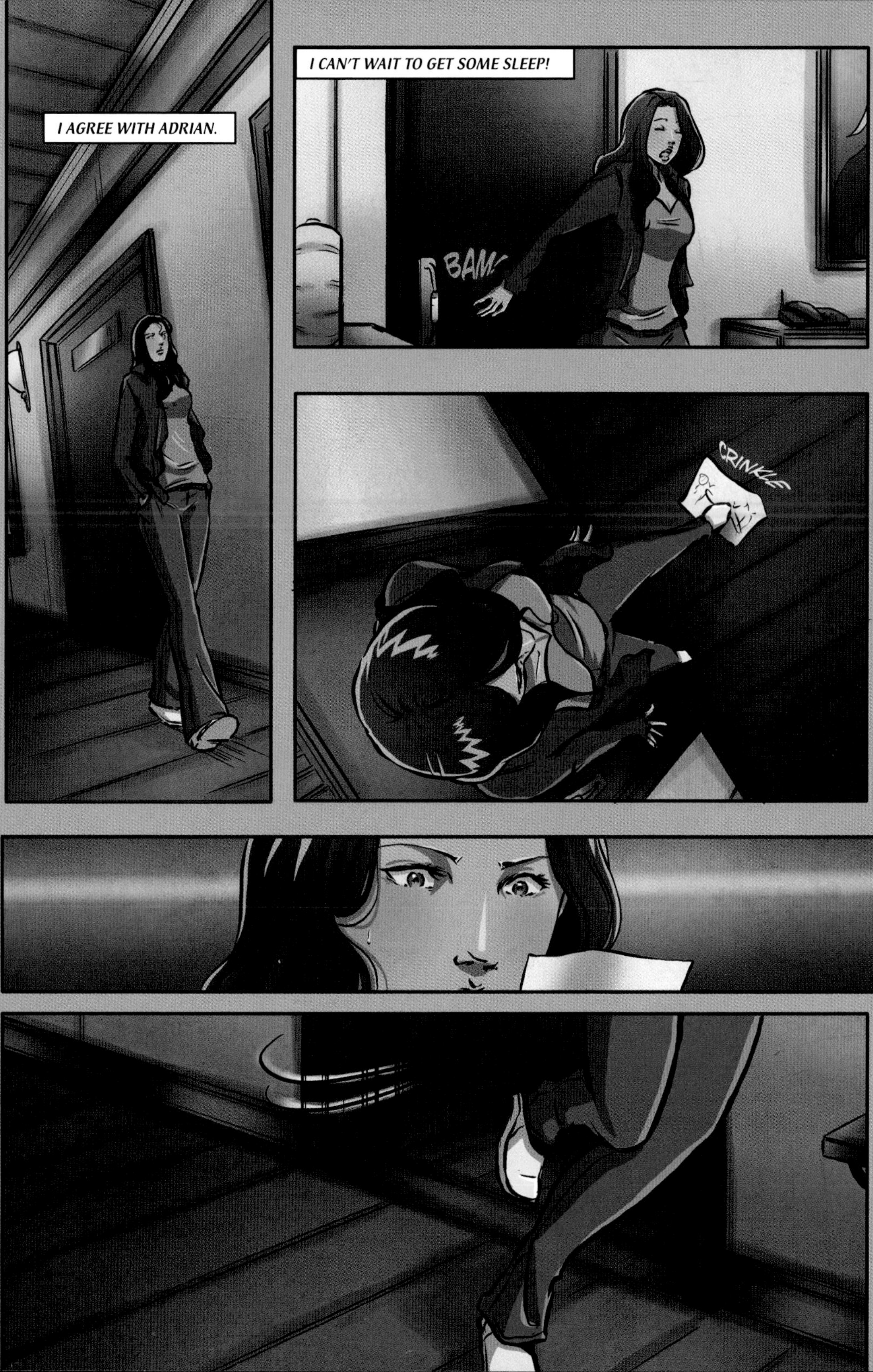
I AGREE WITH ADRIAN.
I CAN'T WAIT TO GET SOME SLEEP!
BAM!
CRINKLE

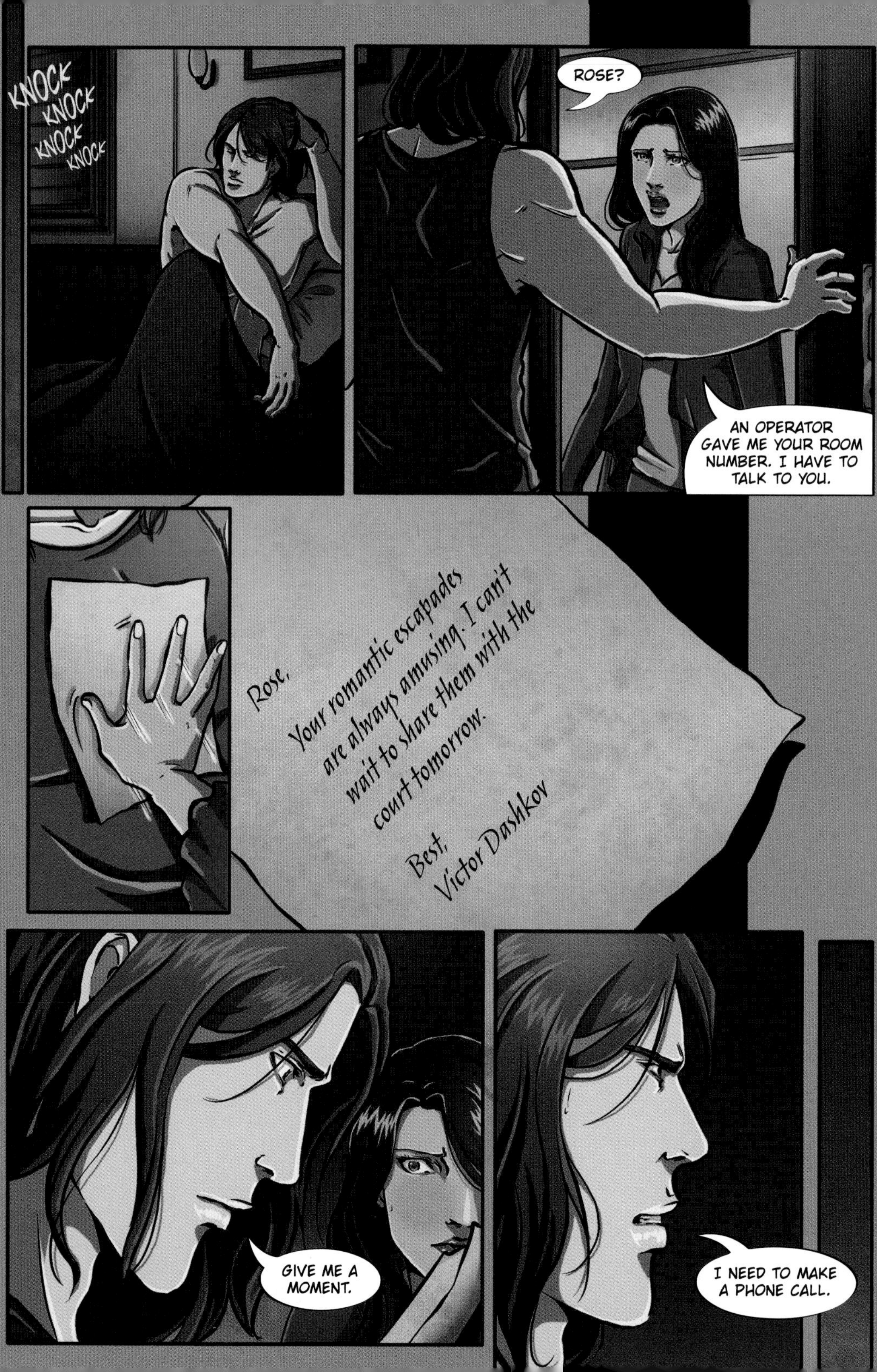
KNOCK KNOCK KNOCK KNOCK
ROSE?
AN OPERATOR GAVE ME YOUR ROOM NUMBER. I HAVE TO TALK TO YOU.
Rose,
Your romantic escapades are always amusing. I can't wait to share them with the court tomorrow.
Best,
Victor Dashkov
GIVE ME A MOMENT.
I NEED TO MAKE A PHONE CALL.

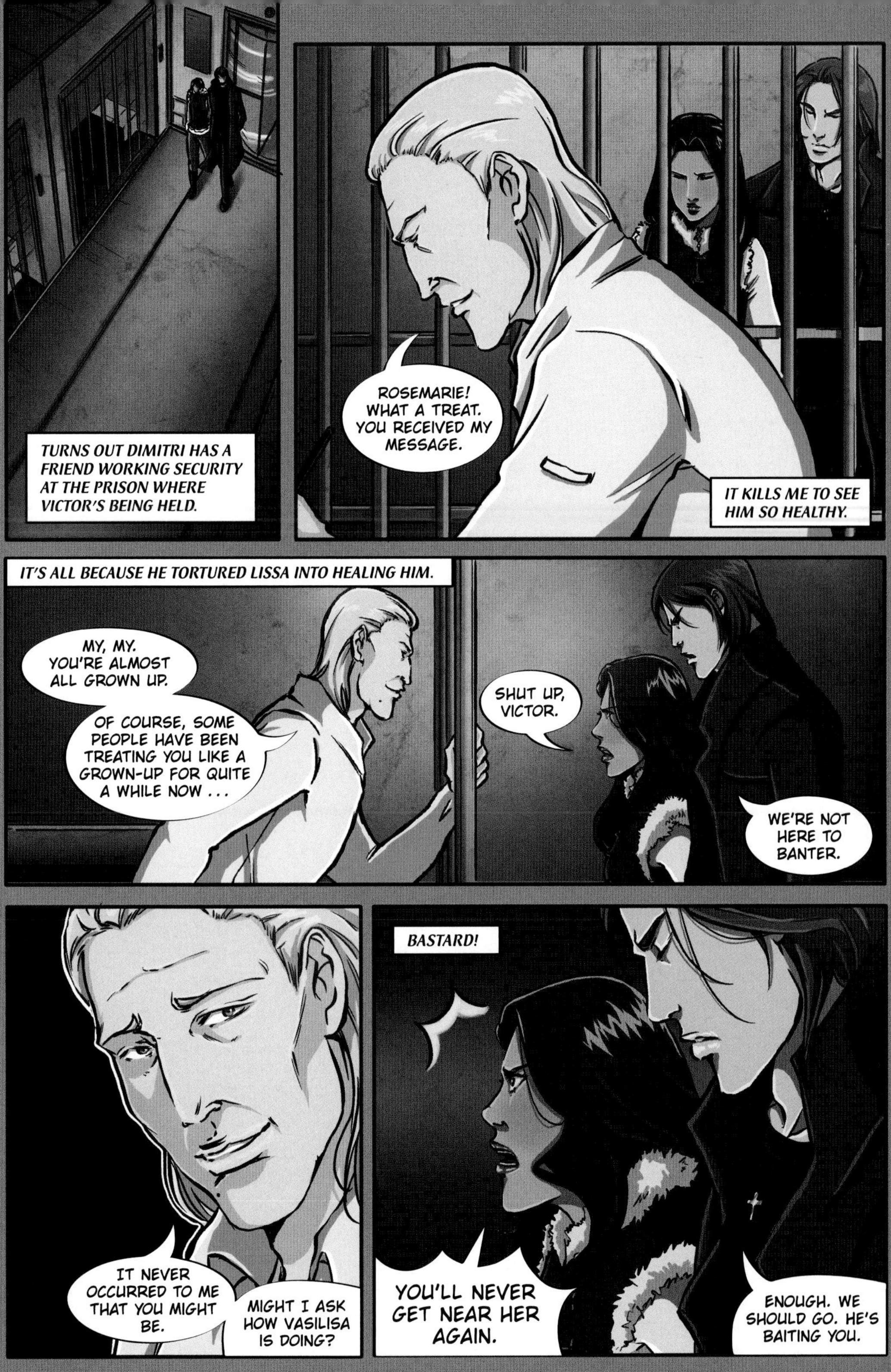
TURNS OUT DIMITRI HAS A FRIEND WORKING SECURITY AT THE PRISON WHERE VICTOR'S BEING HELD.
ROSEMARIE! WHAT A TREAT. YOU RECEIVED MY MESSAGE.
IT KILLS ME TO SEE HIM SO HEALTHY.
IT'S ALL BECAUSE HE TORTURED LISSA INTO HEALING HIM.
MY, MY. YOU'RE ALMOST ALL GROWN UP.
OF COURSE, SOME PEOPLE HAVE BEEN TREATING YOU LIKE A GROWN-UP FOR QUITE A WHILE NOW . . .
SHUT UP, VICTOR.
WE'RE NOT HERE TO BANTER.
IT NEVER OCCURRED TO ME THAT YOU MIGHT BE.
MIGHT I ASK HOW VASILISA IS DOING?
BASTARD!
YOU'LL NEVER GET NEAR HER AGAIN.
ENOUGH. WE SHOULD GO. HE'S BAITING YOU.

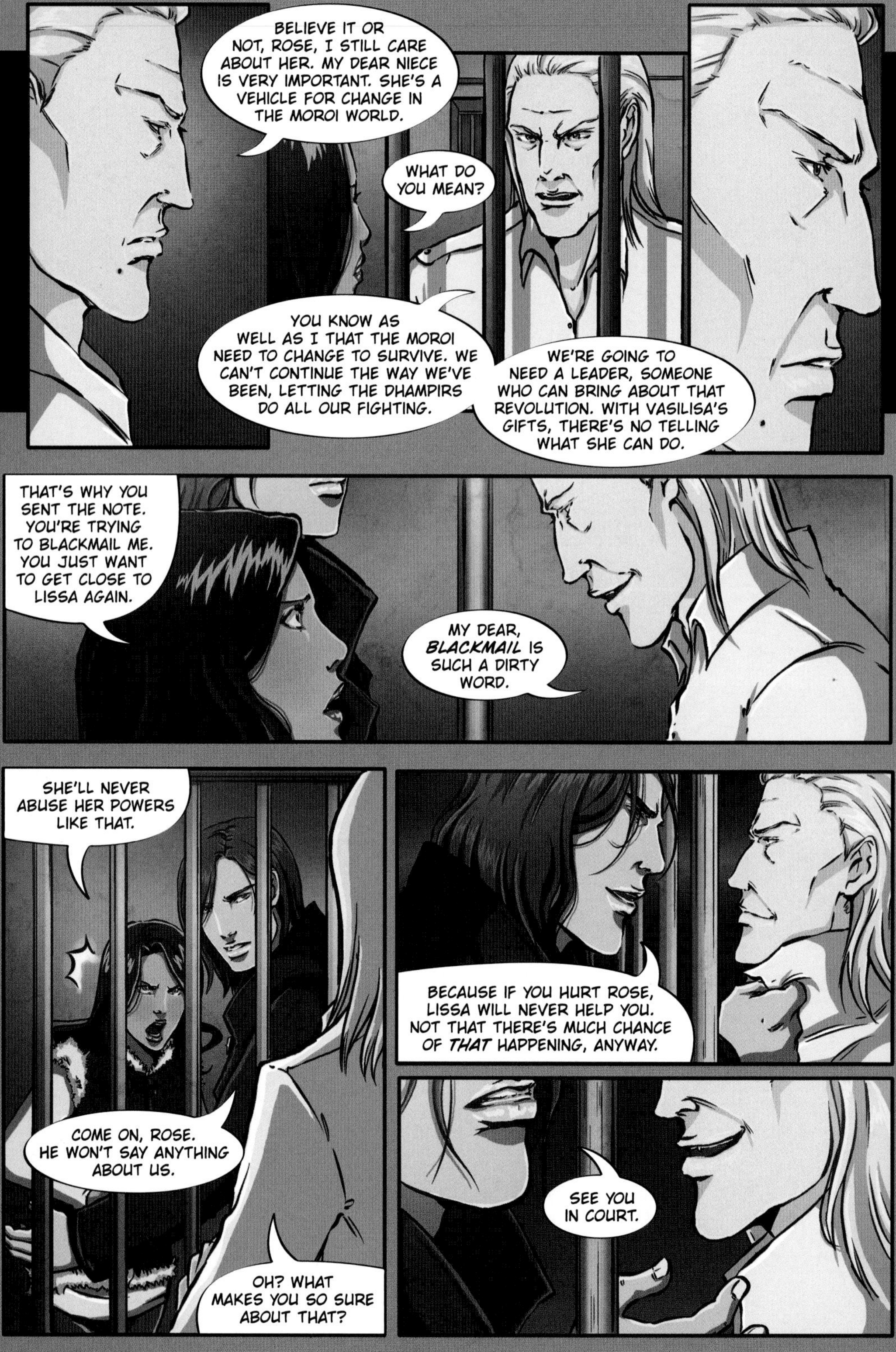
BELIEVE IT OR NOT, ROSE, I STILL CARE ABOUT HER. MY DEAR NIECE IS VERY IMPORTANT. SHE'S A VEHICLE FOR CHANGE IN THE MOROI WORLD.
WHAT DO YOU MEAN?
YOU KNOW AS WELL AS I THAT THE MOROI NEED TO CHANGE TO SURVIVE. WE CAN'T CONTINUE THE WAY WE'VE BEEN, LETTING THE DHAMPIRS DO ALL OUR FIGHTING.
WE'RE GOING TO NEED A LEADER, SOMEONE WHO CAN BRING ABOUT THAT REVOLUTION. WITH VASILISA'S GIFTS, THERE'S NO TELLING WHAT SHE CAN DO.
THAT'S WHY YOU SENT THE NOTE. YOU'RE TRYING TO BLACKMAIL ME. YOU JUST WANT TO GET CLOSE TO LISSA AGAIN.
MY DEAR, *BLACKMAIL* IS SUCH A DIRTY WORD.
SHE'LL NEVER ABUSE HER POWERS LIKE THAT.
COME ON, ROSE. HE WON'T SAY ANYTHING ABOUT US.
OH? WHAT MAKES YOU SO SURE ABOUT THAT?
BECAUSE IF YOU HURT ROSE, LISSA WILL NEVER HELP YOU. NOT THAT THERE'S MUCH CHANCE OF *THAT* HAPPENING, ANYWAY.
SEE YOU IN COURT.

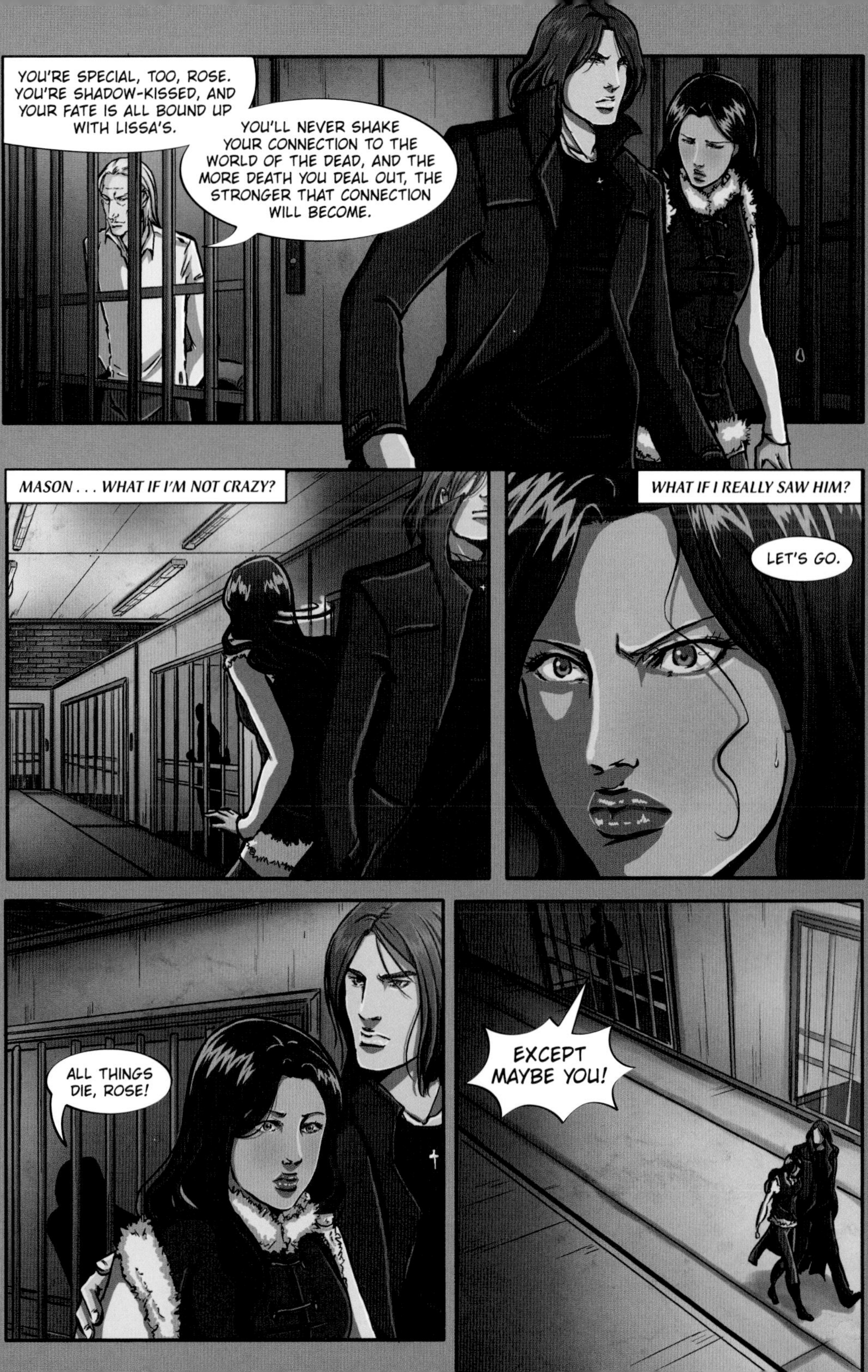
YOU'RE SPECIAL, TOO, ROSE. YOU'RE SHADOW-KISSED, AND YOUR FATE IS ALL BOUND UP WITH LISSA'S.
YOU'LL NEVER SHAKE YOUR CONNECTION TO THE WORLD OF THE DEAD, AND THE MORE DEATH YOU DEAL OUT, THE STRONGER THAT CONNECTION WILL BECOME.
MASON . . . WHAT IF I'M NOT CRAZY?
WHAT IF I REALLY SAW HIM?
LET'S GO.
ALL THINGS DIE, ROSE!
EXCEPT MAYBE YOU!

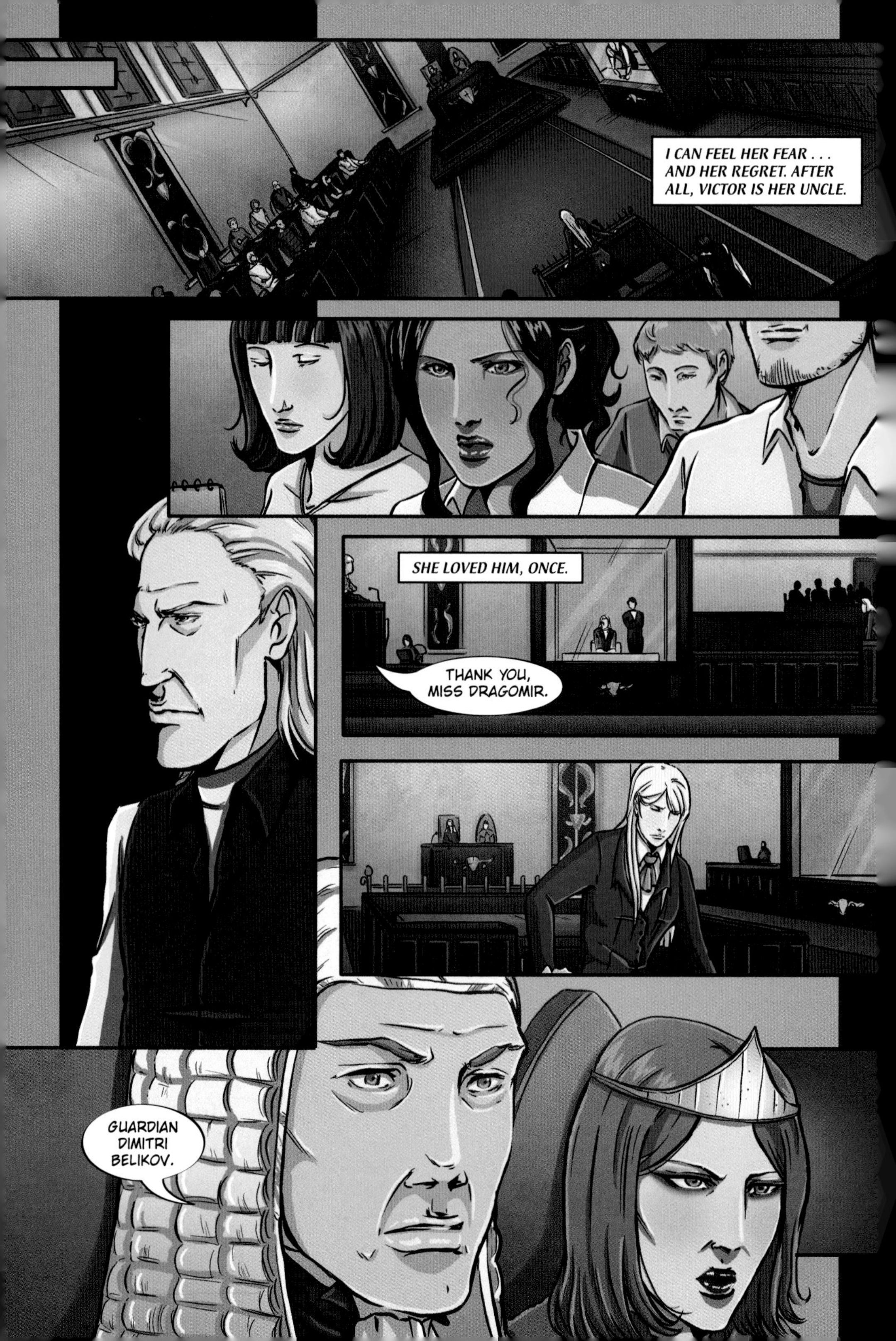
I CAN FEEL HER FEAR . . . AND HER REGRET. AFTER ALL, VICTOR IS HER UNCLE.
SHE LOVED HIM, ONCE.
THANK YOU, MISS DRAGOMIR.
GUARDIAN DIMITRI BELIKOV.

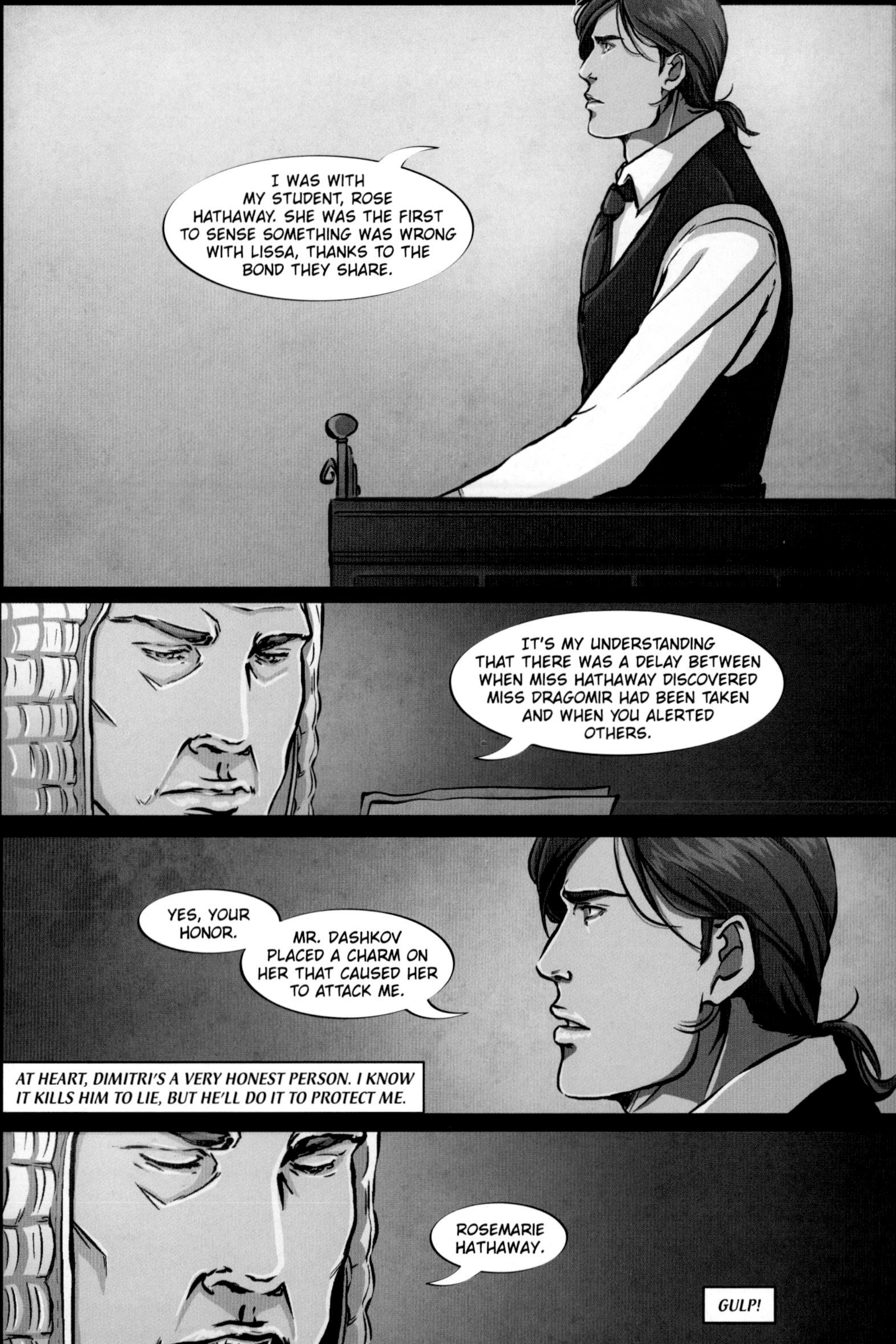
I WAS WITH MY STUDENT, ROSE HATHAWAY. SHE WAS THE FIRST TO SENSE SOMETHING WAS WRONG WITH LISSA, THANKS TO THE BOND THEY SHARE.
IT'S MY UNDERSTANDING THAT THERE WAS A DELAY BETWEEN WHEN MISS HATHAWAY DISCOVERED MISS DRAGOMIR HAD BEEN TAKEN AND WHEN YOU ALERTED OTHERS.
YES, YOUR HONOR.
MR. DASHKOV PLACED A CHARM ON HER THAT CAUSED HER TO ATTACK ME.
AT HEART, DIMITRI'S A VERY HONEST PERSON. I KNOW IT KILLS HIM TO LIE, BUT HE'LL DO IT TO PROTECT ME.
ROSEMARIE HATHAWAY.
GULP!

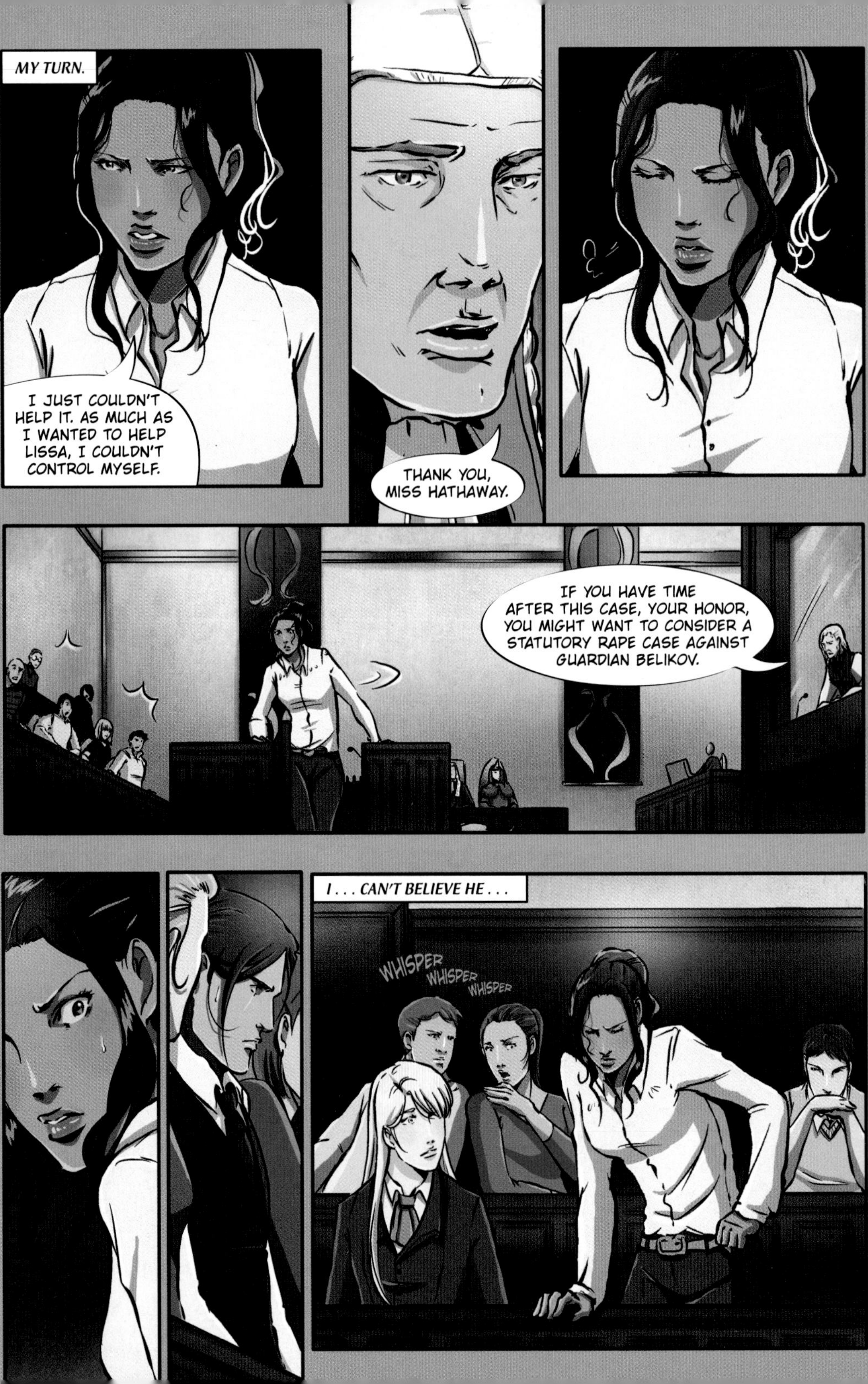
MY TURN.
I JUST COULDN'T HELP IT. AS MUCH AS I WANTED TO HELP LISSA, I COULDN'T CONTROL MYSELF.
THANK YOU, MISS HATHAWAY.
IF YOU HAVE TIME AFTER THIS CASE, YOUR HONOR, YOU MIGHT WANT TO CONSIDER A STATUTORY RAPE CASE AGAINST GUARDIAN BELIKOV.
I . . . CAN'T BELIEVE HE . . .
WHISPER
WHISPER
WHISPER

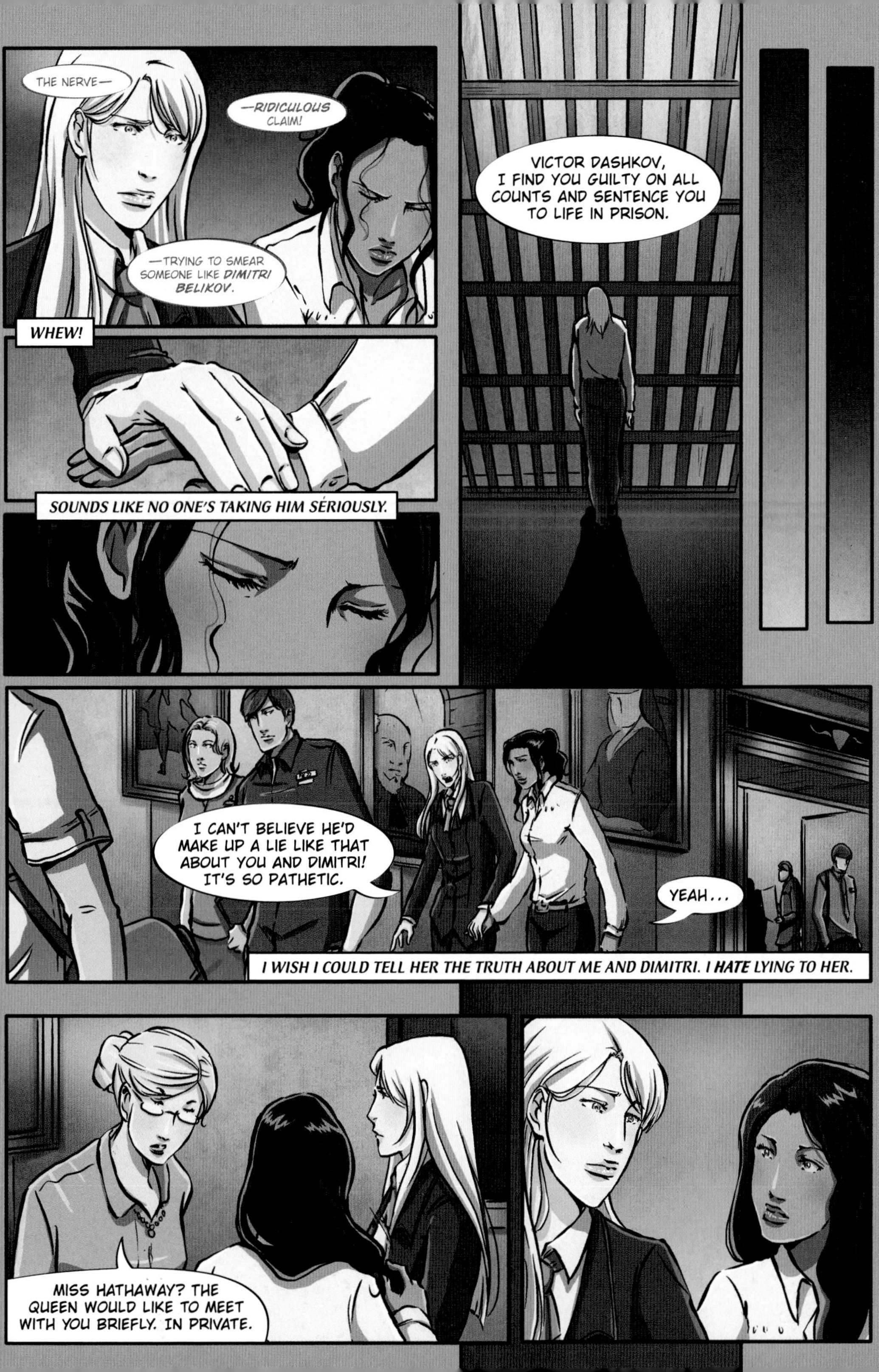
THE NERVE—
—RIDICULOUS CLAIM!
—TRYING TO SMEAR SOMEONE LIKE DIMITRI BELIKOV.
WHEW!
SOUNDS LIKE NO ONE'S TAKING HIM SERIOUSLY.
VICTOR DASHKOV, I FIND YOU GUILTY ON ALL COUNTS AND SENTENCE YOU TO LIFE IN PRISON.
I CAN'T BELIEVE HE'D MAKE UP A LIE LIKE THAT ABOUT YOU AND DIMITRI! IT'S SO PATHETIC.
YEAH...
I WISH I COULD TELL HER THE TRUTH ABOUT ME AND DIMITRI. I HATE LYING TO HER.
MISS HATHAWAY? THE QUEEN WOULD LIKE TO MEET WITH YOU BRIEFLY. IN PRIVATE.

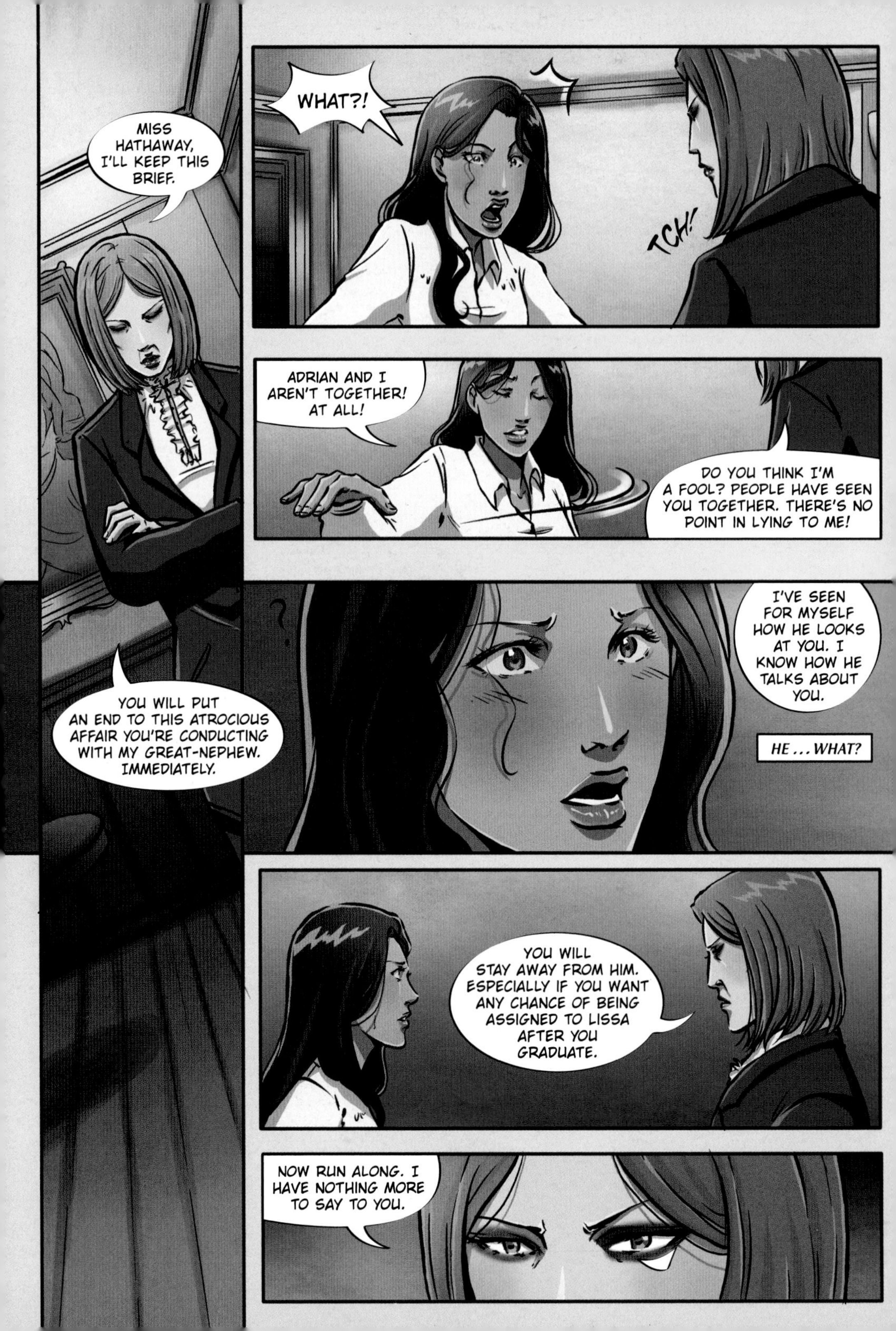
MISS HATHAWAY, I'LL KEEP THIS BRIEF.
WHAT?!
TCH!
ADRIAN AND I AREN'T TOGETHER! AT ALL!
DO YOU THINK I'M A FOOL? PEOPLE HAVE SEEN YOU TOGETHER. THERE'S NO POINT IN LYING TO ME!
YOU WILL PUT AN END TO THIS ATROCIOUS AFFAIR YOU'RE CONDUCTING WITH MY GREAT-NEPHEW. IMMEDIATELY.
?
I'VE SEEN FOR MYSELF HOW HE LOOKS AT YOU. I KNOW HOW HE TALKS ABOUT YOU.
HE . . . WHAT?
YOU WILL STAY AWAY FROM HIM. ESPECIALLY IF YOU WANT ANY CHANCE OF BEING ASSIGNED TO LISSA AFTER YOU GRADUATE.
NOW RUN ALONG. I HAVE NOTHING MORE TO SAY TO YOU.

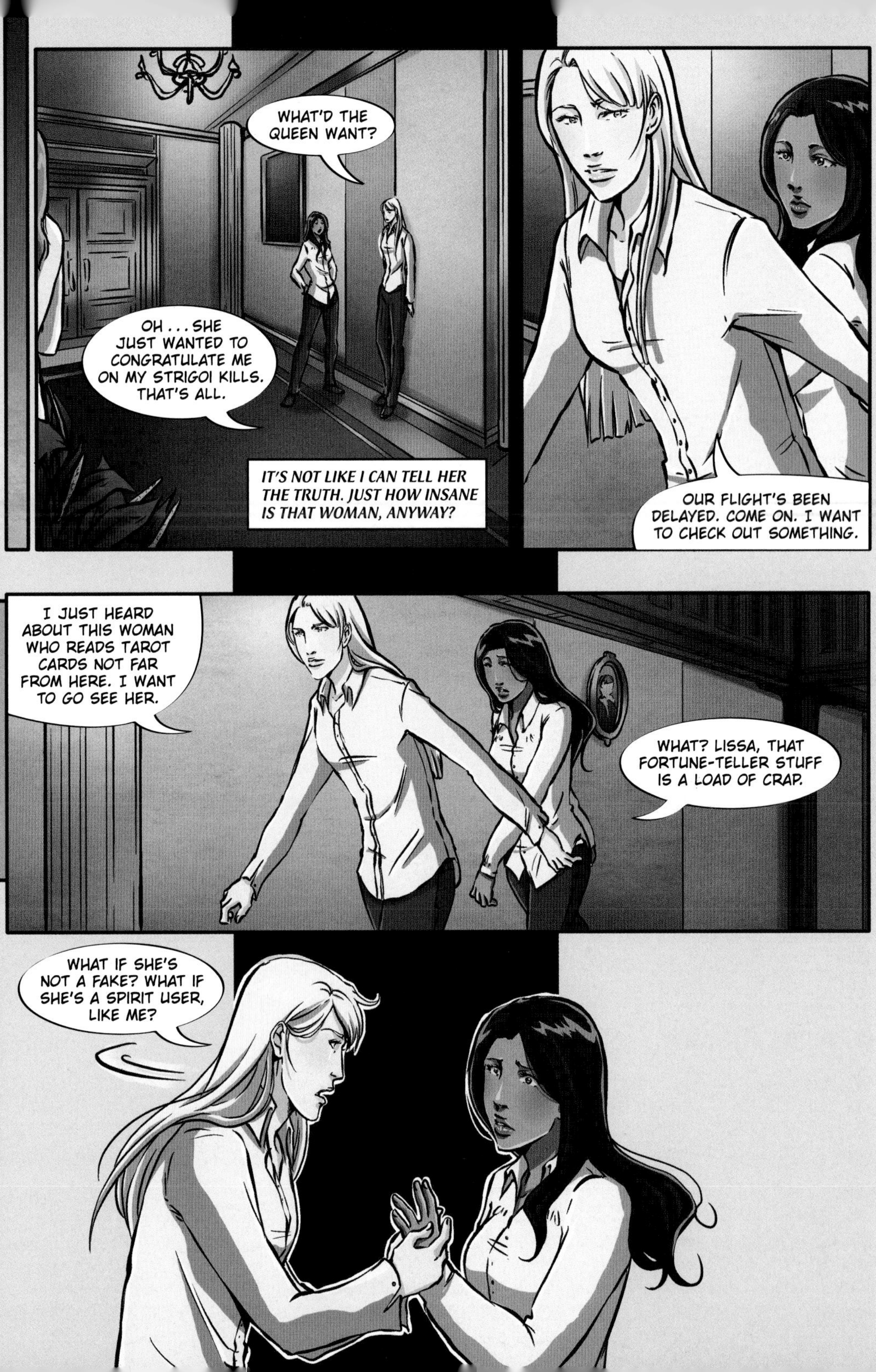
WHAT'D THE QUEEN WANT?
OH . . . SHE JUST WANTED TO CONGRATULATE ME ON MY STRIGOI KILLS. THAT'S ALL.
IT'S NOT LIKE I CAN TELL HER THE TRUTH. JUST HOW INSANE IS THAT WOMAN, ANYWAY?
OUR FLIGHT'S BEEN DELAYED. COME ON. I WANT TO CHECK OUT SOMETHING.
I JUST HEARD ABOUT THIS WOMAN WHO READS TAROT CARDS NOT FAR FROM HERE. I WANT TO GO SEE HER.
WHAT? LISSA, THAT FORTUNE-TELLER STUFF IS A LOAD OF CRAP.
WHAT IF SHE'S NOT A FAKE? WHAT IF SHE'S A SPIRIT USER, LIKE ME?

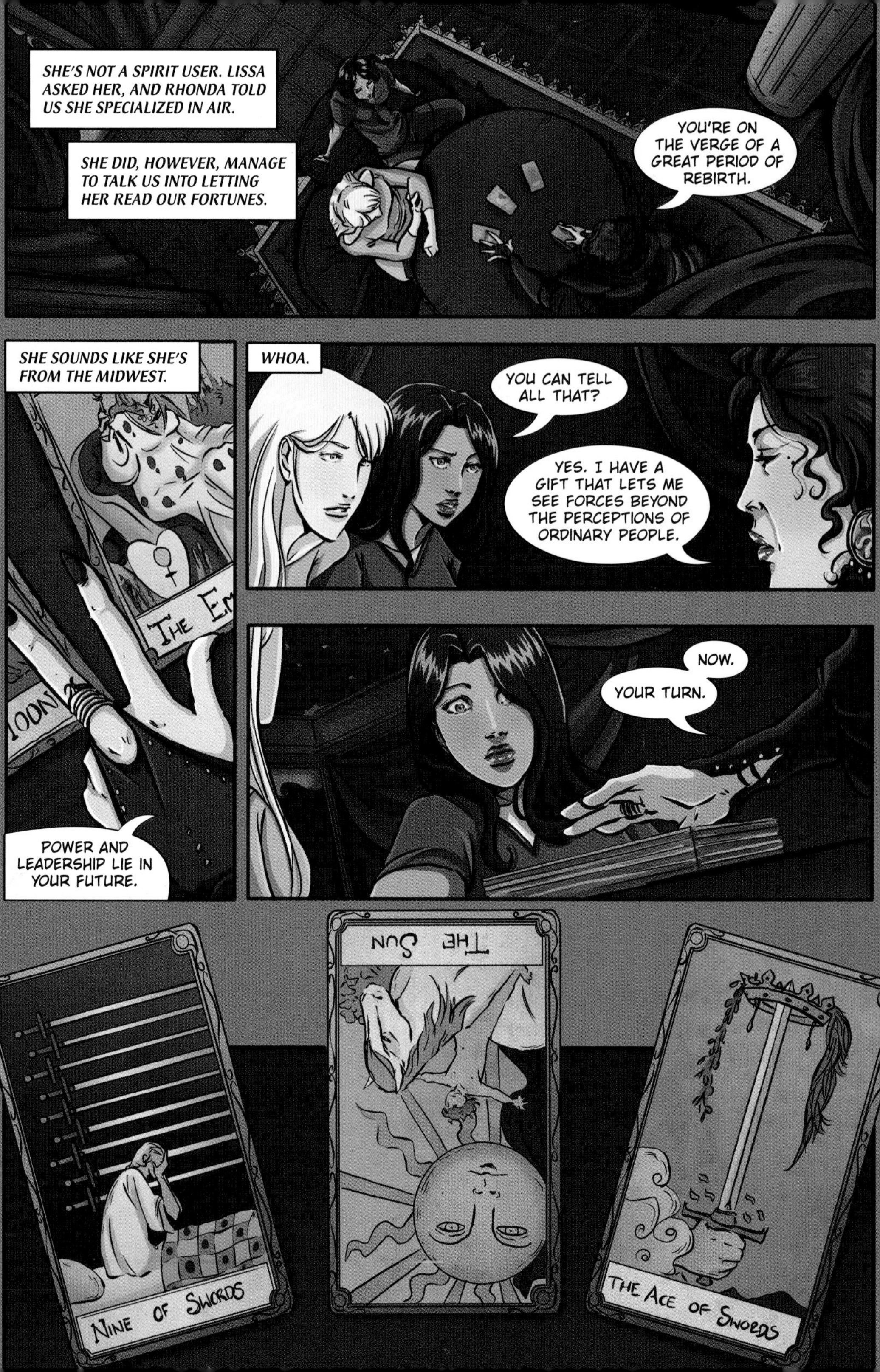

SHE'S NOT A SPIRIT USER. LISSA ASKED HER, AND RHONDA TOLD US SHE SPECIALIZED IN AIR.
SHE DID, HOWEVER, MANAGE TO TALK US INTO LETTING HER READ OUR FORTUNES.
YOU'RE ON THE VERGE OF A GREAT PERIOD OF REBIRTH.
SHE SOUNDS LIKE SHE'S FROM THE MIDWEST.
THE EM
MOON
POWER AND LEADERSHIP LIE IN YOUR FUTURE.
WHOA.
YOU CAN TELL ALL THAT?
YES. I HAVE A GIFT THAT LETS ME SEE FORCES BEYOND THE PERCEPTIONS OF ORDINARY PEOPLE.
NOW.
YOUR TURN.
NINE OF SWORDS
THE SUN
THE ACE OF SWORDS

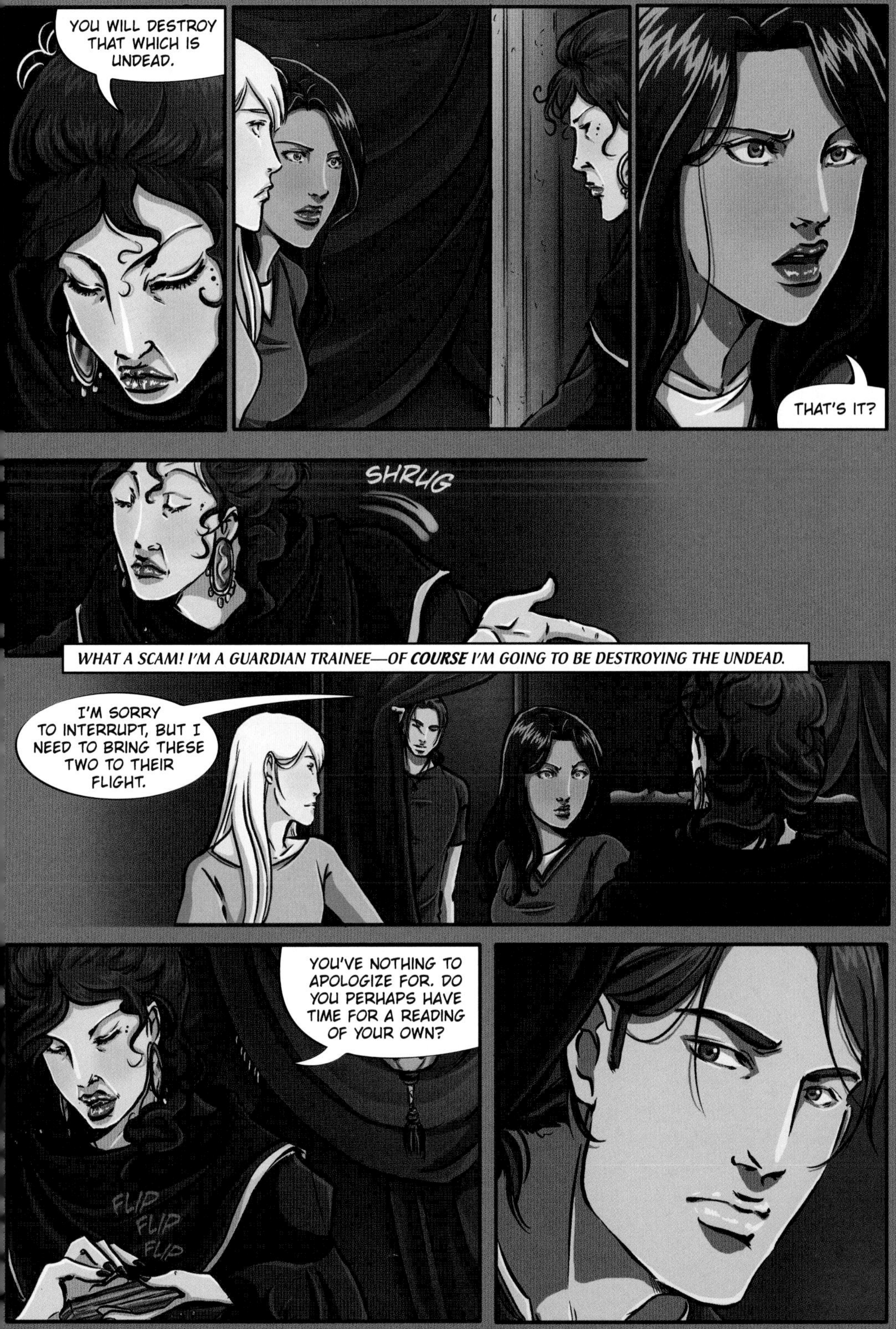
YOU WILL DESTROY THAT WHICH IS UNDEAD.
THAT'S IT?
SHRUG
WHAT A SCAM! I'M A GUARDIAN TRAINEE—OF COURSE I'M GOING TO BE DESTROYING THE UNDEAD.
I'M SORRY TO INTERRUPT, BUT I NEED TO BRING THESE TWO TO THEIR FLIGHT.
YOU'VE NOTHING TO APOLOGIZE FOR. DO YOU PERHAPS HAVE TIME FOR A READING OF YOUR OWN?
FLIP FLIP FLIP

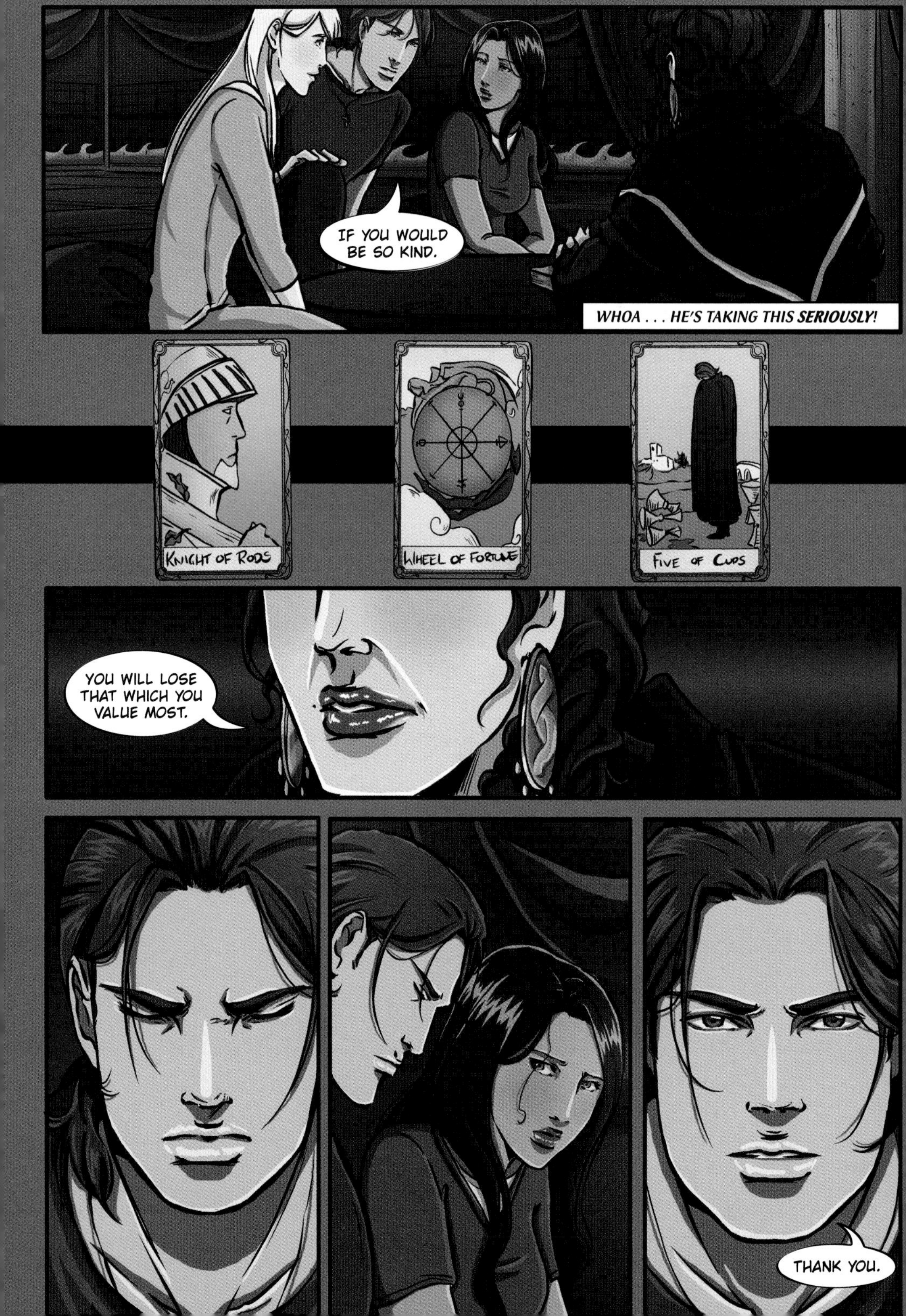
IF YOU WOULD BE SO KIND.
WHOA . . . HE'S TAKING THIS SERIOUSLY!
KNIGHT OF RODS
WHEEL OF FORTUNE
FIVE OF CUPS
YOU WILL LOSE THAT WHICH YOU VALUE MOST.
THANK YOU.

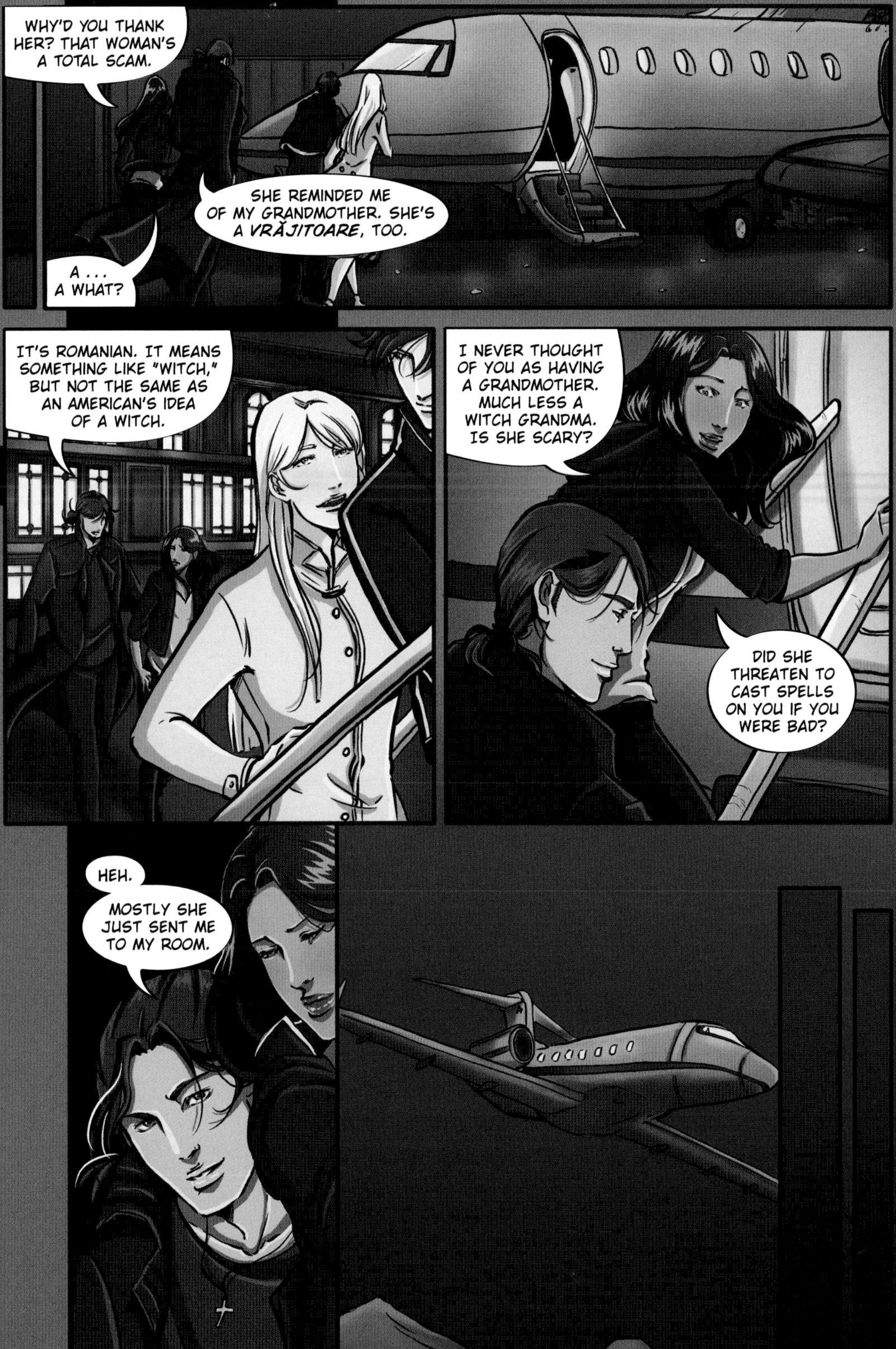
WHY'D YOU THANK HER? THAT WOMAN'S A TOTAL SCAM.
SHE REMINDED ME OF MY GRANDMOTHER. SHE'S A *VRĂJITOARE*, TOO.
A . . . A WHAT?
IT'S ROMANIAN. IT MEANS SOMETHING LIKE "WITCH," BUT NOT THE SAME AS AN AMERICAN'S IDEA OF A WITCH.
I NEVER THOUGHT OF YOU AS HAVING A GRANDMOTHER. MUCH LESS A WITCH GRANDMA. IS SHE SCARY?
DID SHE THREATEN TO CAST SPELLS ON YOU IF YOU WERE BAD?
HEH.
MOSTLY SHE JUST SENT ME TO MY ROOM.

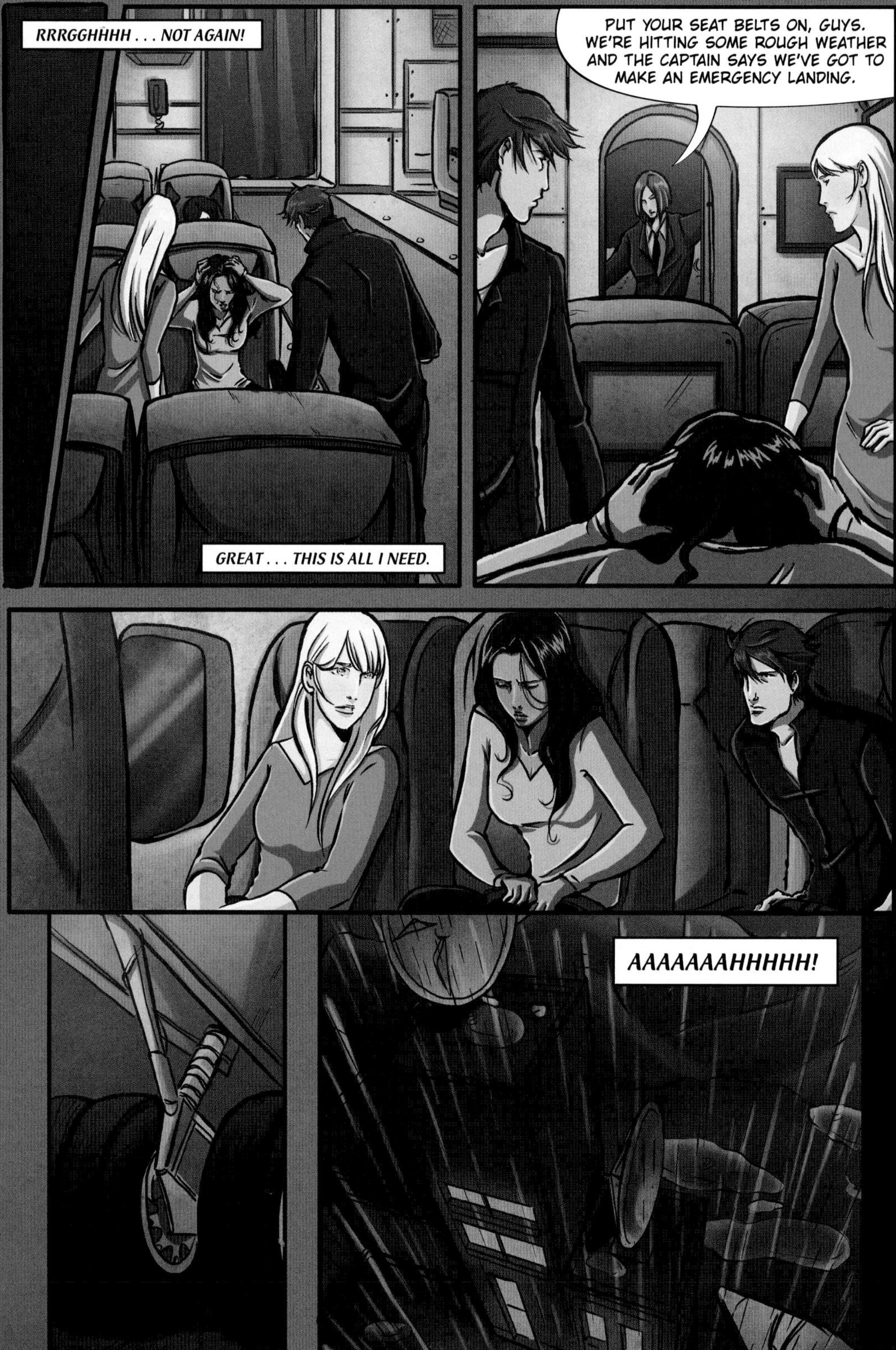
RRRGGHHHH . . . NOT AGAIN!
GREAT . . . THIS IS ALL I NEED.
PUT YOUR SEAT BELTS ON, GUYS. WE'RE HITTING SOME ROUGH WEATHER AND THE CAPTAIN SAYS WE'VE GOT TO MAKE AN EMERGENCY LANDING.
AAAAAAAHHHHH!

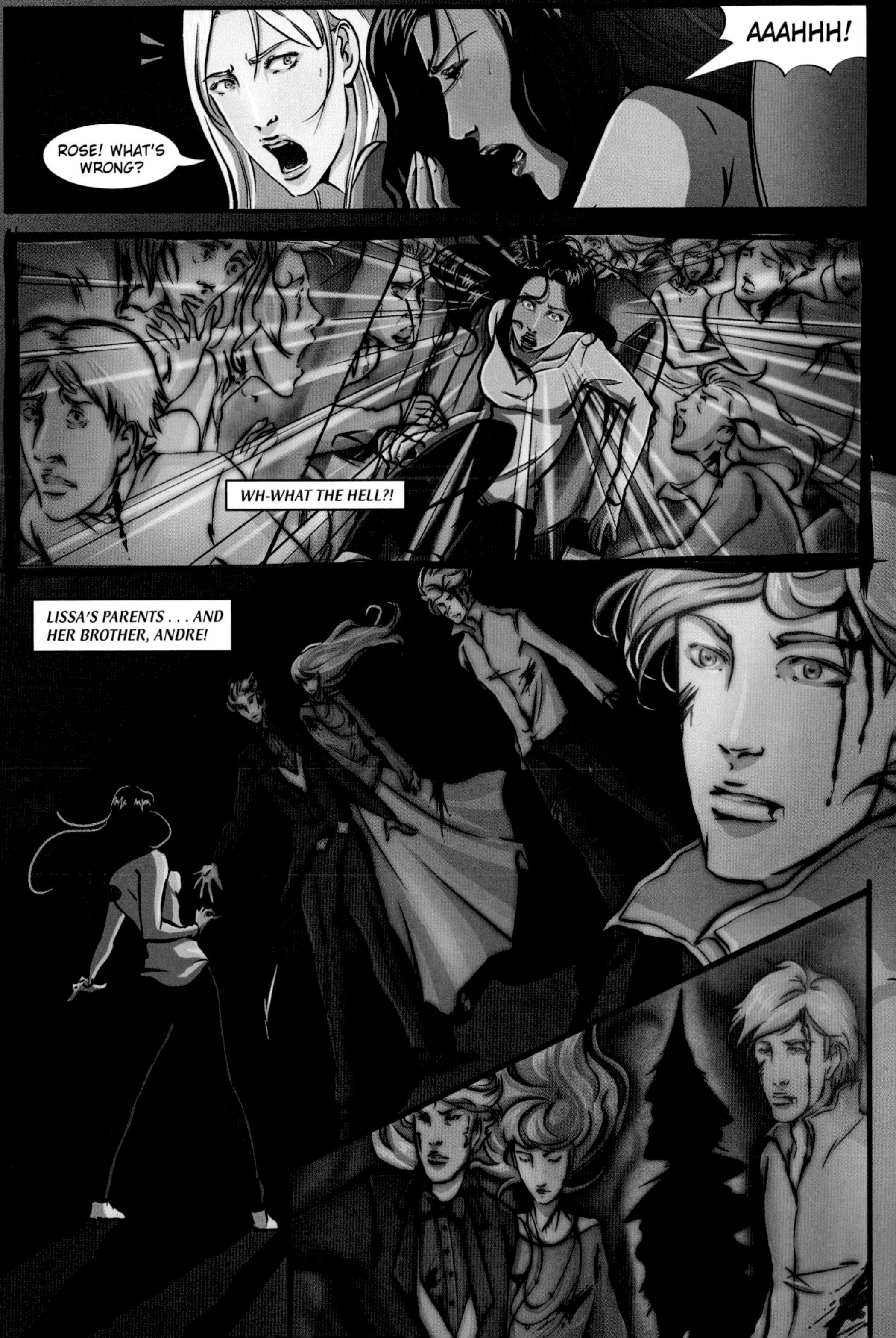
AAAHHH!
ROSE! WHAT'S WRONG?
WH-WHAT THE HELL?!
LISSA'S PARENTS . . . AND HER BROTHER, ANDRE!

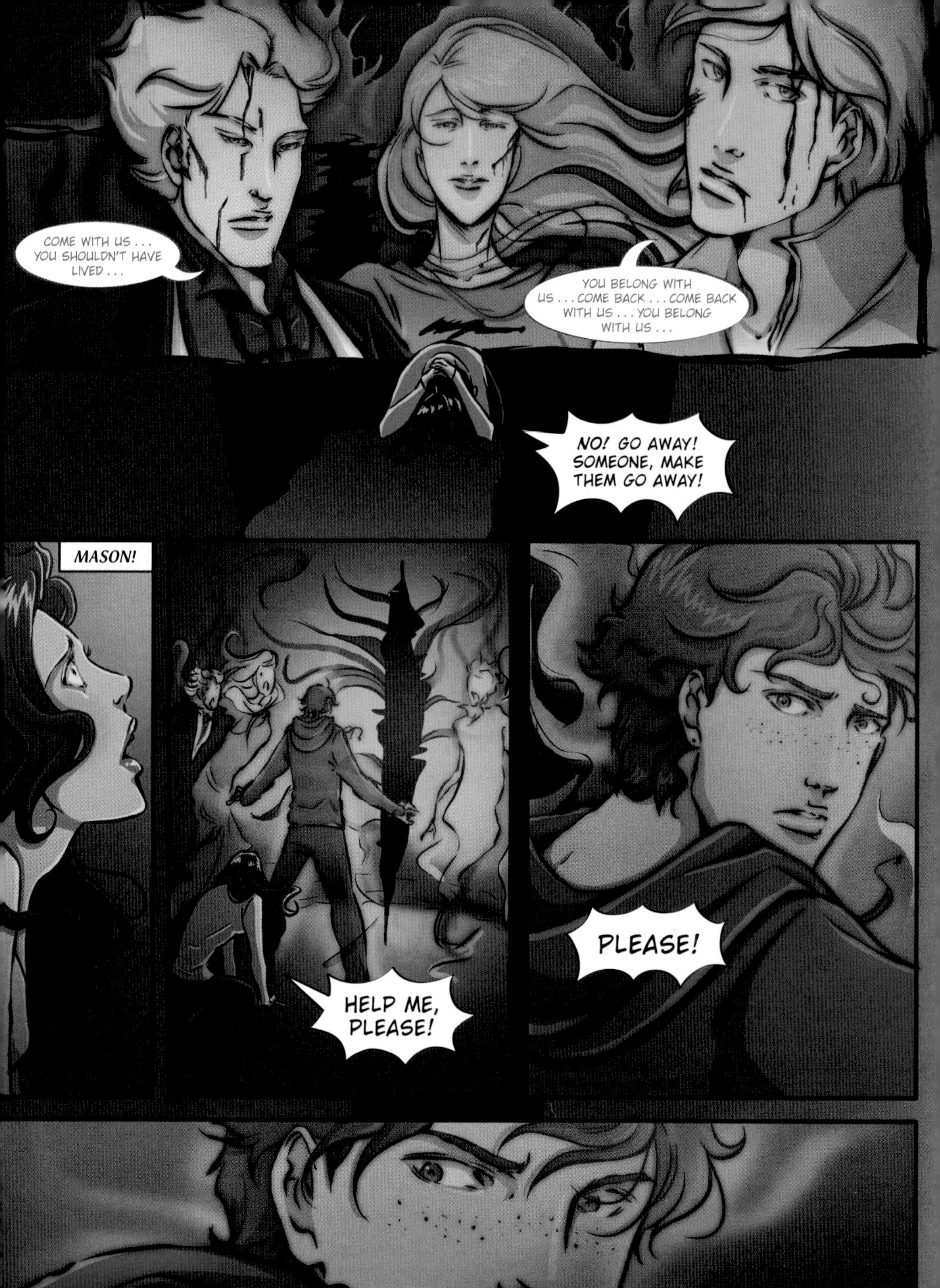
COME WITH US . . . YOU SHOULDN'T HAVE LIVED . . .
YOU BELONG WITH US . . . COME BACK . . . COME BACK WITH US . . . YOU BELONG WITH US . . .
NO! GO AWAY! SOMEONE, MAKE THEM GO AWAY!
MASON!
HELP ME, PLEASE!
PLEASE!

[redacted]

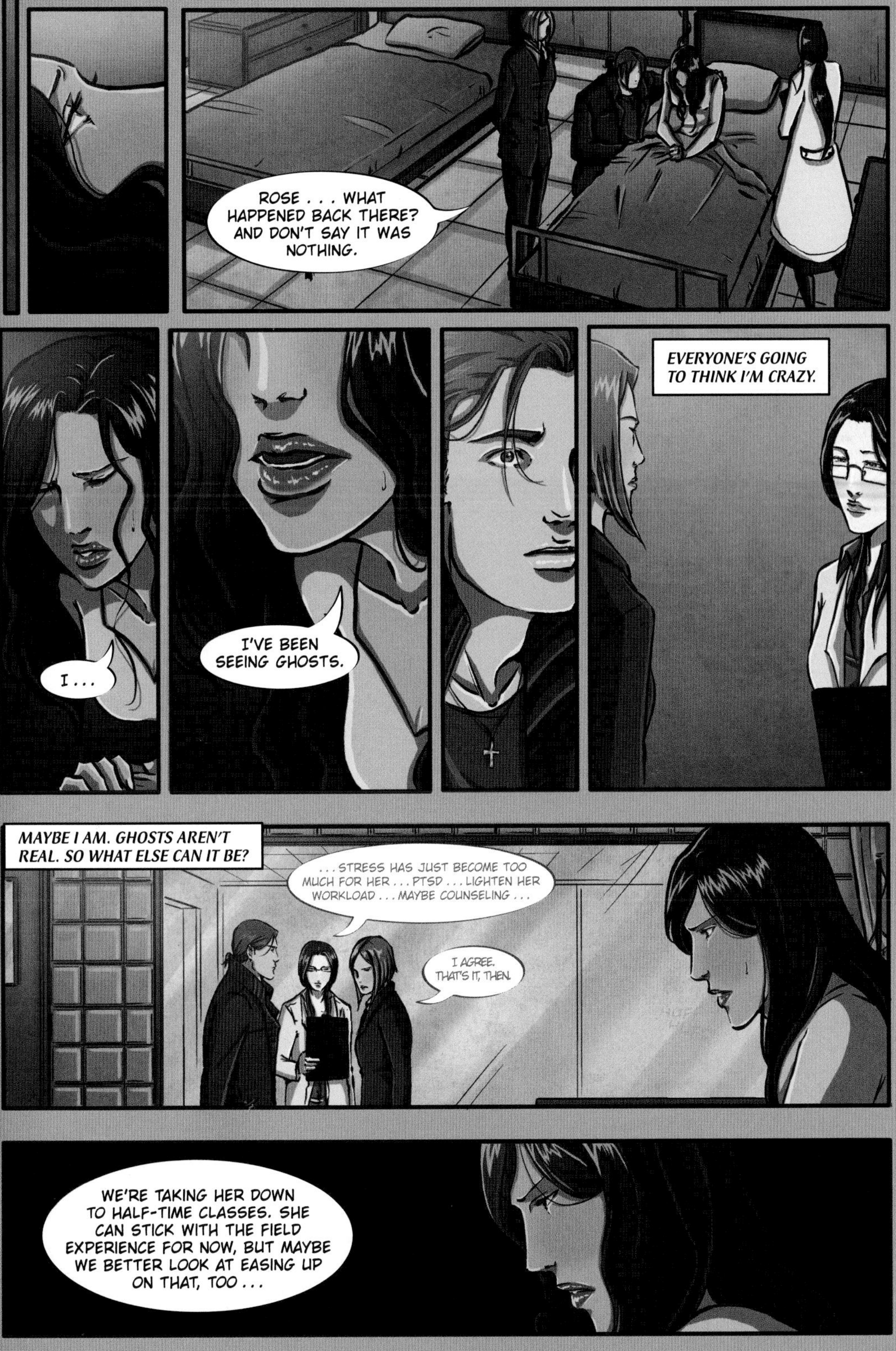
ROSE . . . WHAT HAPPENED BACK THERE? AND DON'T SAY IT WAS NOTHING.
I . . .
I'VE BEEN SEEING GHOSTS.
EVERYONE'S GOING TO THINK I'M CRAZY.
MAYBE I AM. GHOSTS AREN'T REAL. SO WHAT ELSE CAN IT BE?
. . . STRESS HAS JUST BECOME TOO MUCH FOR HER . . . PTSD . . . LIGHTEN HER WORKLOAD . . . MAYBE COUNSELING . . .
I AGREE. THAT'S IT, THEN.
WE'RE TAKING HER DOWN TO HALF-TIME CLASSES. SHE CAN STICK WITH THE FIELD EXPERIENCE FOR NOW, BUT MAYBE WE BETTER LOOK AT EASING UP ON THAT, TOO . . .

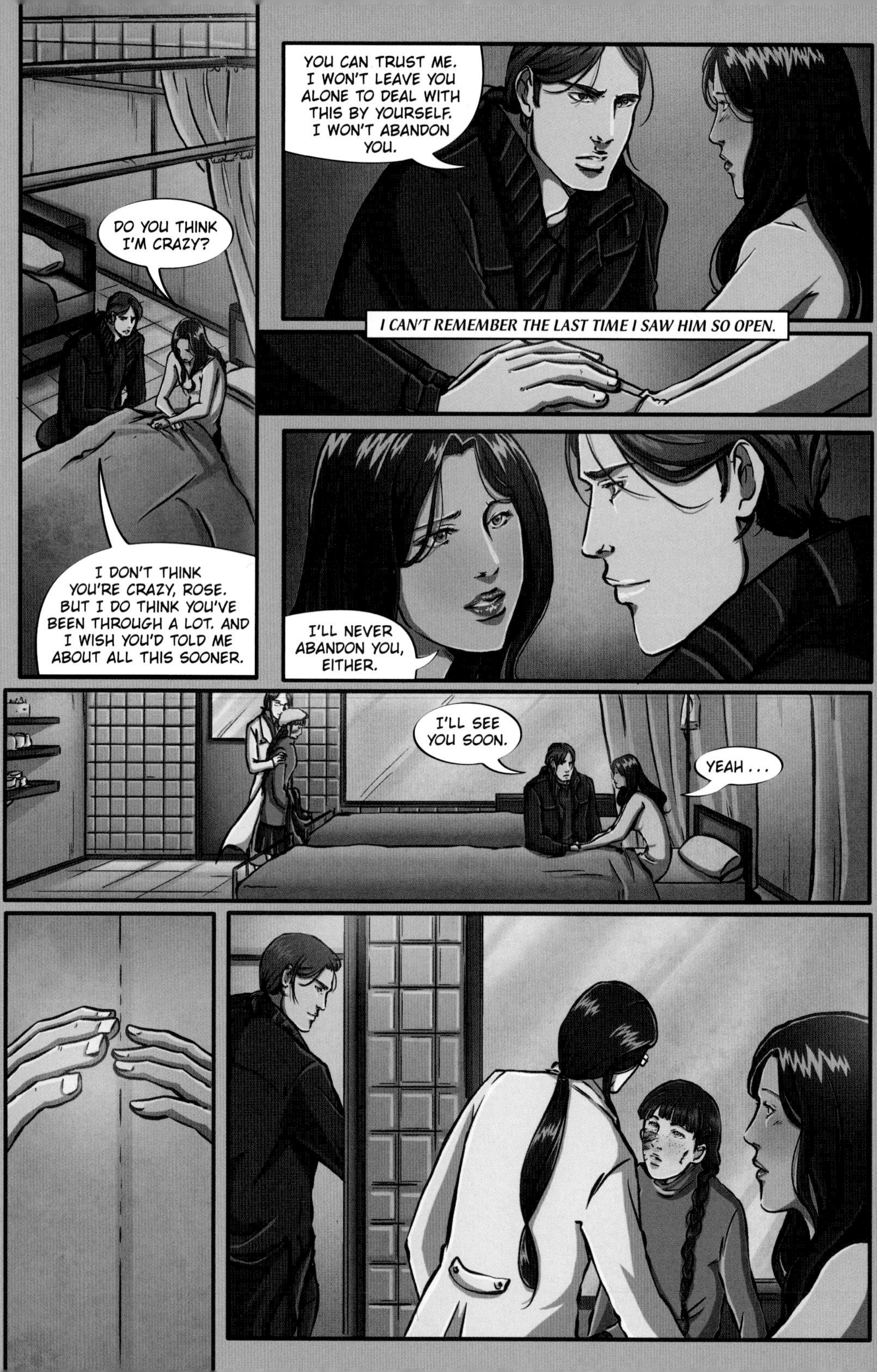
DO YOU THINK I'M CRAZY?
I DON'T THINK YOU'RE CRAZY, ROSE. BUT I DO THINK YOU'VE BEEN THROUGH A LOT. AND I WISH YOU'D TOLD ME ABOUT ALL THIS SOONER.
YOU CAN TRUST ME. I WON'T LEAVE YOU ALONE TO DEAL WITH THIS BY YOURSELF. I WON'T ABANDON YOU.
I CAN'T REMEMBER THE LAST TIME I SAW HIM SO OPEN.
I'LL NEVER ABANDON YOU, EITHER.
I'LL SEE YOU SOON.
YEAH . . .

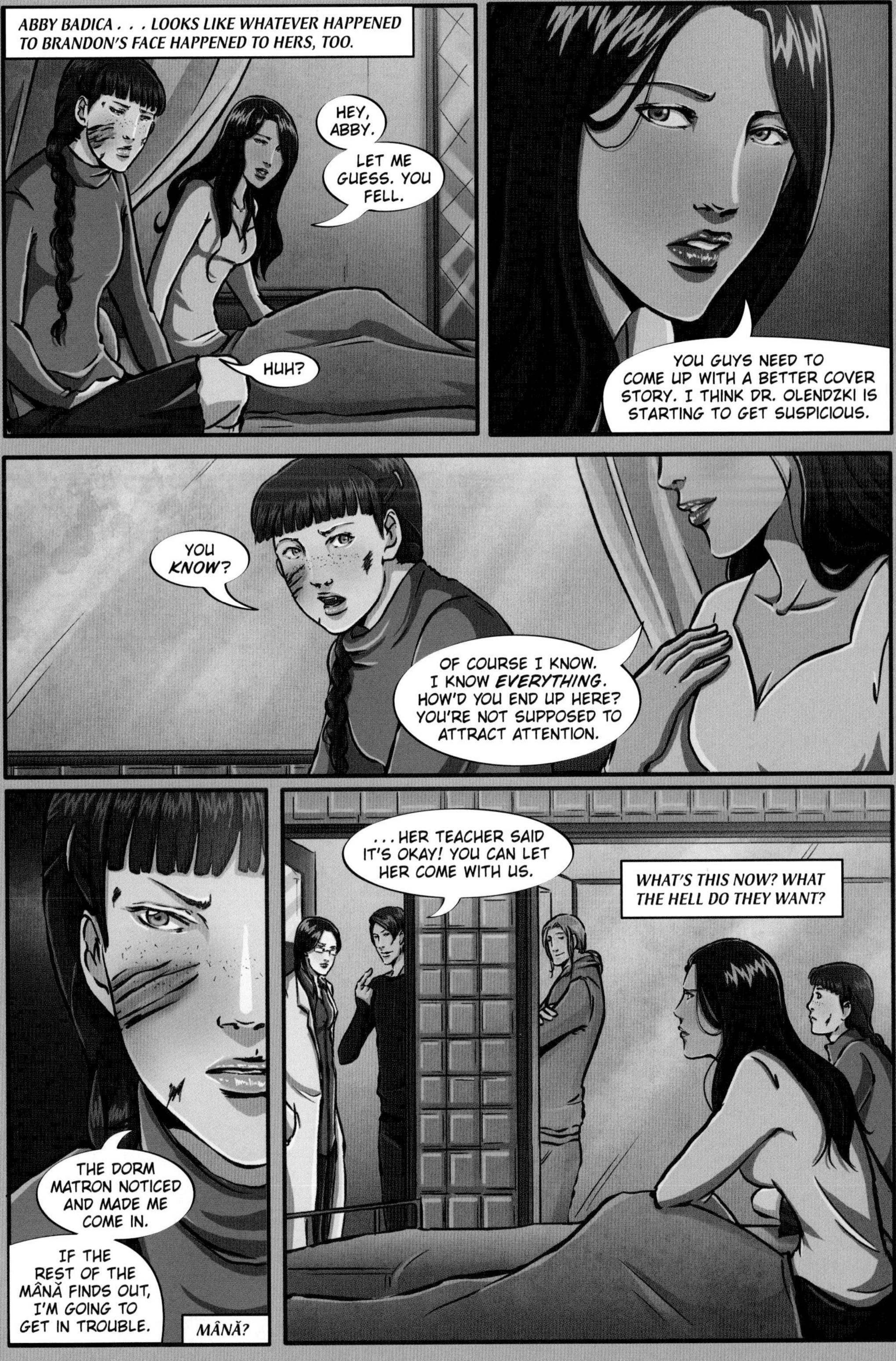
ABBY BADICA . . . LOOKS LIKE WHATEVER HAPPENED TO BRANDON'S FACE HAPPENED TO HERS, TOO.
HEY, ABBY.
LET ME GUESS. YOU FELL.
HUH?
YOU GUYS NEED TO COME UP WITH A BETTER COVER STORY. I THINK DR. OLENDZKI IS STARTING TO GET SUSPICIOUS.
YOU KNOW?
OF COURSE I KNOW. I KNOW EVERYTHING. HOW'D YOU END UP HERE? YOU'RE NOT SUPPOSED TO ATTRACT ATTENTION.
THE DORM MATRON NOTICED AND MADE ME COME IN.
IF THE REST OF THE MÂNĂ FINDS OUT, I'M GOING TO GET IN TROUBLE.
MÂNĂ?
. . . HER TEACHER SAID IT'S OKAY! YOU CAN LET HER COME WITH US.
WHAT'S THIS NOW? WHAT THE HELL DO THEY WANT?

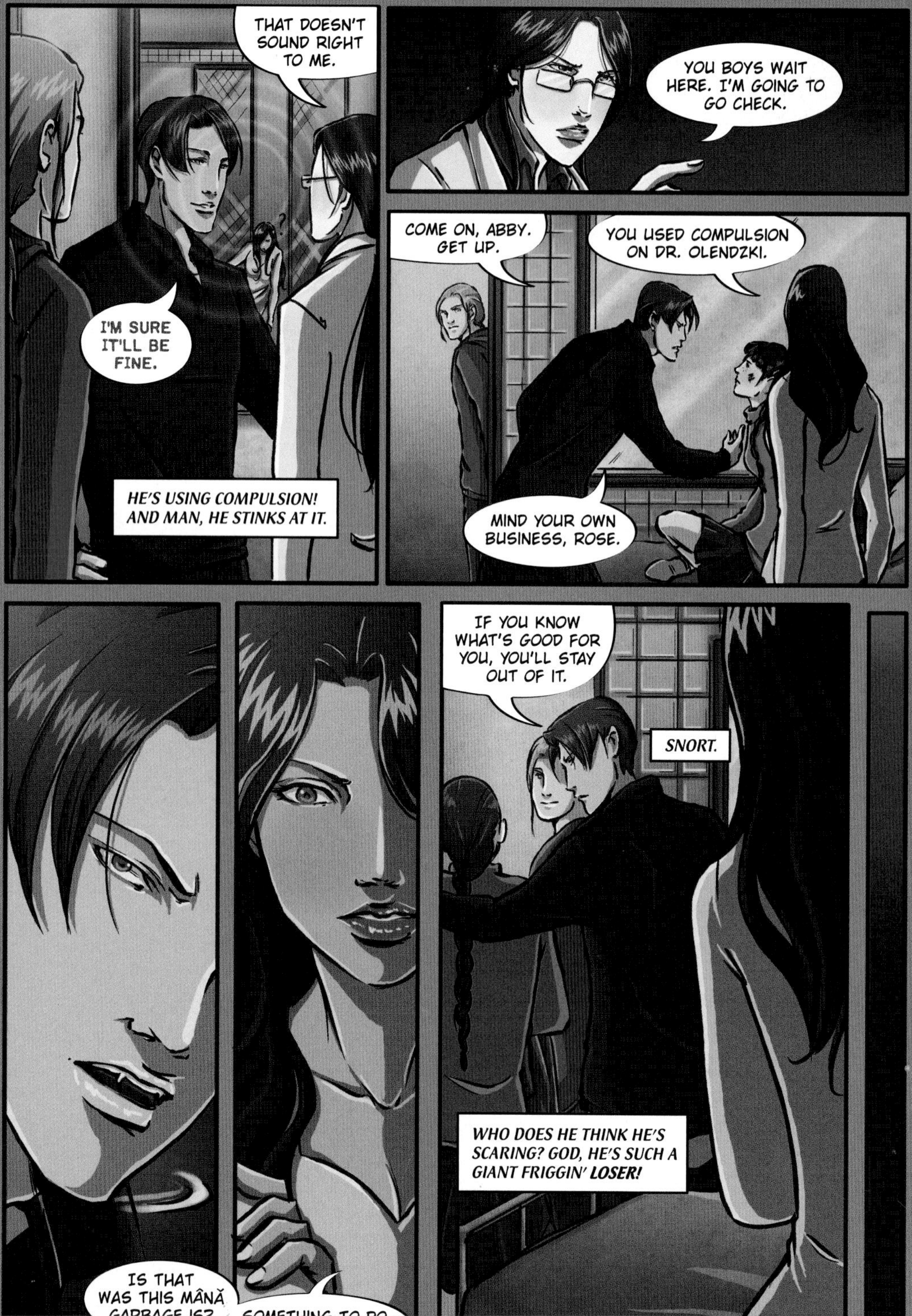
THAT DOESN'T SOUND RIGHT TO ME.
I'M SURE IT'LL BE FINE.
HE'S USING COMPULSION! AND MAN, HE STINKS AT IT.
YOU BOYS WAIT HERE. I'M GOING TO GO CHECK.
COME ON, ABBY. GET UP.
YOU USED COMPULSION ON DR. OLENDZKI.
MIND YOUR OWN BUSINESS, ROSE.
IS THAT WAS THIS MÂNĂ GARBAGE IS?
SOMETHING TO DO WITH COMPULSION?
IF YOU KNOW WHAT'S GOOD FOR YOU, YOU'LL STAY OUT OF IT.
SNORT.
WHO DOES HE THINK HE'S SCARING? GOD, HE'S SUCH A GIANT FRIGGIN' LOSER!

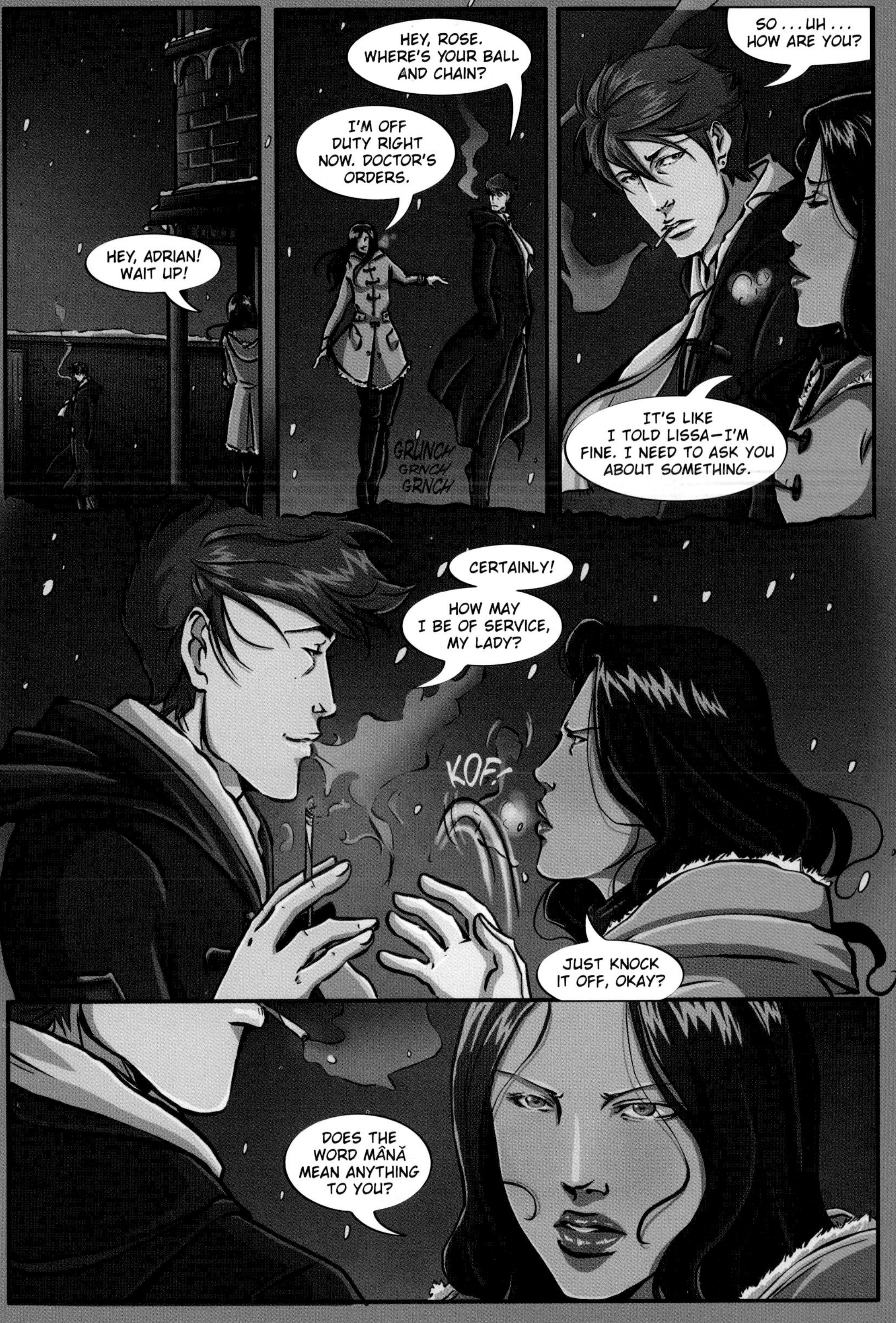
HEY, ADRIAN! WAIT UP!
HEY, ROSE. WHERE'S YOUR BALL AND CHAIN?
I'M OFF DUTY RIGHT NOW. DOCTOR'S ORDERS.
GRUNCH GRNCH GRNCH
SO . . . UH . . . HOW ARE YOU?
IT'S LIKE I TOLD LISSA—I'M FINE. I NEED TO ASK YOU ABOUT SOMETHING.
CERTAINLY!
HOW MAY I BE OF SERVICE, MY LADY?
KOF!
JUST KNOCK IT OFF, OKAY?
DOES THE WORD MÂNĂ MEAN ANYTHING TO YOU?

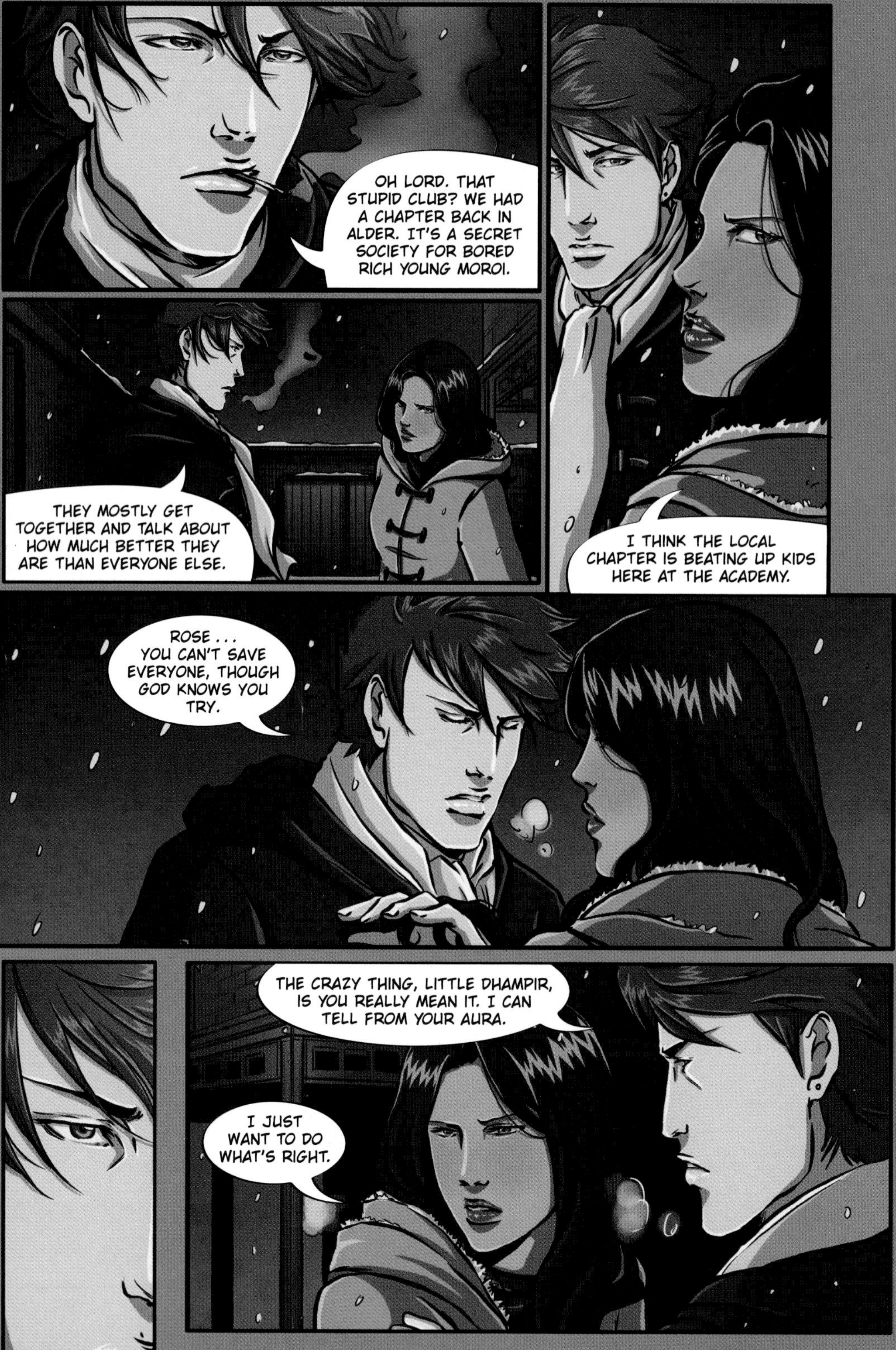
OH LORD. THAT STUPID CLUB? WE HAD A CHAPTER BACK IN ALDER. IT'S A SECRET SOCIETY FOR BORED RICH YOUNG MOROI.
THEY MOSTLY GET TOGETHER AND TALK ABOUT HOW MUCH BETTER THEY ARE THAN EVERYONE ELSE.
I THINK THE LOCAL CHAPTER IS BEATING UP KIDS HERE AT THE ACADEMY.
ROSE . . . YOU CAN'T SAVE EVERYONE, THOUGH GOD KNOWS YOU TRY.
I JUST WANT TO DO WHAT'S RIGHT.
THE CRAZY THING, LITTLE DHAMPIR, IS YOU REALLY MEAN IT. I CAN TELL FROM YOUR AURA.

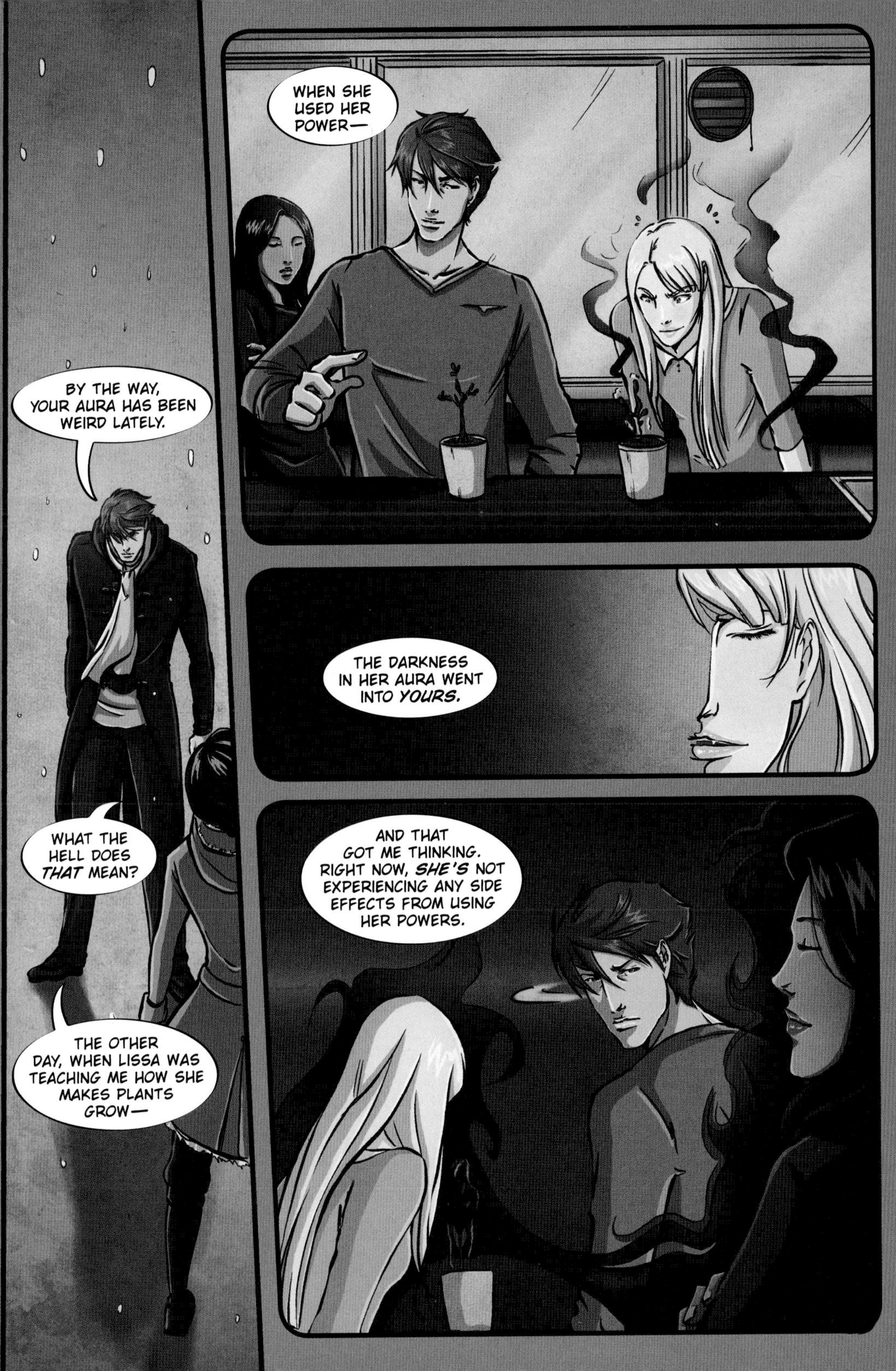
BY THE WAY, YOUR AURA HAS BEEN WEIRD LATELY.
WHAT THE HELL DOES *THAT* MEAN?
THE OTHER DAY, WHEN LISSA WAS TEACHING ME HOW SHE MAKES PLANTS GROW—
WHEN SHE USED HER POWER—
THE DARKNESS IN HER AURA WENT INTO *YOURS.*
AND THAT GOT ME THINKING. RIGHT NOW, *SHE'S* NOT EXPERIENCING ANY SIDE EFFECTS FROM USING HER POWERS.

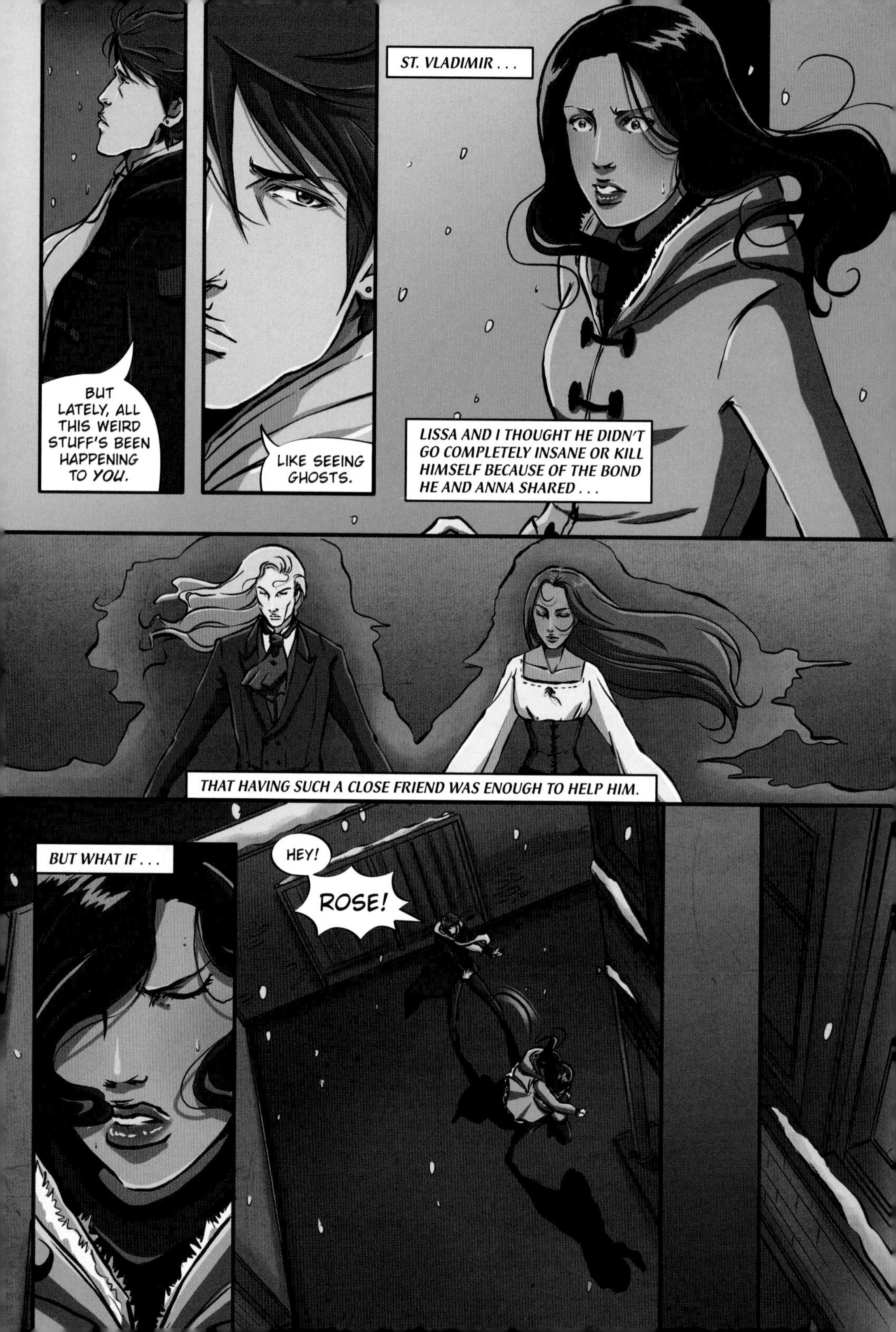
BUT LATELY, ALL THIS WEIRD STUFF'S BEEN HAPPENING TO YOU.
LIKE SEEING GHOSTS.
ST. VLADIMIR . . .
LISSA AND I THOUGHT HE DIDN'T GO COMPLETELY INSANE OR KILL HIMSELF BECAUSE OF THE BOND HE AND ANNA SHARED . . .
THAT HAVING SUCH A CLOSE FRIEND WAS ENOUGH TO HELP HIM.
BUT WHAT IF . . .
HEY!
ROSE!

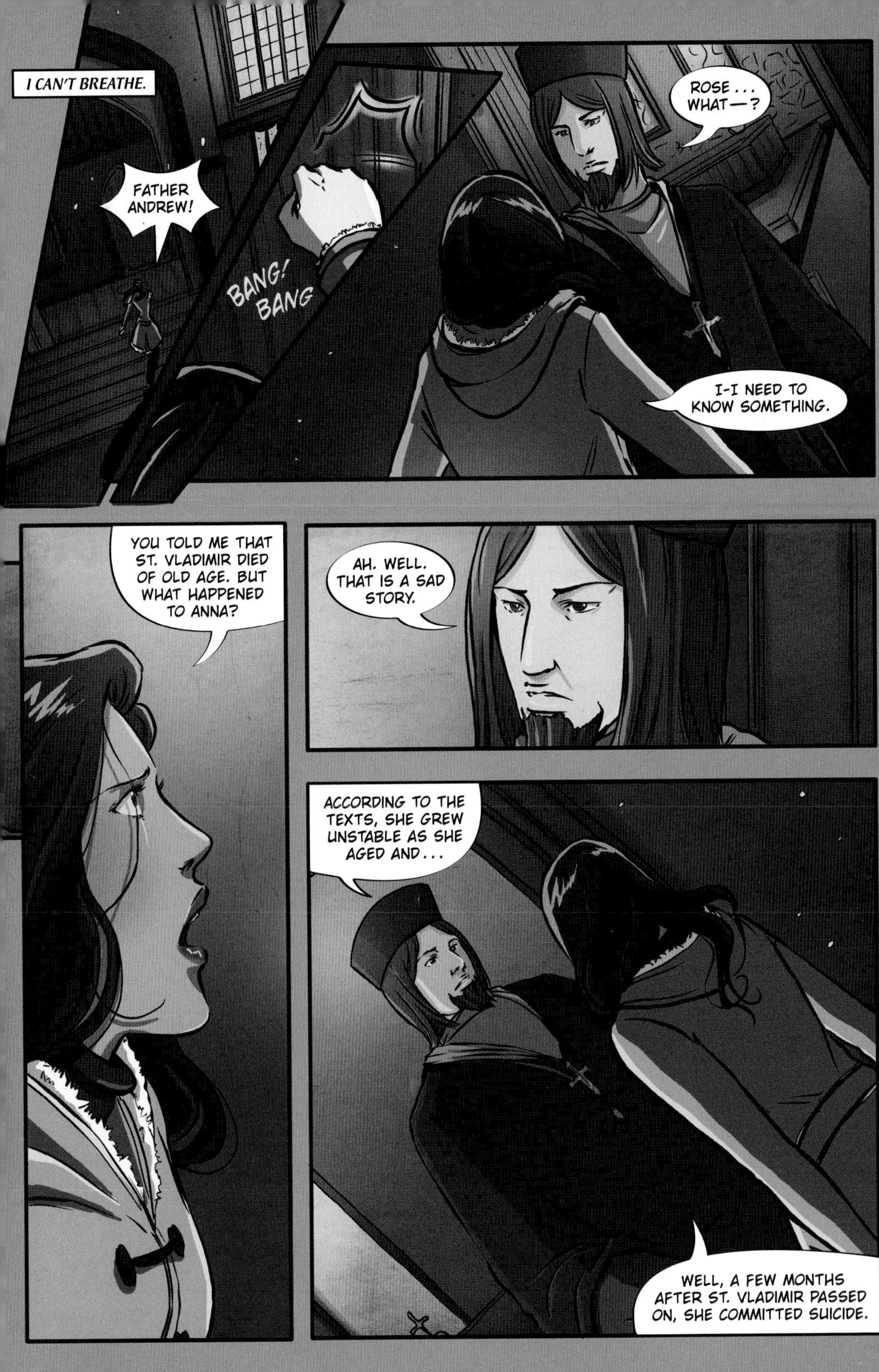
I CAN'T BREATHE.
FATHER ANDREW!
BANG! BANG
ROSE . . . WHAT—?
I-I NEED TO KNOW SOMETHING.
YOU TOLD ME THAT ST. VLADIMIR DIED OF OLD AGE. BUT WHAT HAPPENED TO ANNA?
AH. WELL. THAT IS A SAD STORY.
ACCORDING TO THE TEXTS, SHE GREW UNSTABLE AS SHE AGED AND . . .
WELL, A FEW MONTHS AFTER ST. VLADIMIR PASSED ON, SHE COMMITTED SUICIDE.

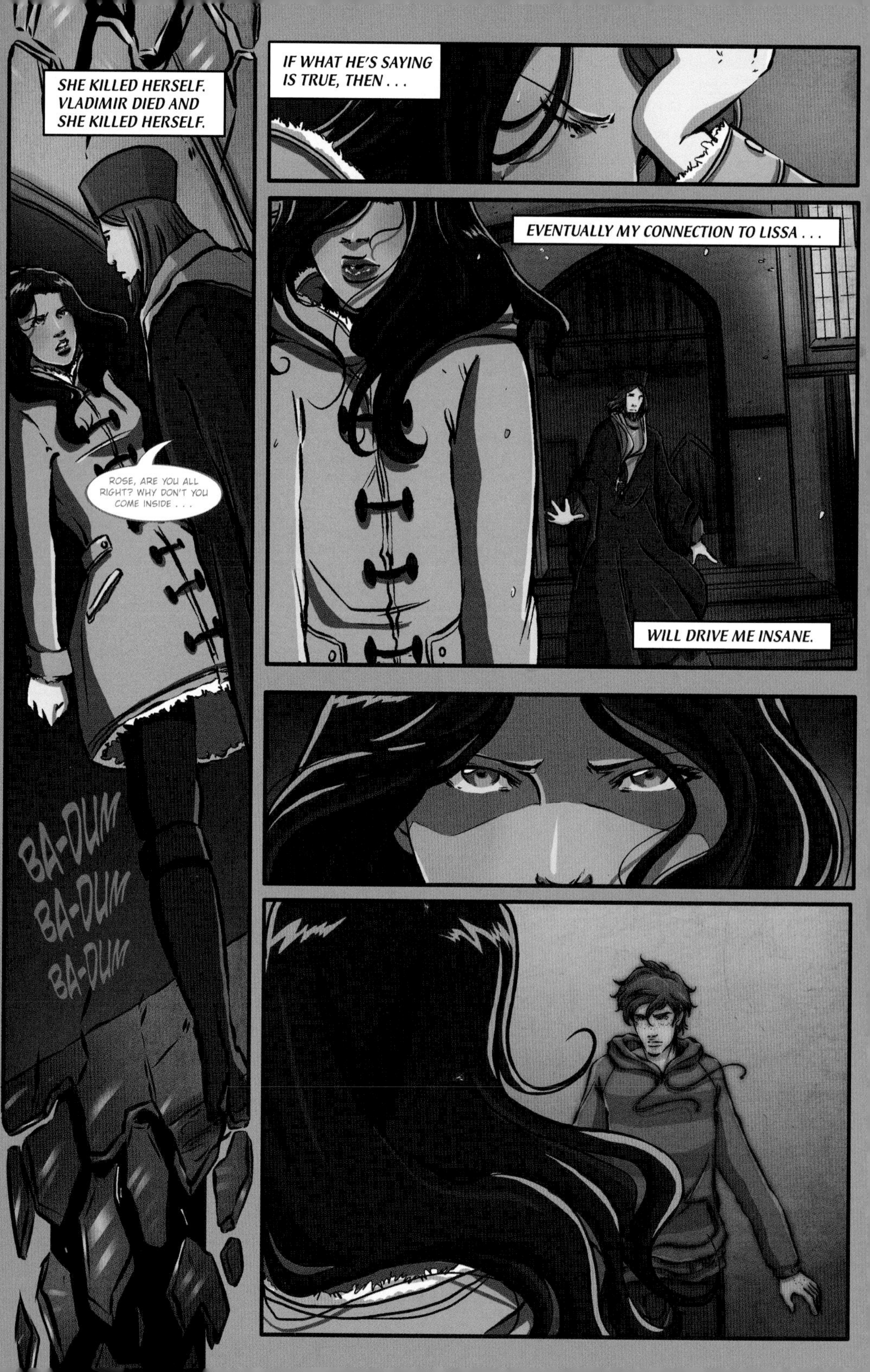
SHE KILLED HERSELF. VLADIMIR DIED AND SHE KILLED HERSELF.
ROSE, ARE YOU ALL RIGHT? WHY DON'T YOU COME INSIDE . . .
BA-DUM
BA-DUM
BA-DUM
IF WHAT HE'S SAYING IS TRUE, THEN . . .
EVENTUALLY MY CONNECTION TO LISSA . . .
WILL DRIVE ME INSANE.

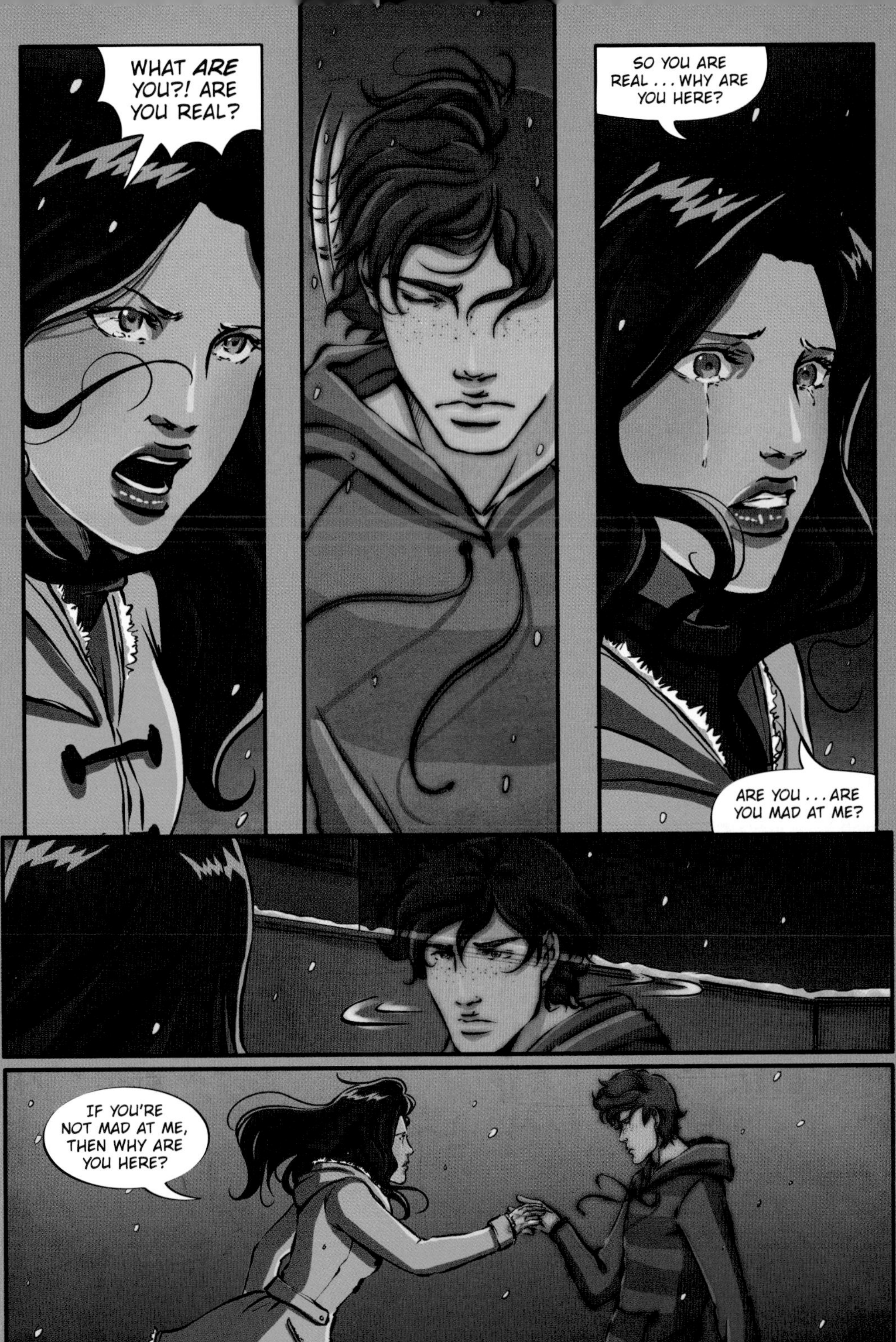
WHAT ARE YOU?! ARE YOU REAL?
SO YOU ARE REAL . . . WHY ARE YOU HERE?
ARE YOU . . . ARE YOU MAD AT ME?
IF YOU'RE NOT MAD AT ME, THEN WHY ARE YOU HERE?

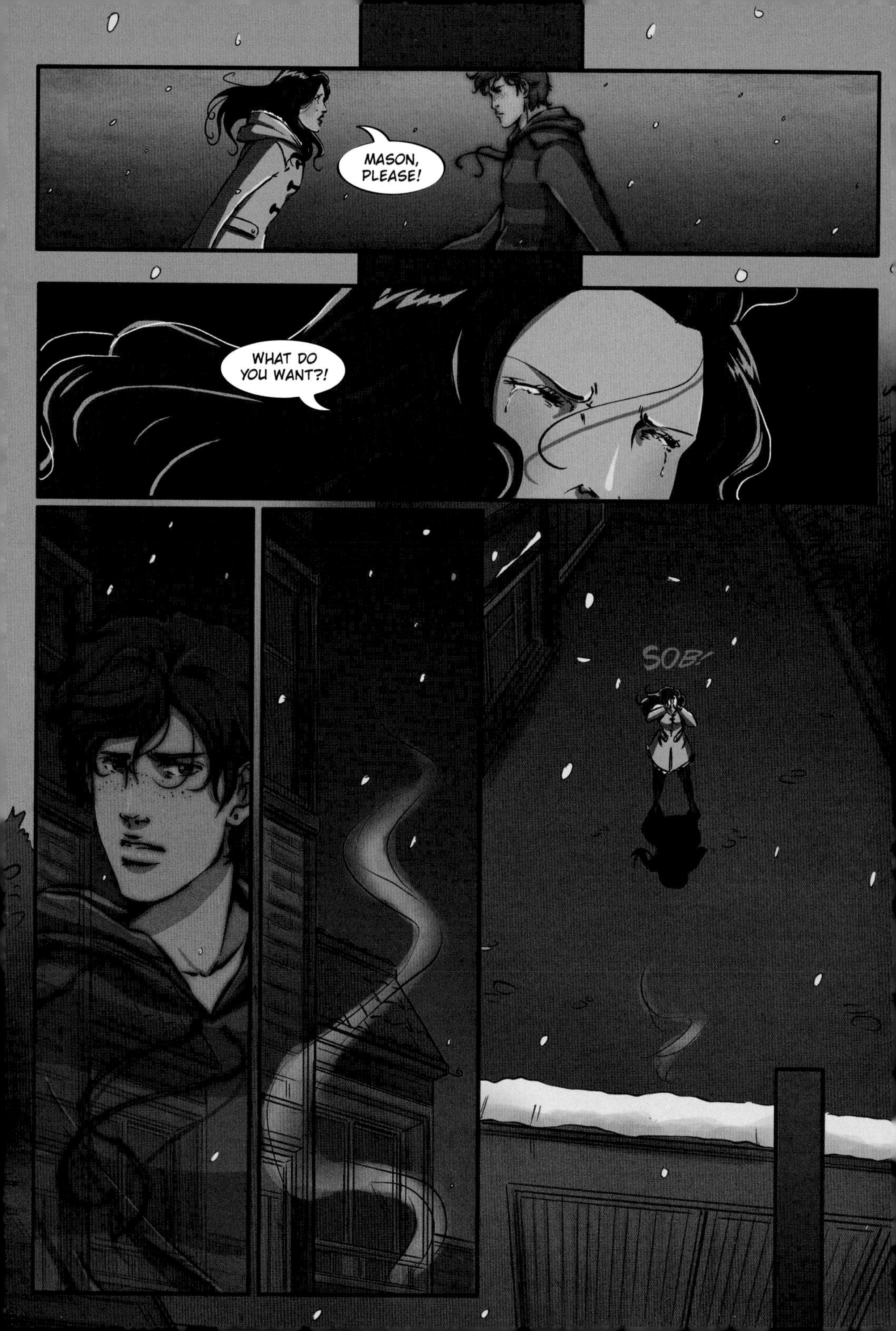
MASON, PLEASE!
WHAT DO YOU WANT?!
SOB!

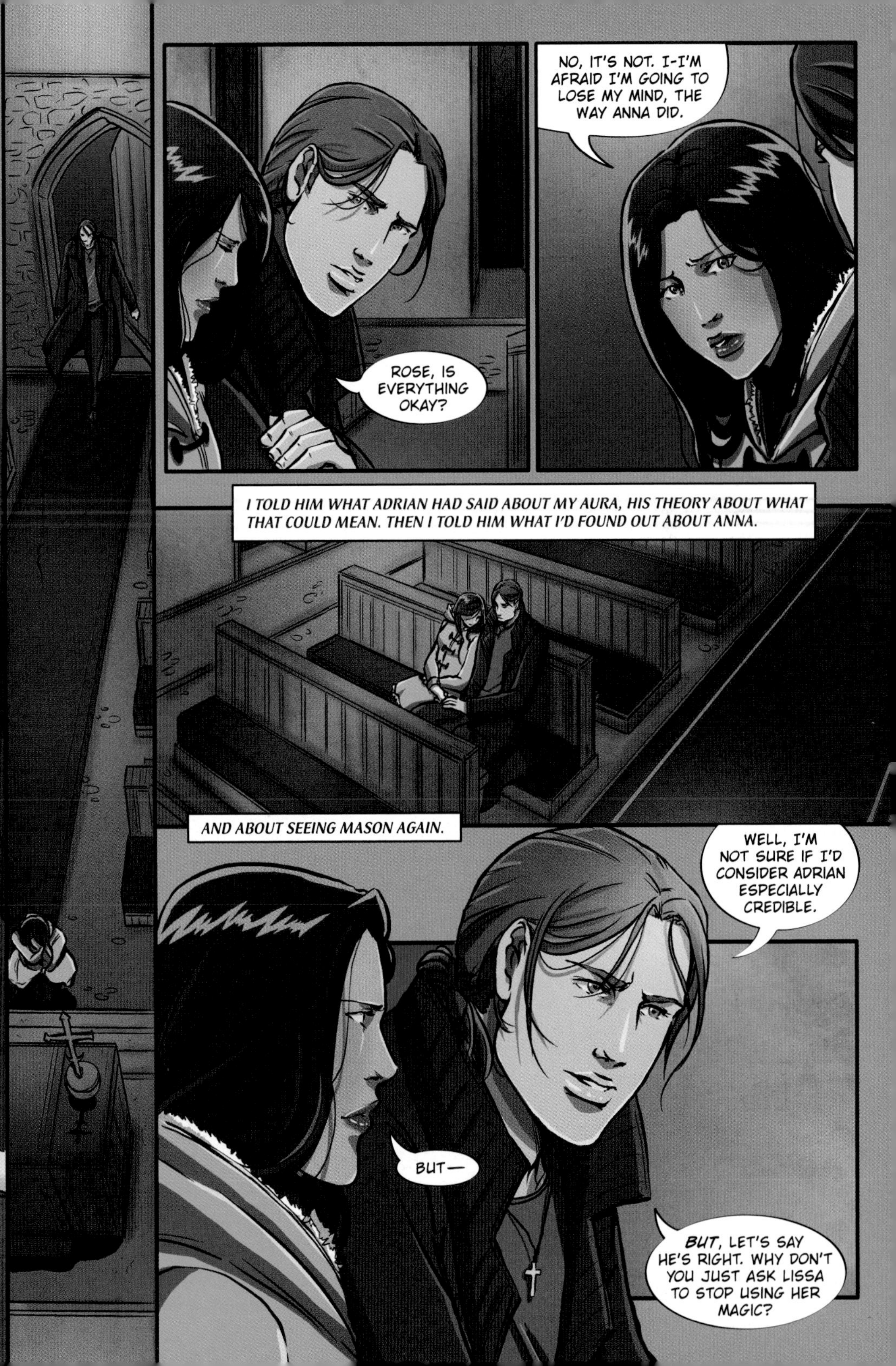
ROSE, IS EVERYTHING OKAY?
NO, IT'S NOT. I-I'M AFRAID I'M GOING TO LOSE MY MIND, THE WAY ANNA DID.
I TOLD HIM WHAT ADRIAN HAD SAID ABOUT MY AURA, HIS THEORY ABOUT WHAT THAT COULD MEAN. THEN I TOLD HIM WHAT I'D FOUND OUT ABOUT ANNA.
AND ABOUT SEEING MASON AGAIN.
WELL, I'M NOT SURE IF I'D CONSIDER ADRIAN ESPECIALLY CREDIBLE.
BUT—
BUT, LET'S SAY HE'S RIGHT. WHY DON'T YOU JUST ASK LISSA TO STOP USING HER MAGIC?

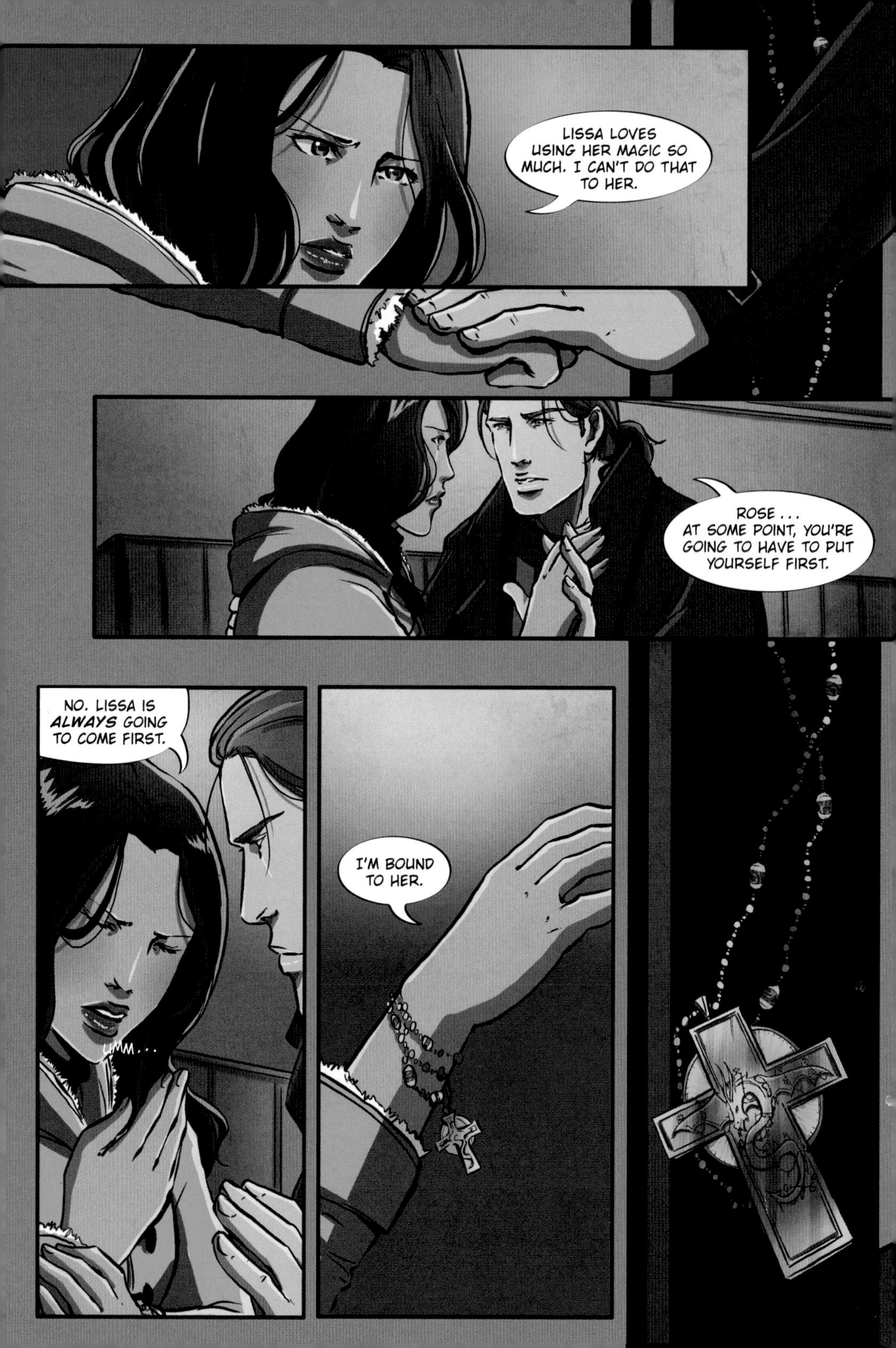
LISSA LOVES USING HER MAGIC SO MUCH. I CAN'T DO THAT TO HER.
ROSE . . . AT SOME POINT, YOU'RE GOING TO HAVE TO PUT YOURSELF FIRST.
NO. LISSA IS *ALWAYS* GOING TO COME FIRST.
UMM . . .
I'M BOUND TO HER.

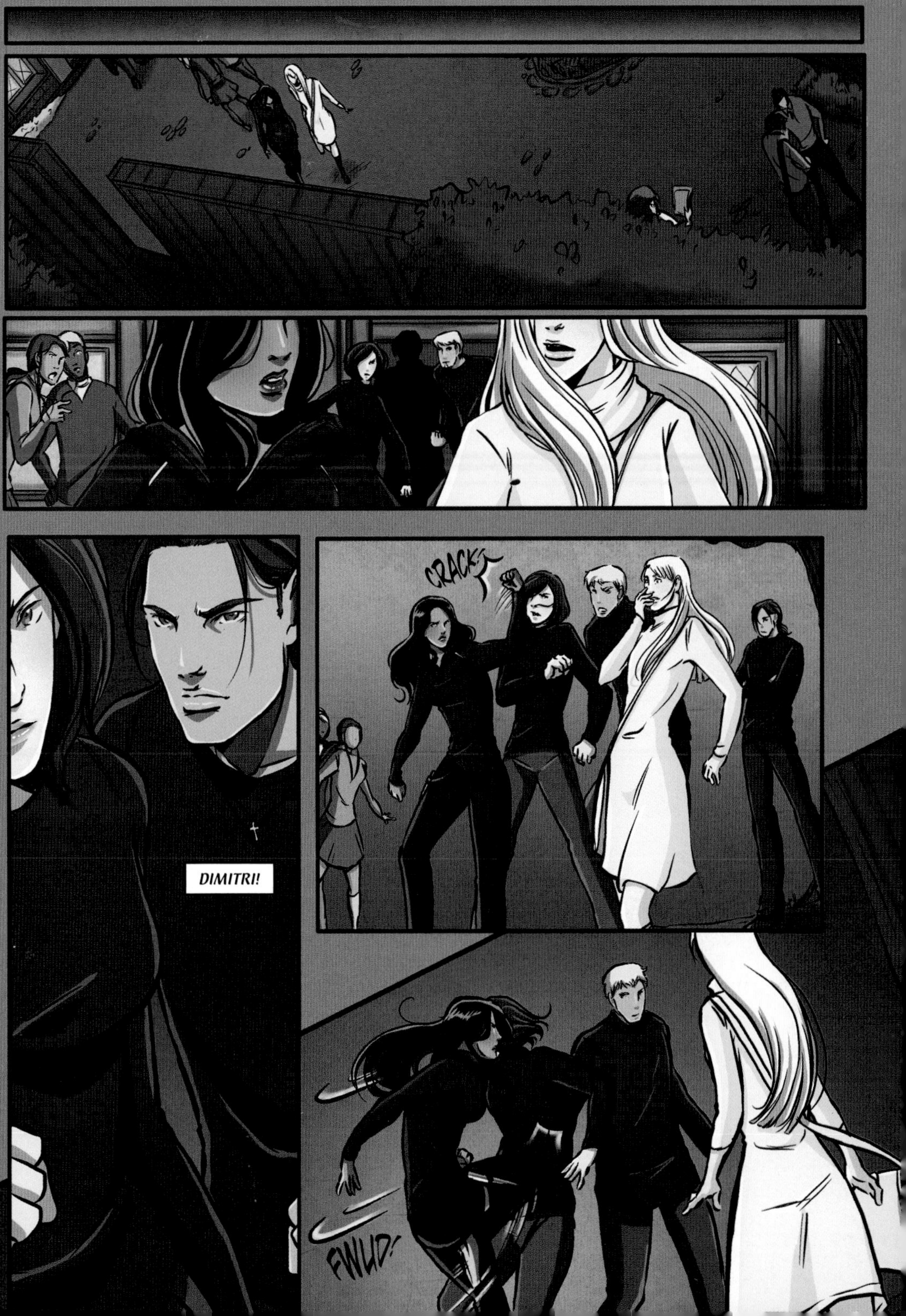
DIMITRI!
CRACK!
FWUD!

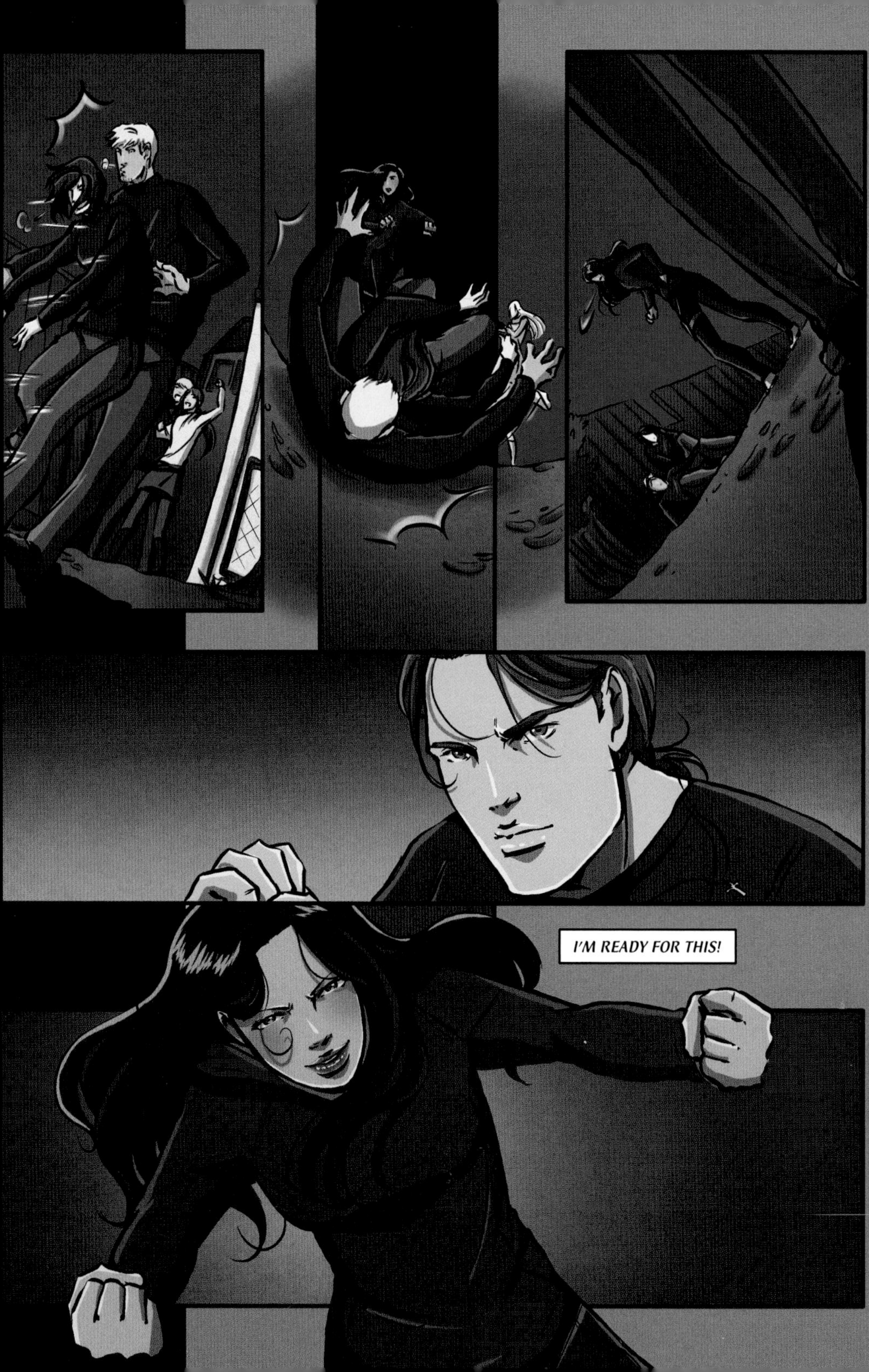
I'M READY FOR THIS!

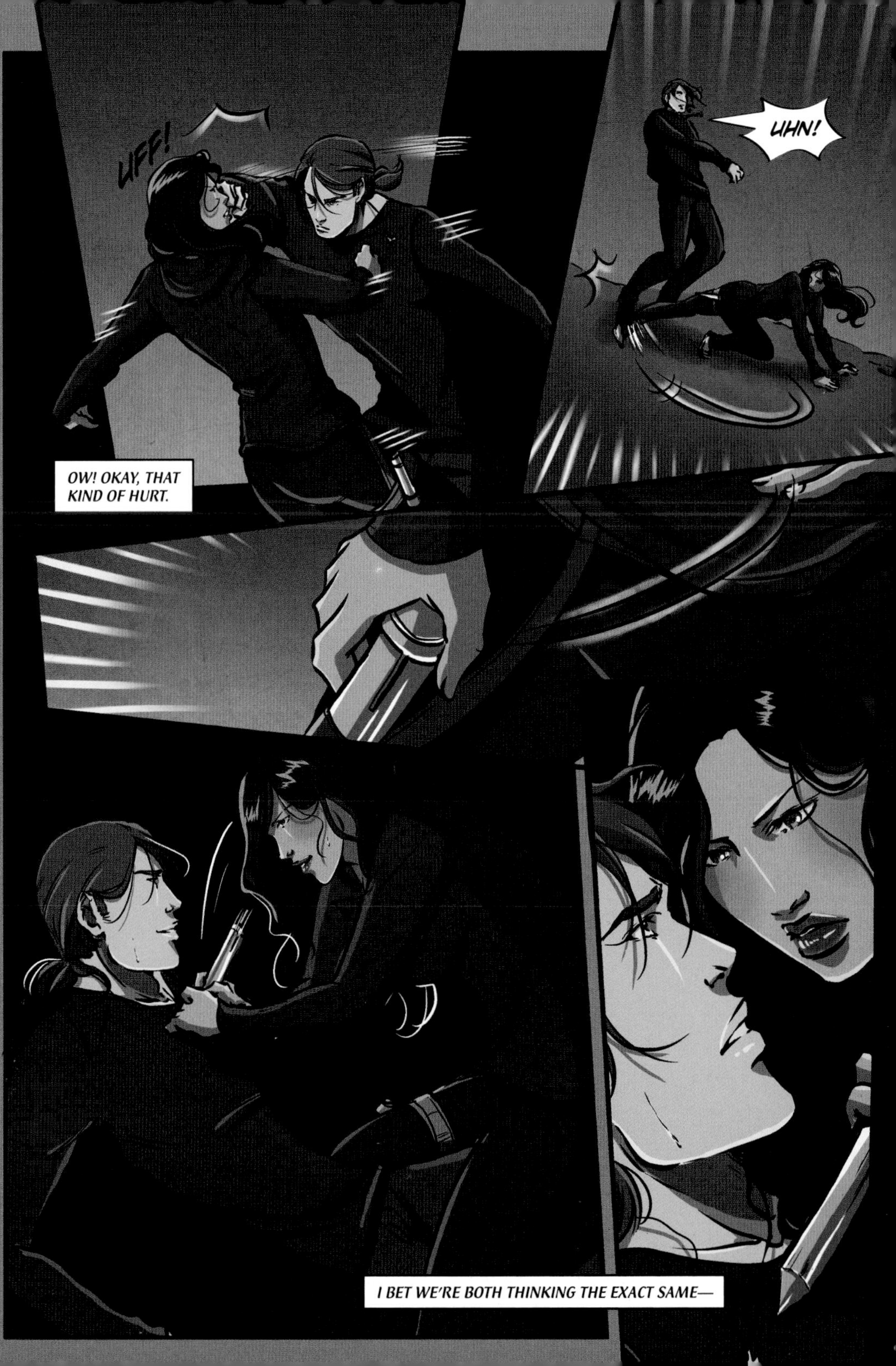
UFF!
UHN!
OW! OKAY, THAT KIND OF HURT.
I BET WE'RE BOTH THINKING THE EXACT SAME—

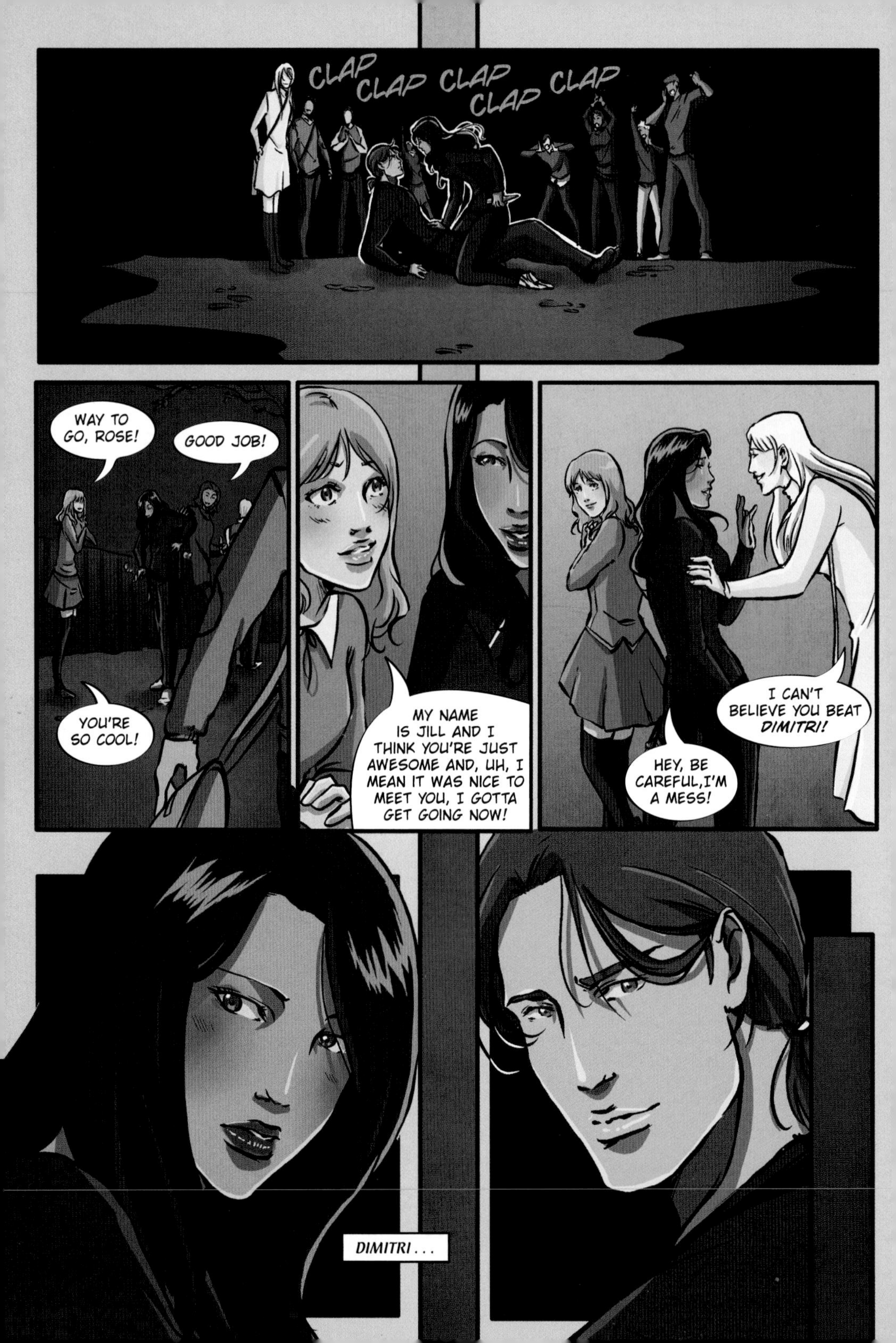
CLAP CLAP CLAP CLAP CLAP
WAY TO GO, ROSE!
GOOD JOB!
YOU'RE SO COOL!
MY NAME IS JILL AND I THINK YOU'RE JUST AWESOME AND, UH, I MEAN IT WAS NICE TO MEET YOU, I GOTTA GET GOING NOW!
I CAN'T BELIEVE YOU BEAT DIMITRI!
HEY, BE CAREFUL, I'M A MESS!
DIMITRI . . .

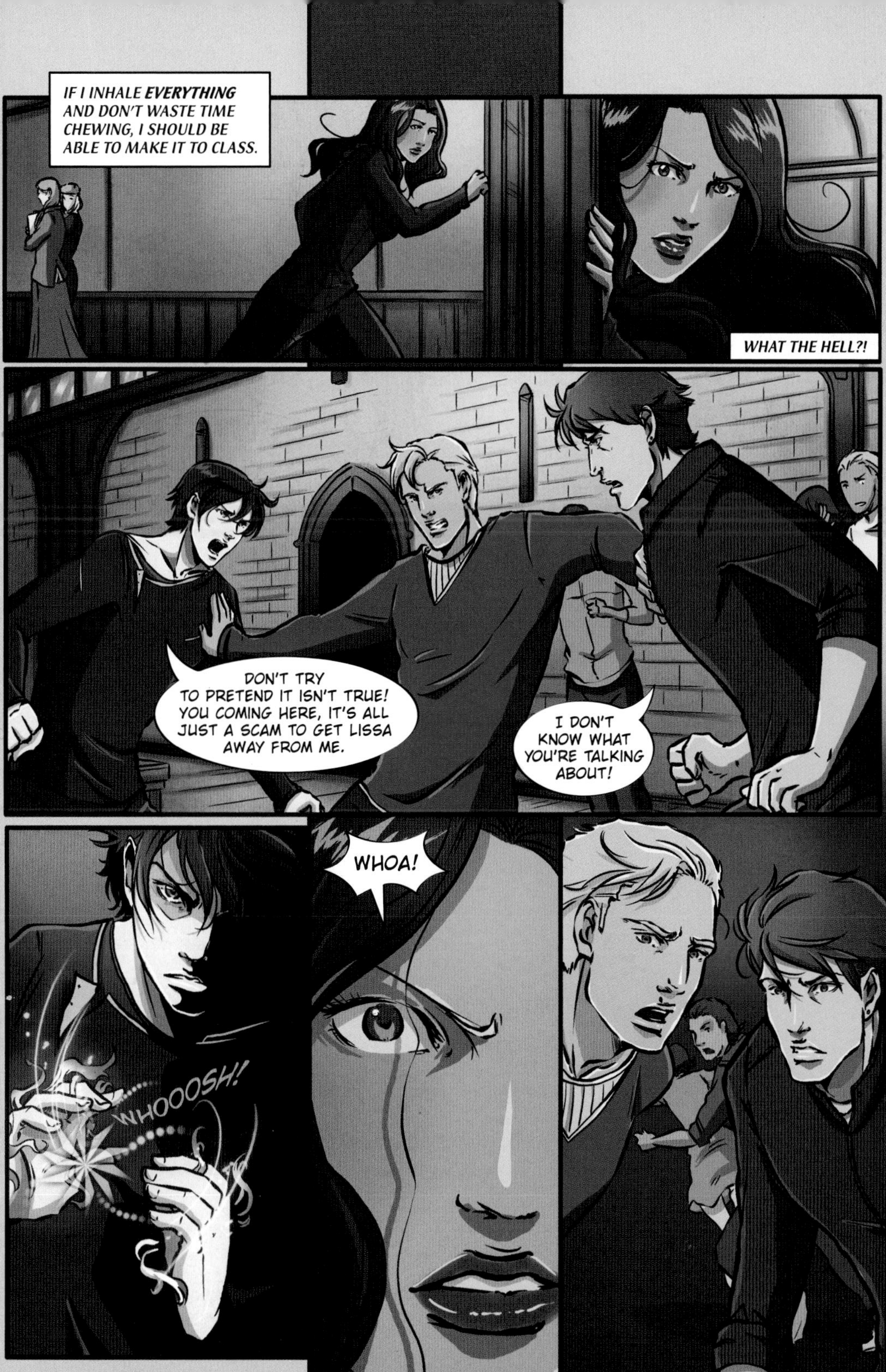
IF I INHALE **EVERYTHING** AND DON'T WASTE TIME CHEWING, I SHOULD BE ABLE TO MAKE IT TO CLASS.
WHAT THE HELL?!
DON'T TRY TO PRETEND IT ISN'T TRUE! YOU COMING HERE, IT'S ALL JUST A SCAM TO GET LISSA AWAY FROM ME.
I DON'T KNOW WHAT YOU'RE TALKING ABOUT!
WHOA!
WHOOOSH!

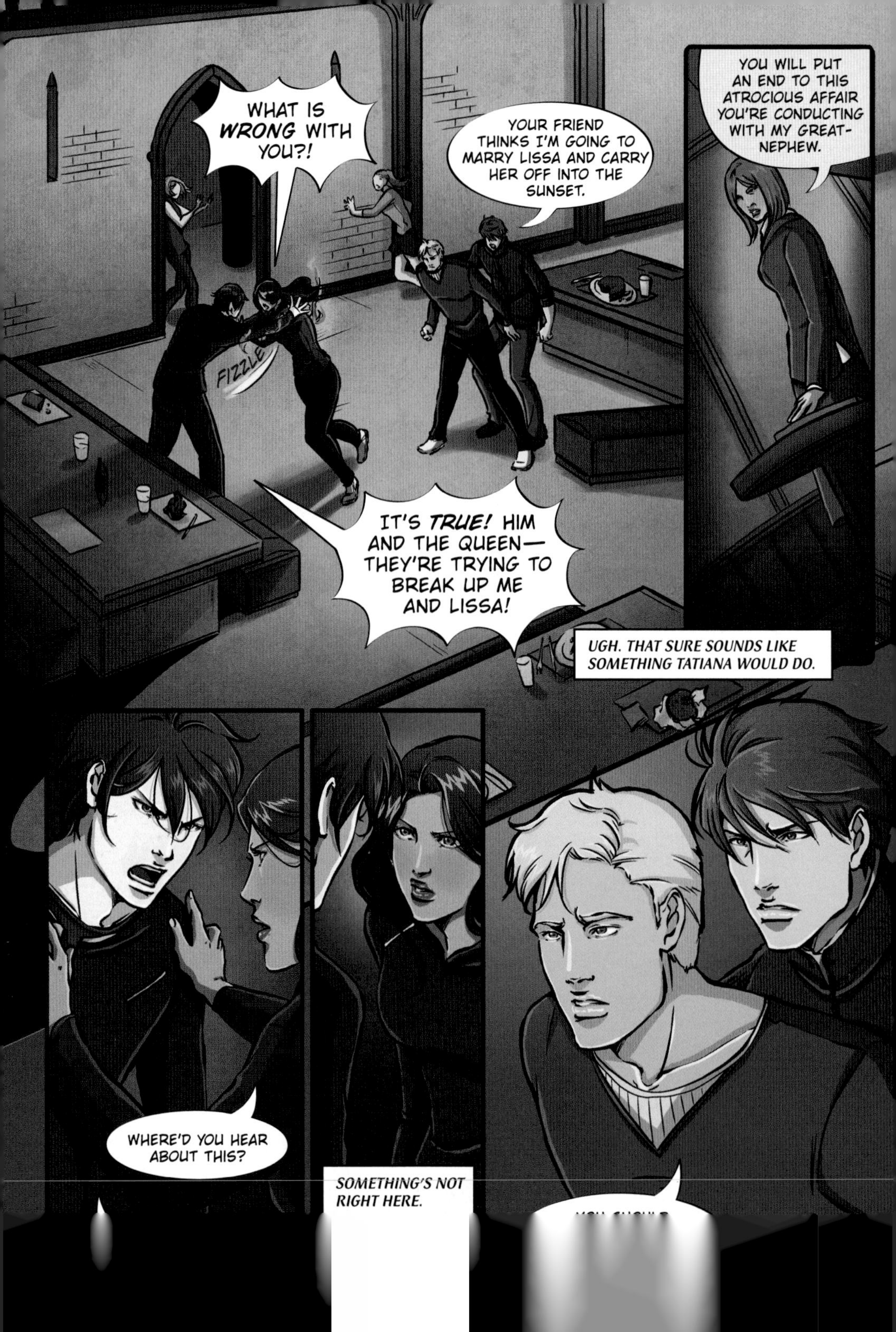
WHAT IS *WRONG* WITH YOU?!
YOUR FRIEND THINKS I'M GOING TO MARRY LISSA AND CARRY HER OFF INTO THE SUNSET.
YOU WILL PUT AN END TO THIS ATROCIOUS AFFAIR YOU'RE CONDUCTING WITH MY GREAT-NEPHEW.
FIZZLE
IT'S *TRUE!* HIM AND THE QUEEN— THEY'RE TRYING TO BREAK UP ME AND LISSA!
UGH. THAT SURE SOUNDS LIKE SOMETHING TATIANA WOULD DO.
WHERE'D YOU HEAR ABOUT THIS?
SOMETHING'S NOT RIGHT HERE.

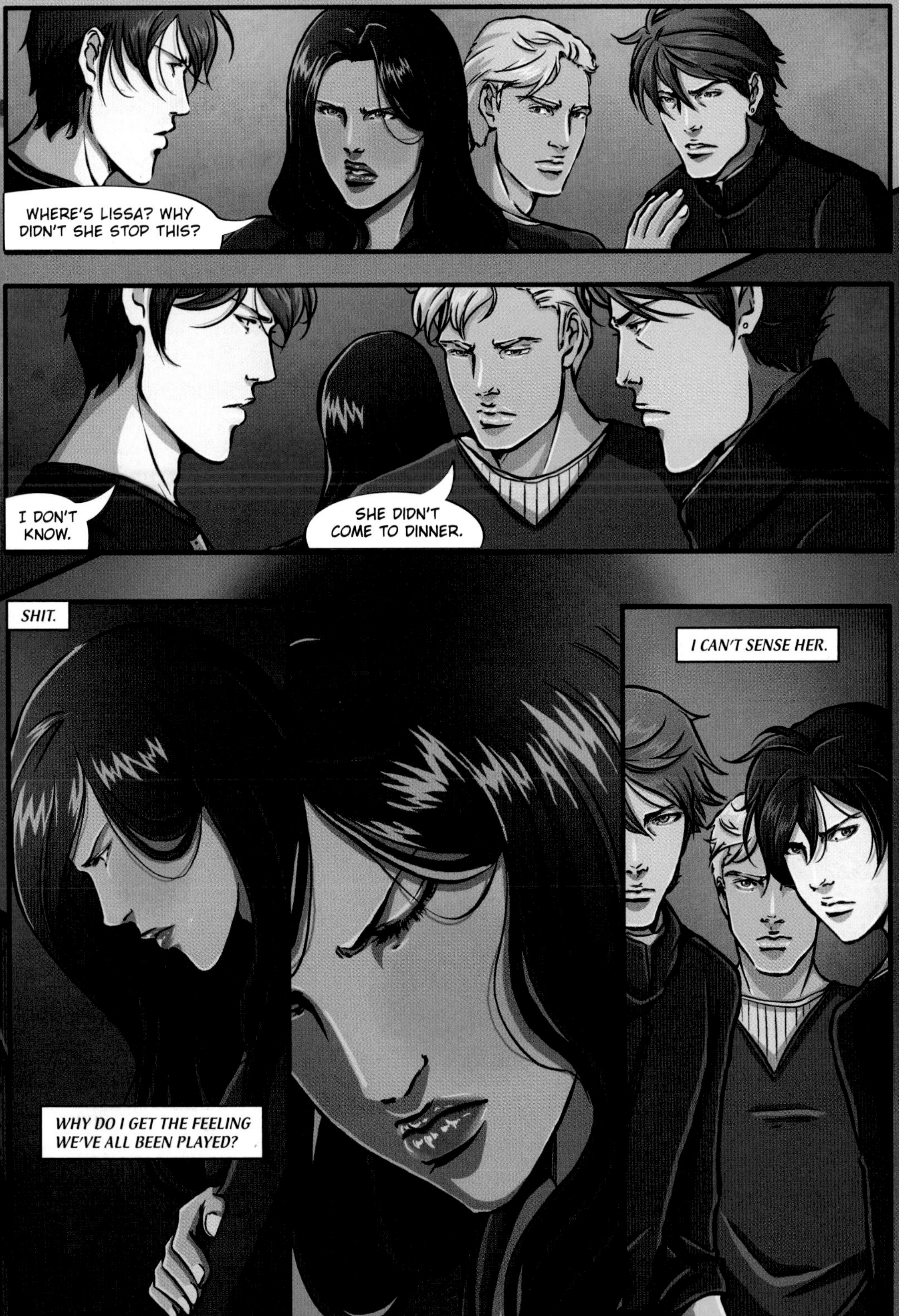
WHERE'S LISSA? WHY DIDN'T SHE STOP THIS?
I DON'T KNOW.
SHE DIDN'T COME TO DINNER.
SHIT.
I CAN'T SENSE HER.
WHY DO I GET THE FEELING WE'VE ALL BEEN PLAYED?

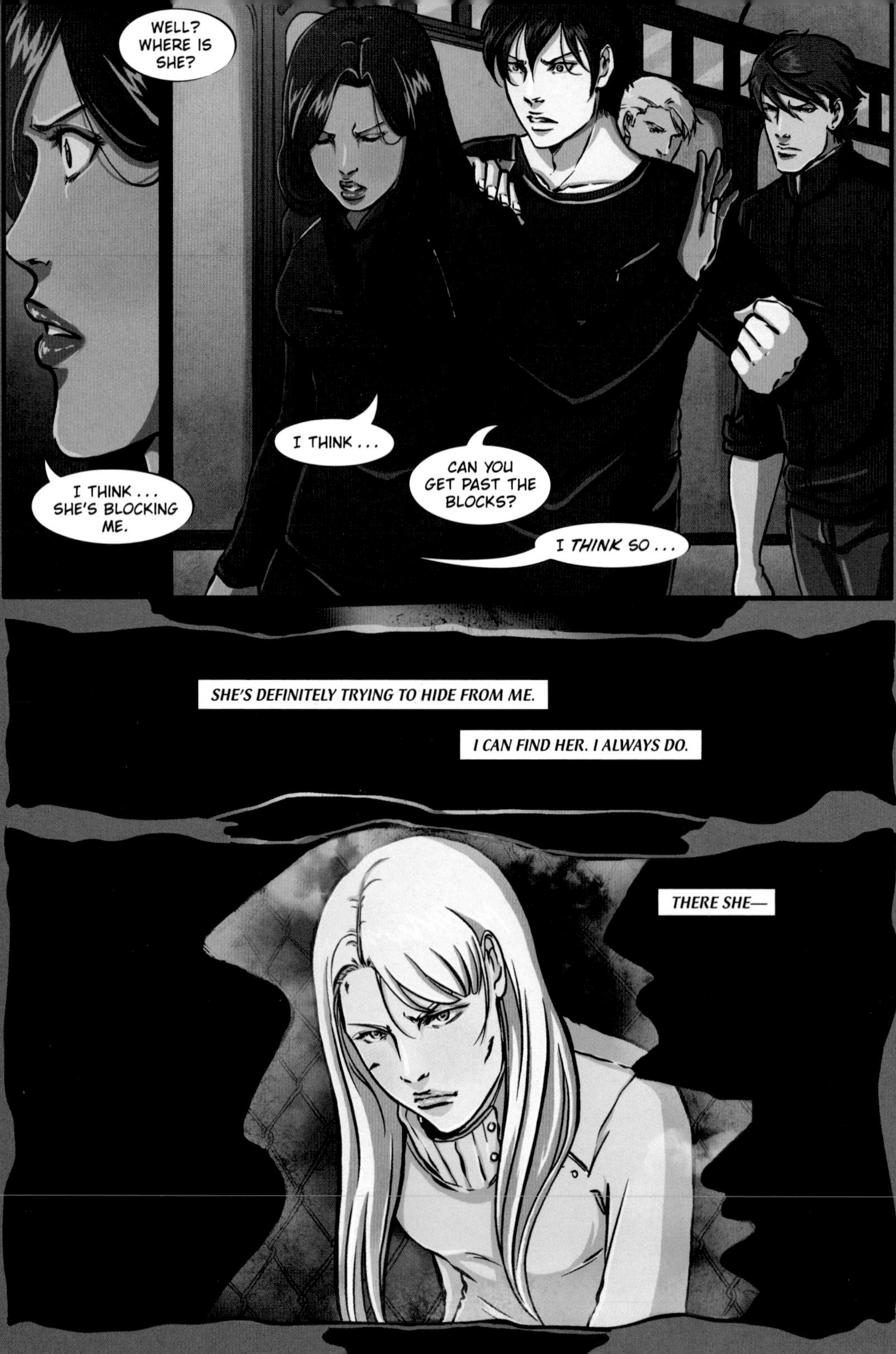
WELL? WHERE IS SHE?
I THINK . . . SHE'S BLOCKING ME.
I THINK . . .
CAN YOU GET PAST THE BLOCKS?
I *THINK* SO . . .
SHE'S DEFINITELY TRYING TO HIDE FROM ME.
I CAN FIND HER. I ALWAYS DO.
THERE SHE—

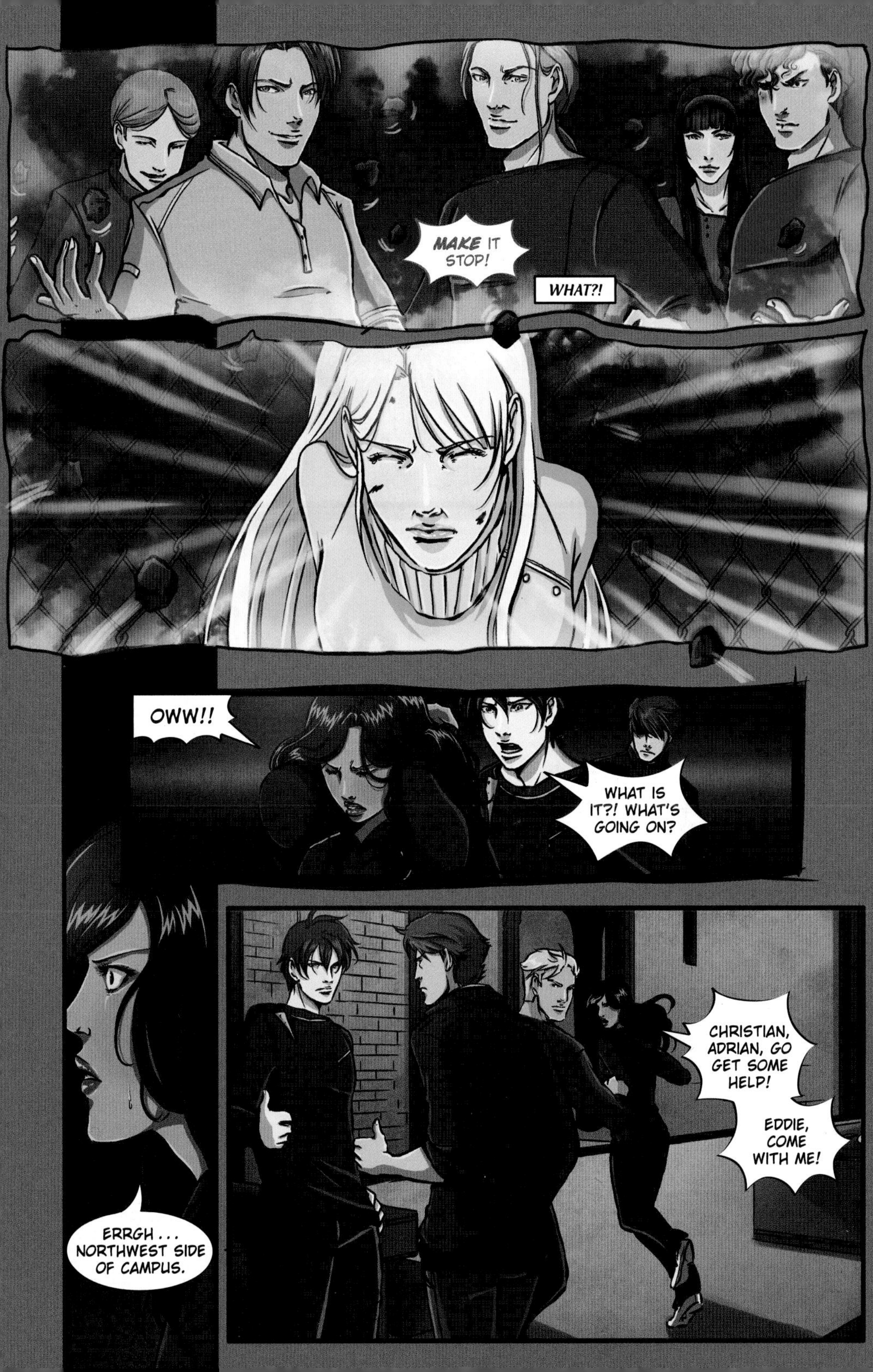
MAKE IT STOP!
WHAT?!
OWW!!
WHAT IS IT?! WHAT'S GOING ON?
ERRGH . . . NORTHWEST SIDE OF CAMPUS.
CHRISTIAN, ADRIAN, GO GET SOME HELP!
EDDIE, COME WITH ME!

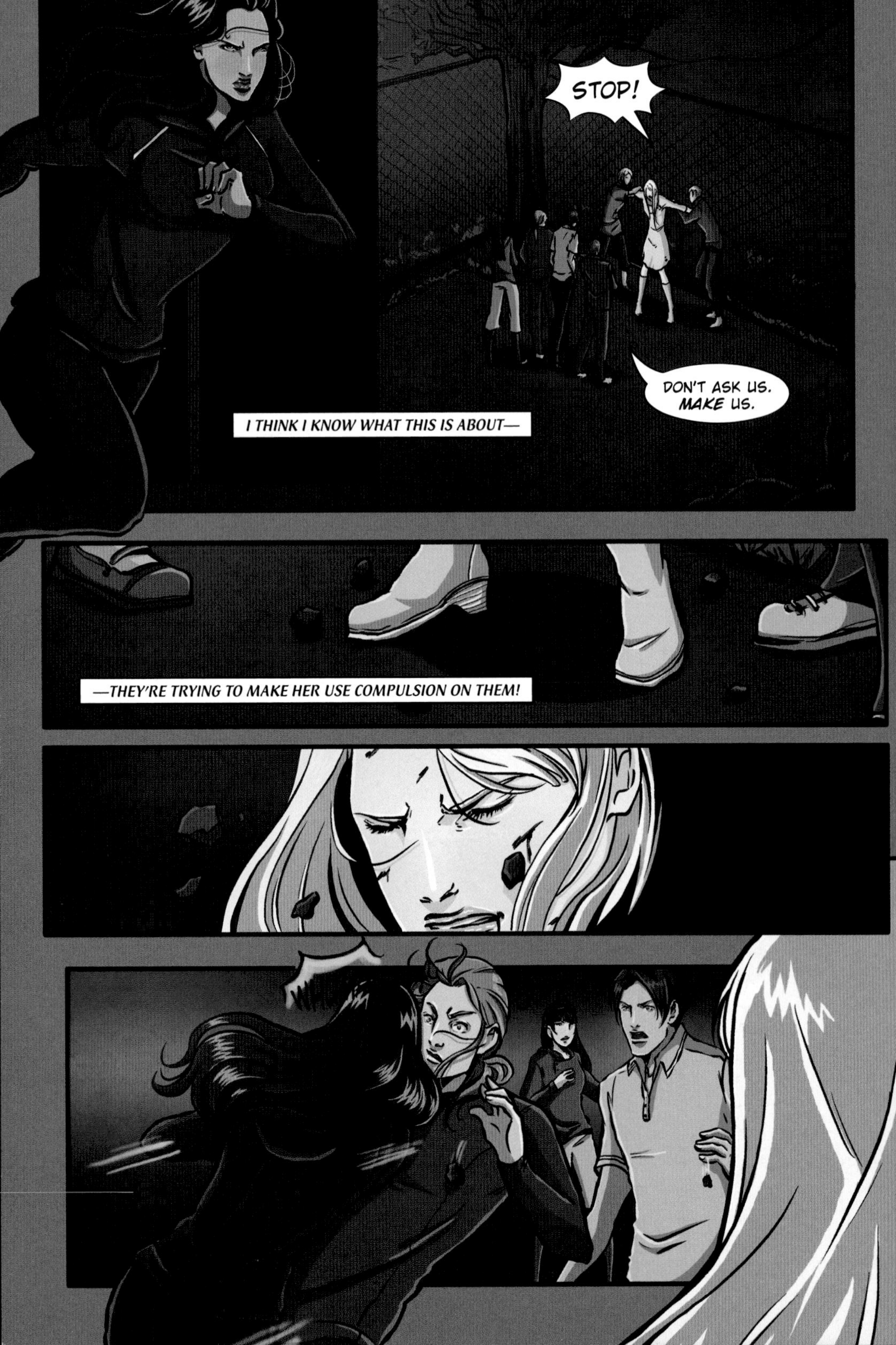
STOP!
DON'T ASK US. MAKE US.
I THINK I KNOW WHAT THIS IS ABOUT—
—THEY'RE TRYING TO MAKE HER USE COMPULSION ON THEM!

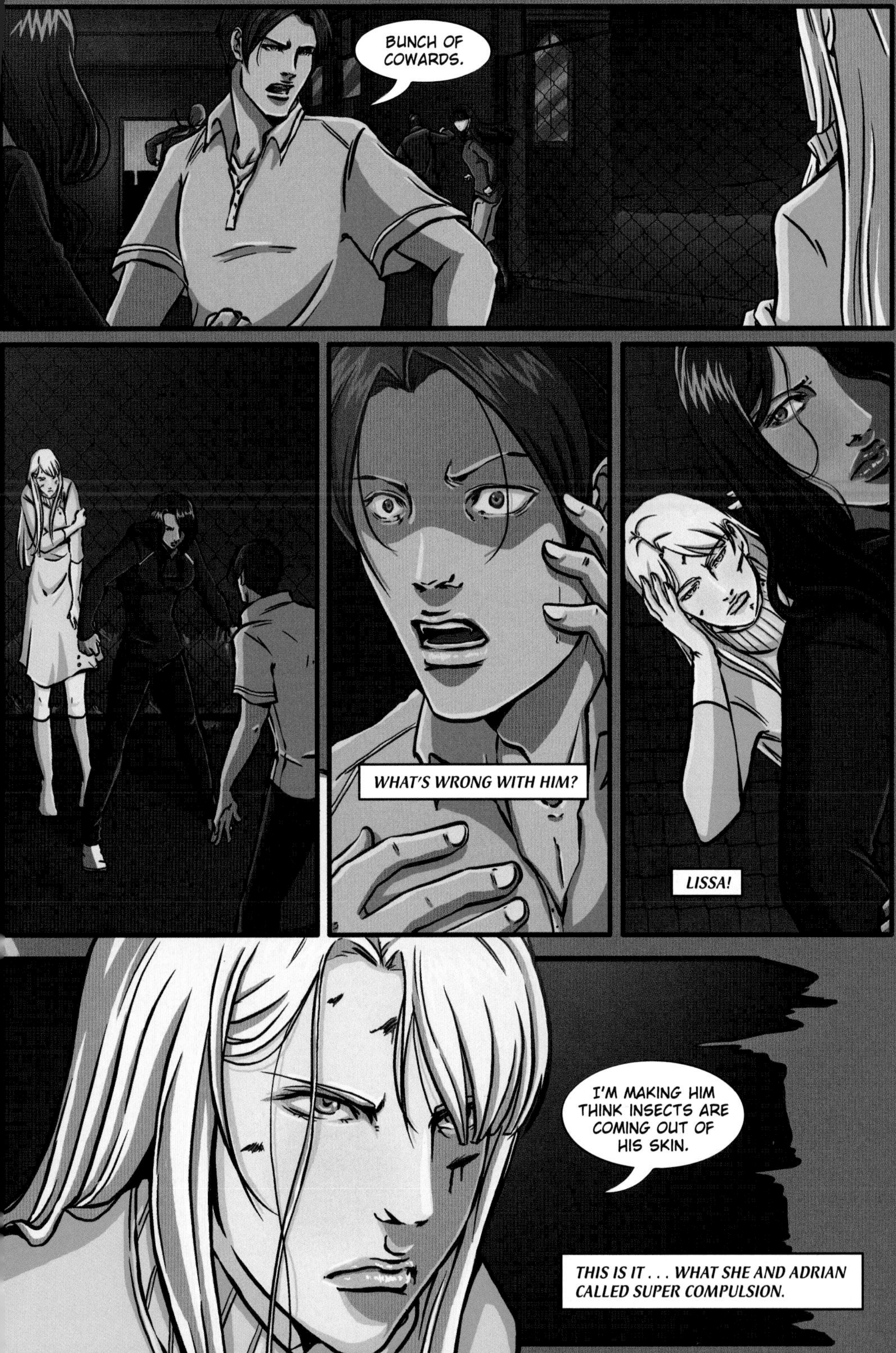
BUNCH OF COWARDS.
WHAT'S WRONG WITH HIM?
LISSA!
I'M MAKING HIM THINK INSECTS ARE COMING OUT OF HIS SKIN.
THIS IS IT . . . WHAT SHE AND ADRIAN CALLED SUPER COMPULSION.

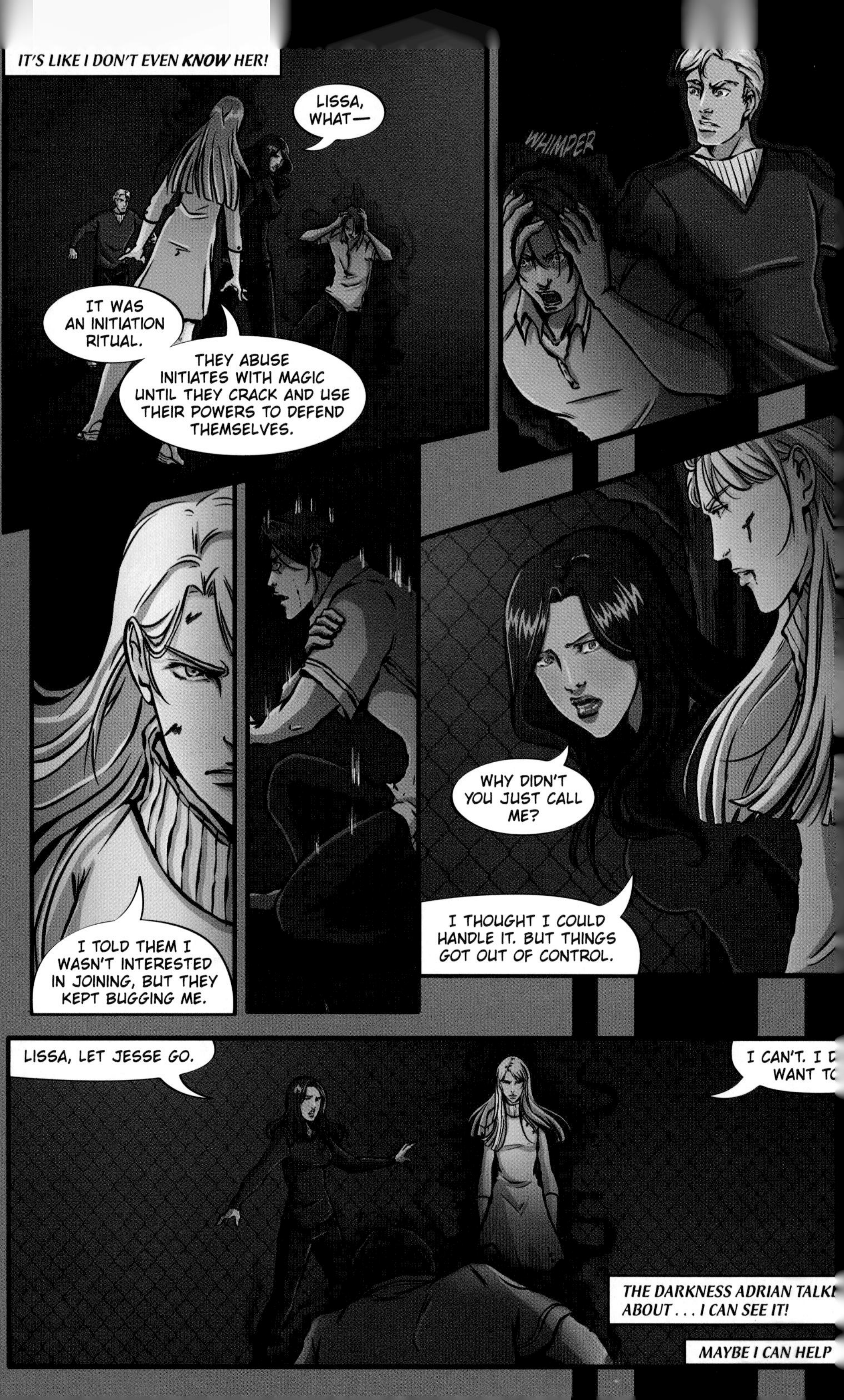

IT'S LIKE I DON'T EVEN KNOW HER!
LISSA, WHAT—
IT WAS AN INITIATION RITUAL.
THEY ABUSE INITIATES WITH MAGIC UNTIL THEY CRACK AND USE THEIR POWERS TO DEFEND THEMSELVES.
WHIMPER
I TOLD THEM I WASN'T INTERESTED IN JOINING, BUT THEY KEPT BUGGING ME.
WHY DIDN'T YOU JUST CALL ME?
I THOUGHT I COULD HANDLE IT. BUT THINGS GOT OUT OF CONTROL.
LISSA, LET JESSE GO.
I CAN'T. I D
WANT TO
THE DARKNESS ADRIAN TALK
ABOUT . . . I CAN SEE IT!
MAYBE I CAN HELP

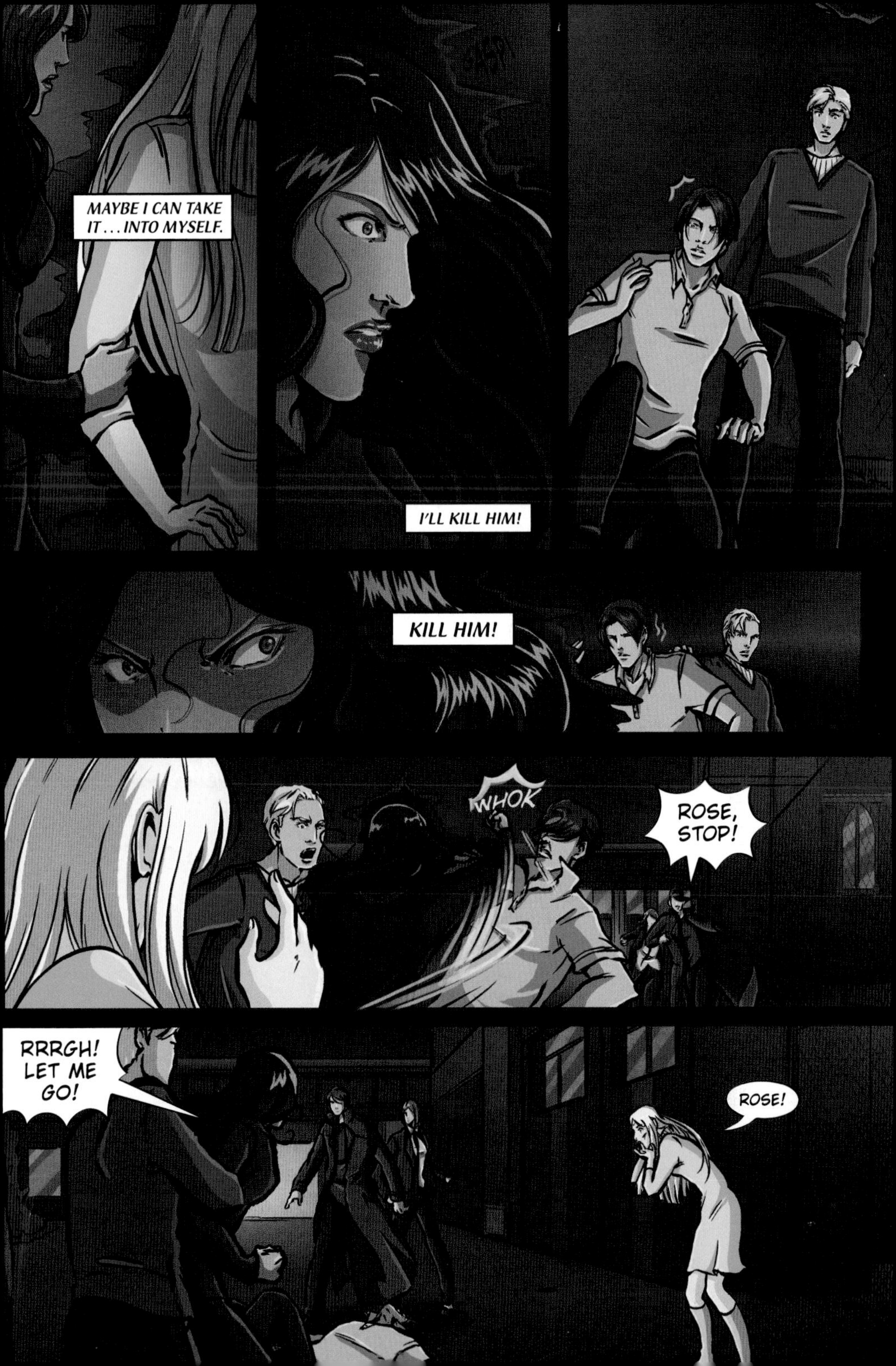
MAYBE I CAN TAKE IT . . . INTO MYSELF.
I'LL KILL HIM!
KILL HIM!
WHOK
ROSE, STOP!
RRRGH! LET ME GO!
ROSE!

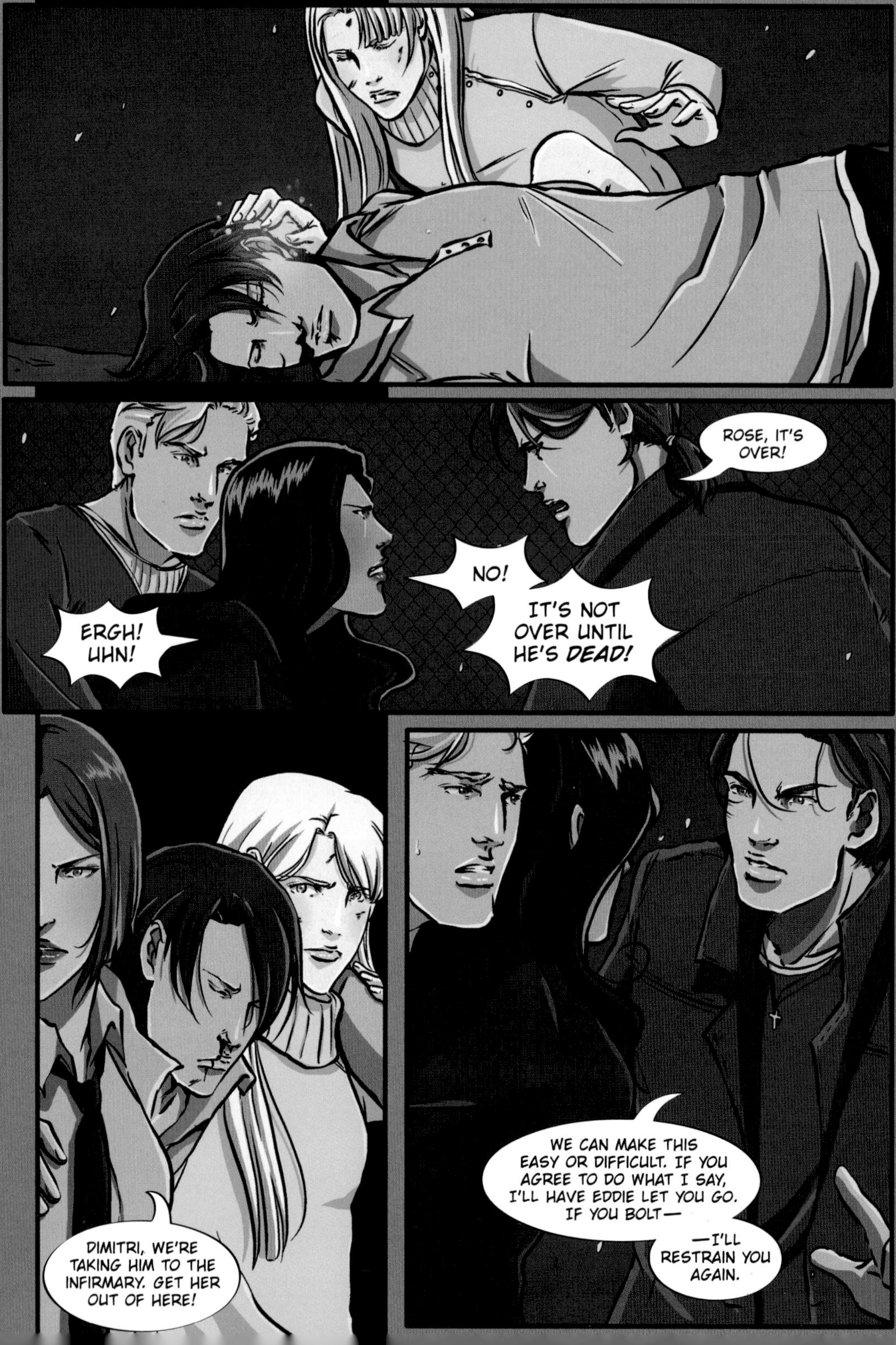
ROSE, IT'S OVER!
ERGH! UHN!
NO!
IT'S NOT OVER UNTIL HE'S *DEAD!*
DIMITRI, WE'RE TAKING HIM TO THE INFIRMARY. GET HER OUT OF HERE!
WE CAN MAKE THIS EASY OR DIFFICULT. IF YOU AGREE TO DO WHAT I SAY, I'LL HAVE EDDIE LET YOU GO. IF YOU BOLT—
—I'LL RESTRAIN YOU AGAIN.

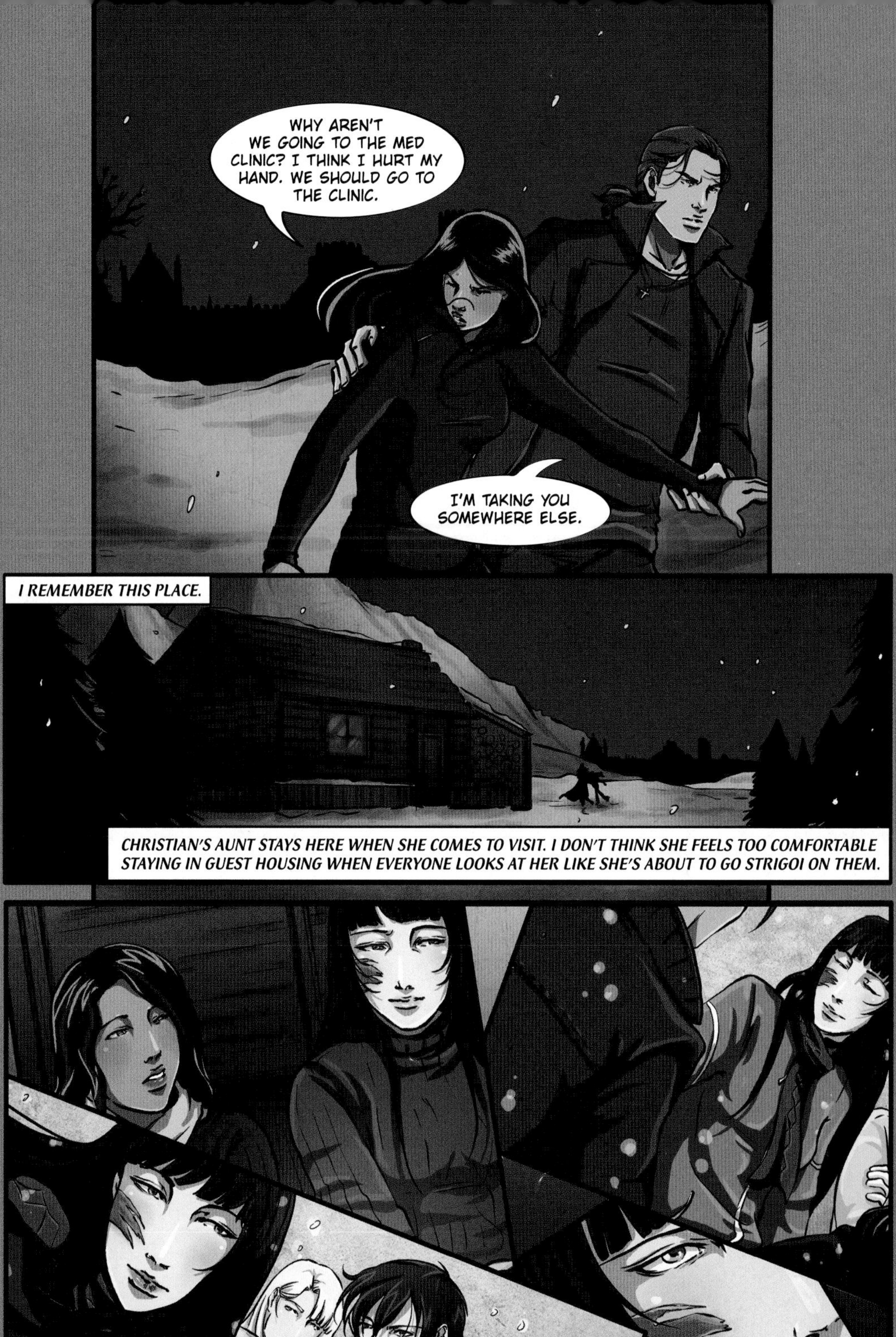
WHY AREN'T WE GOING TO THE MED CLINIC? I THINK I HURT MY HAND. WE SHOULD GO TO THE CLINIC.
I'M TAKING YOU SOMEWHERE ELSE.
I REMEMBER THIS PLACE.
CHRISTIAN'S AUNT STAYS HERE WHEN SHE COMES TO VISIT. I DON'T THINK SHE FEELS TOO COMFORTABLE STAYING IN GUEST HOUSING WHEN EVERYONE LOOKS AT HER LIKE SHE'S ABOUT TO GO STRIGOI ON THEM.

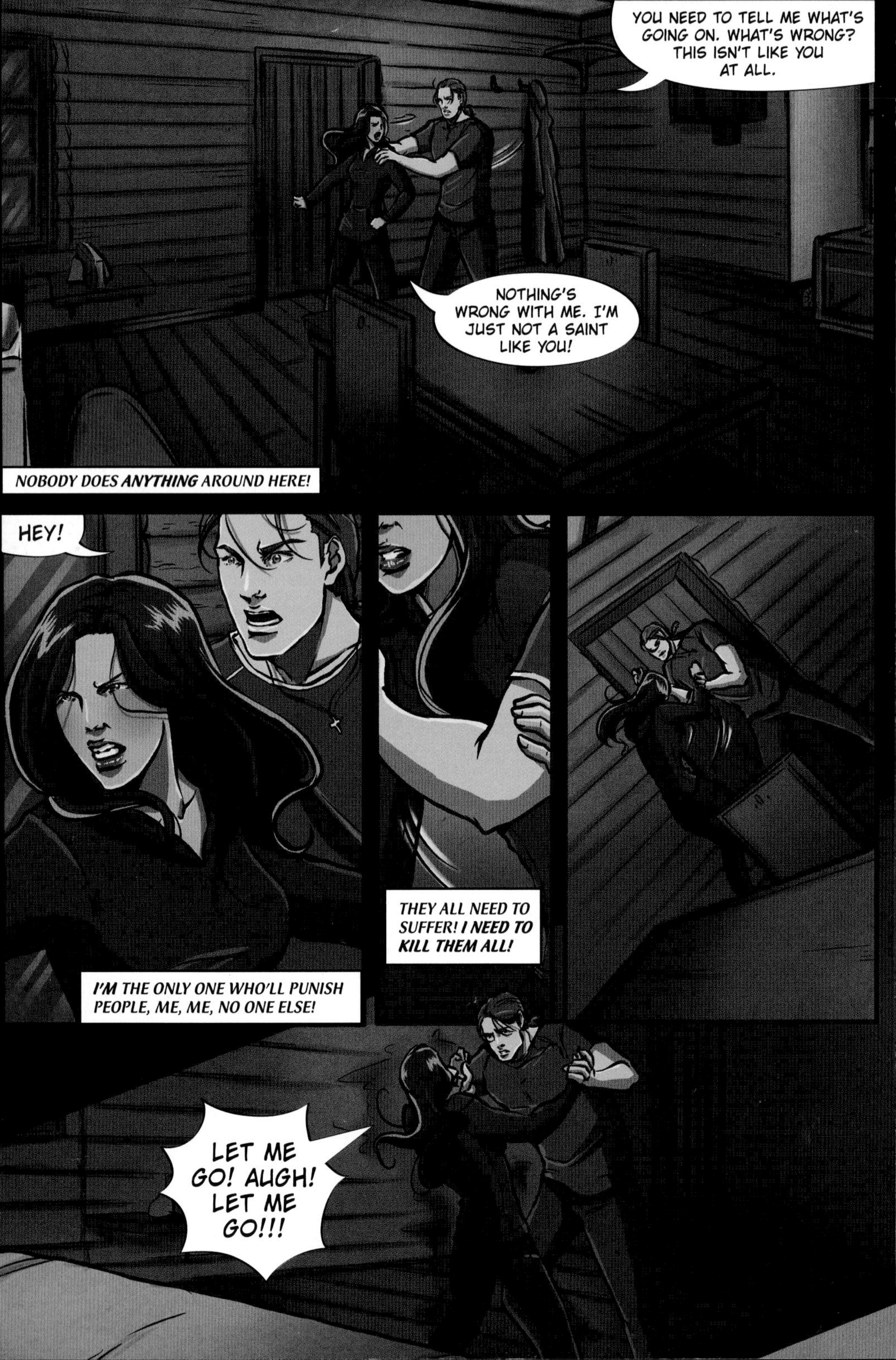
YOU NEED TO TELL ME WHAT'S GOING ON. WHAT'S WRONG? THIS ISN'T LIKE YOU AT ALL.
NOTHING'S WRONG WITH ME. I'M JUST NOT A SAINT LIKE YOU!
NOBODY DOES *ANYTHING* AROUND HERE!
HEY!
I'M THE ONLY ONE WHO'LL PUNISH PEOPLE, ME, ME, NO ONE ELSE!
THEY ALL NEED TO SUFFER! **I NEED TO KILL THEM ALL!**
LET ME GO! AUGH! LET ME GO!!!

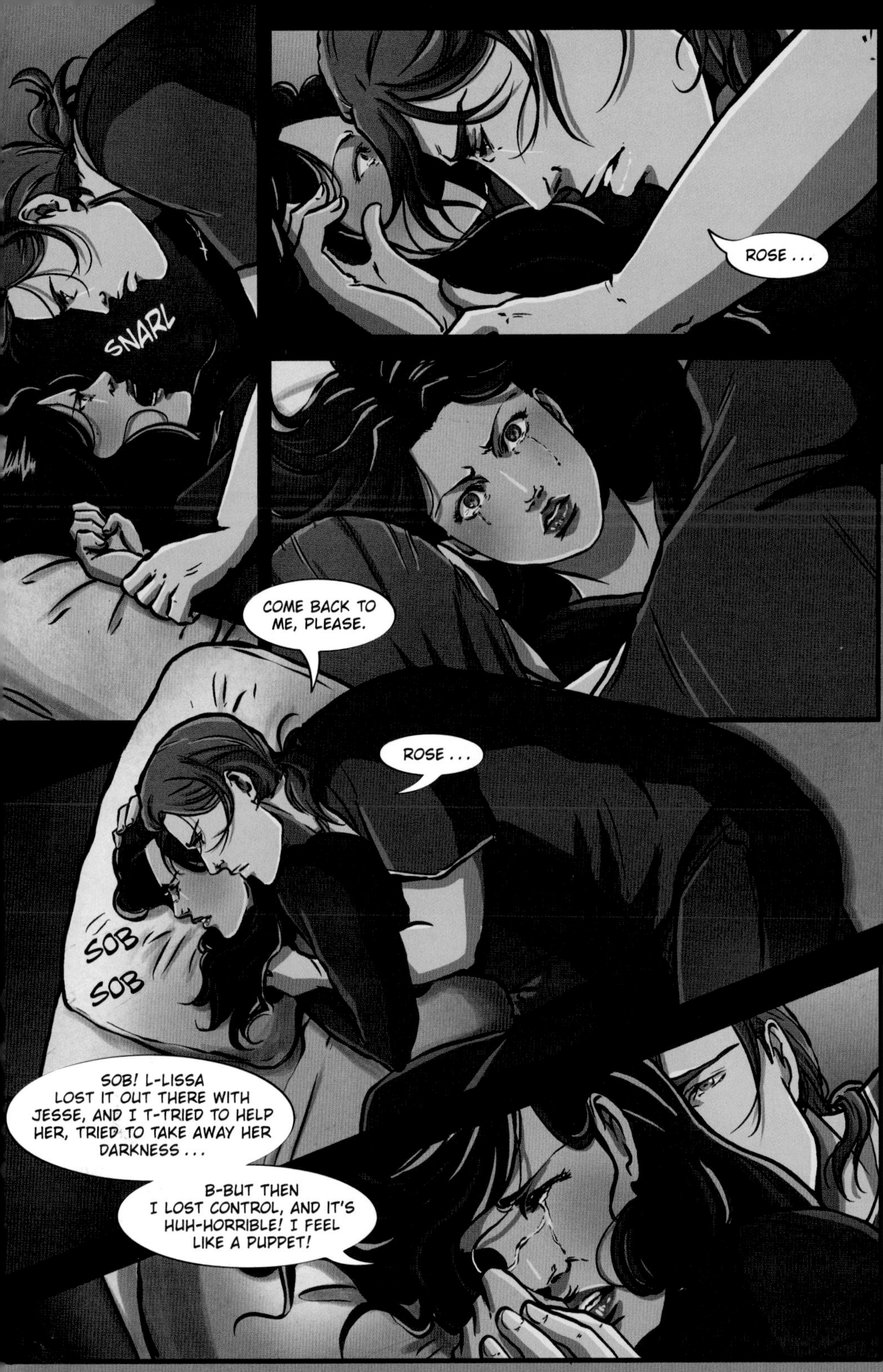
SNARL
ROSE . . .
COME BACK TO ME, PLEASE.
ROSE . . .
SOB
SOB
SOB! L-LISSA LOST IT OUT THERE WITH JESSE, AND I T-TRIED TO HELP HER, TRIED TO TAKE AWAY HER DARKNESS . . .
B-BUT THEN I LOST CONTROL, AND IT'S HUH-HORRIBLE! I FEEL LIKE A PUPPET!

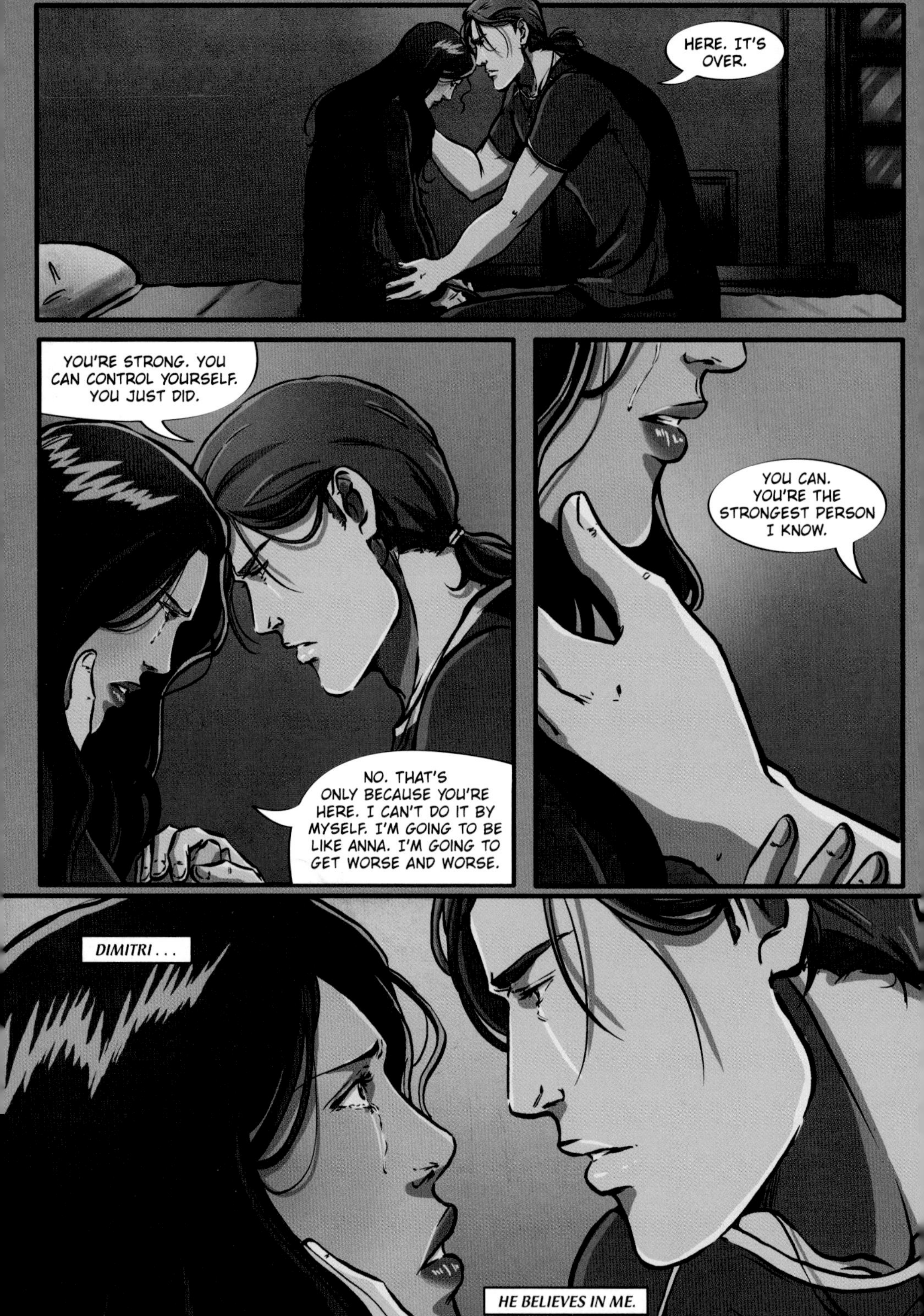
HERE. IT'S OVER.
YOU'RE STRONG. YOU CAN CONTROL YOURSELF. YOU JUST DID.
NO. THAT'S ONLY BECAUSE YOU'RE HERE. I CAN'T DO IT BY MYSELF. I'M GOING TO BE LIKE ANNA. I'M GOING TO GET WORSE AND WORSE.
YOU CAN. YOU'RE THE STRONGEST PERSON I KNOW.
DIMITRI . . .
HE BELIEVES IN ME.

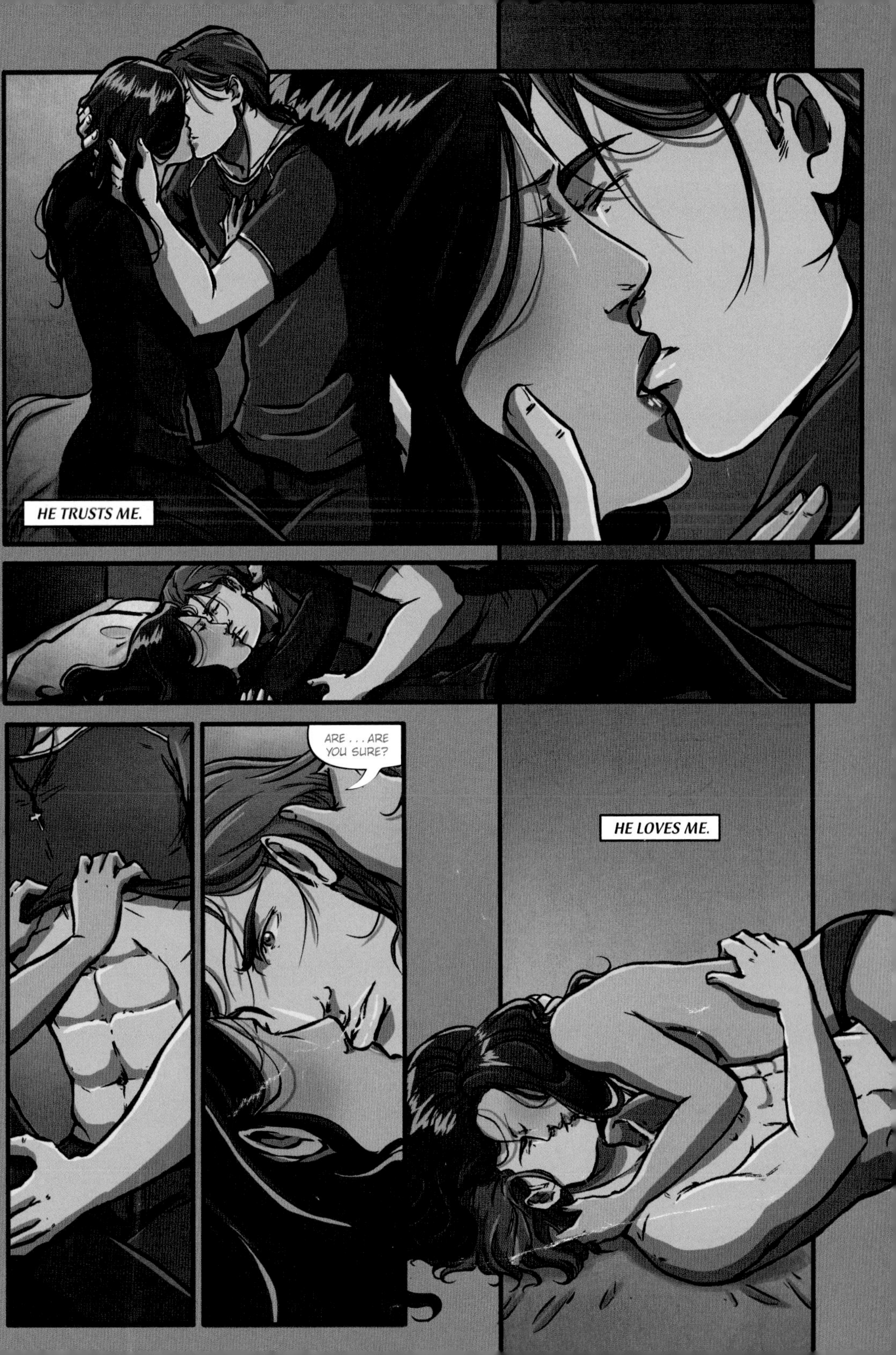
HE TRUSTS ME.
ARE . . . ARE YOU SURE?
HE LOVES ME.

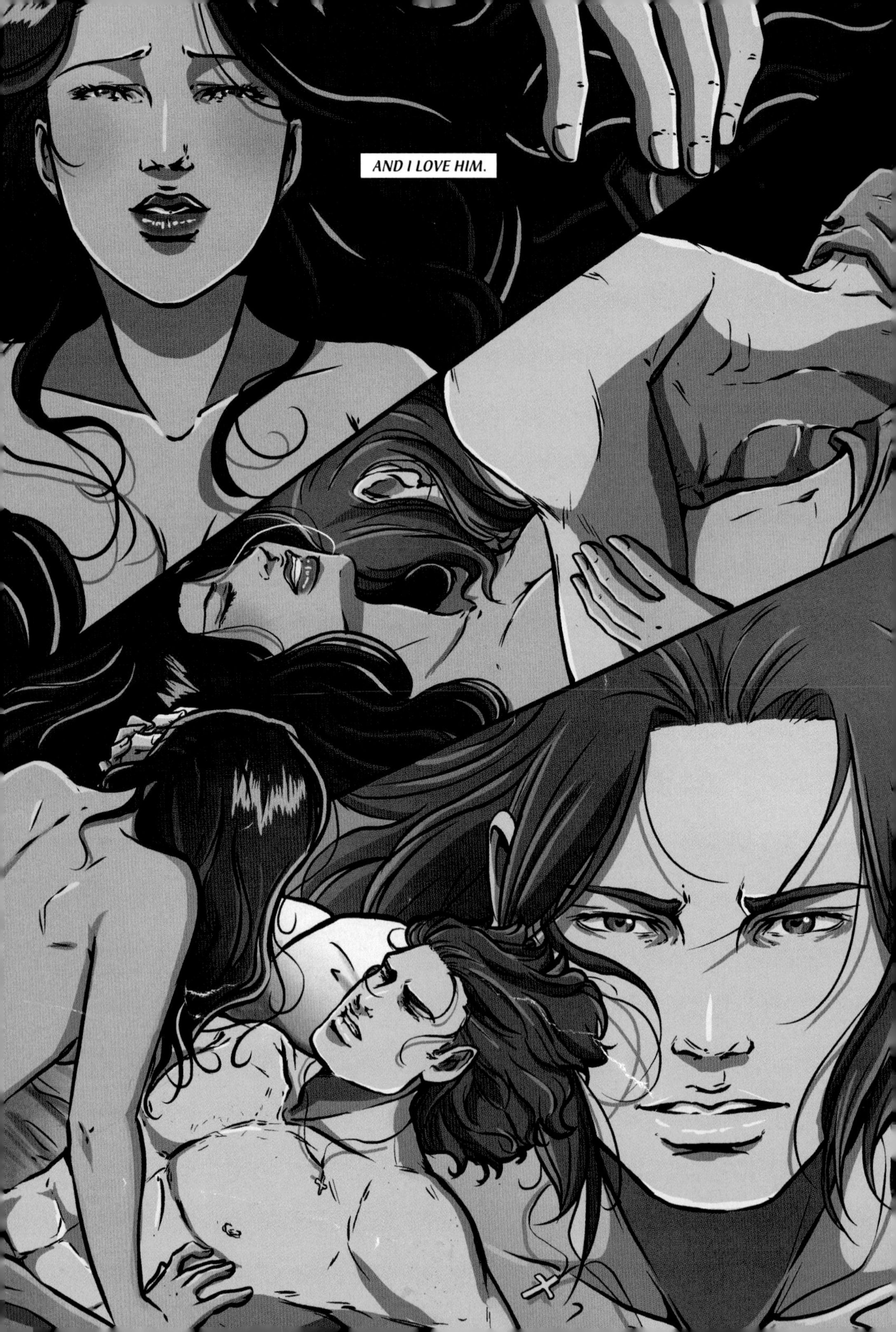
AND I LOVE HIM.

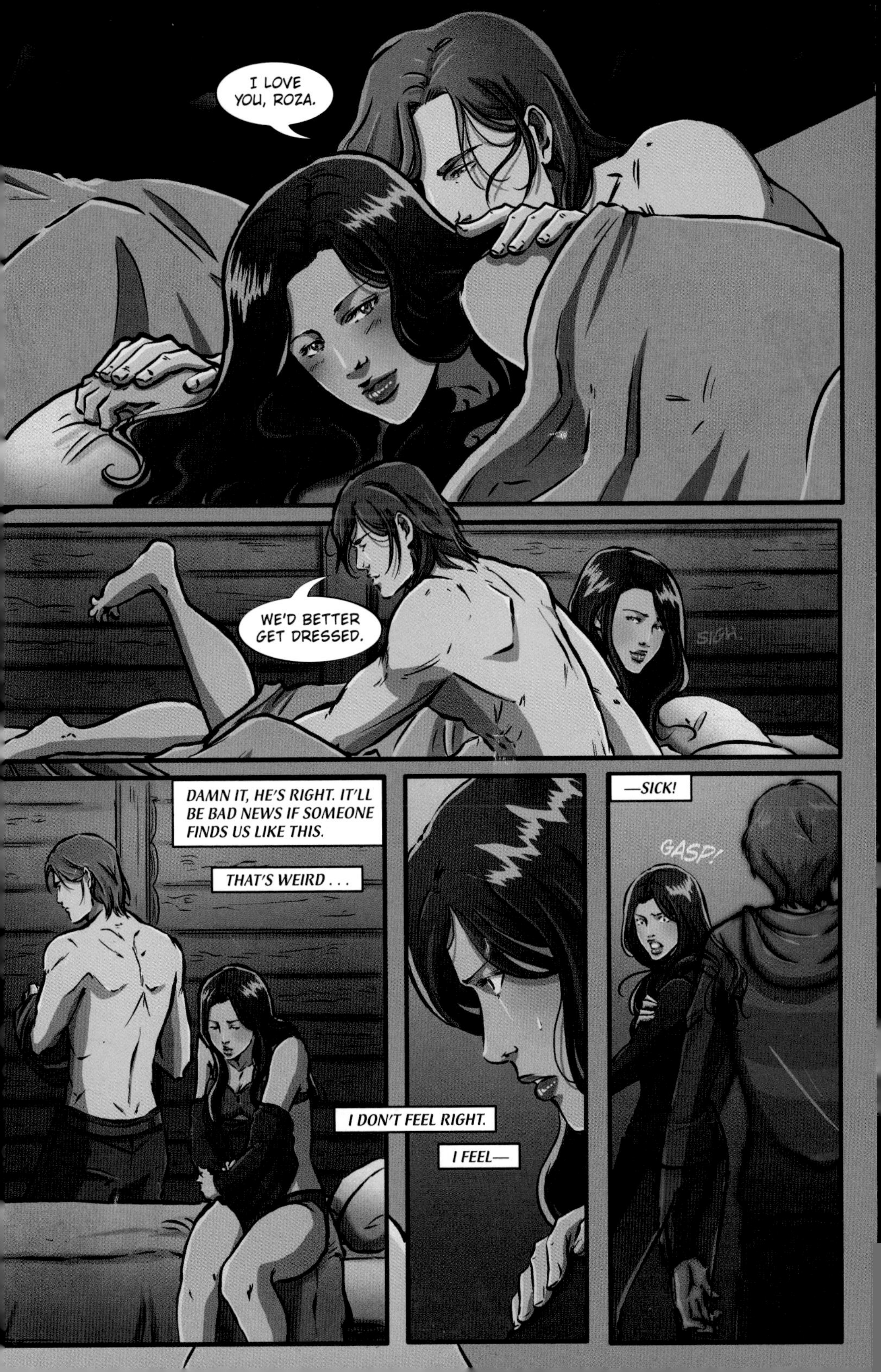
I LOVE YOU, ROZA.
WE'D BETTER GET DRESSED.
SIGH.
DAMN IT, HE'S RIGHT. IT'LL BE BAD NEWS IF SOMEONE FINDS US LIKE THIS.
THAT'S WEIRD . . .
I DON'T FEEL RIGHT.
I FEEL—
—SICK!
GASP!

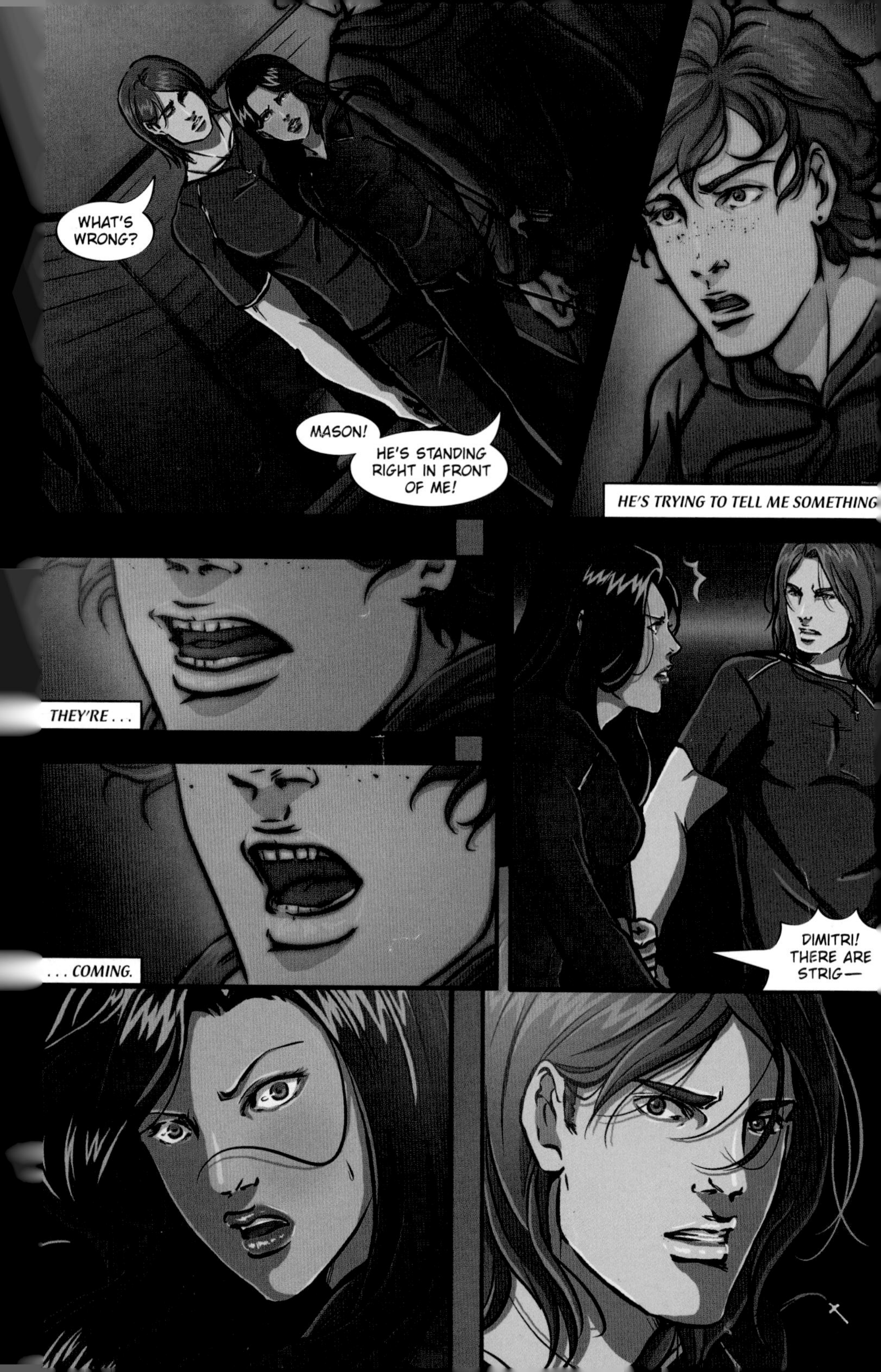
WHAT'S WRONG?
MASON!
HE'S STANDING RIGHT IN FRONT OF ME!
HE'S TRYING TO TELL ME SOMETHING
THEY'RE . . .
. . . COMING.
DIMITRI! THERE ARE STRIG—

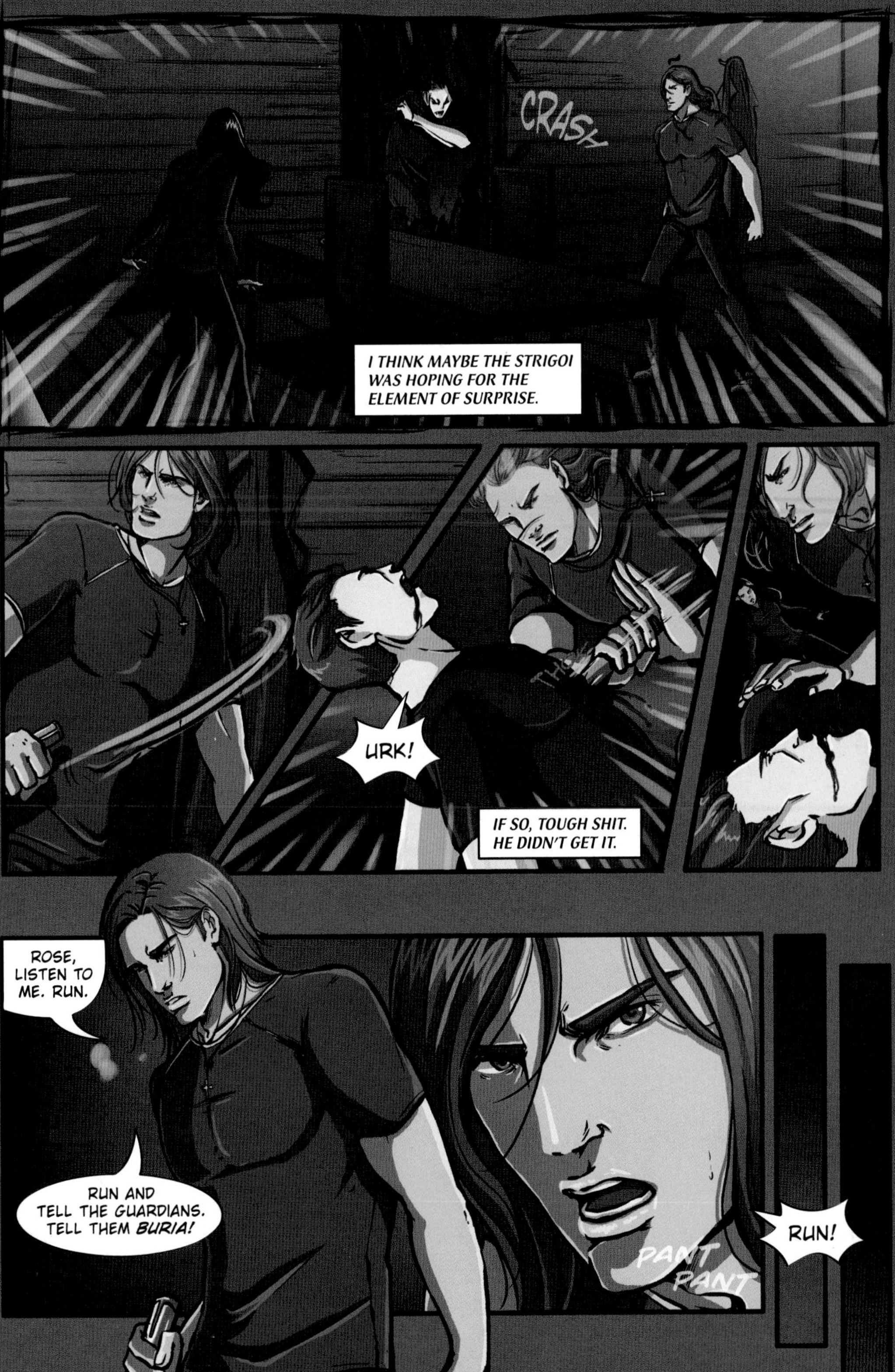
CRASH
I THINK MAYBE THE STRIGOI WAS HOPING FOR THE ELEMENT OF SURPRISE.
URK!
IF SO, TOUGH SHIT. HE DIDN'T GET IT.
ROSE, LISTEN TO ME. RUN.
RUN AND TELL THE GUARDIANS. TELL THEM *BURIA!*
RUN!
PANT PANT

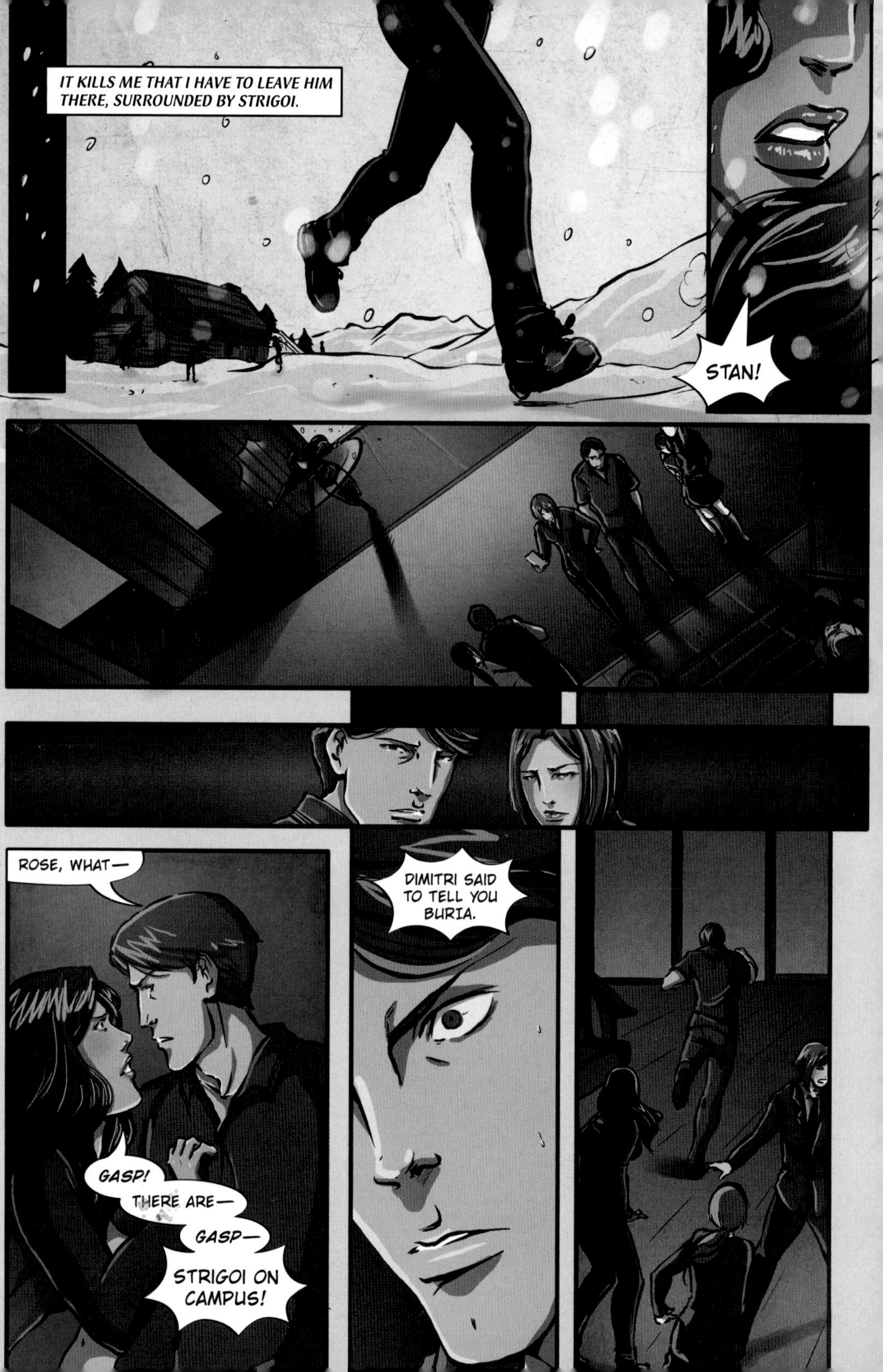
IT KILLS ME THAT I HAVE TO LEAVE HIM THERE, SURROUNDED BY STRIGOI.
STAN!
ROSE, WHAT—
GASP!
THERE ARE—
GASP—
STRIGOI ON CAMPUS!
DIMITRI SAID TO TELL YOU BURIA.

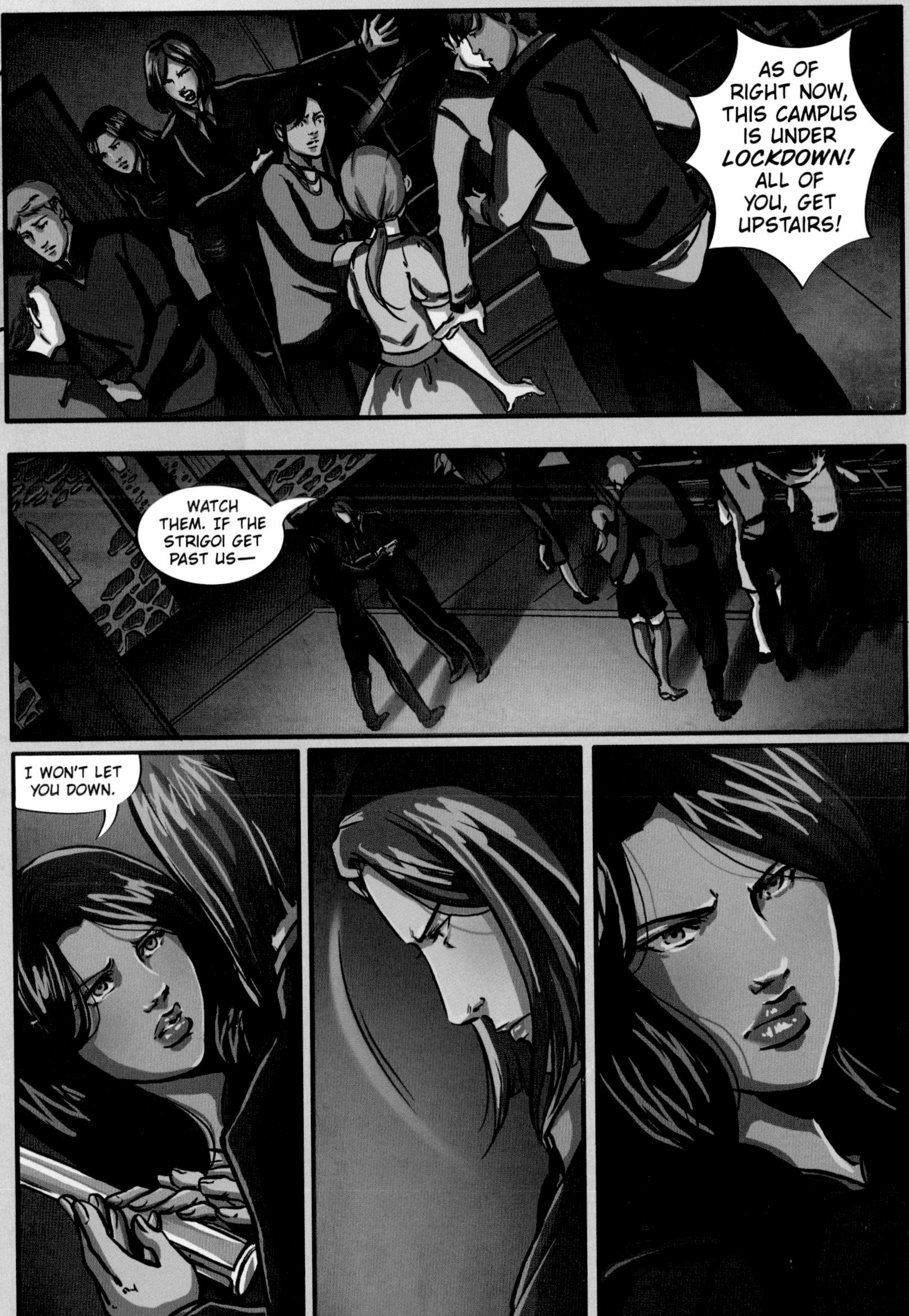
AS OF RIGHT NOW, THIS CAMPUS IS UNDER *LOCKDOWN!* ALL OF YOU, GET UPSTAIRS!
WATCH THEM. IF THE STRIGOI GET PAST US—
I WON'T LET YOU DOWN.

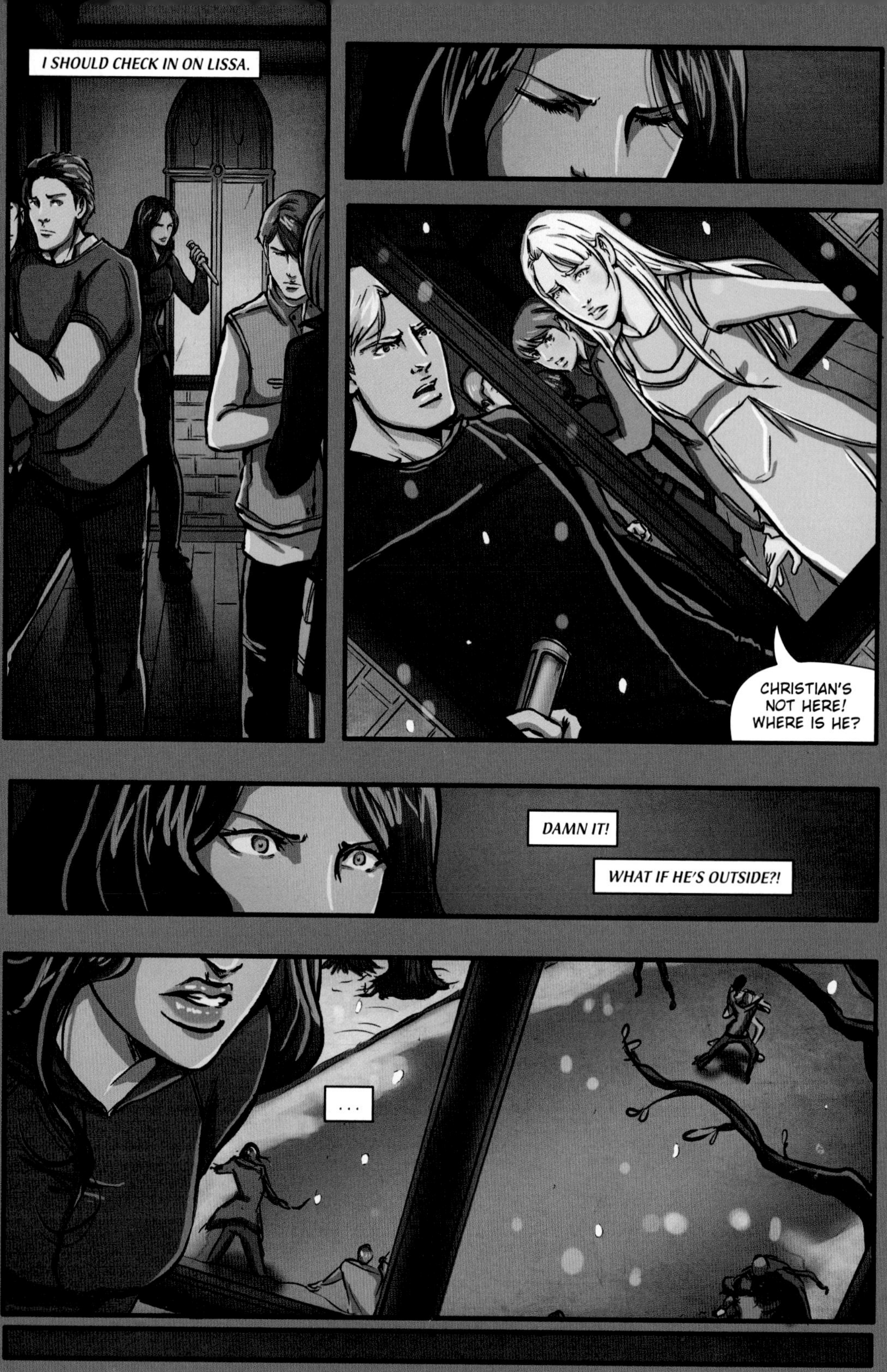
I SHOULD CHECK IN ON LISSA.
CHRISTIAN'S NOT HERE! WHERE IS HE?
DAMN IT!
WHAT IF HE'S OUTSIDE?!
...

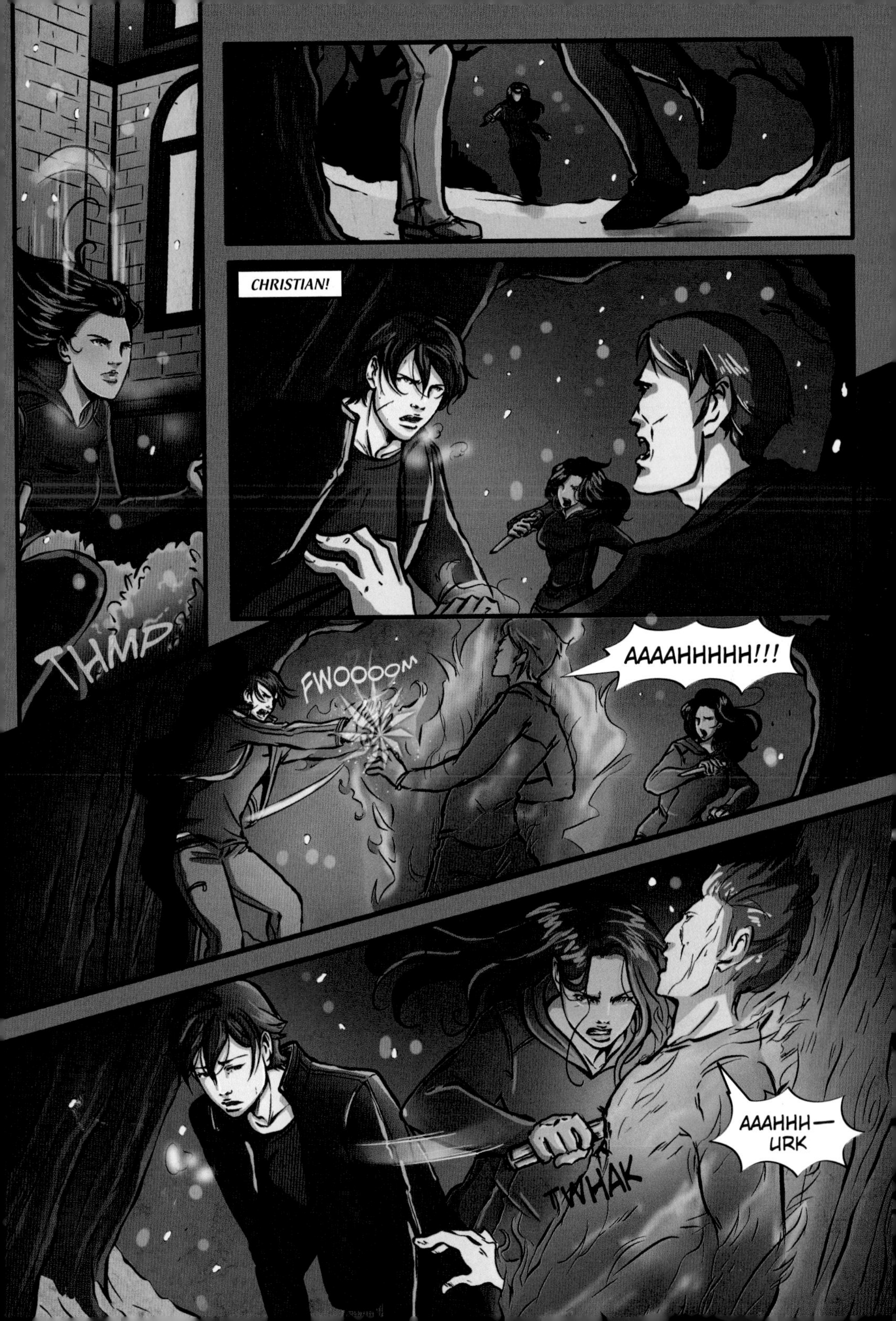
CHRISTIAN!
THMP
FWOOOOM
AAAAHHHHH!!!
AAAHHH—
URK
TWHAK

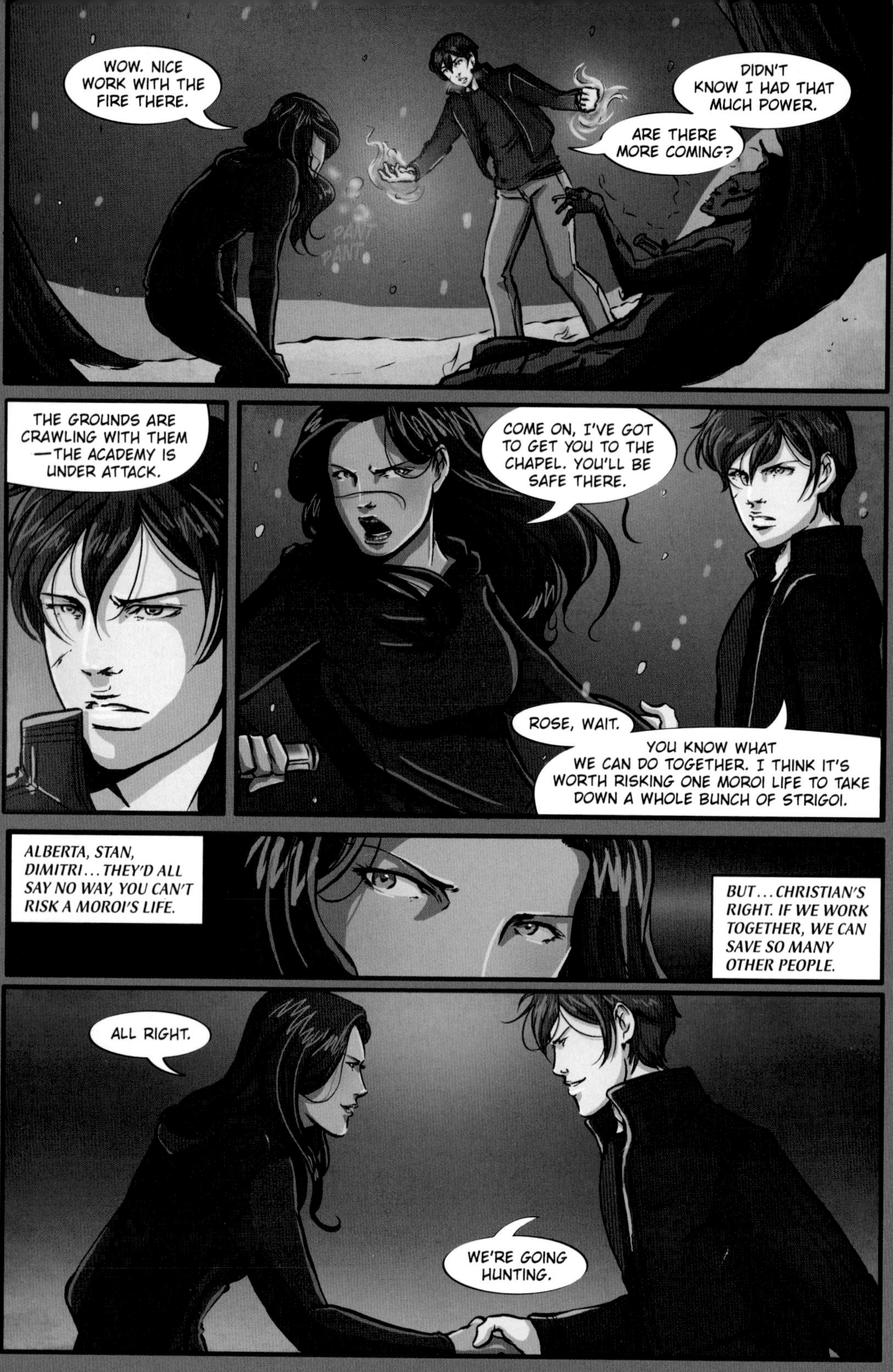
WOW. NICE WORK WITH THE FIRE THERE.
DIDN'T KNOW I HAD THAT MUCH POWER.
ARE THERE MORE COMING?
PANT PANT
THE GROUNDS ARE CRAWLING WITH THEM—THE ACADEMY IS UNDER ATTACK.
COME ON, I'VE GOT TO GET YOU TO THE CHAPEL. YOU'LL BE SAFE THERE.
ROSE, WAIT.
YOU KNOW WHAT WE CAN DO TOGETHER. I THINK IT'S WORTH RISKING ONE MOROI LIFE TO TAKE DOWN A WHOLE BUNCH OF STRIGOI.
ALBERTA, STAN, DIMITRI... THEY'D ALL SAY NO WAY, YOU CAN'T RISK A MOROI'S LIFE.
BUT... CHRISTIAN'S RIGHT. IF WE WORK TOGETHER, WE CAN SAVE SO MANY OTHER PEOPLE.
ALL RIGHT.
WE'RE GOING HUNTING.

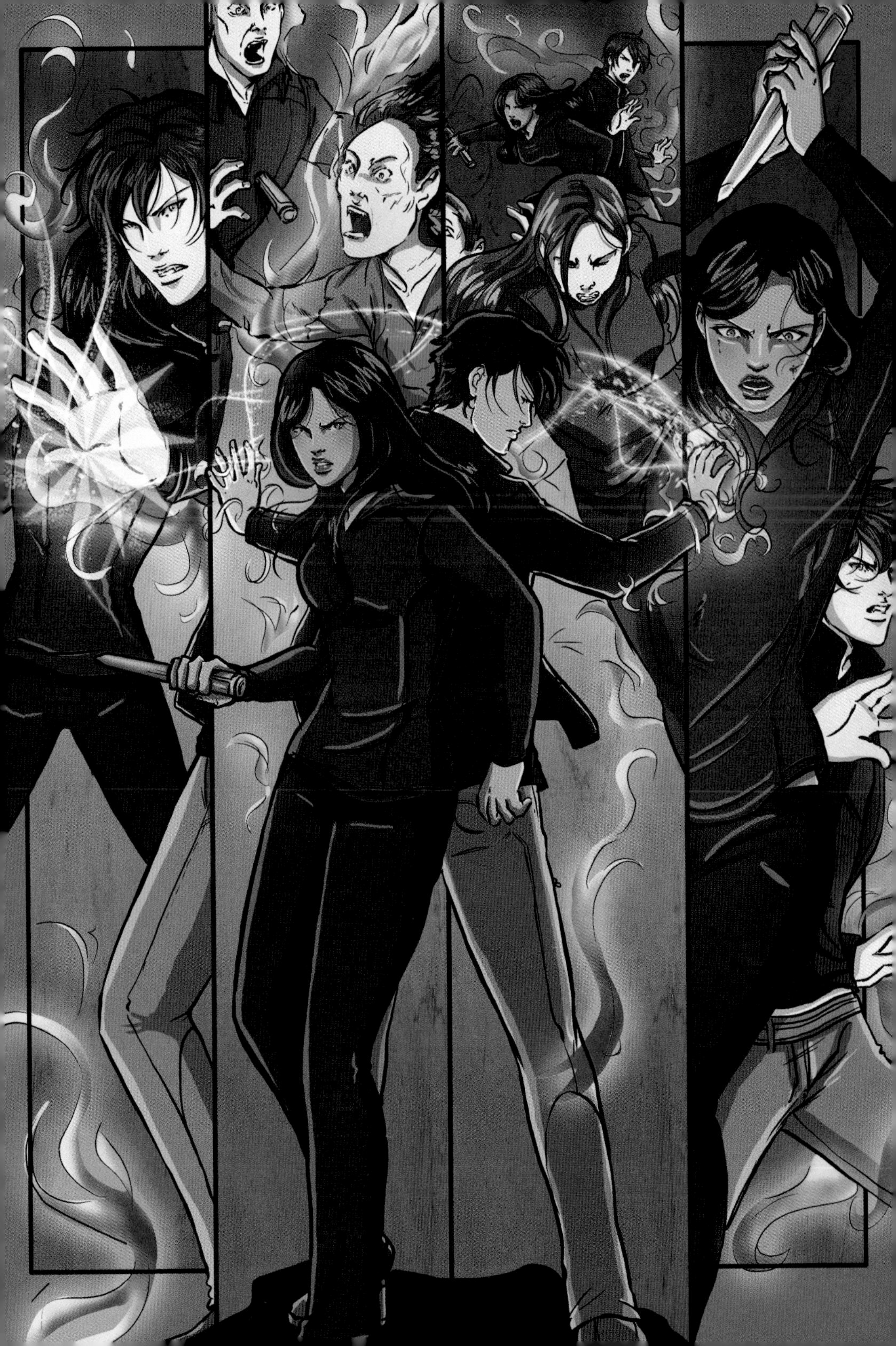

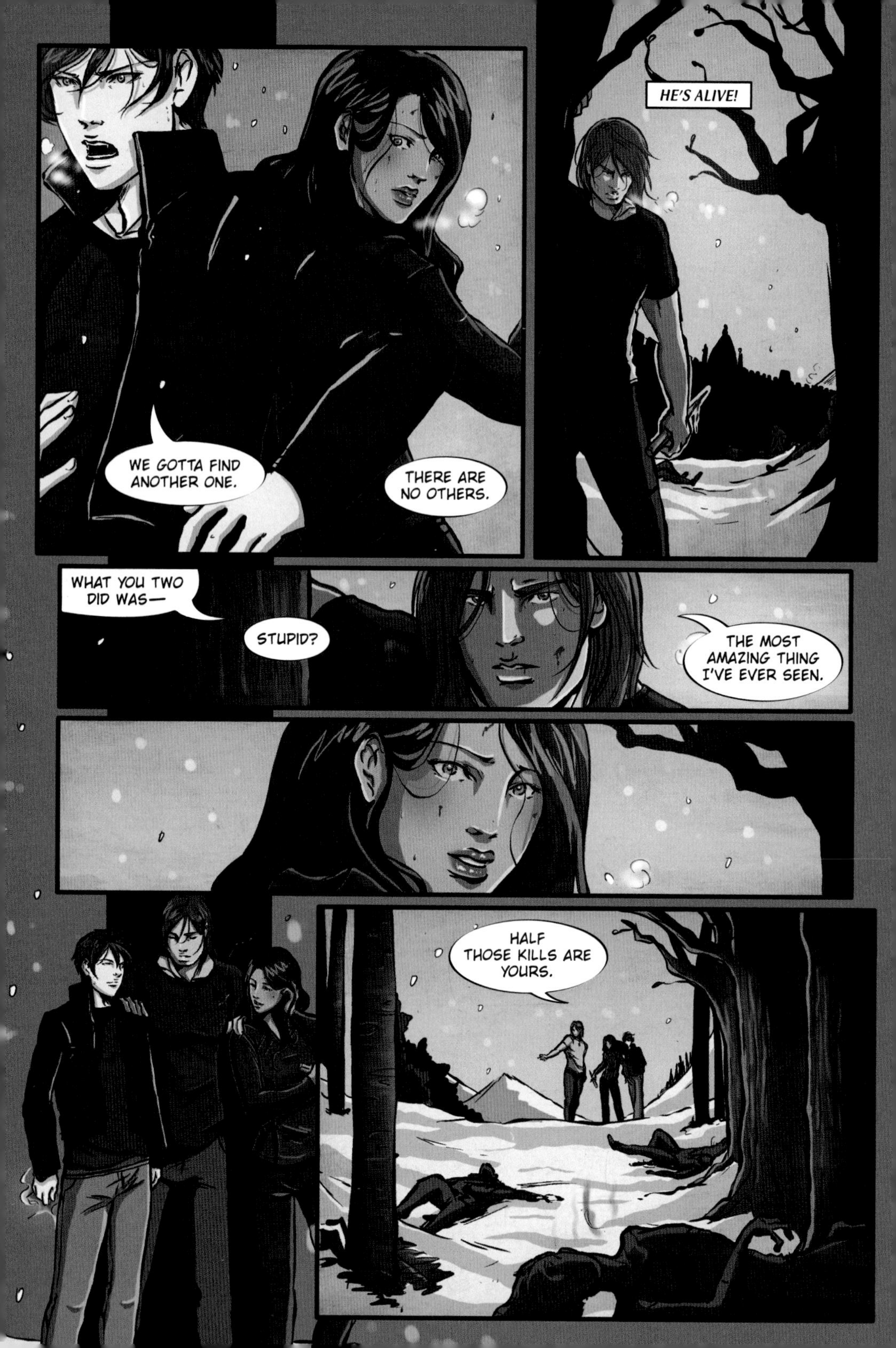
WE GOTTA FIND ANOTHER ONE.
THERE ARE NO OTHERS.
HE'S ALIVE!
WHAT YOU TWO DID WAS—
STUPID?
THE MOST AMAZING THING I'VE EVER SEEN.
HALF THOSE KILLS ARE YOURS.

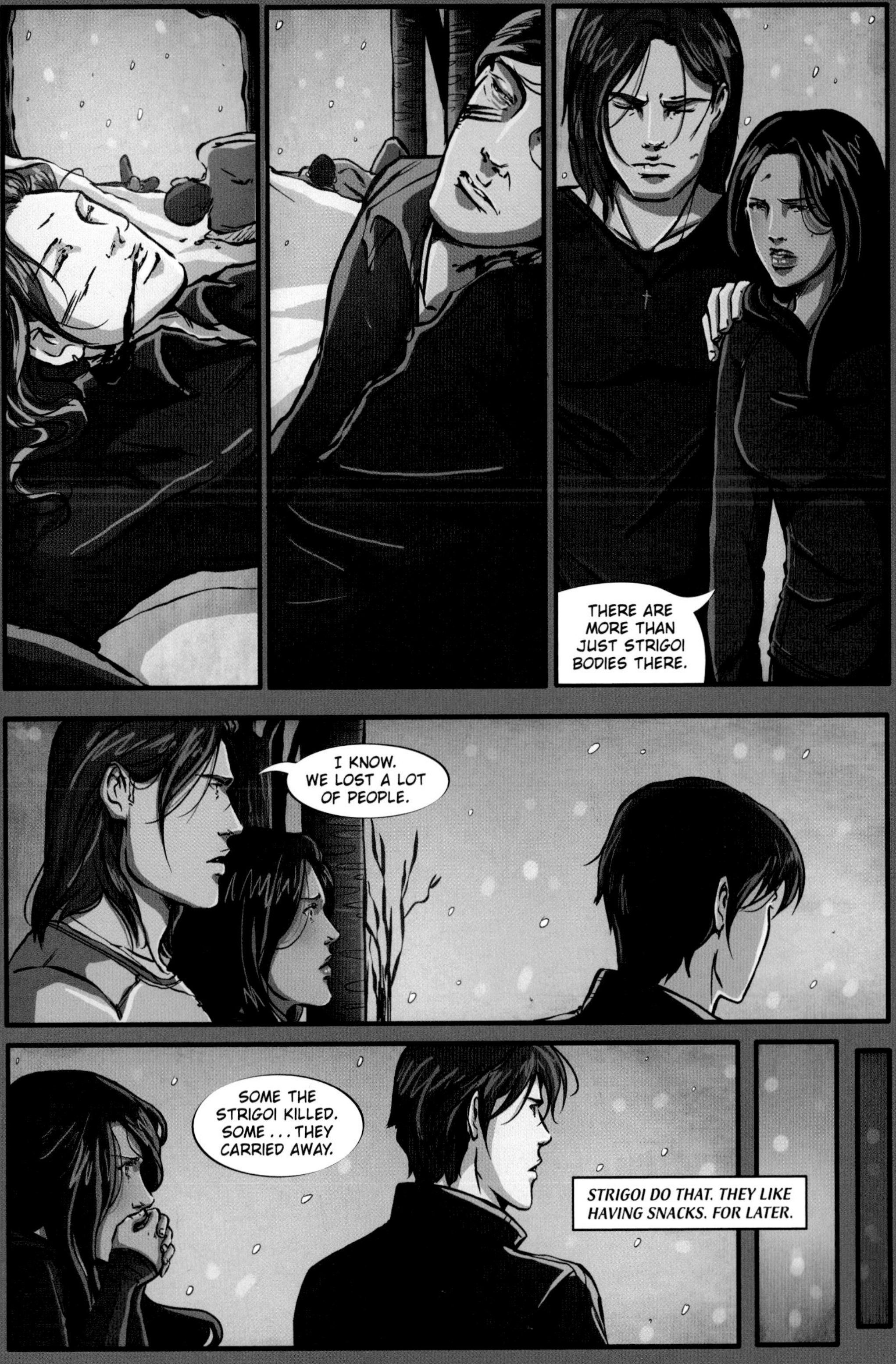

THERE ARE MORE THAN JUST STRIGOI BODIES THERE.
I KNOW. WE LOST A LOT OF PEOPLE.
SOME THE STRIGOI KILLED. SOME . . . THEY CARRIED AWAY.
STRIGOI DO THAT. THEY LIKE HAVING SNACKS. FOR LATER.

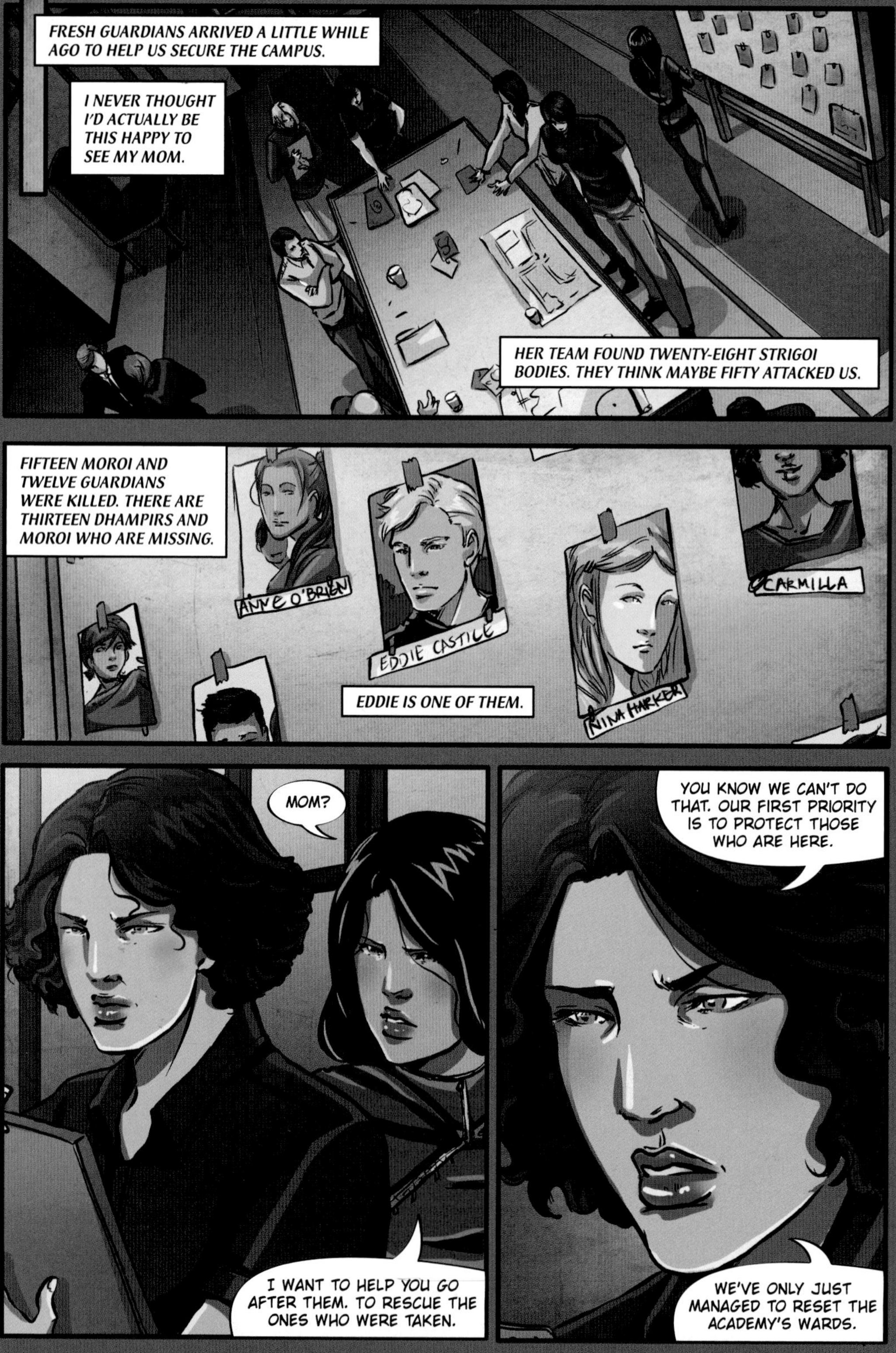
FRESH GUARDIANS ARRIVED A LITTLE WHILE AGO TO HELP US SECURE THE CAMPUS.
I NEVER THOUGHT I'D ACTUALLY BE THIS HAPPY TO SEE MY MOM.
HER TEAM FOUND TWENTY-EIGHT STRIGOI BODIES. THEY THINK MAYBE FIFTY ATTACKED US.
FIFTEEN MOROI AND TWELVE GUARDIANS WERE KILLED. THERE ARE THIRTEEN DHAMPIRS AND MOROI WHO ARE MISSING.
ANNE O'BRIEN
EDDIE CASTILE
NINA HARKER
CARMILLA
EDDIE IS ONE OF THEM.
MOM?
I WANT TO HELP YOU GO AFTER THEM. TO RESCUE THE ONES WHO WERE TAKEN.
YOU KNOW WE CAN'T DO THAT. OUR FIRST PRIORITY IS TO PROTECT THOSE WHO ARE HERE.
WE'VE ONLY JUST MANAGED TO RESET THE ACADEMY'S WARDS.

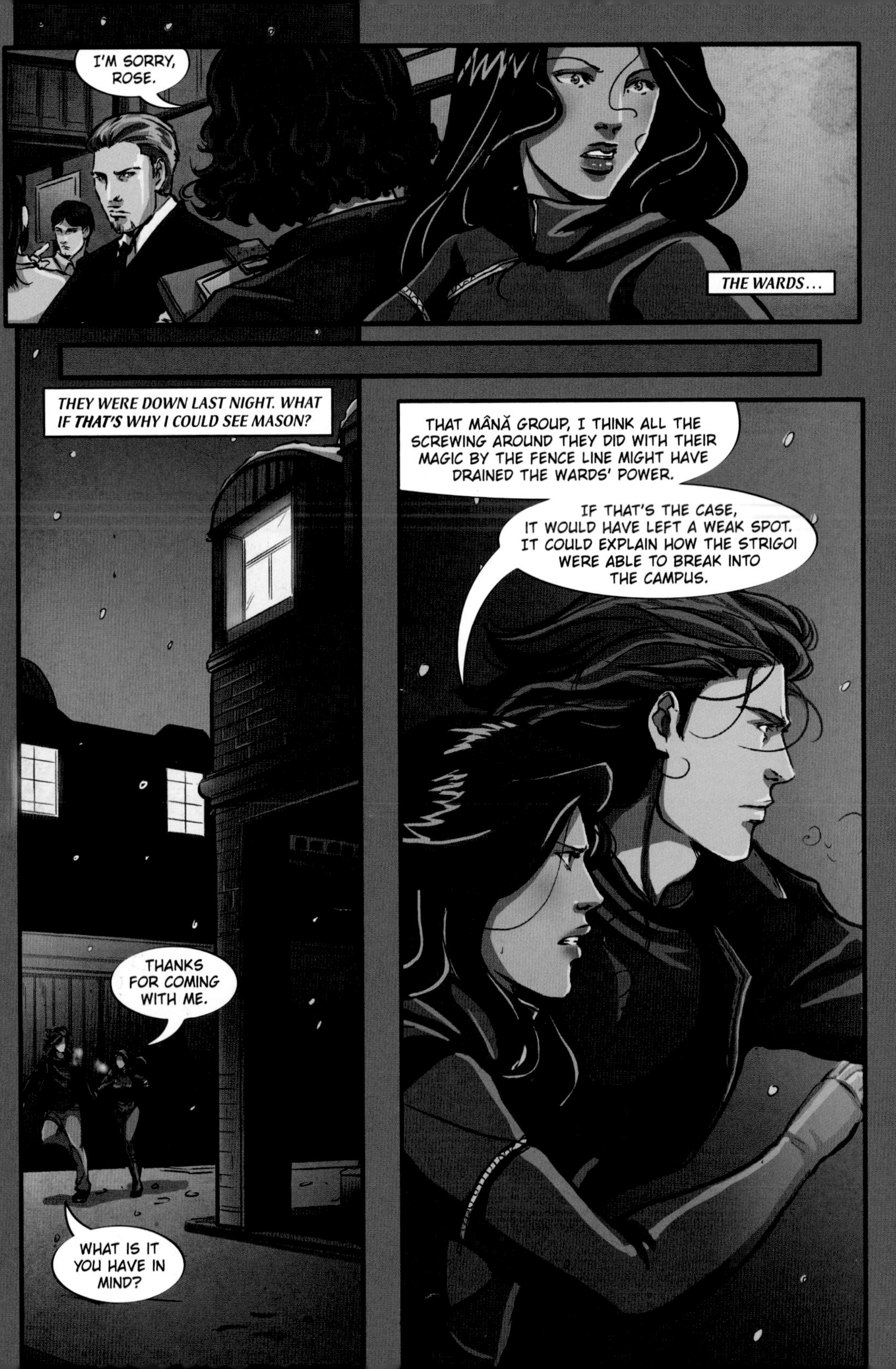
I'M SORRY, ROSE.
THE WARDS . . .
THEY WERE DOWN LAST NIGHT. WHAT IF THAT'S WHY I COULD SEE MASON?
THANKS FOR COMING WITH ME.
WHAT IS IT YOU HAVE IN MIND?
THAT MÂNĂ GROUP, I THINK ALL THE SCREWING AROUND THEY DID WITH THEIR MAGIC BY THE FENCE LINE MIGHT HAVE DRAINED THE WARDS' POWER.
IF THAT'S THE CASE, IT WOULD HAVE LEFT A WEAK SPOT. IT COULD EXPLAIN HOW THE STRIGOI WERE ABLE TO BREAK INTO THE CAMPUS.

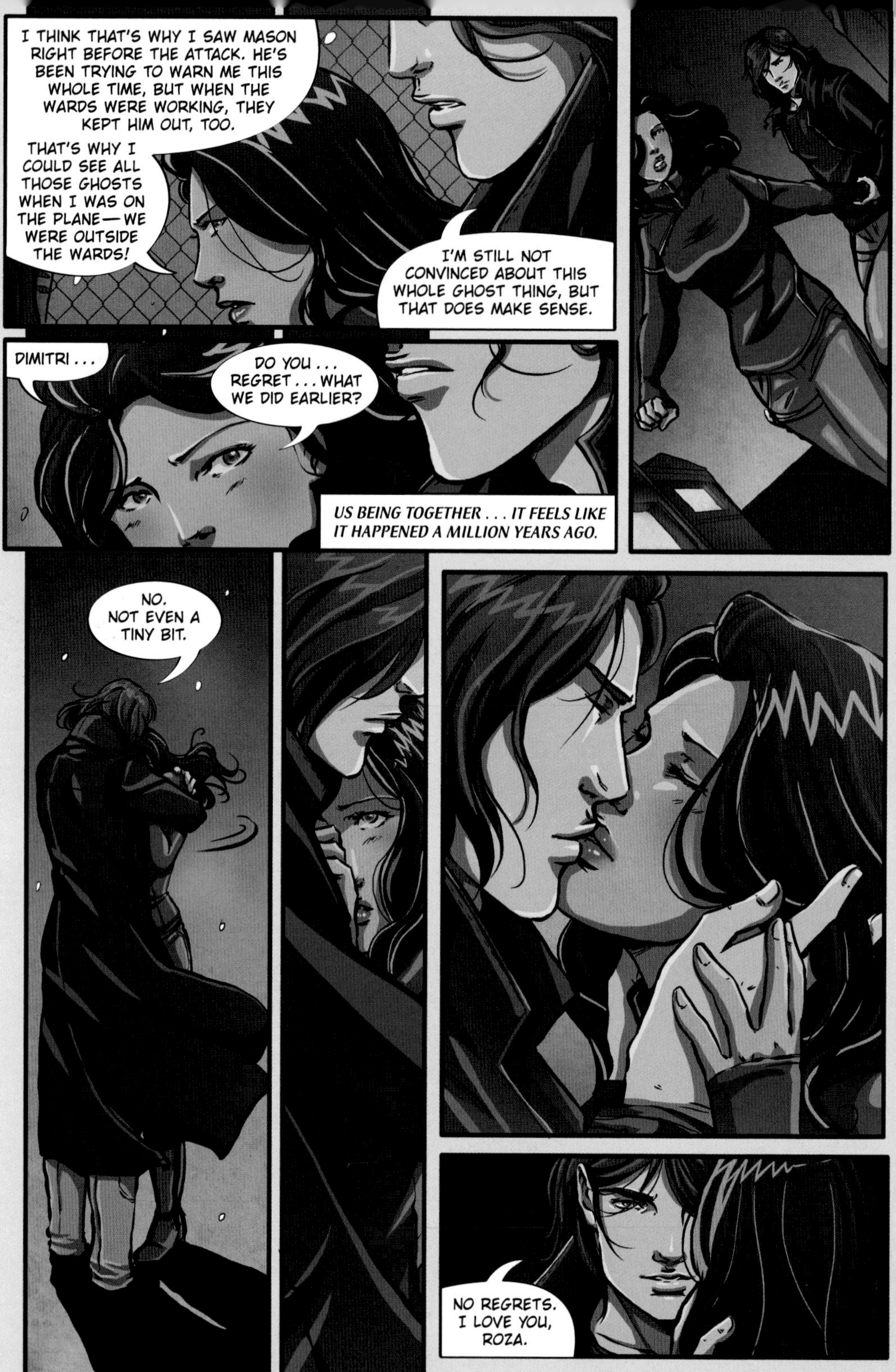
I THINK THAT'S WHY I SAW MASON RIGHT BEFORE THE ATTACK. HE'S BEEN TRYING TO WARN ME THIS WHOLE TIME, BUT WHEN THE WARDS WERE WORKING, THEY KEPT HIM OUT, TOO.
THAT'S WHY I COULD SEE ALL THOSE GHOSTS WHEN I WAS ON THE PLANE—WE WERE OUTSIDE THE WARDS!
I'M STILL NOT CONVINCED ABOUT THIS WHOLE GHOST THING, BUT THAT DOES MAKE SENSE.
DIMITRI . . .
DO YOU . . . REGRET . . . WHAT WE DID EARLIER?
US BEING TOGETHER . . . IT FEELS LIKE IT HAPPENED A MILLION YEARS AGO.
NO. NOT EVEN A TINY BIT.
NO REGRETS. I LOVE YOU, ROZA.

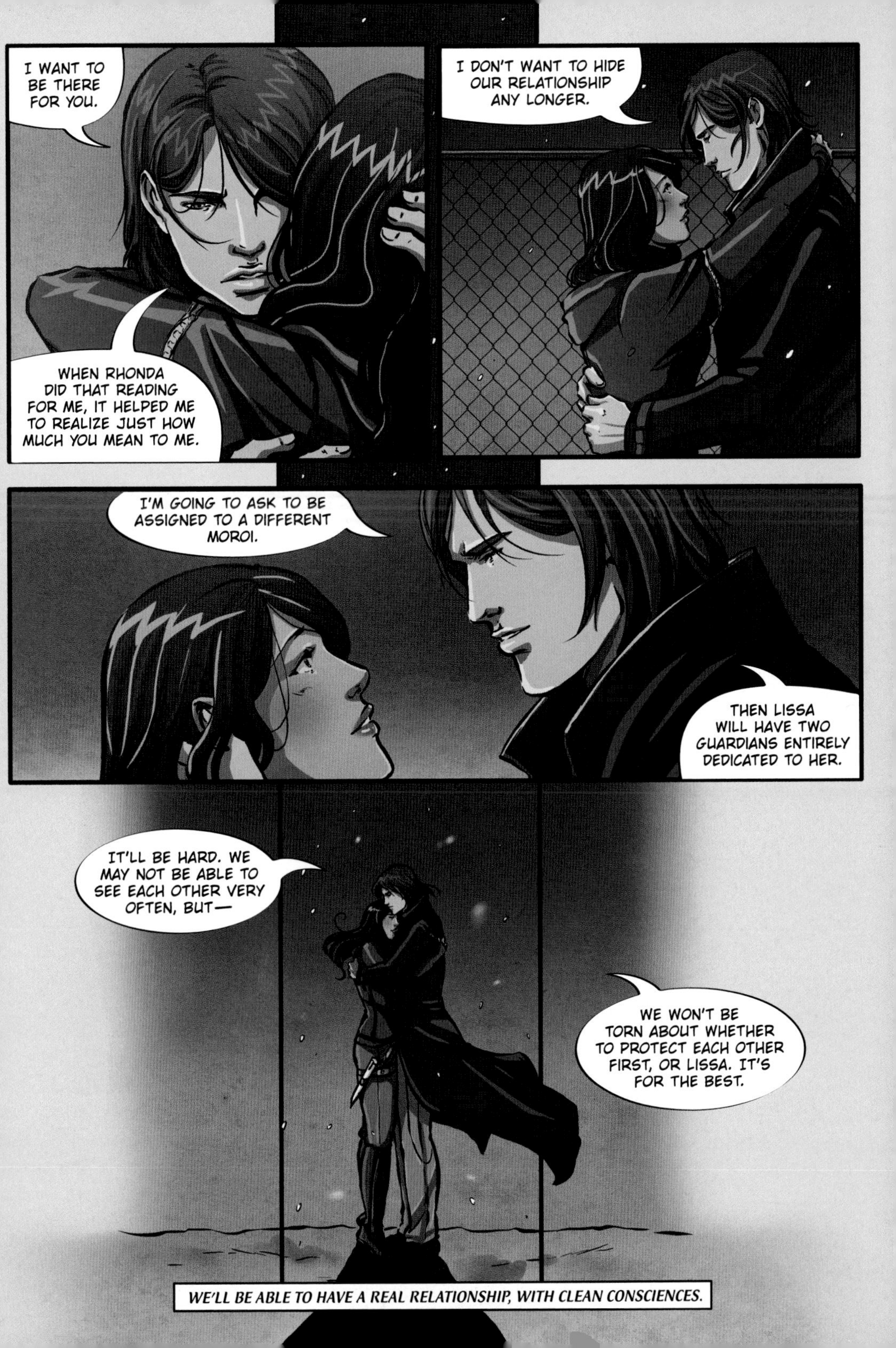
I WANT TO BE THERE FOR YOU.
WHEN RHONDA DID THAT READING FOR ME, IT HELPED ME TO REALIZE JUST HOW MUCH YOU MEAN TO ME.
I DON'T WANT TO HIDE OUR RELATIONSHIP ANY LONGER.
I'M GOING TO ASK TO BE ASSIGNED TO A DIFFERENT MOROI.
THEN LISSA WILL HAVE TWO GUARDIANS ENTIRELY DEDICATED TO HER.
IT'LL BE HARD. WE MAY NOT BE ABLE TO SEE EACH OTHER VERY OFTEN, BUT—
WE WON'T BE TORN ABOUT WHETHER TO PROTECT EACH OTHER FIRST, OR LISSA. IT'S FOR THE BEST.
WE'LL BE ABLE TO HAVE A REAL RELATIONSHIP, WITH CLEAN CONSCIENCES.

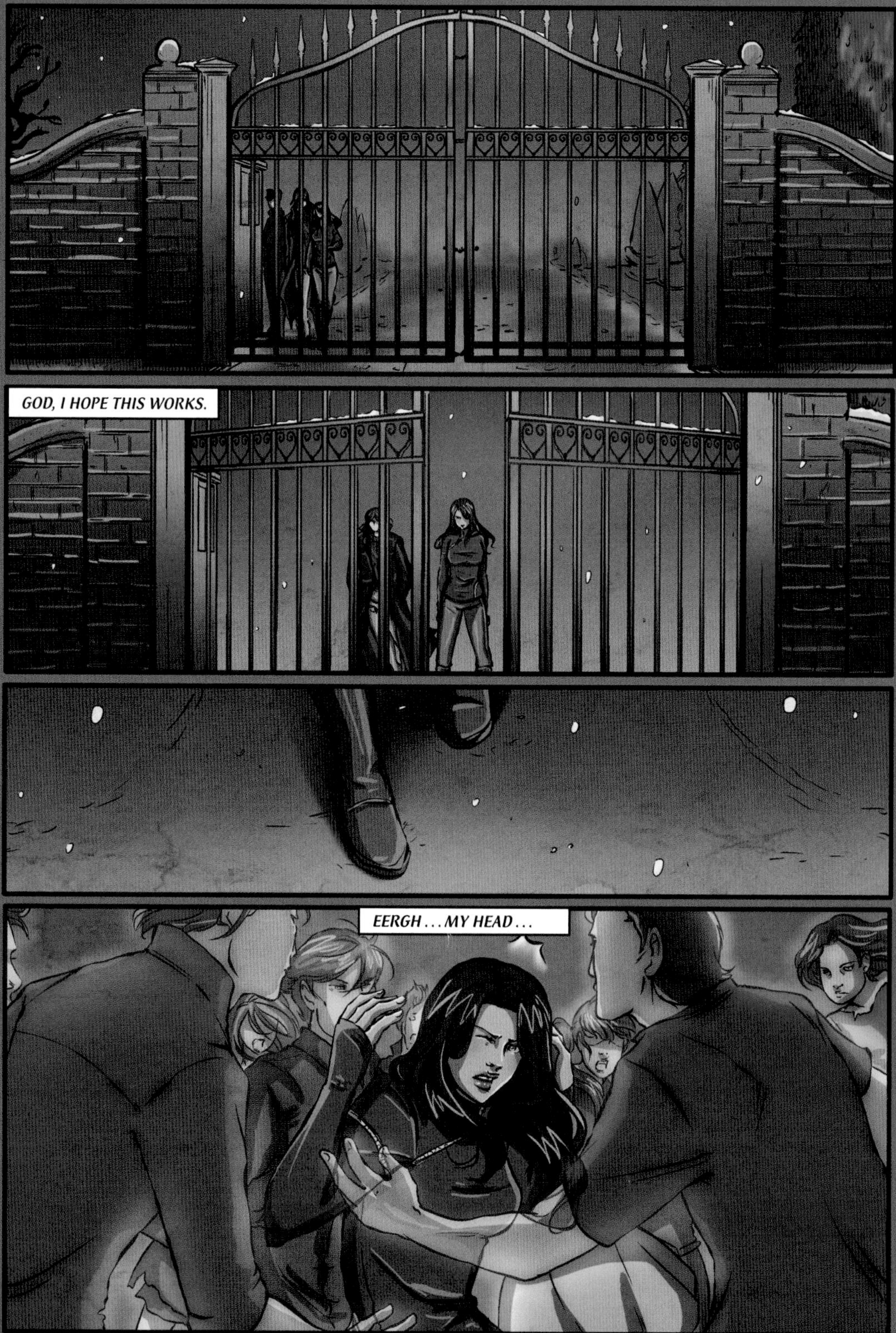
GOD, I HOPE THIS WORKS.
EERGH . . . MY HEAD . . .

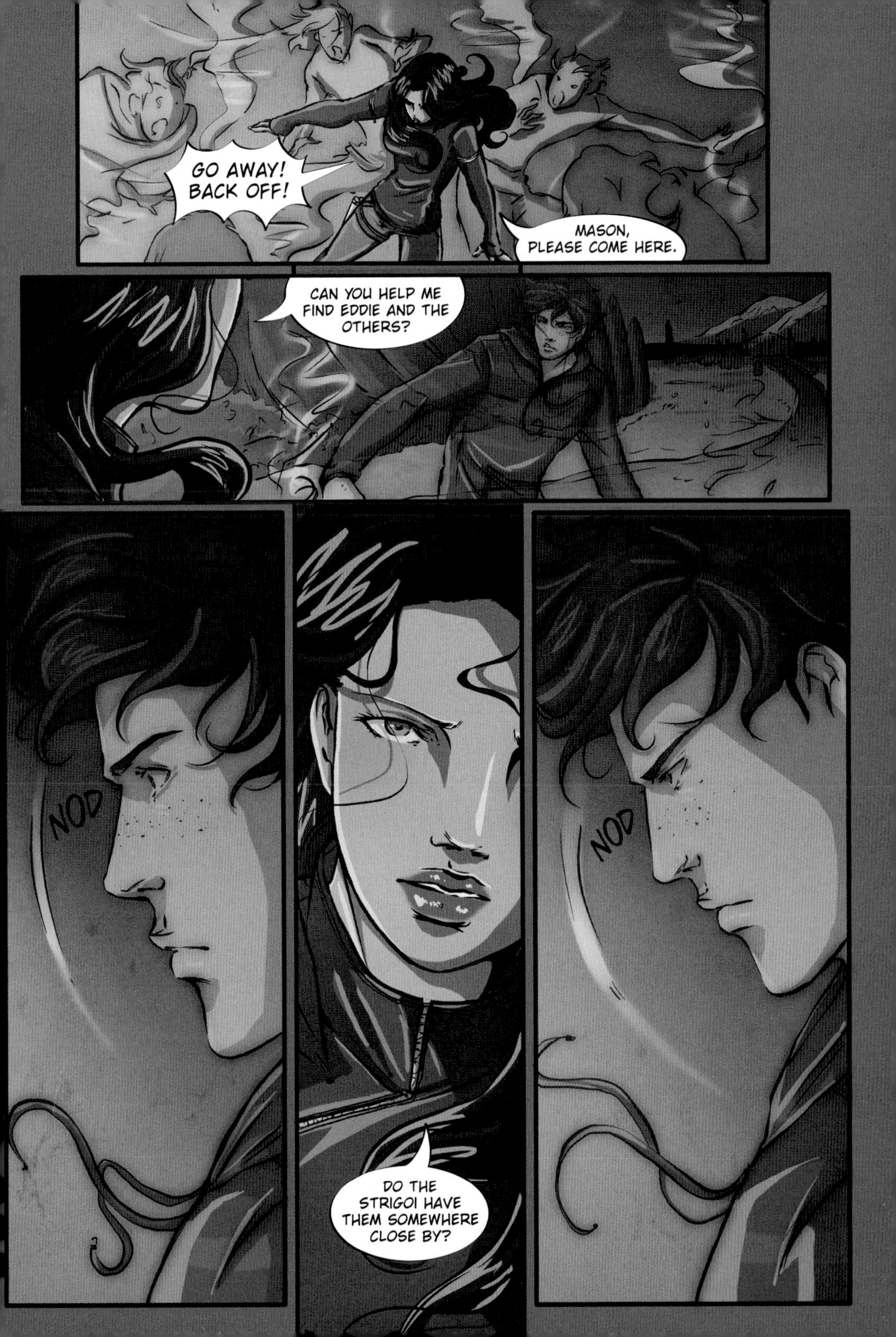
GO AWAY! BACK OFF!
MASON, PLEASE COME HERE.
CAN YOU HELP ME FIND EDDIE AND THE OTHERS?
NOD
DO THE STRIGOI HAVE THEM SOMEWHERE CLOSE BY?
NOD

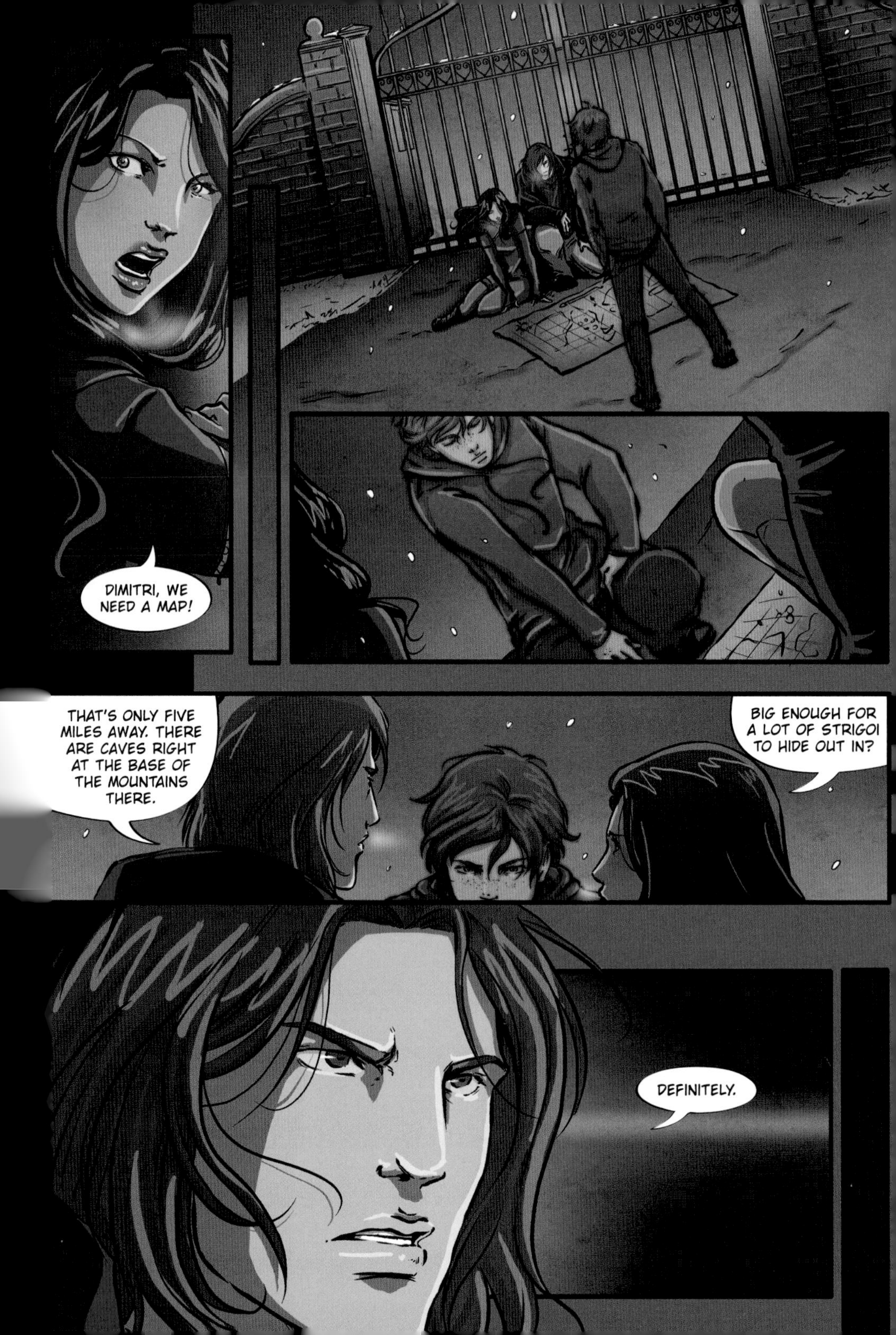
DIMITRI, WE NEED A MAP!
THAT'S ONLY FIVE MILES AWAY. THERE ARE CAVES RIGHT AT THE BASE OF THE MOUNTAINS THERE.
BIG ENOUGH FOR A LOT OF STRIGOI TO HIDE OUT IN?
DEFINITELY.

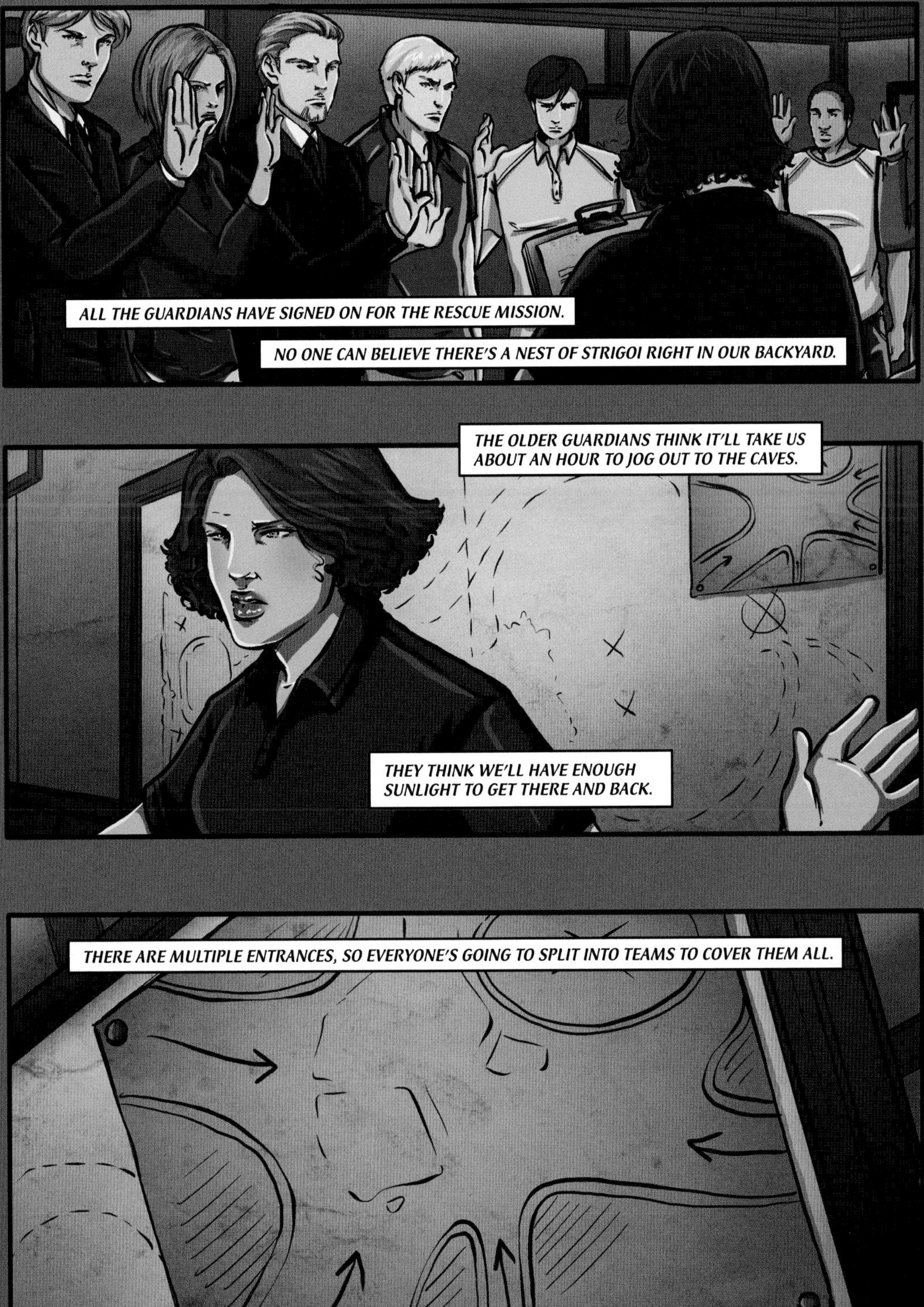
ALL THE GUARDIANS HAVE SIGNED ON FOR THE RESCUE MISSION.
NO ONE CAN BELIEVE THERE'S A NEST OF STRIGOI RIGHT IN OUR BACKYARD.
THE OLDER GUARDIANS THINK IT'LL TAKE US ABOUT AN HOUR TO JOG OUT TO THE CAVES.
THEY THINK WE'LL HAVE ENOUGH SUNLIGHT TO GET THERE AND BACK.
THERE ARE MULTIPLE ENTRANCES, SO EVERYONE'S GOING TO SPLIT INTO TEAMS TO COVER THEM ALL.

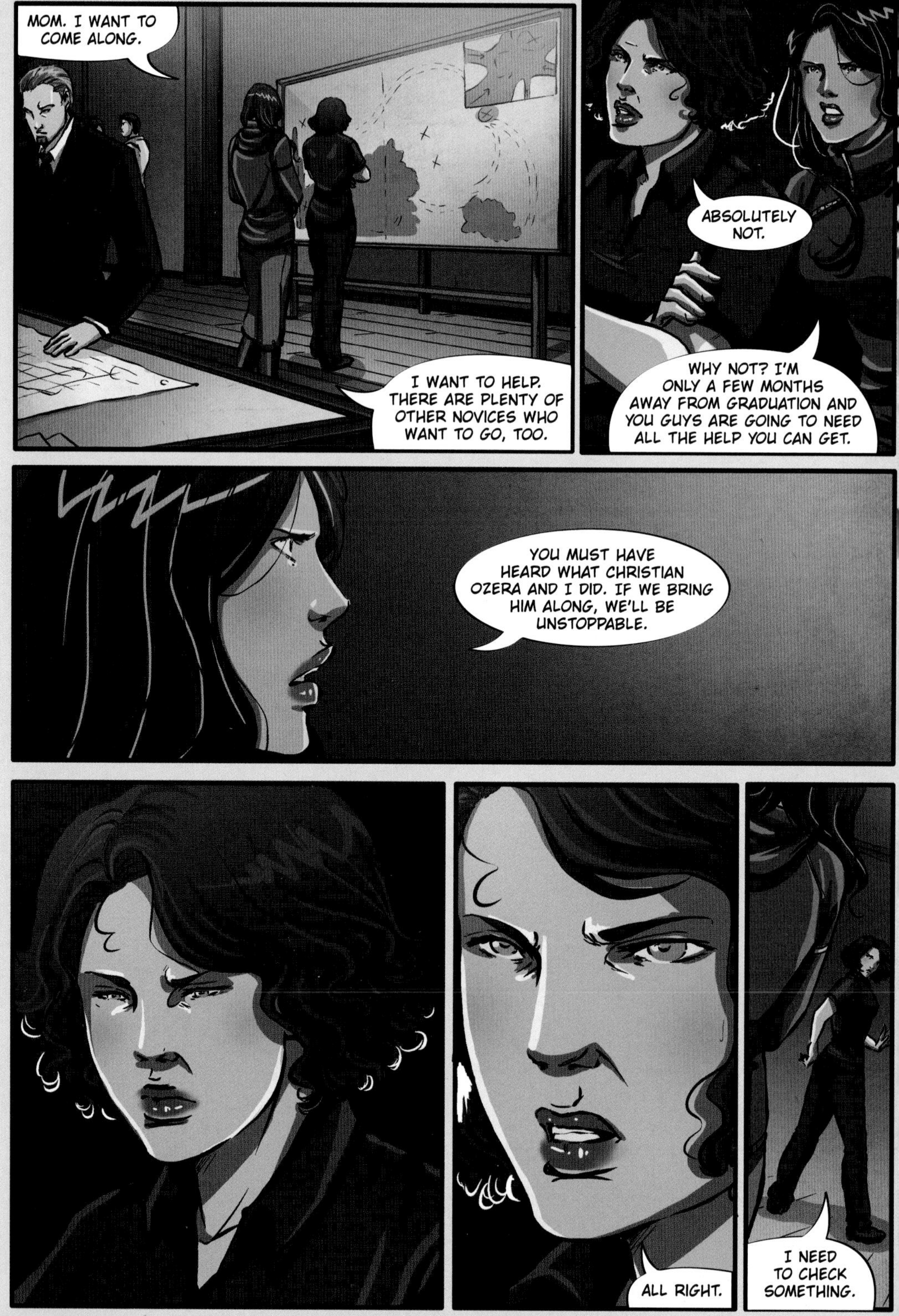
MOM. I WANT TO COME ALONG.
I WANT TO HELP. THERE ARE PLENTY OF OTHER NOVICES WHO WANT TO GO, TOO.
ABSOLUTELY NOT.
WHY NOT? I'M ONLY A FEW MONTHS AWAY FROM GRADUATION AND YOU GUYS ARE GOING TO NEED ALL THE HELP YOU CAN GET.
YOU MUST HAVE HEARD WHAT CHRISTIAN OZERA AND I DID. IF WE BRING HIM ALONG, WE'LL BE UNSTOPPABLE.
ALL RIGHT.
I NEED TO CHECK SOMETHING.

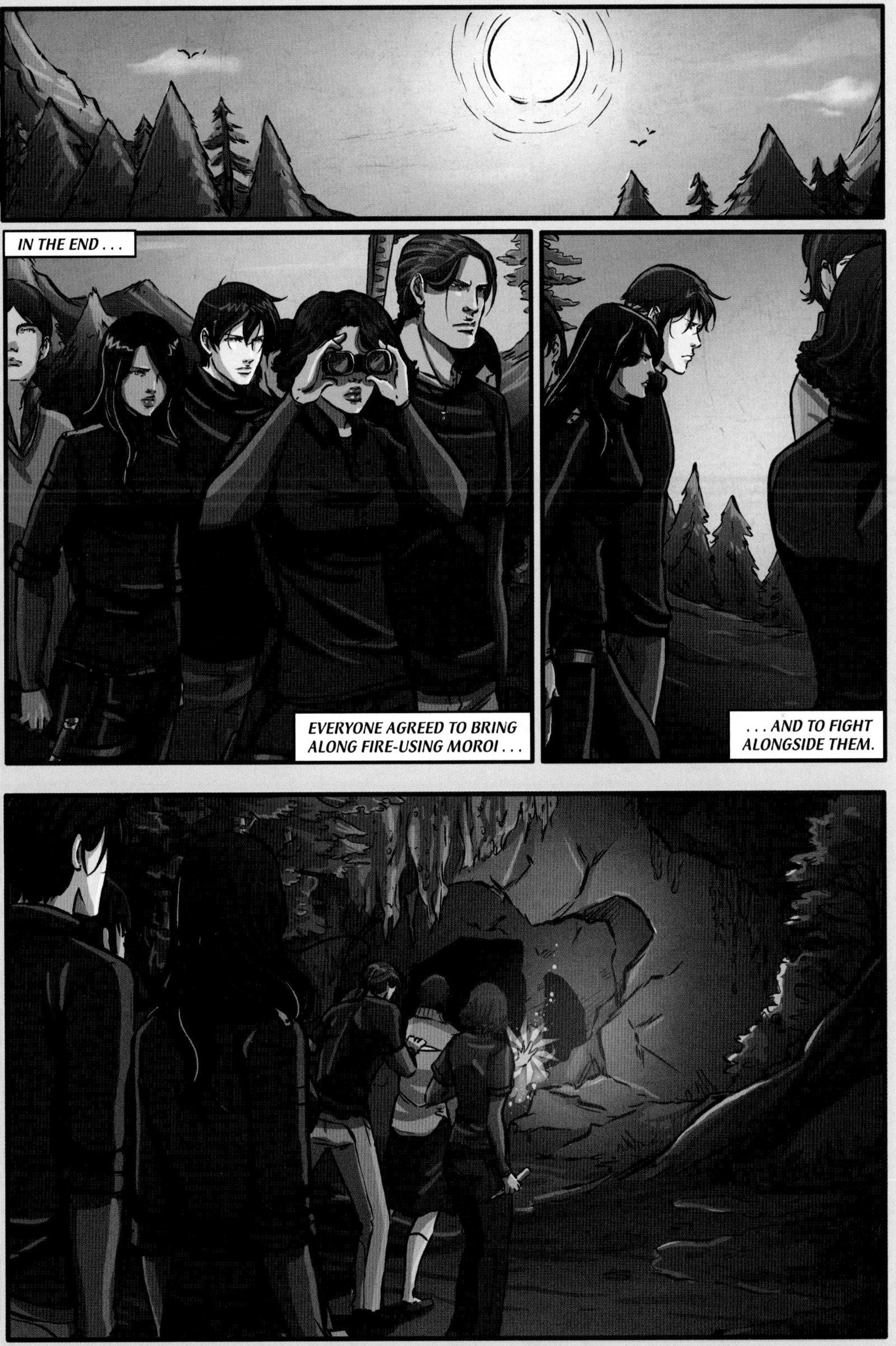
IN THE END . . .
EVERYONE AGREED TO BRING ALONG FIRE-USING MOROI . . .
. . . AND TO FIGHT ALONGSIDE THEM.

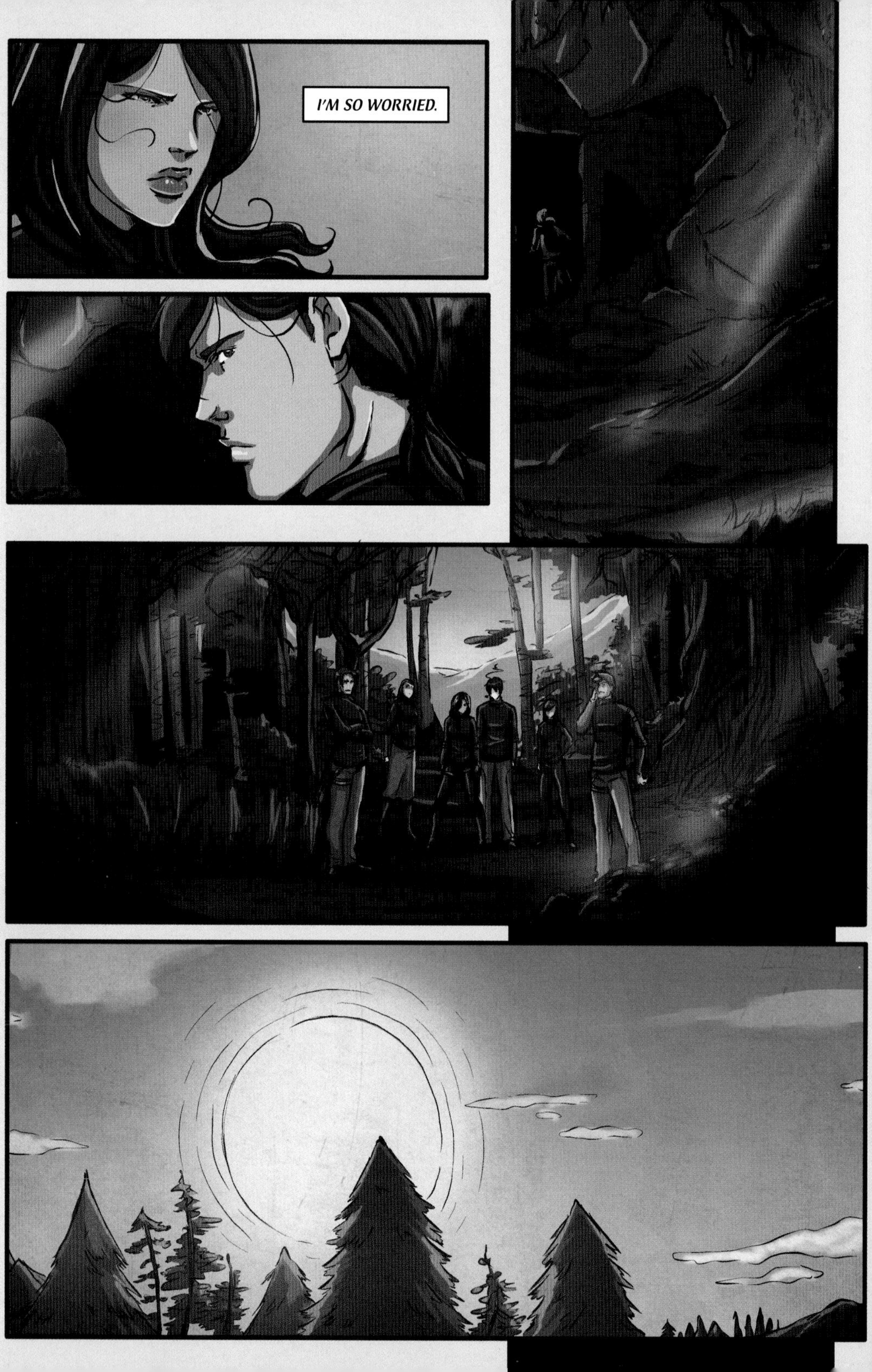
I'M SO WORRIED.

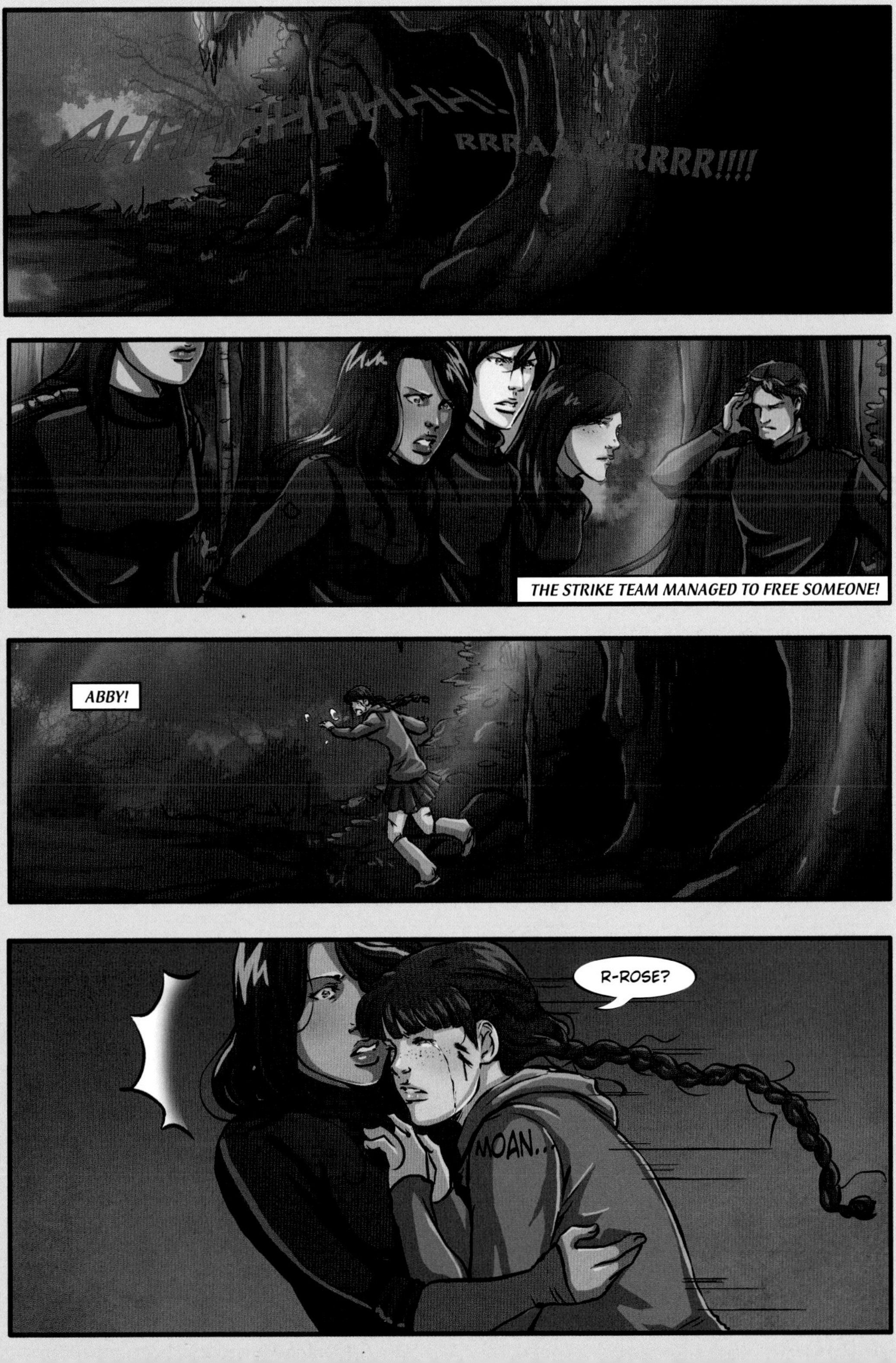

AHHH HHHHHHH!!
RRRA RRRRR!!!!
THE STRIKE TEAM MANAGED TO FREE SOMEONE!
ABBY!
R-ROSE?
MOAN...

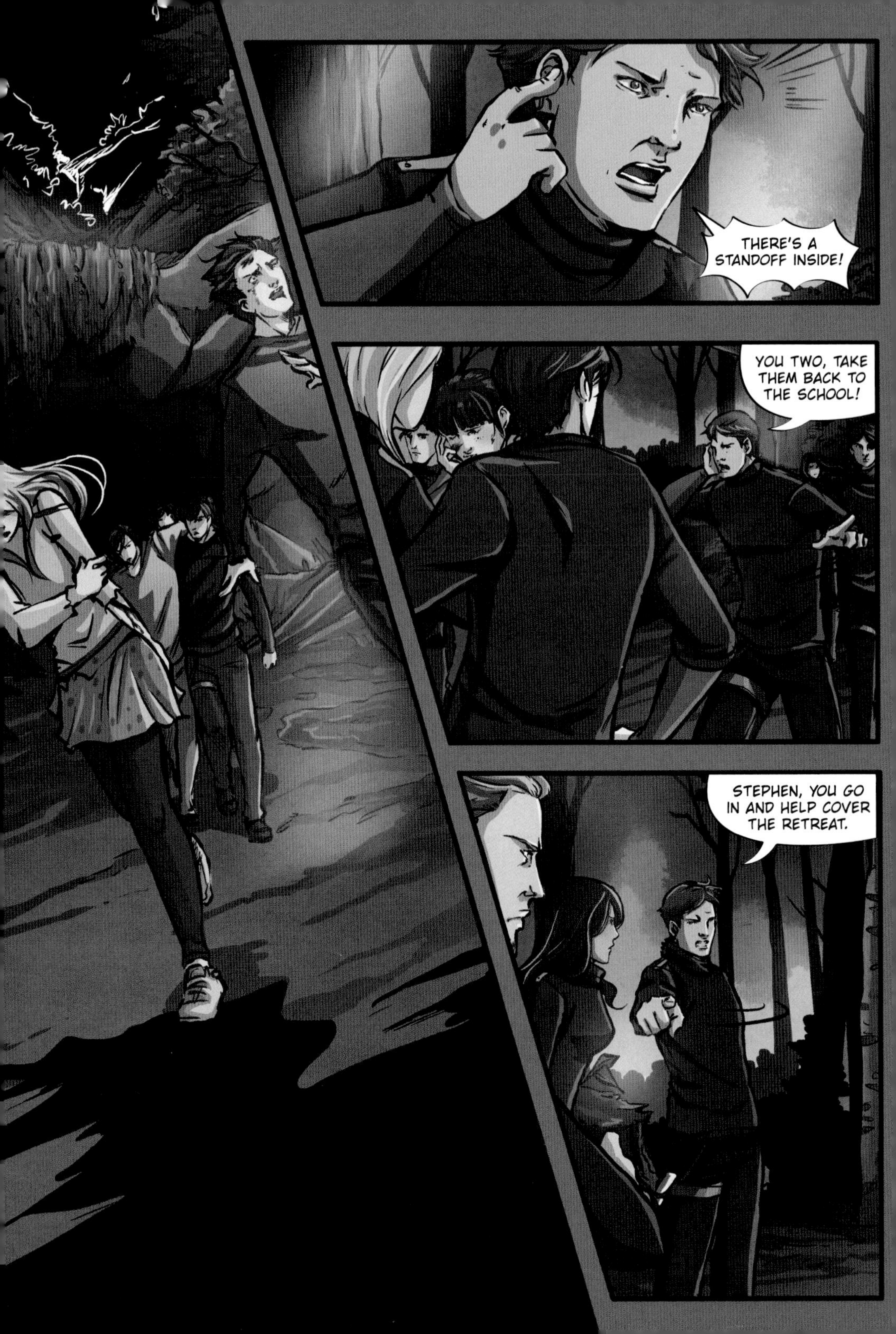
THERE'S A STANDOFF INSIDE!
YOU TWO, TAKE THEM BACK TO THE SCHOOL!
STEPHEN, YOU GO IN AND HELP COVER THE RETREAT.

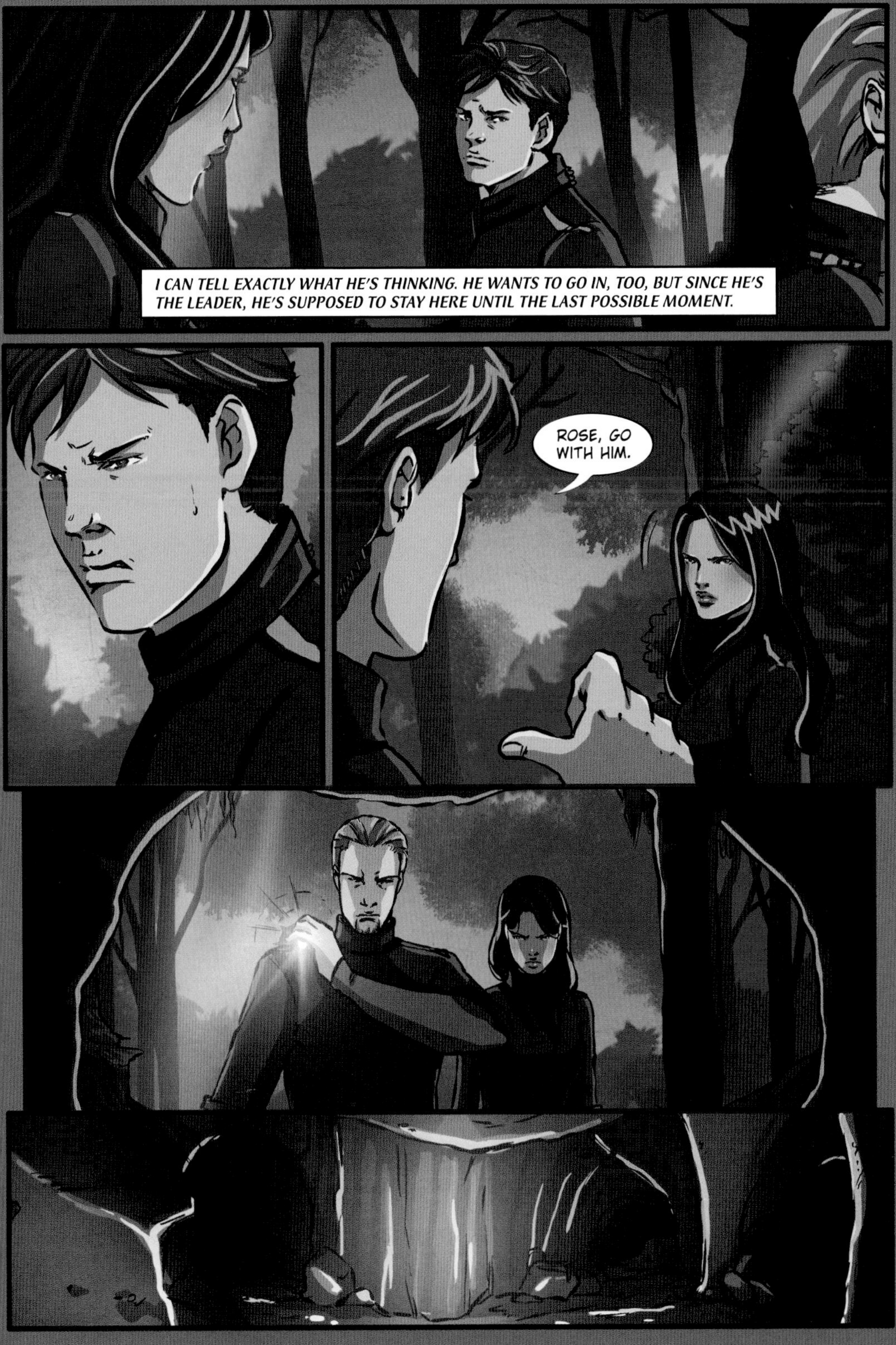
I CAN TELL EXACTLY WHAT HE'S THINKING. HE WANTS TO GO IN, TOO, BUT SINCE HE'S THE LEADER, HE'S SUPPOSED TO STAY HERE UNTIL THE LAST POSSIBLE MOMENT.
ROSE, GO WITH HIM.

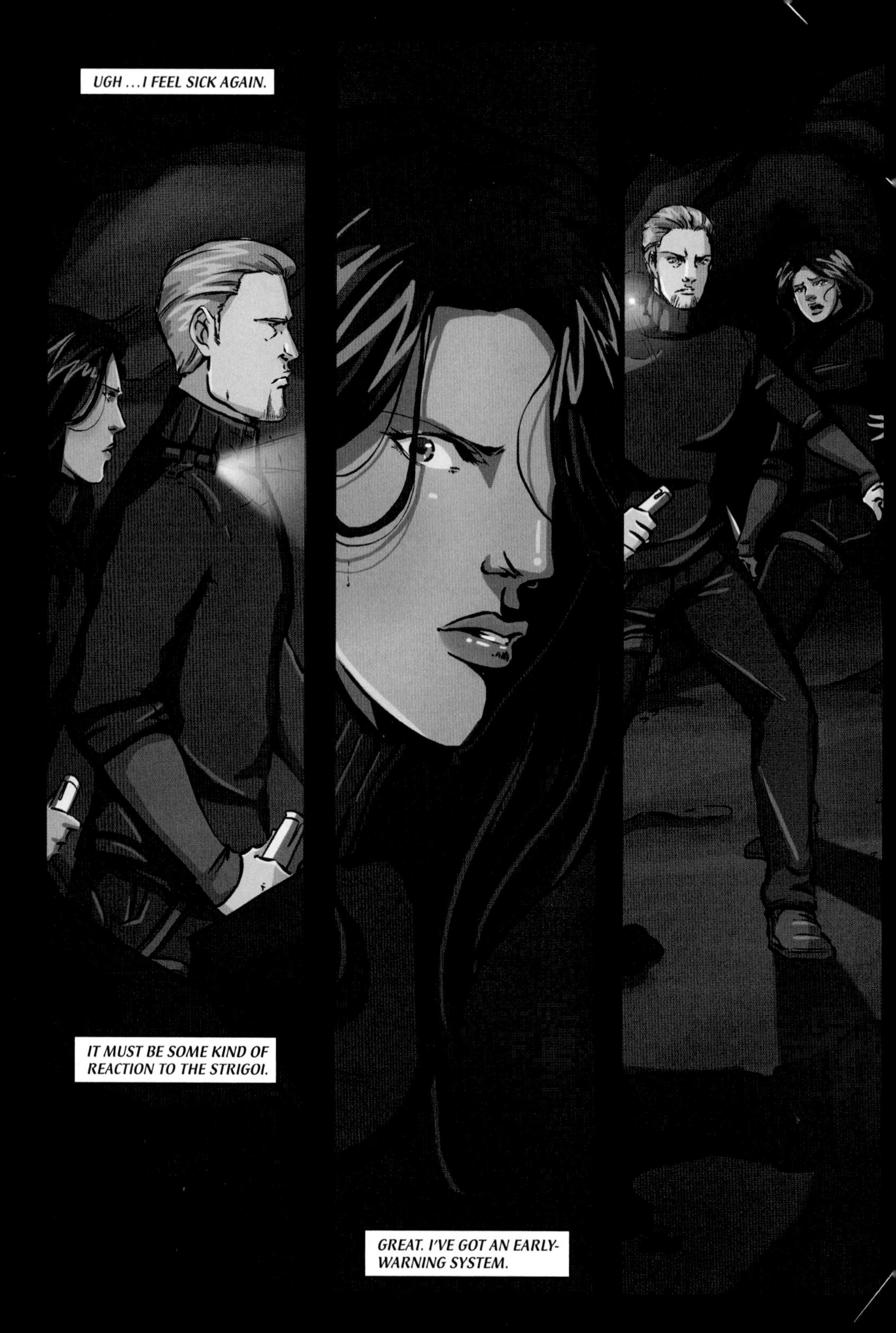
UGH ... I FEEL SICK AGAIN.
IT MUST BE SOME KIND OF REACTION TO THE STRIGOI.
GREAT. I'VE GOT AN EARLY-WARNING SYSTEM.

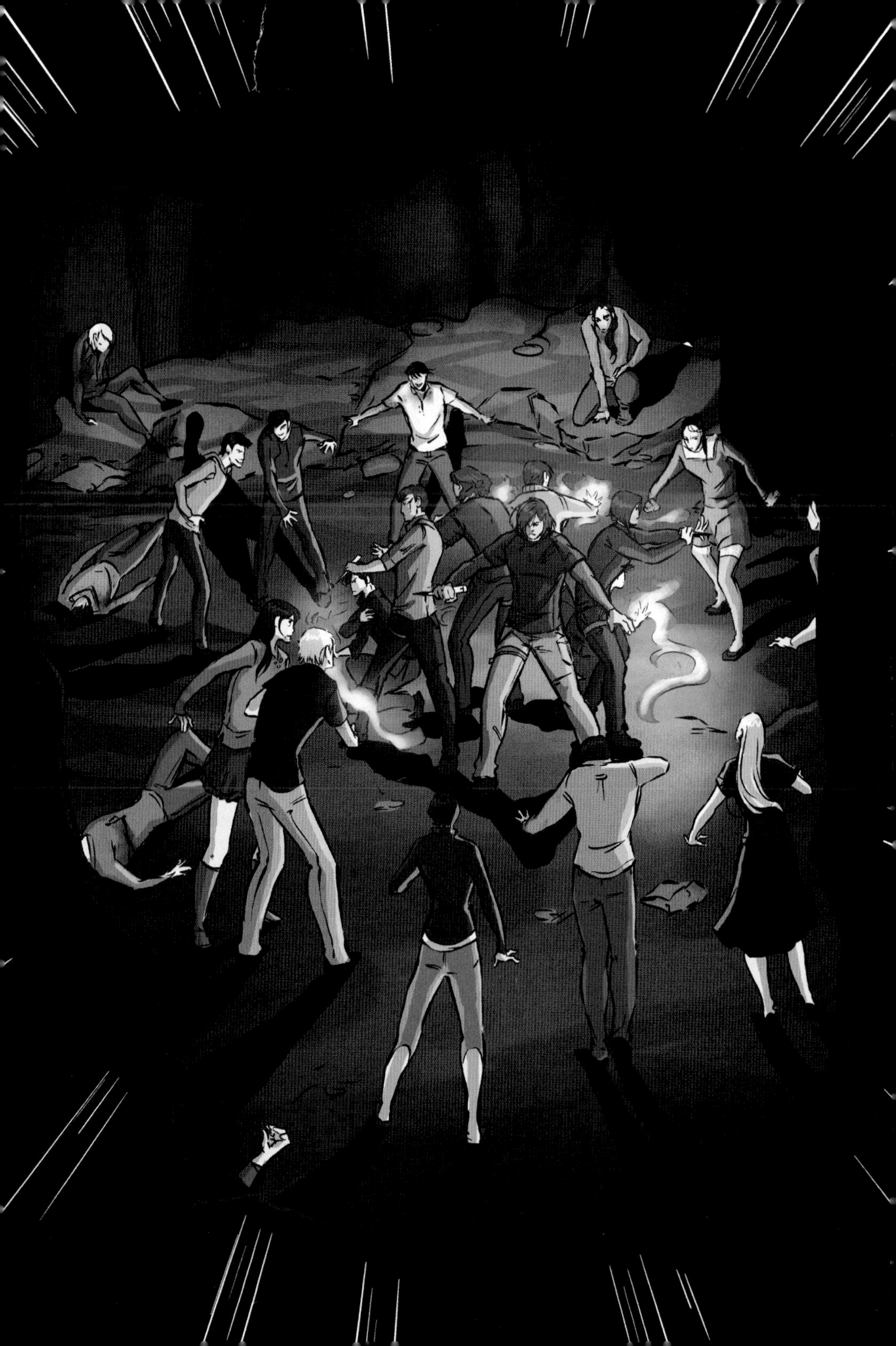

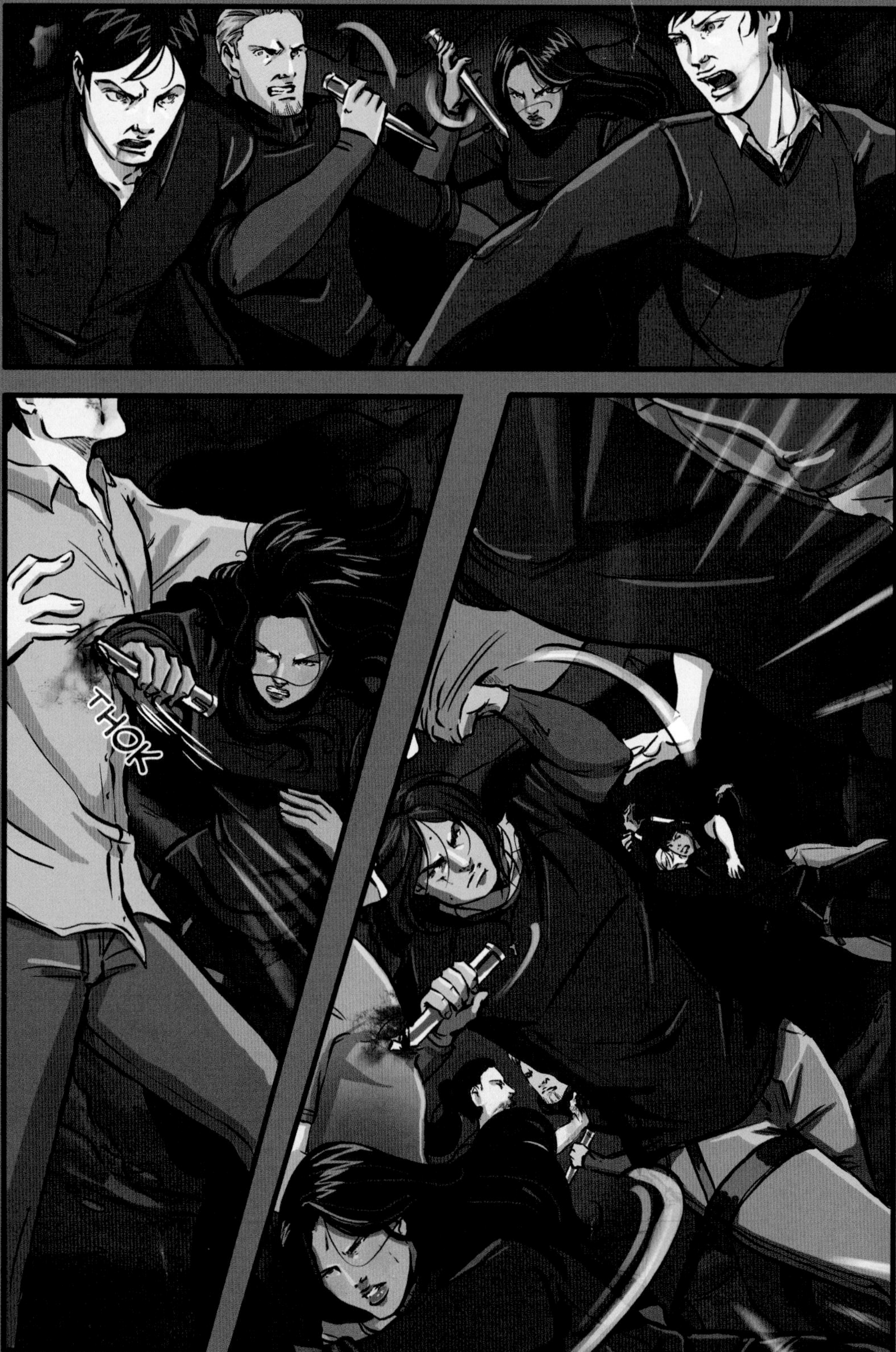
THOK

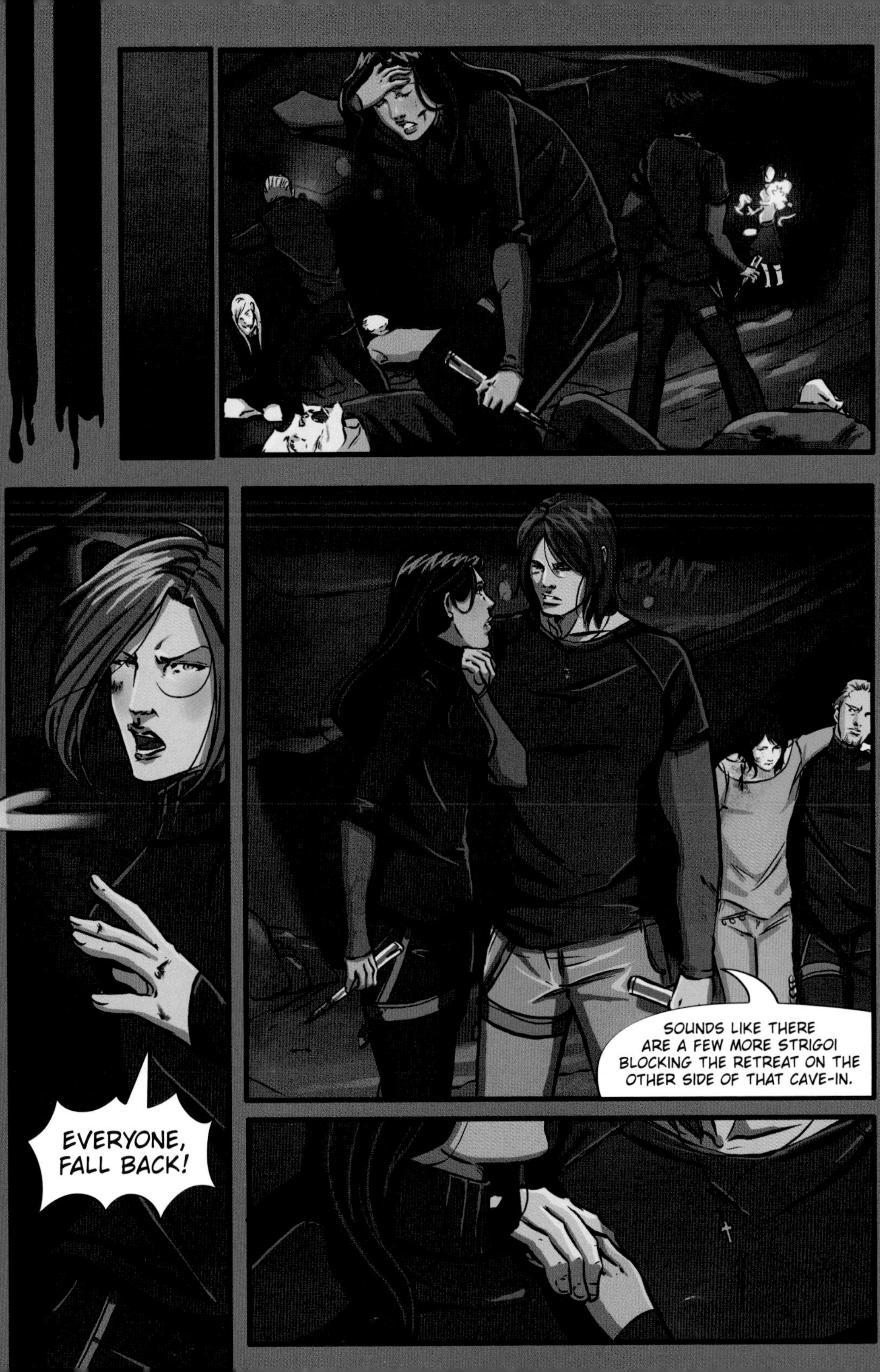
EVERYONE, FALL BACK!
PANT
SOUNDS LIKE THERE ARE A FEW MORE STRIGOI BLOCKING THE RETREAT ON THE OTHER SIDE OF THAT CAVE-IN.

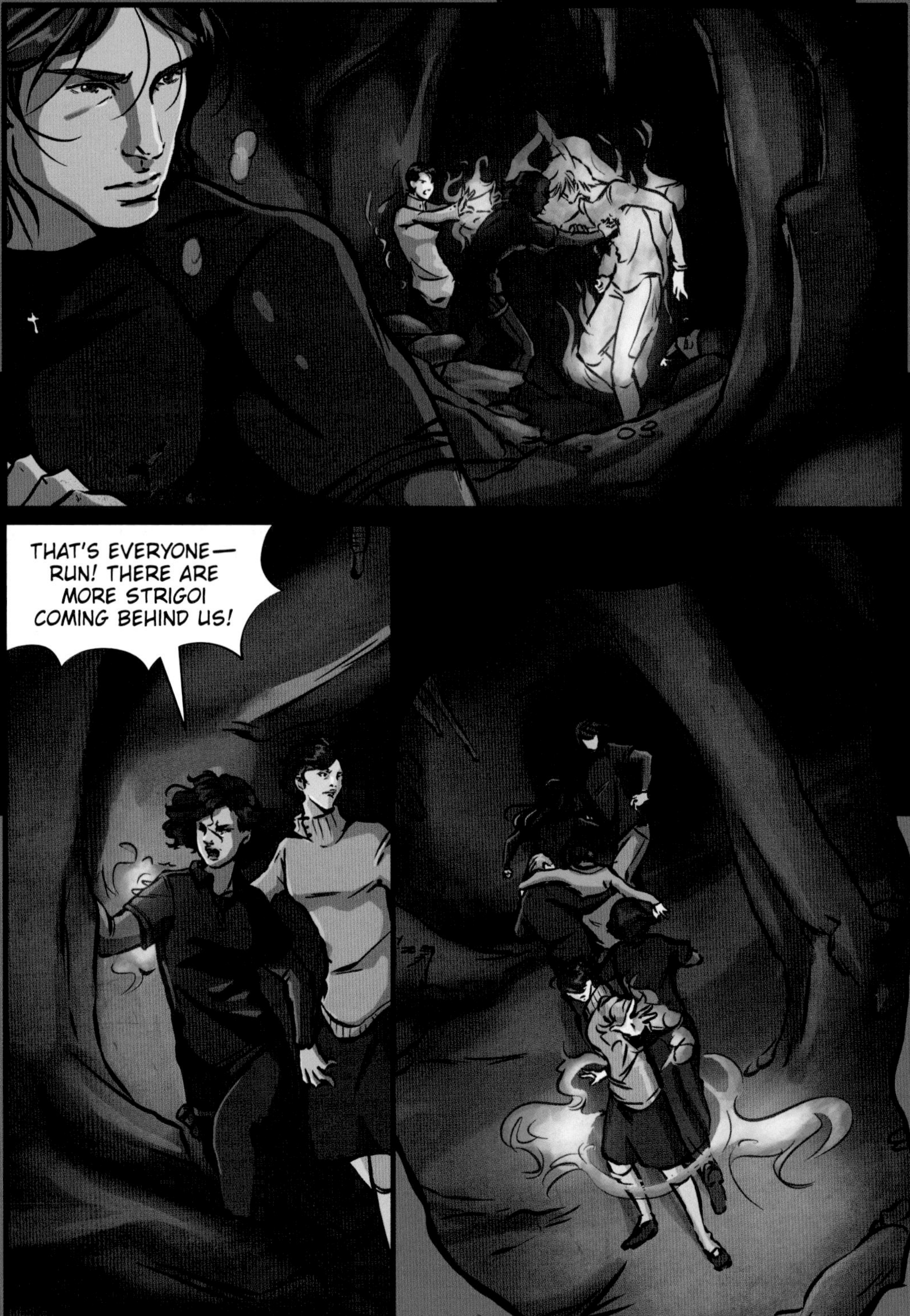
THAT'S EVERYONE—RUN! THERE ARE MORE STRIGOI COMING BEHIND US!

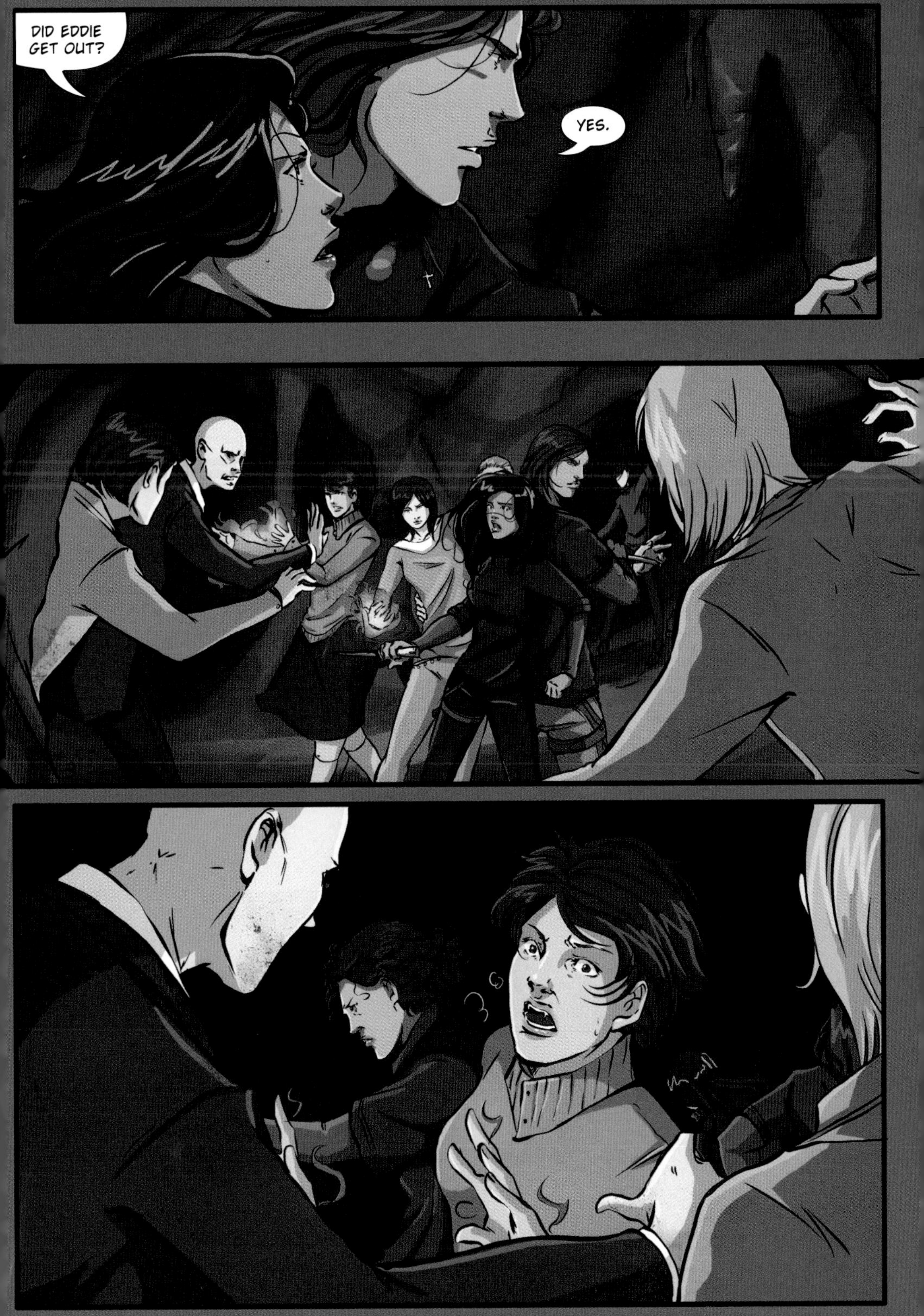
DID EDDIE GET OUT?
YES.

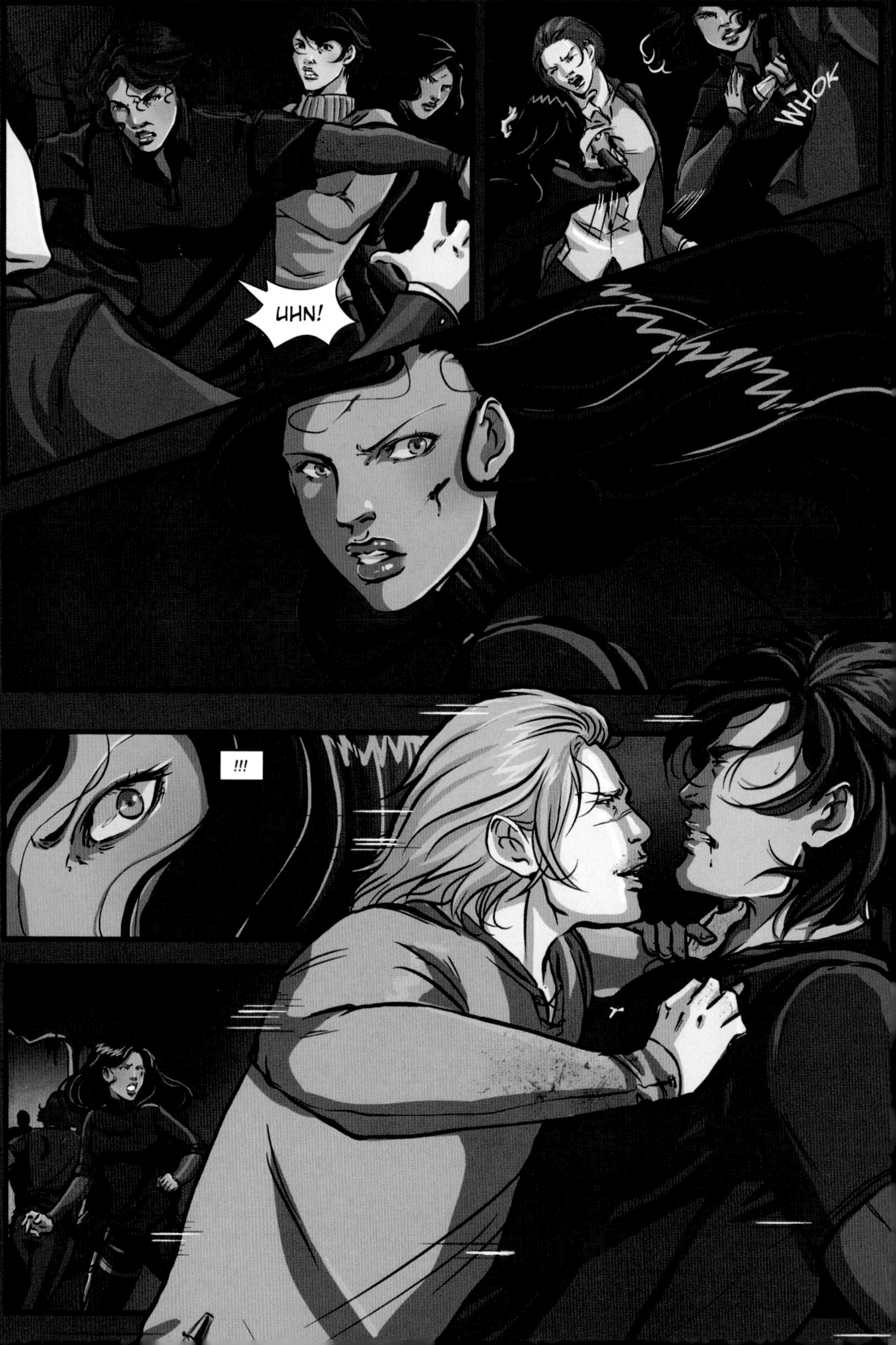
WHOK
UHN!
!!!

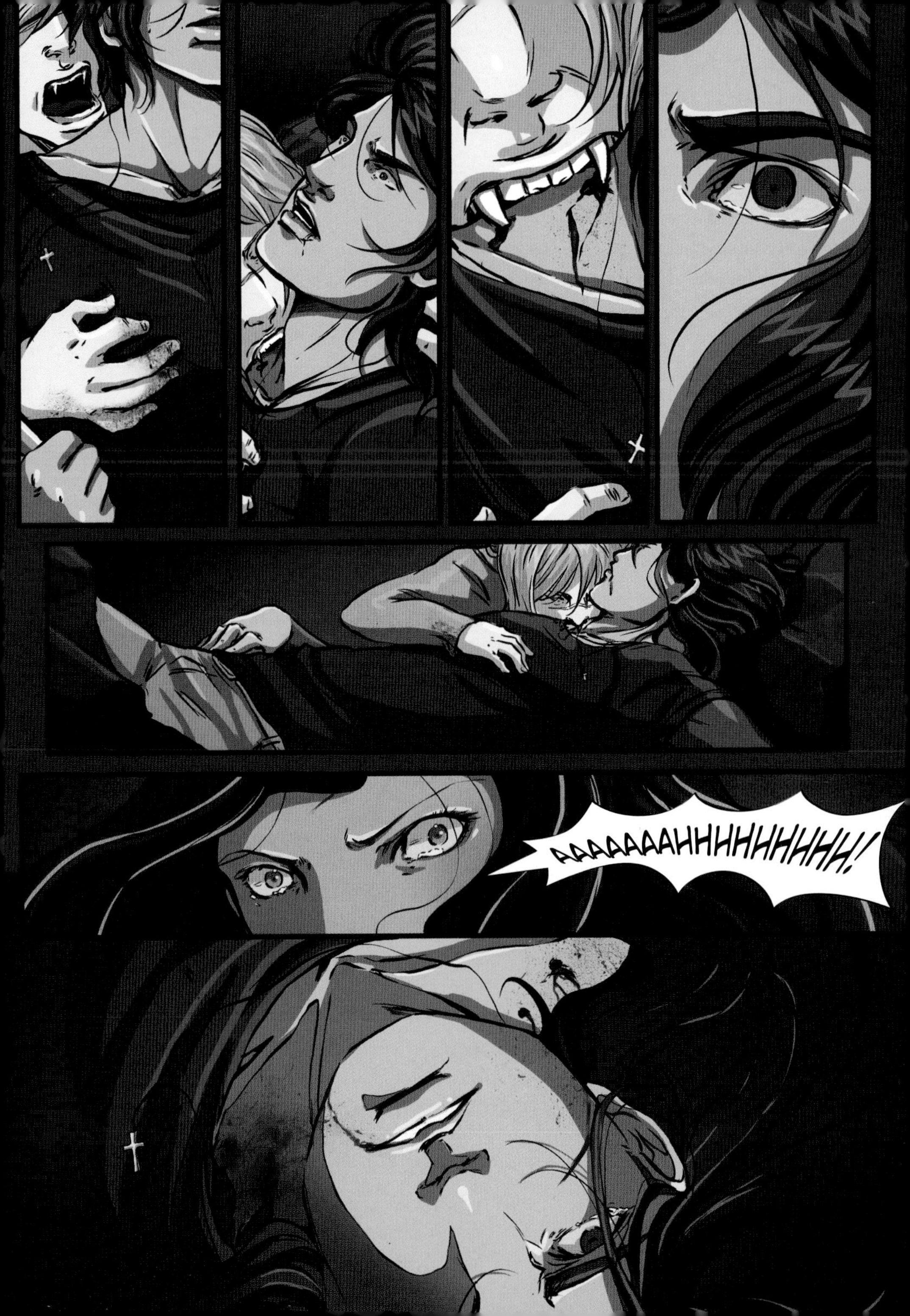
AAAAAAAHHHHHHHH!

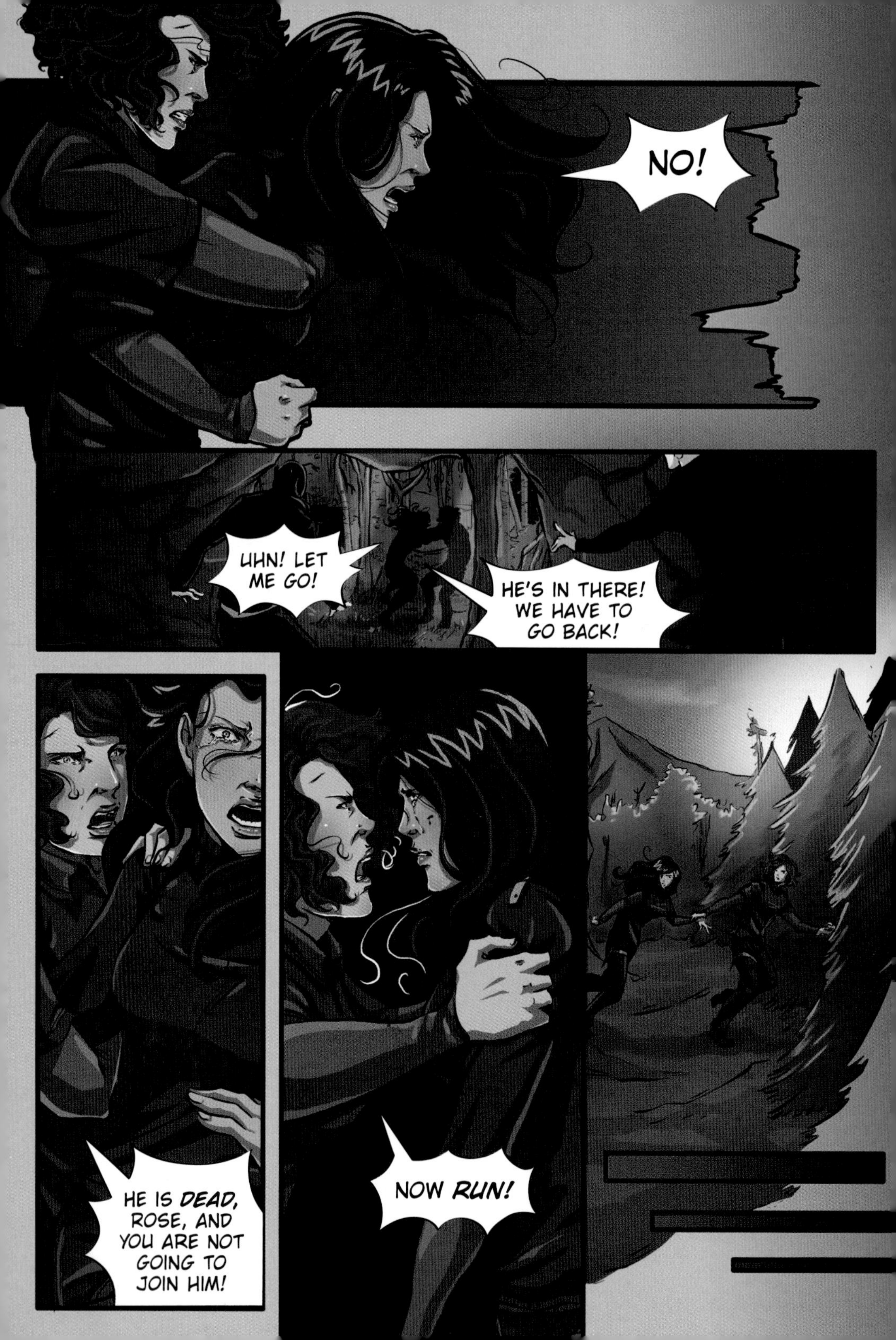
NO!
UHN! LET ME GO!
HE'S IN THERE! WE HAVE TO GO BACK!
HE IS *DEAD*, ROSE, AND YOU ARE NOT GOING TO JOIN HIM!
NOW *RUN!*

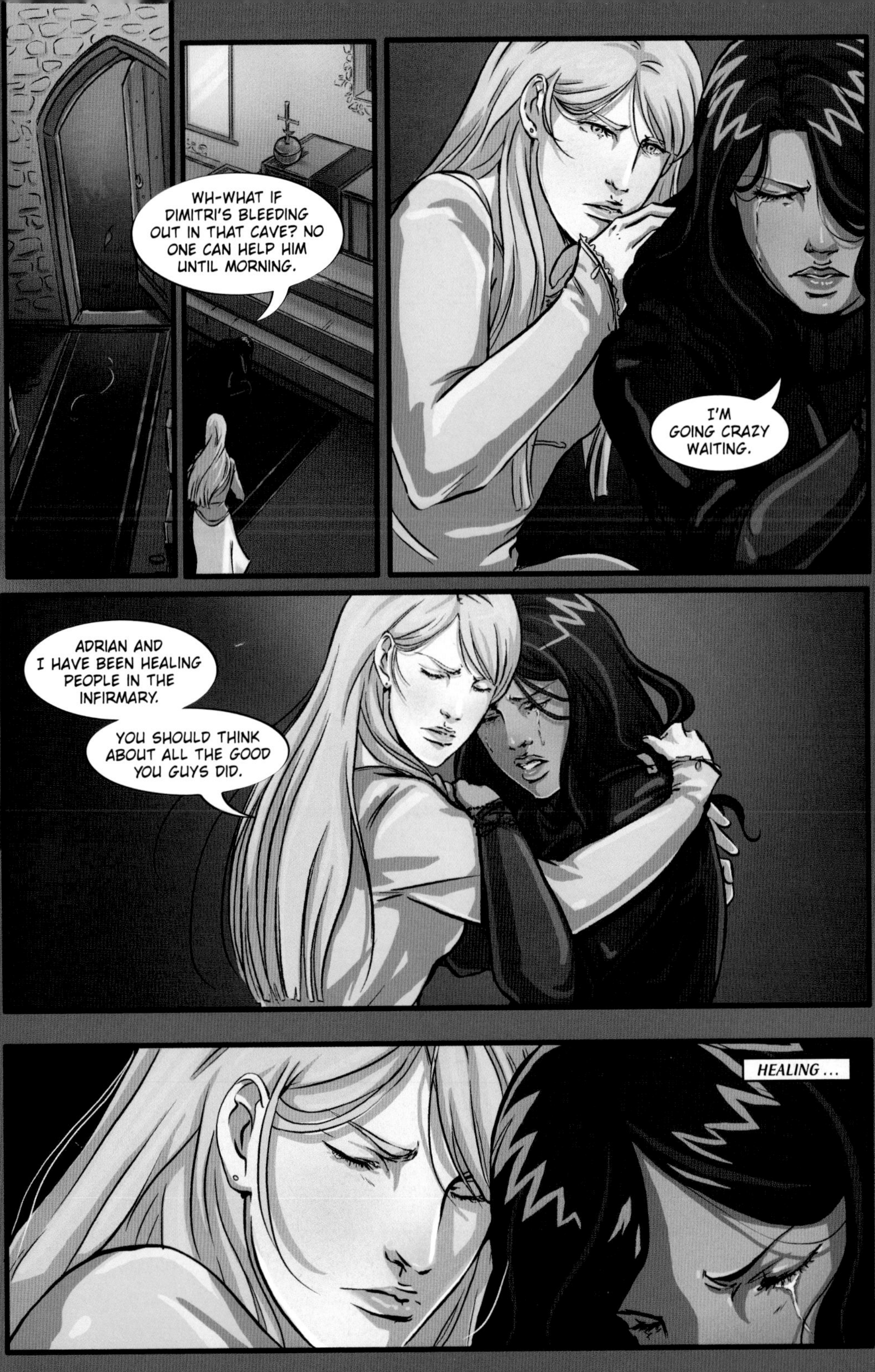
WH-WHAT IF DIMITRI'S BLEEDING OUT IN THAT CAVE? NO ONE CAN HELP HIM UNTIL MORNING.
I'M GOING CRAZY WAITING.
ADRIAN AND I HAVE BEEN HEALING PEOPLE IN THE INFIRMARY.
YOU SHOULD THINK ABOUT ALL THE GOOD YOU GUYS DID.
HEALING . . .

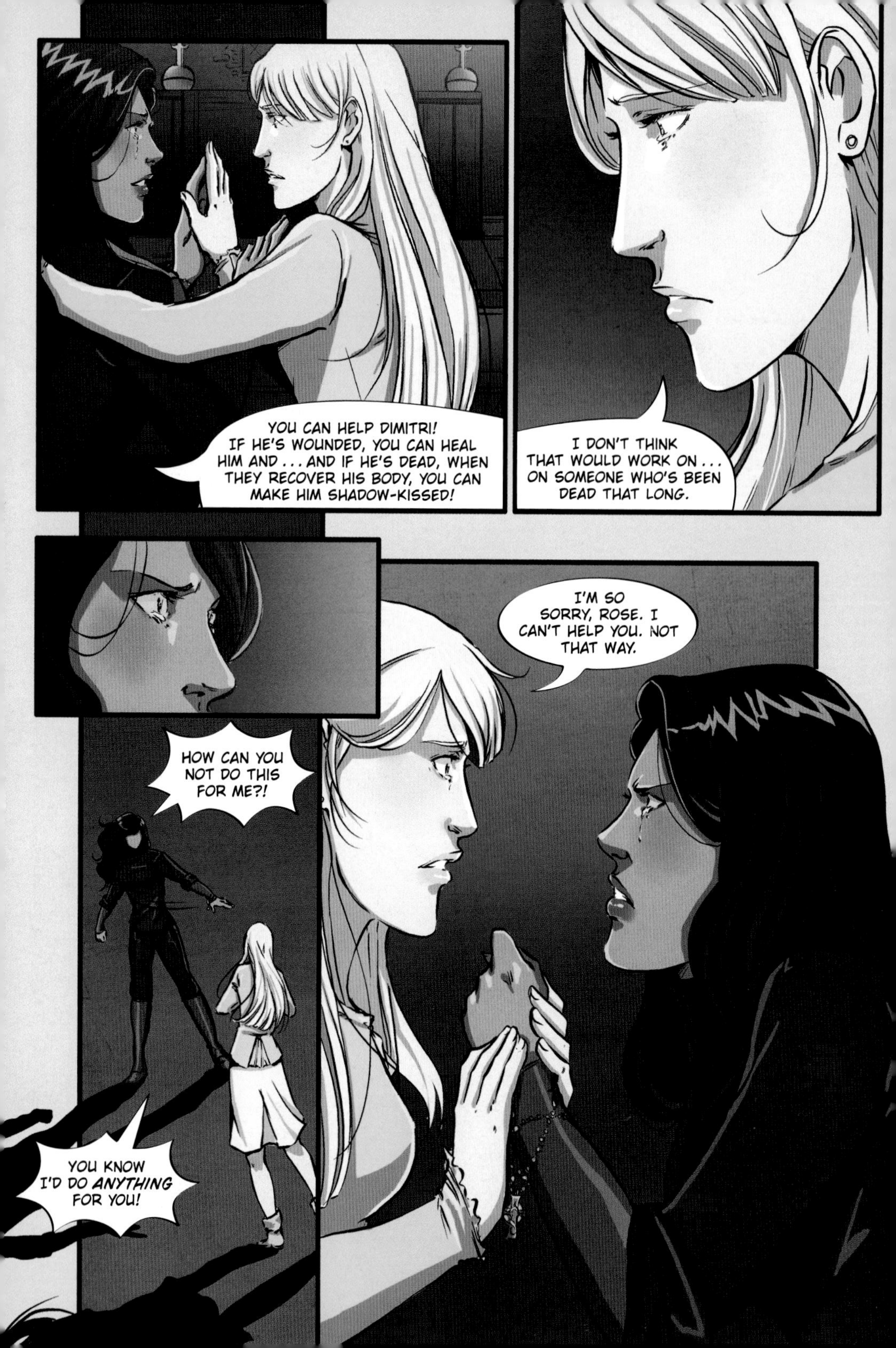

YOU CAN HELP DIMITRI! IF HE'S WOUNDED, YOU CAN HEAL HIM AND . . . AND IF HE'S DEAD, WHEN THEY RECOVER HIS BODY, YOU CAN MAKE HIM SHADOW-KISSED!
I DON'T THINK THAT WOULD WORK ON . . . ON SOMEONE WHO'S BEEN DEAD THAT LONG.
I'M SO SORRY, ROSE. I CAN'T HELP YOU. NOT THAT WAY.
HOW CAN YOU NOT DO THIS FOR ME?!
YOU KNOW I'D DO *ANYTHING* FOR YOU!

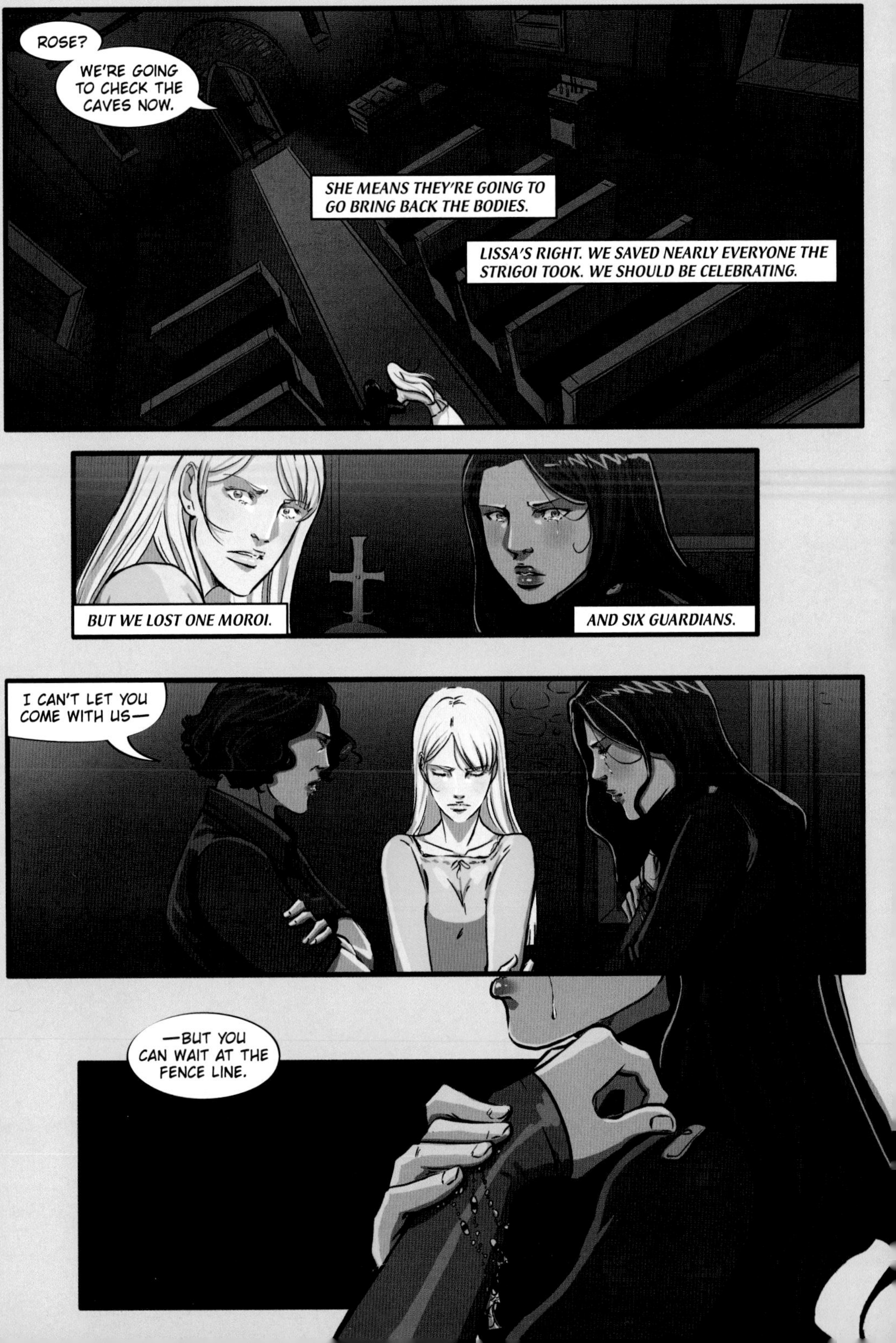
ROSE?
WE'RE GOING TO CHECK THE CAVES NOW.
SHE MEANS THEY'RE GOING TO GO BRING BACK THE BODIES.
LISSA'S RIGHT. WE SAVED NEARLY EVERYONE THE STRIGOI TOOK. WE SHOULD BE CELEBRATING.
BUT WE LOST ONE MOROI.
AND SIX GUARDIANS.
I CAN'T LET YOU COME WITH US—
—BUT YOU CAN WAIT AT THE FENCE LINE.

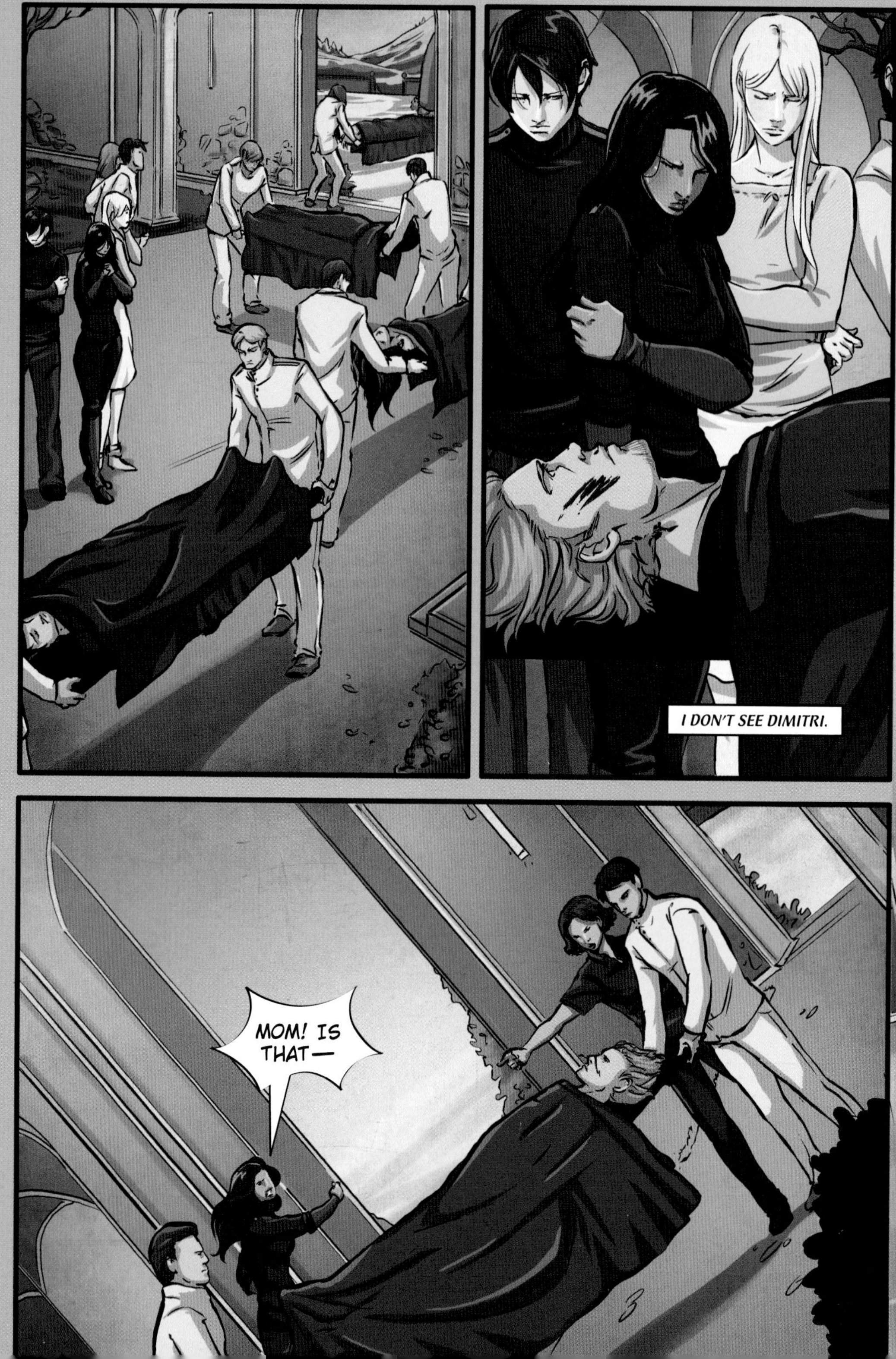
I DON'T SEE DIMITRI.
MOM! IS THAT—

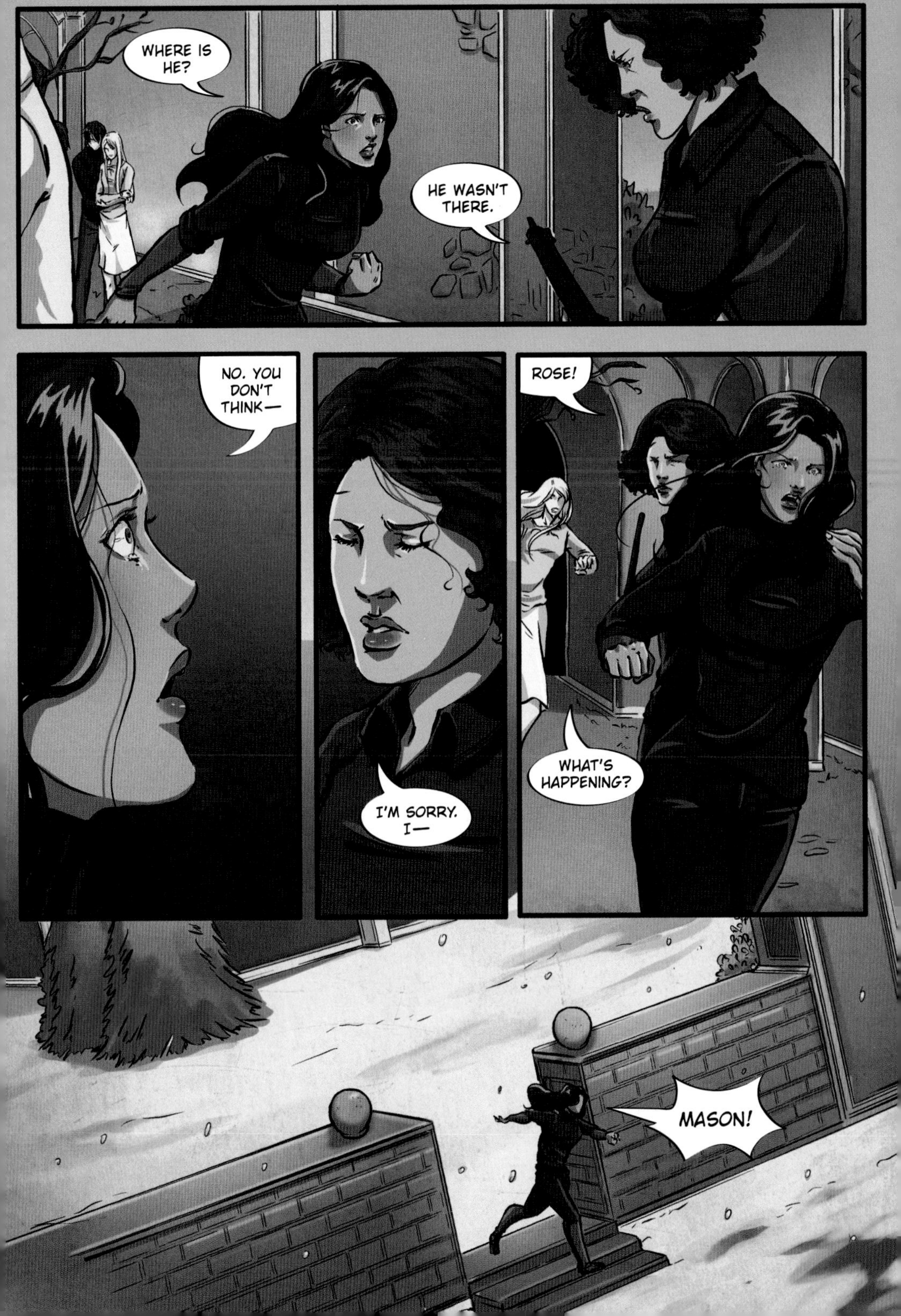
WHERE IS HE?
HE WASN'T THERE.
NO. YOU DON'T THINK—
I'M SORRY. I—
ROSE!
WHAT'S HAPPENING?
MASON!

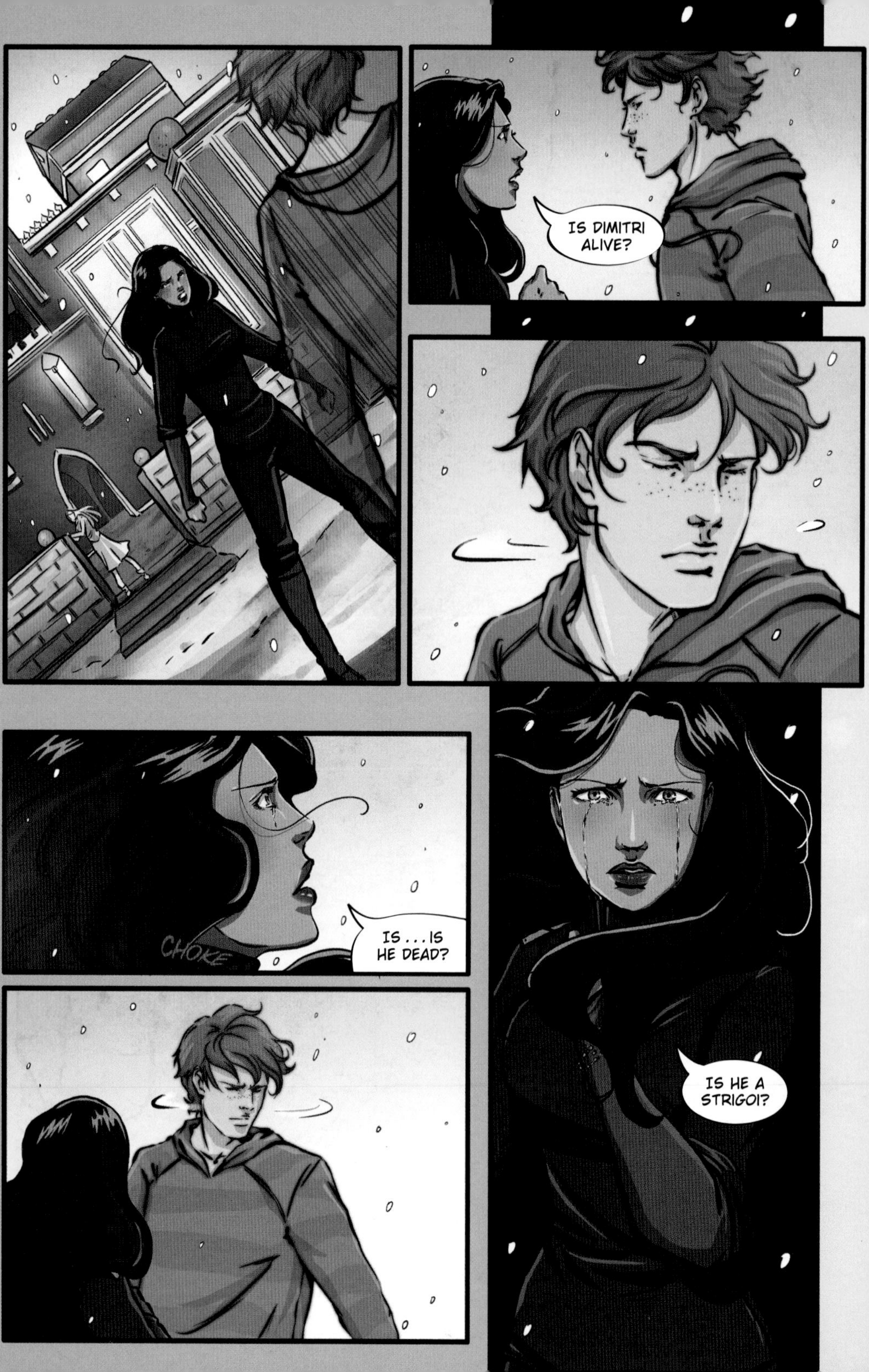
IS DIMITRI ALIVE?
CHOKE
IS . . . IS HE DEAD?
IS HE A STRIGOI?

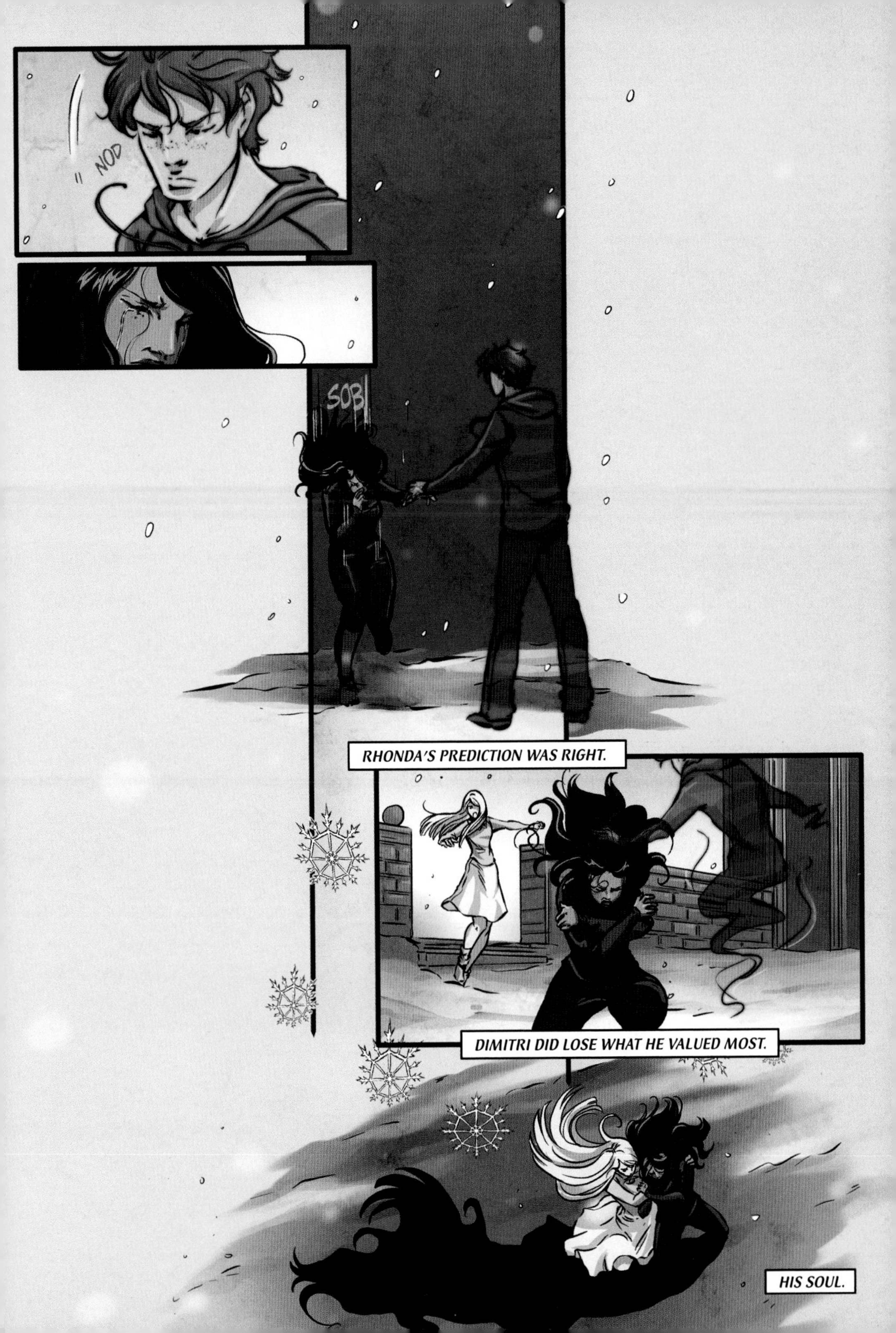
NOD
SOB
RHONDA'S PREDICTION WAS RIGHT.
DIMITRI DID LOSE WHAT HE VALUED MOST.
HIS SOUL.

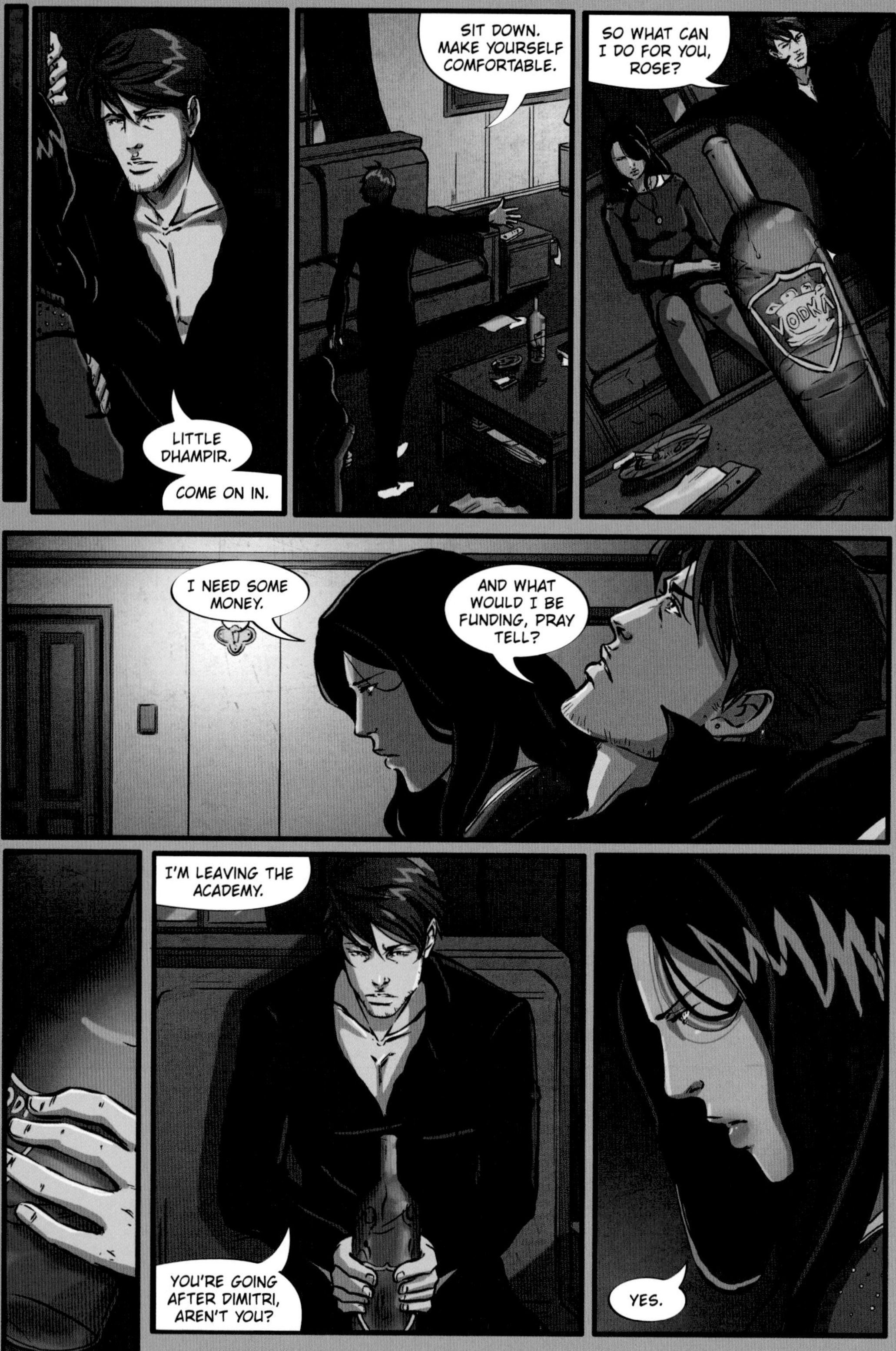
LITTLE DHAMPIR.
COME ON IN.
SIT DOWN. MAKE YOURSELF COMFORTABLE.
SO WHAT CAN I DO FOR YOU, ROSE?
VODKA
I NEED SOME MONEY.
AND WHAT WOULD I BE FUNDING, PRAY TELL?
I'M LEAVING THE ACADEMY.
YOU'RE GOING AFTER DIMITRI, AREN'T YOU?
YES.

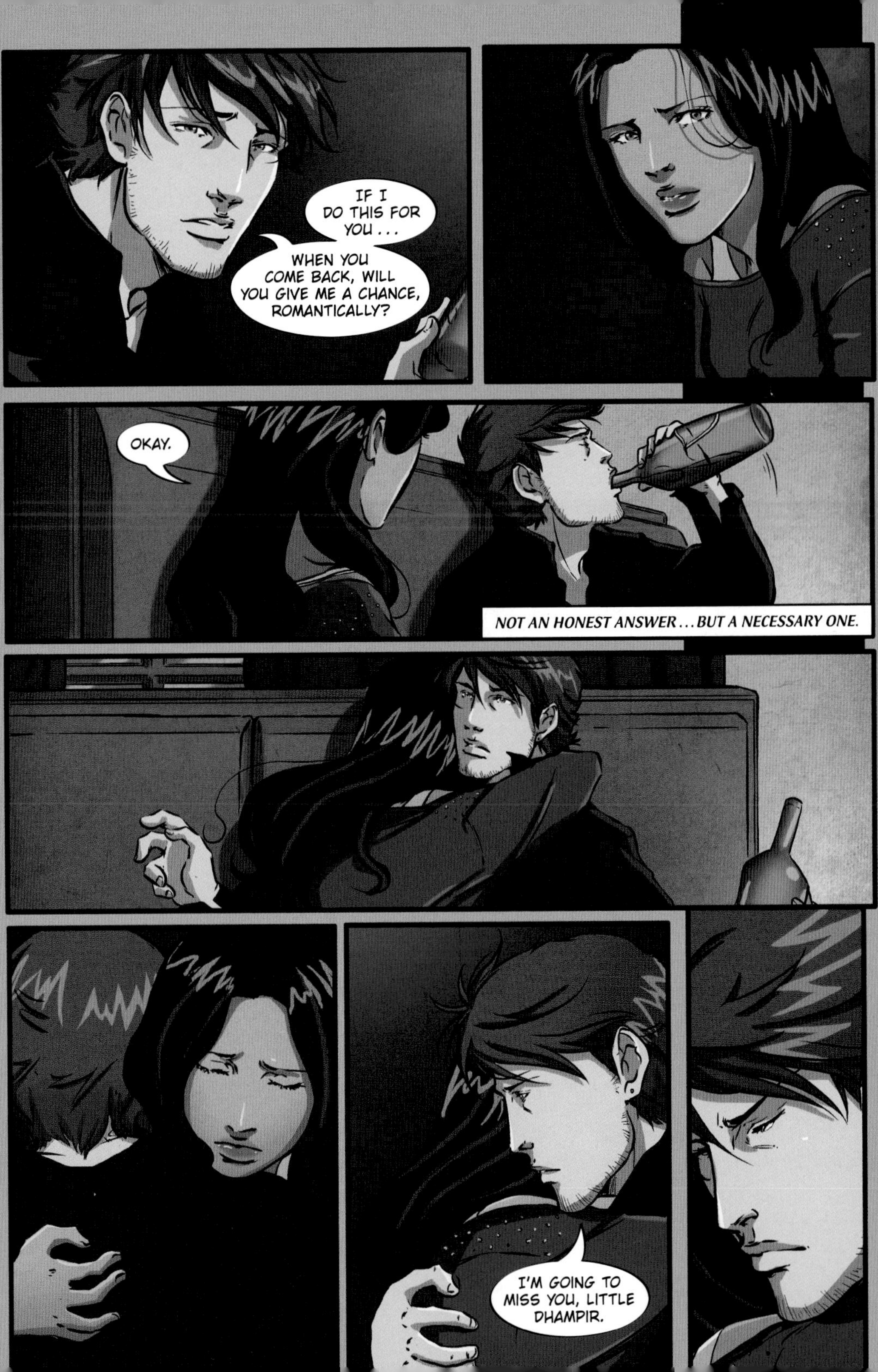
IF I DO THIS FOR YOU . . .
WHEN YOU COME BACK, WILL YOU GIVE ME A CHANCE, ROMANTICALLY?
OKAY.
NOT AN HONEST ANSWER . . . BUT A NECESSARY ONE.
I'M GOING TO MISS YOU, LITTLE DHAMPIR.

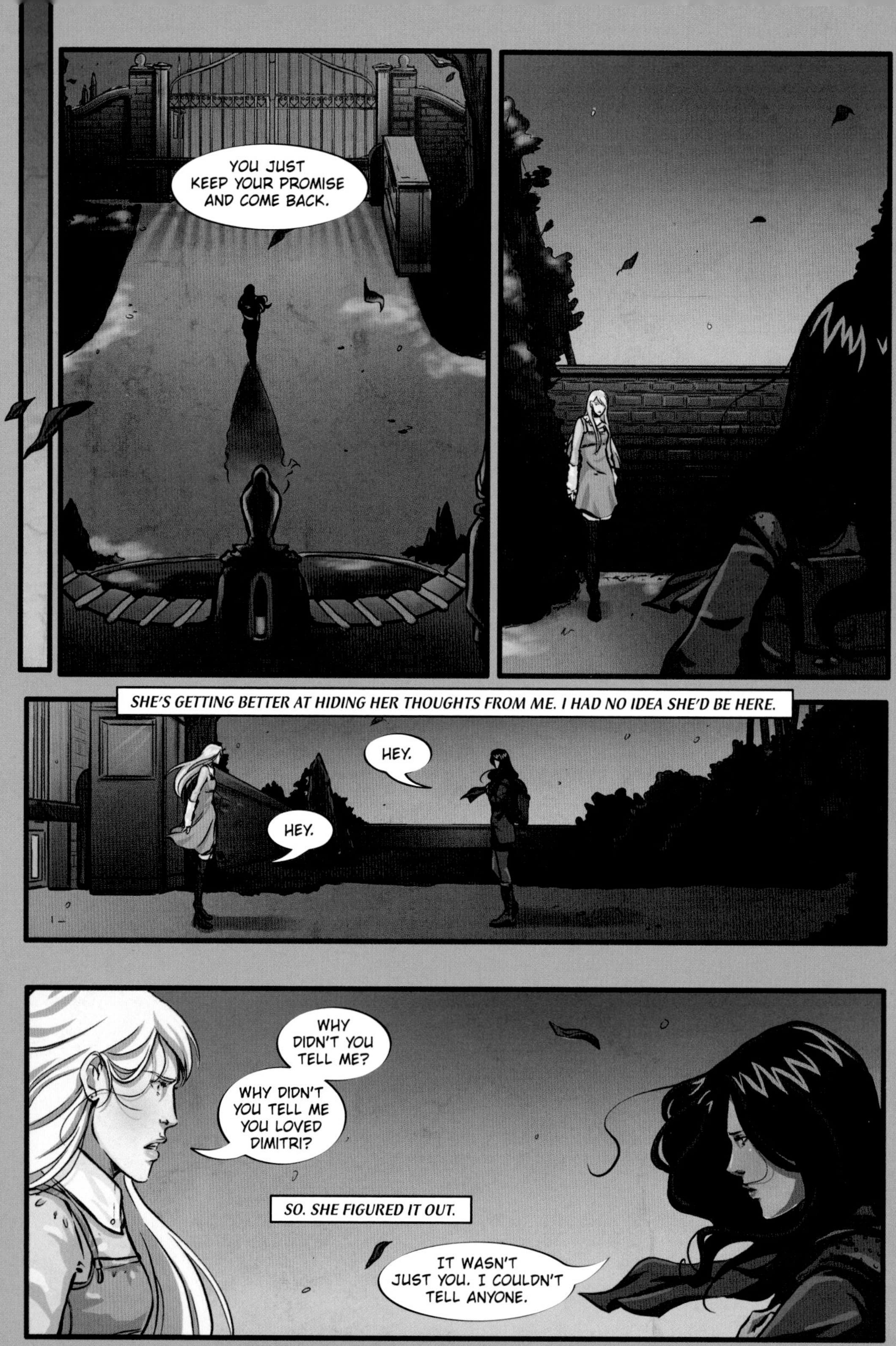
YOU JUST KEEP YOUR PROMISE AND COME BACK.
SHE'S GETTING BETTER AT HIDING HER THOUGHTS FROM ME. I HAD NO IDEA SHE'D BE HERE.
HEY.
HEY.
WHY DIDN'T YOU TELL ME?
WHY DIDN'T YOU TELL ME YOU LOVED DIMITRI?
SO. SHE FIGURED IT OUT.
IT WASN'T JUST YOU. I COULDN'T TELL ANYONE.

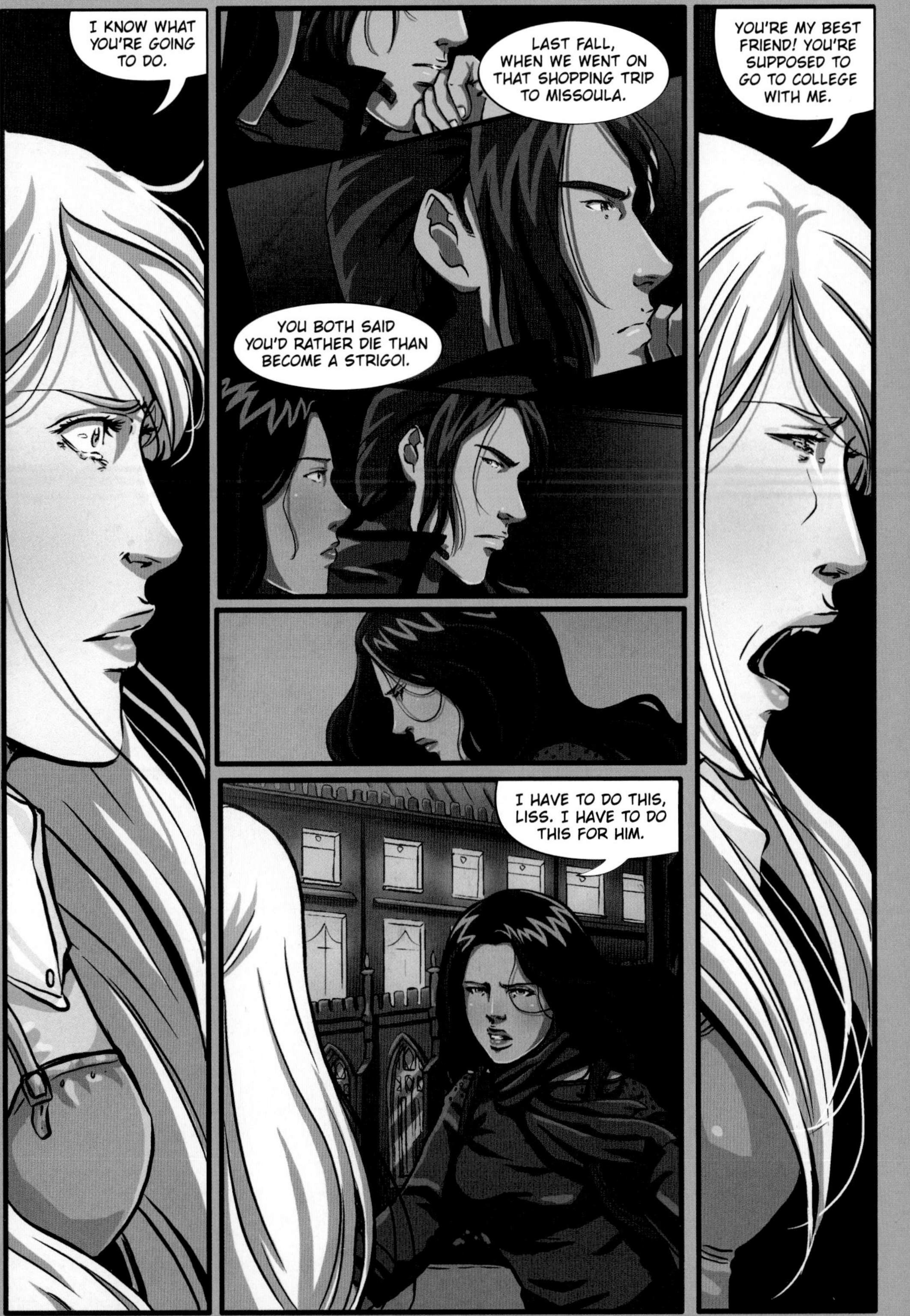
I KNOW WHAT YOU'RE GOING TO DO.
LAST FALL, WHEN WE WENT ON THAT SHOPPING TRIP TO MISSOULA.
YOU BOTH SAID YOU'D RATHER DIE THAN BECOME A STRIGOI.
I HAVE TO DO THIS, LISS. I HAVE TO DO THIS FOR HIM.
YOU'RE MY BEST FRIEND! YOU'RE SUPPOSED TO GO TO COLLEGE WITH ME.

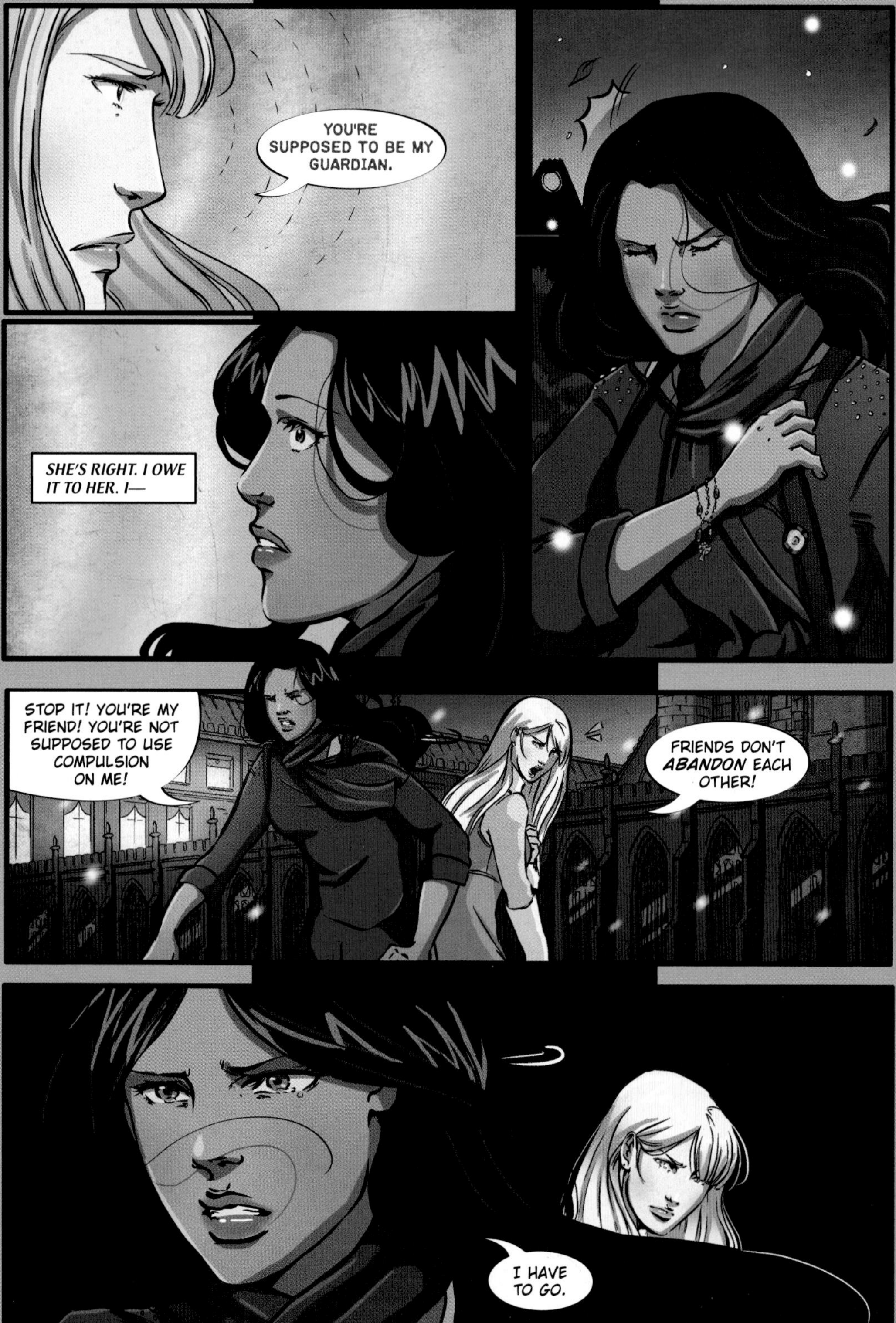
YOU'RE SUPPOSED TO BE MY GUARDIAN.
SHE'S RIGHT. I OWE IT TO HER. I—
STOP IT! YOU'RE MY FRIEND! YOU'RE NOT SUPPOSED TO USE COMPULSION ON ME!
FRIENDS DON'T ABANDON EACH OTHER!
I HAVE TO GO.

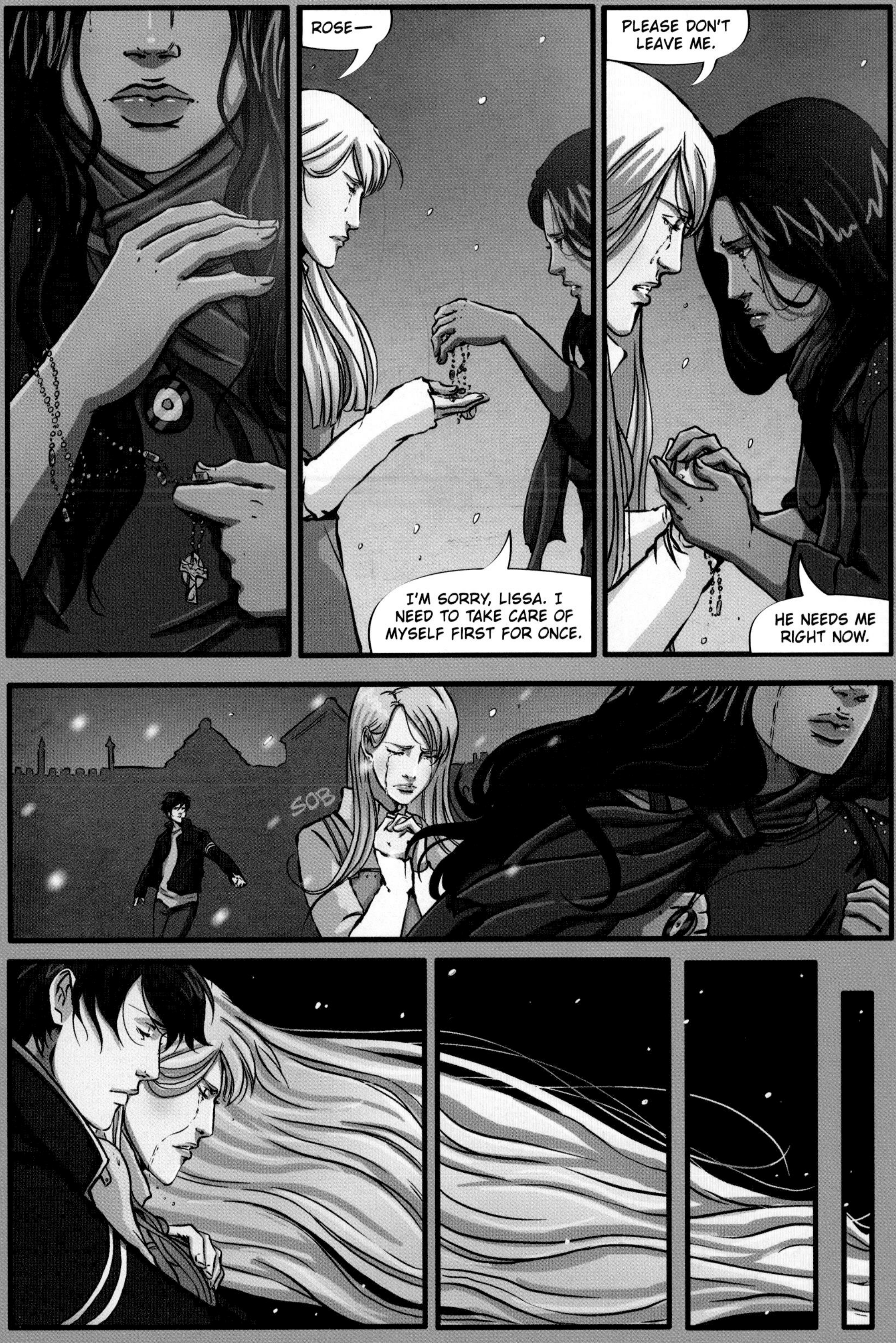
ROSE—
I'M SORRY, LISSA. I NEED TO TAKE CARE OF MYSELF FIRST FOR ONCE.
PLEASE DON'T LEAVE ME.
HE NEEDS ME RIGHT NOW.
SOB

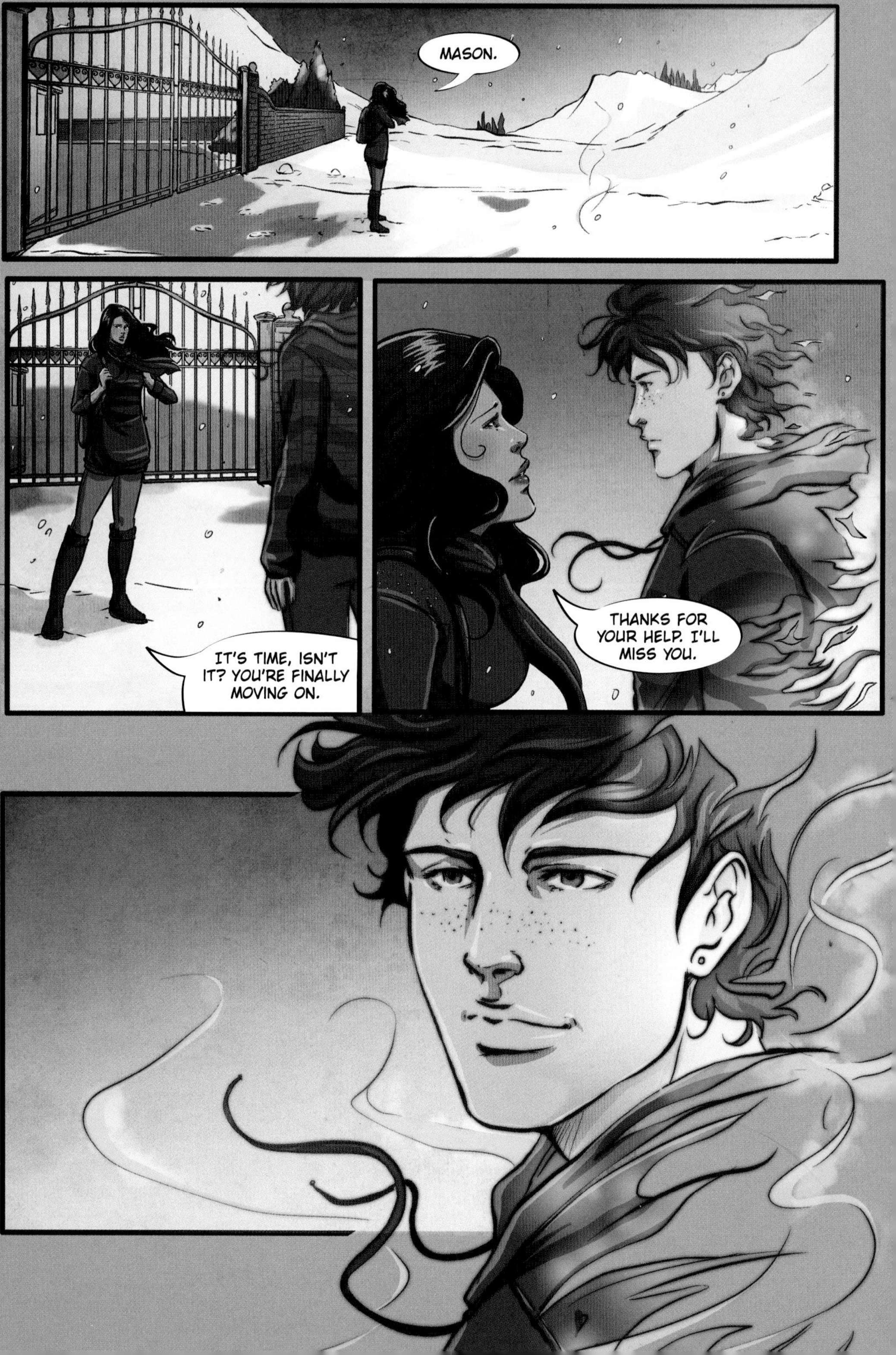
MASON.
IT'S TIME, ISN'T IT? YOU'RE FINALLY MOVING ON.
THANKS FOR YOUR HELP. I'LL MISS YOU.

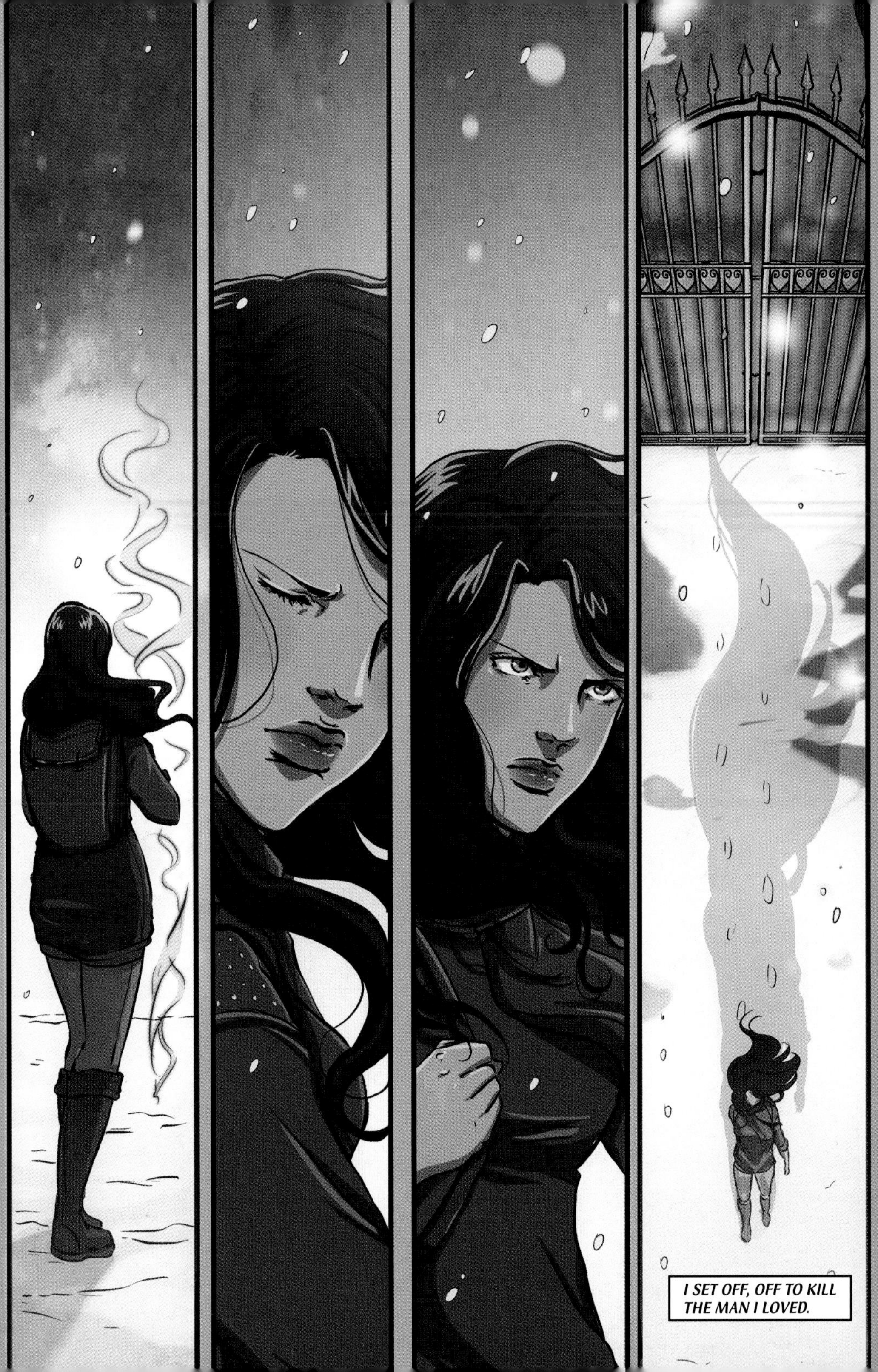
I SET OFF, OFF TO KILL THE MAN I LOVED.

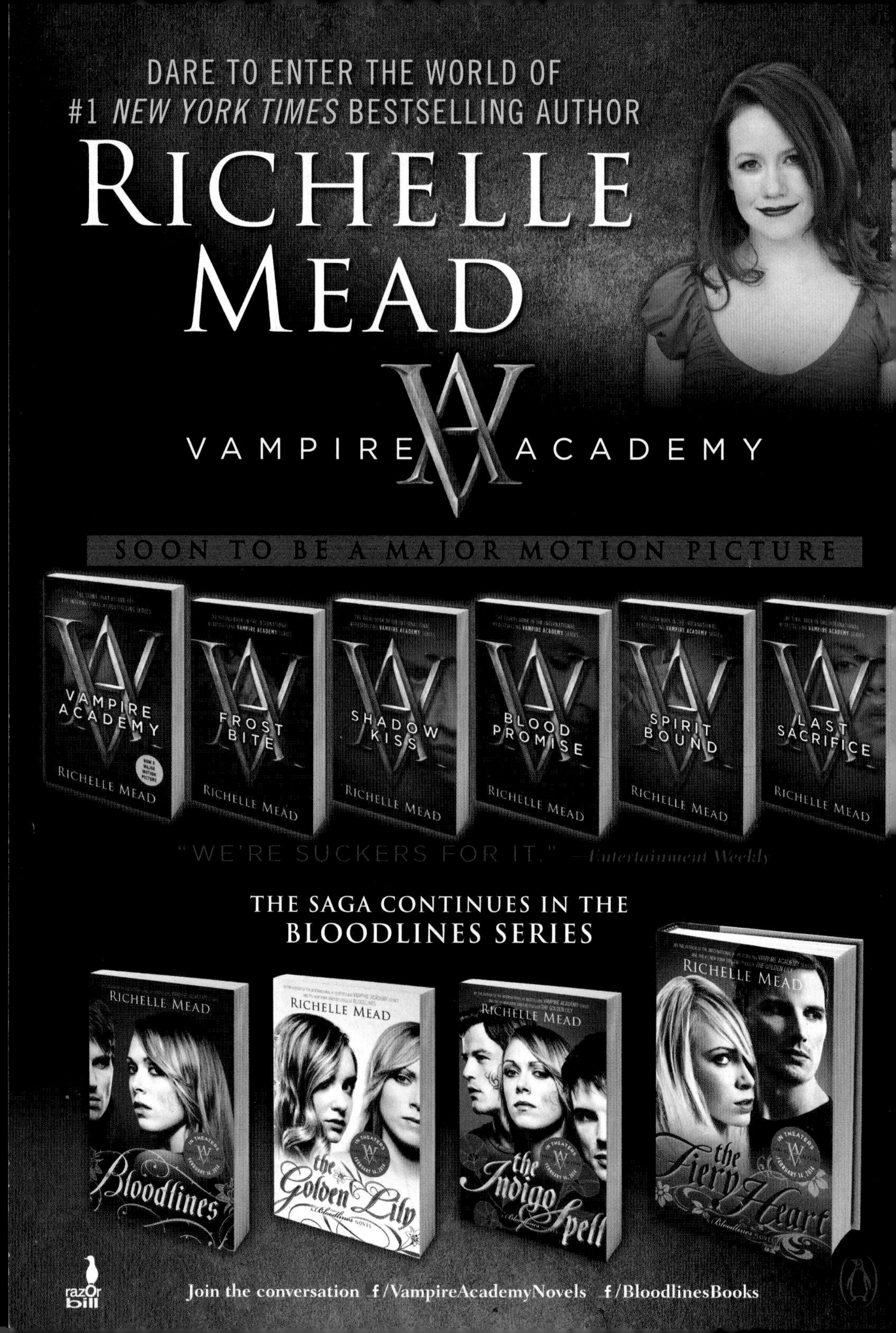
DARE TO ENTER THE WORLD OF
#1 NEW YORK TIMES BESTSELLING AUTHOR
RICHELLE MEAD
VAMPIRE ACADEMY
SOON TO BE A MAJOR MOTION PICTURE
VAMPIRE ACADEMY RICHELLE MEAD
FROSTBITE RICHELLE MEAD
SHADOW KISS RICHELLE MEAD
BLOOD PROMISE RICHELLE MEAD
SPIRIT BOUND RICHELLE MEAD
LAST SACRIFICE RICHELLE MEAD
"WE'RE SUCKERS FOR IT." —Entertainment Weekly
THE SAGA CONTINUES IN THE
BLOODLINES SERIES
RICHELLE MEAD Bloodlines
RICHELLE MEAD the Golden Lily
RICHELLE MEAD the Indigo Spell
RICHELLE MEAD the Fiery Heart
razOr bill
Join the conversation f/VampireAcademyNovels f/BloodlinesBooks

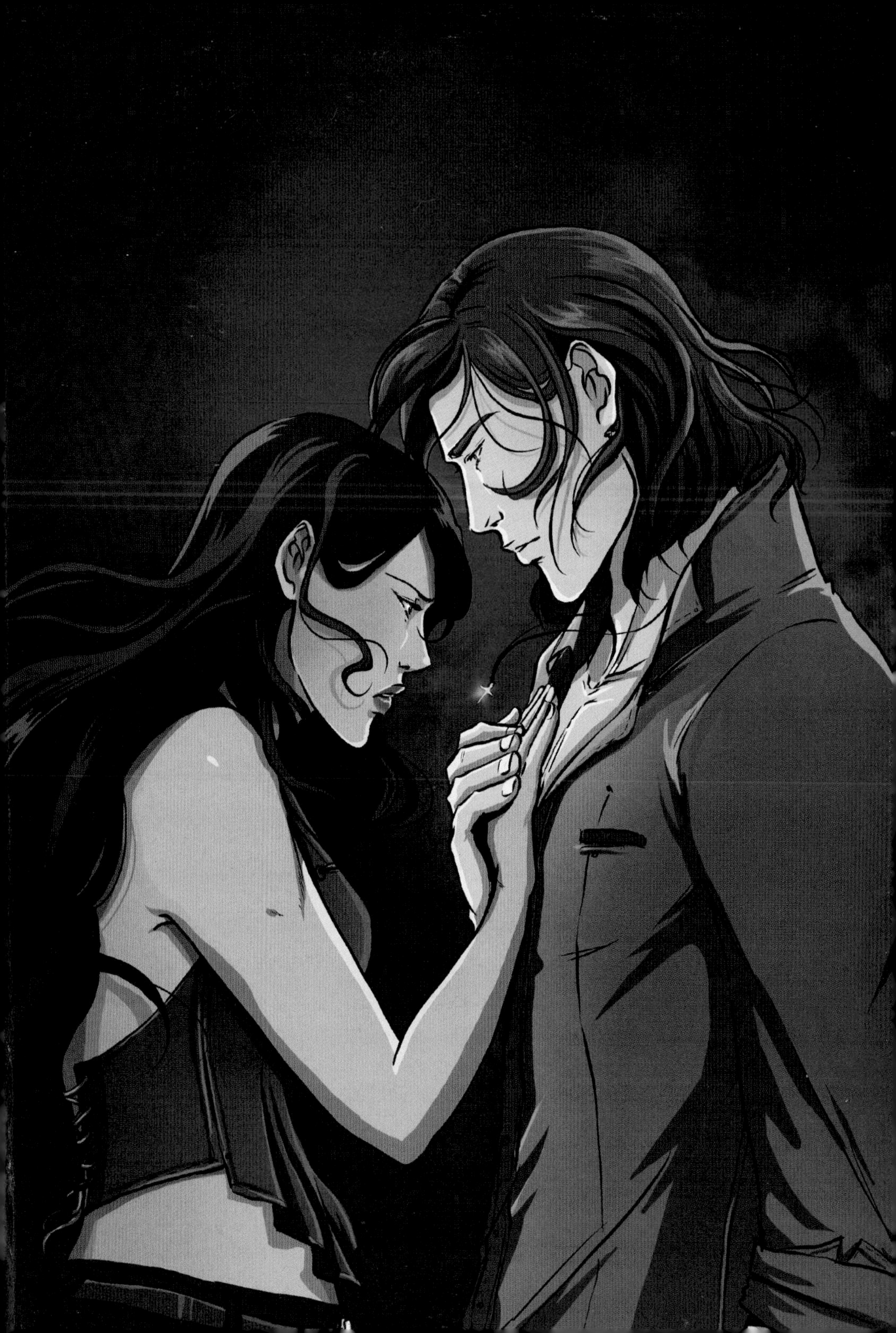